The Complaint

Tom Breen

AF427326

BBRADFORD BOOKS

Copyright © 2013, 2015, 2024; Tom Breen
All Rights Reserved

No part of this book may be reproduced or transmitted in any form or by any means, electronic or mechanical, including photocopying, recording or by any information storage and retrieval system without permission in writing from the publisher.

BBradford Books—Port Jefferson Station, NY
Paperback ISBN: 979-8-9865185-3-4
Hardcover ISBN: 979-8-9865185-4-1
eBook ISBN: 979-8-9865185-5-8
Library of Congress Control Number: 2023921047
Title: *The Complaint*
Author: Tom Breen
Digital distribution | 2024
Paperback | 2024
Hardcover | 2024

This is a work of fiction. The characters, names, incidents, places, and dialogue are products of the author's imagination, and are not to be construed as real.

Dedication

This book is dedicated to my dear wife of forty-four years, Deidre E. Breen.

I have always marveled at her intellect and memory, but it is her capacity to love that is most endearing.

Acknowledgment

I would like to thank the College of the Holy Cross in Worcester, Massachusetts. The Jesuits always did their best to teach the proper use of English and I am forever grateful for their efforts—I hope this book doesn't fall embarrassingly short of their high standards.

Plus, special thanks to Em Hughes, Executive Publisher of New Book Authors Publishing Company, for her insight and experience in navigating the turbulent waters of the publishing world, especially with regard to a revised work.

Also, a note of appreciation to Jean Burke of Fulton Street in NYC—she didn't blink an eye when I first walked into her office with hundreds of pages of handwritten scribble and asked her to turn it into a readable work.

Preface

Considering it has been ten years since THE COMPLAINT was first released, I decided it was a good time to make some necessary revisions.

I corrected the grammatical errors and shortened many lengthy paragraphs. I believe the story is currently more reader friendly, with a better flow to the dialogue.

Over the last decade, I have received a number of helpful comments from readers regarding improvements to the text. I incorporated many of the suggestions in this revised edition. Yet, the plot remains the same; the characters have the same flaws and strengths; and, the conclusion remains untouched.

I had little experience in writing a fictional story when I first started scribbling words on a legal pad in 2011. With time and practice came experience, so the early shortcomings eventually became obvious, necessitating the revisions.

I anticipate that the changes will enhance the reader's level of enjoyment. And, that's my whole purpose in writing—to provide entertainment as an escape from the daily challenges of life.

Thanks for Reading,

Tom Breen
January 2024

Chapter 1

The professional life of an attorney is, on the whole, fairly boring. For that matter, I've found the entire life cycle of lawyering in Manhattan and living on Long Island to be repetitive and mundane.

Maybe Shakespeare had it right when he wrote, in the words of Dick the Butcher, that a top priority should be given to the eradication of lawyers. Of course, Shakespeare was condemning not only the evils inherent in the practice of law, but also lawyers' arrogant sense of entitlement to the highest levels of esteem and influence in the social order of civilized society. But, I guess Dick the Butcher could not have cared less about a lawyer's assumed right to upward mobility, so long as all lawyers expeditiously and quietly went away and did not return. At least it would put us out of our professional misery.

So, what is so unexciting about working as an attorney in downtown Manhattan? Essentially, the problem is this: If you're not in the courtroom, at a deposition or participating in a mediation, then you are strapped to your desk doing mundane paperwork or dealing with emails. While creating words on a piece of paper or in an email may sound challenging, the subject matter of the words is the problem. It simply is not interesting or challenging to write about insurance policies, contracts and quarreling litigants. If and when a lawsuit is filed in court, the paperwork reaches its peak of volume and boredom.

For example, when a dispute is in litigation, the parties

are required to accumulate and send to their adversary all documentation that could reasonably be related to the issues at hand, including all legal papers, correspondence, emails and other electronic communications, such as text messages. This production usually consists of hundreds of thousands of documents, mostly emails and other electronically created communications, all of which have to be accumulated and reviewed. The tedious task can take weeks, if not months.

Being in a courtroom or attending a mediation is an entirely different experience. In those proceedings, lawyers have the opportunity to speak in front of other attorneys, clients, judges and/or mediators while presenting the factual and legal positions of the client who is paying your fee. Litigators articulate their thoughts and opinions in these public forums and everybody is required to act like they are listening, whether the attorney is doing a good job or not. As a rule, I find this type of lawyering to be challenging, enjoyable work.

Yet, my favorite legal activity is participating at a deposition. During a deposition, the attorney will either ask questions of an adversarial party sworn to tell the truth or else defend the deposition as counsel to the witness who is testifying. The attorney asking the questions will attempt to direct his inquiries in a manner that will elicit testimony damaging to the witness's position. In fact, the lawyer will endeavor to ask questions that will cause the witness to hurt his or her case no matter how the questions are answered. If you are counsel to the witness, your job is to object to such questions and state on the record why the question is confusing or argumentative, or just plain intended to get the witness to say something he or she doesn't really believe to be true. Whereas, if you are the lawyer asking the questions, the key is to keep hammering away at the question you want answered until you either get a response or the witness and the witness's lawyer storm out of the deposition in a pique of anger. It really is fun.

So, for twenty-five years this has been my professional life and I think I have held up fairly well. I'm still trim, about 6'3", although my face has started to droop around the corners of my mouth. I'm fortunate to still have most of the wavy, black hair that covers the top of my ears and dangles unpredictably over my forehead above thick eyebrows. My eyelids cover the top of my brown pupils, but this is offset by long eyelashes that somehow naturally curve upward at the ends.

It all creates a facial appearance that some women have said makes me appear vulnerable and perhaps even sad, although I don't believe either emotional state accurately describes my true nature. With regard to the opposite sex, I try to rely on my engaging conversation and wit to attract women, usually without great success.

Notwithstanding, I was lucky enough to eventually meet and marry my wife of twenty years. Shortly after our marriage, we purchased our home in Port Jefferson, Long Island.

Looking back, I realize now that a basic appreciation of home, family and the mundane, repetitive pattern of work and play all provide a comforting and reassuring cushion to the inevitable moments of disappointment and heartache in life. Being as thick-headed and shallow as I am, I was unable to appreciate that simple truth of life until I experienced the unsettling events that started to unfold beginning in November 2008.

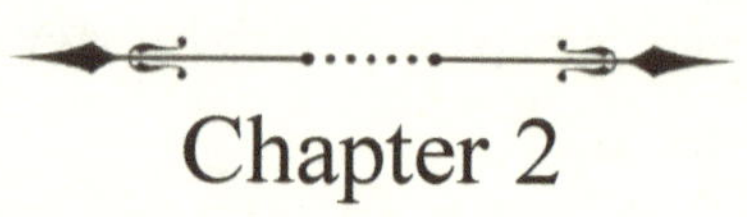

Chapter 2

It's early November 2008, and I'm looking out the window of my law office on the 45th floor of 40 Wall Street in downtown Manhattan. The view is spectacular. It's about 4:30 p.m. and the sun is starting to set. The remaining sunlight gives a bright reddish-pink hue to the Brooklyn Bridge and the Manhattan Bridge, both spanning gracefully above the East River.

The building at 40 Wall Street, currently renamed the Trump Building, is a 70-story skyscraper. It was completed in 1930 and was the world's tallest building for about a month in May of 1930. By the end of May, the Chrysler Building, and then the Empire State Building in 1931, exceeded the height of 40 Wall Street. I guess the builders of 40 Wall Street had a great plan that didn't succeed for long. But, it is difficult to feel sorry for the failed goal of being the tallest when considering enormously expensive, ego-driven structures, rather than disappointed teenagers unable to make the front line on the school's basketball team.

Although the view is magnificent, gazing out the window of my office always reminds me of the horror of September 11, 2001, when two huge passenger jets crashed full speed into the Twin Towers of the World Trade Center on a sun-drenched day with a brilliantly blue sky, untouched by clouds.

On September 11, 2001, I was scheduled to fly from LaGuardia Airport to Orlando for the mediation of a lawsuit pending in South Florida. The mediation was canceled a few days before 9/11, leaving me with a non-refundable American Airlines ticket. So, on the morning of 9/11, before I went to work, I decided to walk over to the American Airlines ticket-sales counter in the lobby of the World Trade Center to hopefully convince the American Airlines agent to refund the non-refundable ticket.

That morning, I had taken my usual commuter train to Penn Station and then the Seventh Avenue subway downtown to the Wall Street Station. Upon exiting the subway station, I walked through Chase Manhattan Bank Plaza towards the World Trade Center. Once I got to Broadway, traffic was stopped and hundreds of people were looking up at a huge hole in the southwest face of the South Tower.

Although the six-story gap had been caused by a jet crashing into the building, no part of the airplane was visible. Flames rose from around the edges of a huge black void where the plane had pierced the building, with thick, dark smoke rising from the destroyed floors. The North Tower was also burning, but only the side opposite the impact could be seen from where I stood. It was shocking to see people in the windows above the burning hole desperately waving downward. I stared helplessly and wondered how the firemen were going to rescue the distraught victims so high up in the Towers. Soon, a policeman came by and told the crowd to move away and go back to work to avoid falling debris from the fire. I left as instructed. If I had not, I would have still been standing near the base of the Towers when they collapsed.

Also, it did not help my 9/11 anxieties that in 1946 a United States Army plane had crashed into the 58th floor of 40 Wall Street in a fog, killing five people.

Each day at the office I tell myself to just stop thinking about such ill-fated events and get back to reading whatever unremarkable legal decision or contract is on my desk. Sometimes it works, sometimes it doesn't.

My thoughts that day were interrupted by a young lady entering my office. "Excuse me, Mr. Bradford, do you have a minute?"

I turned away from the window and towards the entrance of my office. Mary Douglas, an associate at the firm, was standing across from my desk.

"Mary, please call me Brian. The formality of addressing me as Mr. Bradford makes me feel old and dull, however true it may actually be."

I've mentioned this to her before, but she usually forgets my request, on purpose or otherwise.

"Okay—Brian. I just wanted to remind you about the meeting tomorrow with the doctor representatives of the New York/New Jersey Medical Association," she mentioned.

"Yes, I remember," I replied. "Thanks for reconfirming with me."

I've known Mary for about three years and, as a rule, have done my best to keep our interaction on a professional level. Mary is single, with straight, long blond hair that flows down her back. Her large hazel eyes combine with a pretty smile and an attractive figure. Basically, the whole package is darn good.

The thought crossed my mind to tell her she looked nice but, of course, such a comment would probably be misinterpreted. The problem is that there is a double standard that must be complied with. A woman can quite appropriately comment that she likes your tie or suit. However, in the office, I cannot come out and say: "Ms.

Douglas, that is a very pretty blouse you have on today."

Anything said to a woman about looks or clothing has the potential to be considered an inappropriate and sexist remark in the workplace. This includes all of the following: "I like your hair—the curls are really pretty," or "Your perfume smells great," and especially not, "The fishnet stockings really go well with your four-inch pink Jimmy Choo high heels."

Bottom line, at the office a man is required to just shut up and not express any of the thoughts that uncontrollably pop into his male mind on a continuously recurring basis.

Getting back to tomorrow's meeting, I reminded Mary that I would meet her in the conference room fifteen minutes before the 10 a.m. start time.

"Good night, Mr.... I mean Brian, see you then," Mary said, as she left my office.

The appointment was originally made during a telephone call I received from Doctor Martin Brown. The doctor was complaining about his bills being severely underpaid by a health care insurance company. It seemed odd to me at the time. Mostly, the public would find it laughable that a doctor is whining that he or she is not making enough money. But I told myself to keep an open mind and booked the appointment.

My day was completed, so I headed to the elevator to begin my commute home to Port Jefferson. I intended to get plenty of rest before my meeting with Dr. Brown. Little did I realize the life altering events that would follow.

Chapter 3

I began my commute by taking the Long Island Railroad from Pennsylvania Station, known as Penn Station, to a town called Ronkonkoma in Suffolk County.

Penn Station is an underground commuter rail complex located at 8th Avenue and 31st Street in Midtown Manhattan. Access to the trains requires you to descend about three stories below street level. The claustrophobic terminal, which contains numerous gates leading down to the tracks, has low ceilings and cramped windowless walkways that are unable to comfortably handle the hordes of people arriving at rush hour each morning and evening.

Prior to its demolition, the original Penn Station, opened in 1910, was an extraordinary structure. According to Wikipedia, it was an outstanding "masterpiece of the Beaux-Arts style," with a magnificent concourse, a breathtaking main entrance over 61 feet in height and a "main waiting room on the scale of St. Peter's Basilica in Rome." Adorned with continuous, mammoth Roman columns and huge stone eagles weighing several tons, it was an epic construction of grace and majesty with a curved ceiling 150 feet high. Pictures of the old Penn Station revealed a huge public area with an enormous sense of spaciousness that created the sensation of being outdoors while being enclosed inside the terminal.

Remarkably, plans are in place to raise the ceilings, expand the hallways and create a modern, sun-drenched Train Hall in the U.S. Post Office connected underground to Penn Station.

Of course, not being able to leave well enough alone, some builder had a great idea to demolish it all, starting in 1963, in order to build high-rise office buildings and a new Madison Square Garden. Talk about regrets and mistakes, that act of history had plenty of both. But the good news is that a landmark designation movement began shortly after the demolition. A lesson in preservation was learned.

Putting the inadequacies of the present terminal aside, the train ride itself was smooth and comfortable, although the Long Island Railroad seems unable to keep its cars pleasantly warm in cold weather. For some reason I can't explain, the air vents in the ceiling of each car consistently blow cold air from the outside directly onto the passengers all winter long. The conductors always give the excuse that they are unable to control it and unable to stop it. One conductor told me the switch that controls ceiling air vents was underneath the train. It seems to be one of the great mysteries of life. One day, I intend to put duct tape over the section of the air vent directly above my seat.

Another problem I have with the train occurs only when I do not have the good fortune to have a woman sit next to me in the adjoining seat. Men have no consideration for staying on their side of the seat when sitting on the attached seats for two. Men spread their legs and arms when seated and take as much room as they can grab from your side of the seat, even though the continuous seat cushion that connects the two adjoining seats has a slight rise in the middle, clearly marking the boundaries of each seat.

This uncivilized male activity also includes a constant elbow to my ribs each time the seat glutton next to me turns a page of the newspaper with arms outstretched. Plus, the absolute worst seat hogs are men with laptops. In order to type on the keyboard, the seat predator must extend his arms away from his body with his elbow again poking me in the side. Soon, one of these seat scavengers is going to find his computer tossed down the middle aisle of the train car.

Women, on the other hand, are especially considerate and conscious of "your space" and "my space" boundaries. They never have any part of their anatomy cross the middle line between the seats and make every effort to have a generous "free-zone" between you and her. That alone is a major reason for my high appreciation of the opposite sex.

On the train trip home this evening, I was fortunate to have a pleasant looking middle-aged woman as a seat mate. As I anticipated, she made every effort to keep as much space as possible between us and never once turned to look at me. I was in heaven. Then again, maybe I needed a breath mint.

My last thought about commuter trains is the obnoxious overuse of cell phones by both sexes. It seems acceptable to make a short call home to say "Hi, honey, I'm on the 5:41 out of Penn Station." However, it is quite another matter to talk incessantly about the type of pizza to order that night in a loud, irritating voice.

"Are you sure you don't want pepperoni on half the pie?" "Okay, if no pepperoni, how about onions?"

"What do you mean you don't like onions—we had them last week and you loved them."

It can go on and on until I want to grab the cell phone from his or her ear and smash it under my foot. My theory is those people never got any attention as children and now demand the "spotlight" by conspicuously gabbing so loud the whole train car becomes their captive (or should I say "captured") audience. Someday, I'll probably end up in jail for taking the law into my own hands on the Long Island

Railroad.

I arrived in Ronkonkoma, about fifty miles from Penn Station, after a train ride of about an hour and fifteen minutes. In 1988, the track between Ronkonkoma and Penn Station was electrified for faster, more efficient service. In fact, the fastest ride between the two locations was a morning rush hour train that ran express with no stops after leaving Ronkonkoma and arrived in Penn Station in about 58 minutes.

Of course, such efficient service was too good to be true, and didn't last long. Shortly after the non-stop trip was inaugurated, the LIRR decided to add additional stops, forever making all rides between Penn Station and Ronkonkoma over an hour. All good things always seem to come to an end, but that change I will never understand.

The Ronkonkoma Station is an elaborate, red brick facility with a pedestrian skywalk that extends over the tracks and the adjacent roadway to an adjoining, multi-level parking garage that is safe and convenient. The main building has an impressive curved roof over the entranceway and windows with the word 'RONKONKOMA' in large black letters, that also curve with the contour of the roof.

The station was built with great detail and care. All the building materials were top of the line and installed with evident craftsmanship. The woodwork inside the ticket office spared no expense, with unique curved wood beams in grand display. Unfortunately, maintenance has been less than desired and signs of wear are showing. Hopefully, it won't be allowed to fall into gross disrepair.

From the parking garage in Ronkonkoma, I drove northeast to the Village of Port Jefferson, which the mayor once referred to as "one of the most picturesque of waterside villages to be found on Long Island." The Village is approximately 56 miles east of New York City, nestled next to Port Jefferson Harbor on the north shore.

The deep-water harbor is serviced by a ferry company that transports cars and passengers across Long Island Sound on three huge ferries that travel on an hourly schedule between Port Jefferson and Bridgeport, Connecticut. The Bridgeport-Port Jefferson Steamboat Company has been providing cross-sound ferry service since 1883.

Main Street in Port Jefferson is a lovely, rustic thoroughfare of stores, restaurants and shops that end at the water's edge. The docking pier for the ferries extends into the harbor. The waterfront hotel called "Danford's on the Sound" is located next to the pier. Antique street lights with simulated gas lanterns create the appearance of a small fishing village in the early 1900s. With its close resemblance to a small New England town, there is a substantial tourist trade in the summer.

My wife and I live about four blocks from the ferry terminal in a small, white clapboard house with a large wooden front porch. It is peaceful. The sound of the ferry's horn as it departs the terminal is a consistent nautical comfort.

I entered the front door of the house anticipating an ice cold beer to start the evening with my wife. I'm a fortunate guy. My wife Kimberly, whom I call "Kim," is a very pretty brunette with shoulder-length hair, large, sexy, brown eyes, soft skin and a naturally tan complexion. She works out frequently and keeps herself in very good shape.

After twenty years of marriage, I am (and always have been) very attracted to Kim. My best friend, Marie Carney, introduced us. Marie, God rest her soul, died fifteen years ago from cancer and the memories of her are always with me.

Anyway, Marie and I first met when I was in the eighth grade and she was in the seventh. We both went to St. Mary's High School in Manhasset, Long Island. At that time, St. Mary's had a separate boys' school and girls' school a few blocks apart—forced gender segregation that probably forever damaged the boys' ability to properly relate to women. Eventually, some astute administrator realized that the separation of the sexes was a prehistoric concept and combined the schools.

Over the years, Marie and I often hung out together on weekends. I usually went to Marie's house and watched sporting events with her brothers or talked together and played "Group Therapy." Marie and I never actually dated, although we often double-dated with each of us going out with someone else. There were occasions when we did create some boy-girl mischief between ourselves, but that was the exception rather than the rule.

Both Marie's family and my family grew up in Manhasset on the north shore of the Island. Today, it is a prestigious, wealthy community a short twenty-seven minute ride to New York City on the Long Island Railroad. However, when I grew up in the town many years ago, it was a close-knit, middle-class town of people with mostly modest incomes, although there were some huge estates like the 500-acre John Jay Whitney property. Most of the residents were Irish Catholics with many children. I might not know every person I ran into, but I surely knew his or her brother or sister.

Plandome Road was the main street of the town and, during my teenage years, had all the usual small-town stores most would expect. My family's home on High Meadow Road, in the Norgate section, was only a few short blocks from Plandome Road, St. Mary's Church, the elementary school and the high school. Back then, you got around by walking, riding your bike or occasionally hitchhiking. Since everyone was so familiar, it was easy to get a ride as soon as you stuck out your thumb. Nowadays, I wouldn't recommend it.

After graduation from high school, I attended a small Catholic liberal arts college in Massachusetts. When Marie graduated high school a year later, she attended a girls' college in Westchester, New York. Coincidentally, Kim went to the same college as Marie and they became close friends. One night when I was home from college, Marie called and told me that she and her college friends would be at Kilmeade's Bar on Plandome Road.

I was happy to attend, since Kilmeade's was my favorite bar in Manhasset and also within walking distance of my family's home. In fact, all essential products and services were available on a two or three-block section of Plandome Road: across from Kilmeade's was Phil's Sports Shop (owned by Phil Ruggerio, a legendary Manhasset businessman with a kind heart and pleasant manner), a florist, a liquor store next to Kilmeade's, a religious card store, a newspaper shop on the corner, the Lamplight Bar, Town Hall Pharmacy, Grand Union Supermarket, the public elementary school, and the Town Hall.

But Kilmeade's was my main hang out. It was fairly narrow inside, with a long wooden bar running practically the length of the establishment. There was only room for a few tables against the side wall across from the bar. A few feet past the end of the bar was a small backroom with several more tables and a pool table in the middle. The kitchen was in the rear. Jim Kilmeade was an elderly Irish gentleman with a full head of white hair. He always said loudly in a lingering, Gaelic bellow, "Thank Yoooou" each time a customer purchased a 25¢ draft of beer. Jim's wife and son both worked at the bar, with Jim's wife making her famous oversized sandwiches and hamburgers in the kitchen. It was always friendly, full of kids my same age that I knew by face, if not by name. Plus, it had a familiar "bar smell" of stale beer, booze and old wood.

I first started going to Kilmeade's on Friday afternoons in my senior year of high school (the drinking age was 18). For some reason, the seniors were let out of school on Fridays at 1:00 p.m. and, of course, we would be in Kilmeade's, a short five-minute walk, by 1:05 p.m. I can't imagine why the high school thought it was a good idea to release the seniors so early on a Friday when it was a well-known secret that the local gin mill was our next stop.

One of my most memorable times at Kilmeade's was the night I anxiously waited to learn if I had passed the New York State Bar Examination. Back then, first listing of the names that passed the Bar was printed in the *New York Times* on a pre-designated date. In order to prepare myself to face the test results, I went to Kilmeade's early in the evening to surround myself with friends. Then, I took the Long Island Railroad to New York City so I could grab a first edition of the *New York Times* as it was delivered to Penn Station just after midnight. I purchased a copy of the paper just as the wires that bundled the papers were being cut. To my great joy and/or astonishment, I found my name.

Upon receiving the good news and wondering what hundredth of a percentile of the minimum passing grade I exceeded, I took the train back to Manhasset and rejoined my friends at Kilmeade's to celebrate. What a mistake. Before I knew it, my space at the bar was lined with tequila shots, slices of lemon and salt shakers. I don't remember how many I threw back because I don't remember much of anything after the first few. Hopefully, I had a ton of fun. Of course, the next day I was so terribly ill. I've never had a shot of anything since.

Despite my hangover, I returned to Kilmeade's after Marie called and asked me to join her and her friends from college. Honestly, I was not in the bar two minutes before I first spotted Kimberly and started staring. You know, that blank, expressionless gawk that men constantly bombard on women as the sexes silently cross paths each day of everyday life. Quite inexplicably, "the stare" did not have the usual result of annoying or antagonizing its target (as far as I know).

Marie introduced us and Kim was friendly, engaging and quite proficient at small talk. Of course, she was probably thinking she had to be nice to Marie's closest hometown friend, while all I was thinking were the usual man-type thoughts and checking out her figure (discreetly) at the same time. I'm good at multitasking.

Kim must have sensed my mental salivating because she started to talk about her long-time boyfriend who worked as a bartender in White Plains. In view of the boyfriend situation, I decided my best tactic was to use my status as Marie's best friend to keep in contact with Kim by letter and phone while awaiting any change in her social status. No Facebook back then. Also, I would occasionally run into Kim whenever I visited Marie at their college.

Several years after our first meeting at Kilmeade's, I was driving home from the law school in Boston when I decided to stop at Kim's apartment in Port Washington. After graduation she took a teaching job at the local Catholic elementary school during the week. Since it was Saturday, I hoped she had stayed in town. I didn't think it was a good idea to knock on her door unannounced, so I just kept driving around her block until I was lucky enough to see her leave her apartment building as she walked towards her car. I pulled into her parking lot and said I just happened to be in the neighborhood. Kim decided not to call me a liar. In fact, she asked me if I wanted to go with her to Jones Beach (I astutely hesitated before agreeing to join her in order to give the impression I had to be somewhere else).

Once at the beach, Kim revealed her very sensuous two-piece red bikini and dangling, gold hoop earrings. That sealed the deal for me. Now all I had to do was get rid of the boyfriend. Of course, I never imagined that it would happen that night, while we were having dinner at her apartment.

The boyfriend showed up that night uninvited, knocking on the front door just as the baked chicken was being served. I was in the kitchen. Kim was speaking with the boyfriend in the living room. He must have sensed some withdrawal of affection from Kim because he abruptly left without saying hello or goodbye to me (although we had met on several occasions at the bar where he worked). I didn't know it at the time, but Kim and the boyfriend were already on the way out and my presence that evening merely confirmed the inevitable. From then on, Kim and I were an item.

Fast forward to November 2008, I arrived home and opened the refrigerator door to get the cold beer I had been looking forward to after a long day of work.

"I'm glad you didn't get home too late tonight," Kim called from the other room, knowing that my profession often required late nights at the office.

"I wanted to get to bed early tonight so I'm well rested for the meeting tomorrow," I called back.

I opened my beer and poured Kim a glass of white wine. Kim entered the kitchen and we kissed. Our lips touched only for a moment. Not exactly passionate, but a special ritual we maintained each night.

"I still don't understand why you are meeting with these doctors," Kim mentioned. "You are a defense attorney and the doctors will probably want you to switch sides and file a complaint to collect their unpaid fees. You said the doctor didn't mention a medical malpractice suit against him, so there is no other reason to consult with you other than to start a lawsuit."

"And your question is what?" I responded, a little too aggressively.

"My question is when did you decide to become a collection attorney?"

I was concerned that her inquisitive probing was about to set an edgy tone to the evening. However, her point was essentially correct. But the best approach I've discovered for smooth marital relations was to agree fully and enthusiastically with the points presented by one's spouse.

This applies whether her points were right or wrong but, as I said, she was correct in this instance. In fact, I've exclusively been a defense attorney my entire career, either representing attorneys sued for malpractice or businessmen sued for wrongful acts as directors or officers of public corporations. I never started a lawsuit against anyone except when I cut my finger taking the lid off a can of peanuts. I won the lawsuit. I'm undefeated at least.

"You're right, honey. But it appears this may be a huge case. The doctor I spoke to told me that not only was he being consistently underpaid by the managed health care industry, but hundreds of other doctors were in the same situation."

Basically, I told Kim that the damages suffered by the doctors could add up to millions, so why not hear out the potential client?

"Regardless, Brian, I don't think money should be your motivation for starting a lawsuit, especially when prosecuting a lawsuit hasn't been your practice for the last twenty years," she responded.

Kim then astutely added, "By the way, good luck trying to convince the jury that these wealthy doctors are entitled to collect more money for medical services that have already been paid when the sole purpose is to make them even wealthier. Plus, the jurors probably just got bills from their health care companies raising the premiums on their health insurance."

Kim kept piling on the negatives, seemingly with the purpose of assisting me in my practice of law. Since she clearly was not going to stop telling me all the reasons why it was stupid to make the appointment, I focused on a way to divert the topic of conversation.

"I agree with everything you say, Kim." This is another version of the 'You're right, honey' rule. "I probably should have thought it through more before I agreed to meet, but I said I would and the meeting is the first thing tomorrow."

It seemed to work, since the next series of topics had to do with whether I wanted a baked potato with dinner and about my choice of a TV program. Our usual "workweek" evening conversation. Thank God, we were back on course.

But the truth is that my dearest Kimberly had certainly put many valid questions in my mind regarding why this meeting was not such a good idea. Little did I know then, but I should have followed my wife's cue and immediately sent the following email to Doctor Brown:

"MEETING FOR TOMORROW CANCELLED. DON'T CALL AGAIN, EVER."

The next morning, Kim surprised me with a birthday gift

a week early. Maybe she felt a little guilty over her accurate, but critical, remarks of the night before.

"It's the least I can do to repair the overly sensitive, middle-aged male ego," she said, upon presenting me with a heavy, rectangular box about sixteen inches tall and eight inches wide. The outside of the box was covered entirely in black velvet material.

Upon lifting the lid of the box, I pulled out a solid glass globe about the size of a softball, although much heavier. The land surfaces on the globe were etched in a cloudy white design, with the shape of the oceans left smooth and transparent. There was also a separate, small rectangular base on which the globe was placed for display.

"Thank you. This is stunning. I'll put it on my dresser upstairs," I said.

"But I bought it as a gift for your office," she responded.

"Yes, of course. I will put it on the credenza in my office. Thanks again."

Marriage. It is an acquired taste that fully blossoms after years of learning and interaction. The new globe would be put in my office and nothing would be gained by arguing the point. Besides, if I put it on my dresser I risked being smashed with it during a future marital spat. I was better off with the globe at work. No question about it.

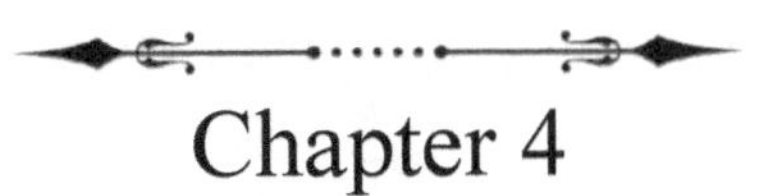

Chapter 4

The morning of my meeting with the doctors was crisp, cool and sunny. I felt full of energy and ready to take on the challenges of the day. This translates to mean I didn't drink too many beers the night before, deviating from my usual behavior.

I dressed as usual in a dark, three-button suit with a bright-colored tie and an Oxford cloth shirt with a button-down collar. Although many lawyers in the office dress casually, I doubt the client is going to believe your legal drivel wearing a shrunken polo/golf shirt and wrinkled khaki pants. Image and credibility are everything in the legal business. It's important to look like you know what you're talking about before you explain to a client what you are talking about.

The meeting was scheduled for the large conference room, also on the 45th floor. It contained a forty-foot conference table surrounded by black leather chairs with high backs and mahogany arms. The four over-sized windows along the wall revealed an array of midtown skyscrapers, including the massive 102-story Empire State Building, the tallest building in New York City since September 11, 2001. The Freedom Tower, also known as One World Trade Center, will eventually exceed the height of the Empire State Building.

Like my building at 40 Wall Street, the Empire State Building was also struck by an airplane in thick fog. It occurred on July 28, 1945 when a B-25 Mitchell bomber struck the building between the 79th and 80th floors. Once again, I needed to either stop thinking so much about these aerial tragedies or just move the location of the law firm to the first floor.

My firm, Alfonso and Ryan, is a small firm of ten partners and fifteen associates. We do defense work for many insurance companies and banks located in downtown Manhattan. The firm does a very good job for our clients and the compensation is sufficient to pay the bills, but will never make me rich enough to retire while still in good health.

My wife wasn't far from the truth when she sensed a change in my professional direction that was motivated, in part, by the possibility of filing a big payday lawsuit. As a rule, thirty-three percent of the recovery is paid to the lawyers. But I didn't have time at the moment for deep self-analysis. I was about to greet the new client that could provide the vehicle to navigate my career adjustment.

I walked into the conference room at 9:45 a.m. and greeted Mary Douglas sitting at the table reading through some files.

"Hello, how are you today?" Consistent with my personal conduct rules, I did not mention that her very sheer, baby-blue blouse was perfectly contoured to her upper torso.

"Oh, fine. I'm actually looking forward to meeting Dr. Brown and hearing about his legal problem. Also, I can't wait to start my vacation next week. My boyfriend and I are going to St. Martin in the Caribbean."

I had an immediate vision of her walking on the very popular "clothing optional" beach known as Orient Beach on the French side of the island, with the other side being the more conservative Dutch St. Maarten.

But, more importantly, I can't understand why a young,

single, professional woman such as Mary would think it acceptable to tell her married, middle-aged boss with presumably middle-class values that she was going to spend the week in a hotel room with her boyfriend in the Caribbean. Not that I'm old-fashioned or naive (I think), but how could she possibly believe this conversation is appropriate with the person she worked for, especially first thing in the morning.

What if a month from now she breaks up with the current boyfriend and then tells me she is taking her summer vacation traveling Europe with "the new man" in her life. This is all too much information. I don't want or need to know about her sleeping companions. The rule should be that I won't ask who you vacation with and you don't volunteer the information. Think of it as the heterosexual version of the "Don't Ask, Don't Tell" policy implemented in the military during the Clinton administration.

Anyway, I like Mary as a person and as a professional, so I changed the topic back to business.

"I think the game plan for the meeting is to just let Dr. Brown, and anyone else he brings, tell us why he came to see us and what he wants us to do for him. The rest we'll just play by ear," I said.

"Okay, I just got an email on my BlackBerry. There are two people downstairs waiting at the security desk. I'll get them and be right back," Mary said.

Five minutes later, into the conference room walked two individuals who introduced themselves as Dr. Martin Brown and Dr. Stanley Hyman. Both were dressed in suits, although Doctor Hyman's was so small it barely fit him.

Dr. Brown was about 5'10" with short grey hair, black-framed glasses, large ears and narrow little eyes that were too close to his large protruding nose. Although he was clearly in his early fifties, he was slim with powerful shoulders that made it look like someone had superimposed an aging face on a youthful body. He walked with an air of purpose and determination.

Dr. Hyman was a little younger and a shorter man, with a stocky build. He had a pale complexion, high forehead and a crew cut. He introduced himself in a deep, muted voice. He immediately annoyed me with both his sweaty hand and a refusal to look me in the eye when I greeted him. It seemed he had other, much more important things on his mind. He appeared more suited to professional wrestling than a white coat and a stethoscope.

"Good morning, I'm Brian. Thanks for coming in. It's a pleasure to meet you both," I said. They didn't see me wipe off the moisture from Dr. Hyman's hand on my pants.

"I'm glad we could finally get together to see if you can help us with our legal problem," Dr. Brown said.

"That's what my firm and I are here for, so feel free to start at the beginning. Take your time and tell me everything. You met Mary downstairs. She will be helping us today as my very competent associate. Please, start your story whenever you feel comfortable. We have no formalities and no time restrictions," I recited as my standard opening remarks to a new client.

"Well, Dr. Hyman and I are representatives of the New York/New Jersey Medical Association that consists of approximately 60,000 doctors, although we also have contact with thousands of additional doctors nationwide. Our professional fees are being significantly underpaid on a consistent basis by managed health care organizations, but especially and most egregiously by the biggest of them all, ZeiiMed, Inc. As doctors, we are sick of it and want you to do something to get it to stop. That's it in a nutshell."

"I understood this was going to be the general subject matter of our discussion, but I need details regarding the billing procedures, the payment methodology and whatever knowledge you have as to how ZeiiMed calculates a payment that is less than what you are owed," I responded.

"Yes, of course. I'll put some meat on the bones," Dr. Brown said. "As you know, most people don't pay their doctor in cash or by check. The patient has health care insurance, usually with ZeiiMed, and just shows the insurance card to the doctor's administrative staff. ZeiiMed, being the huge, all powerful, big-brother company that it is, sends to all licensed doctors a full-color, large print brochure telling the doctors that their medical services will be paid upon acceptance of the patient's ZeiiMed insurance card.

"The problem," Dr. Brown continued, "is that ZeiiMed's propaganda brochure doesn't say how much a doctor will be paid for a particular medical service, but merely states that the payment will be made based on a complex formula that is plugged into a computer to calculate the 'usual, reasonable and customary' rate for doctors in a particular geographical area. All the doctor is required to do is look up a claim code that corresponds to the medical services provided and submit the claim code to ZeiiMed on a ZeiiMed claim form. ZeiiMed does everything else, resulting in a payment that ZeiiMed contends is the exact amount every other doctor is getting for the same service, although it is always significantly below the doctors' posted schedule of charges."

"So, what's the hitch?" I asked, trying to sound well informed and analytical. "It appears you get paid by ZeiiMed the same amount paid to all of your colleagues in the same area for the same service. In other words, Dr. ABC down the street is getting the same as you received for the same service. Isn't that equitable, socialized medicine?"

All my comment did was get the good doctor a little agitated.

"It's not equitable for a number of reasons that I am happy to explain to you," Dr. Brown tersely responded. "First, ZeiiMed doesn't explain to us exactly what information is downloaded into its computers to arrive at the usual, reasonable and customary rates that serve as the foundation for all reimbursements. Not a single doctor that I know has received from ZeiiMed a 'rate' survey form requesting sample fee schedules or other fee information in many years."

So, where does ZeiiMed get the data used to calculate the rates?" I asked.

"Candidly, it appears to us that ZeiiMed feeds its computers data regarding rates and fees that are ten to fifteen years old," Dr. Brown explained. "But ZeiiMed isn't telling and it's impossible to get the unpaid balance of our medical bills from the patient's own pocketbook. Plus, we know for a fact that the damn ZeiiMed computers don't distinguish between the amount paid to highly specialized surgeons for a pre-surgery office visit and the amount paid to a general practitioner treating a cold at a walk-in medical clinic. They both get the same reduced amount for a standard office visit and the computer assumes the length of the office visit is always the same for all. Plus, multiple medical procedures administered to the same patient on the same day are simply disregarded and only one of the procedures gets paid."

"It does seem that ZeiiMed should be required to periodically test its computer database by sending survey forms and information requests to doctors to determine if the doctors on the same skill level are being paid a consistent, appropriate and fair fee for the same medical service with an automatic inflation increase," I commented.

At that point, the very quiet Dr. Hyman spoke up.

"Either they don't do such surveys because ZeiiMed doesn't want accurate, up-to-date rate information or worse, the sampling is done and ZeiiMed purposefully refuses to change the database despite knowledge of its inherent obsolescence. Personally, I think that ZeiiMed intentionally inputs its computer database with old, distorted physician records and payment information knowing that reduced reimbursement payments will result. But it seems no one can prove it so no one can stop it."

Although perspiration was accumulating on Dr. Hyman's over-sized forehead, I played devil's advocate. Lawyers find this very easy to do.

"So, tell ZeiiMed to go to hell. The doctors in your Association are no longer going to accept ZeiiMed's insurance cards from your patients and you're not going to do any business with ZeiiMed."

Dr. Brown again took over, apparently concerned Dr. Hyman's clearly agitated state might lead to heart failure. He certainly didn't want to perform mouth-to-mouth on Hyman.

"It's not that easy, ZeiiMed has, without a doubt, the best insurance premiums in the industry. Companies in New York, New Jersey and across the country jump at the chance to provide health insurance to their employees at inexpensive rates, and no one is cheaper than ZeiiMed. ZeiiMed is like the Wal-Mart of the health insurance industry. No one can compete with its prices."

"Actually, I do know. My law firm shopped around and no one else was close to ZeiiMed's group rate premiums," I noted.

"Exactly, that damn company controls health insurance from coast to coast," Dr. Brown responded, now getting worked up himself.

"I am a cardiac surgeon, which means I'm capable of taking your heart out of your body, placing in on top of your chest, cleaning out your arteries and returning the heart to where it belongs, giving you thirty more years of life. But if this situation with ZeiiMed doesn't change I'm out of business and looking for another profession."

I immediately had the terrifying vision of these really smart doctors suddenly going to law school, eventually saturating the legal marketplace with new shingles on every corner. Something had to be done for these doctors before they squeezed me out of business. Holding in my own panic as best I could, I decided to make a suggestion.

"So, why don't we go after ZeiiMed to recover everything you have been underpaid. Also, we will change the way ZeiiMed does business by getting an injunction to force business changes in the database used by ZeiiMed to calculate its payments to your colleagues."

Of course, I didn't mention that I never filed a major class action lawsuit before. It didn't seem like the ideal time to bring it up.

"Yes," Dr. Hyman said anxiously, "We can recruit thousands of doctors across the country that have the same issue, probably over 700,000 doctors. I envision a national class of all doctors across the country marching into Court against ZeiiMed."

"I can easily calculate the amount of money involved in such a lawsuit," Dr. Brown added. "Suppose each doctor has ten office visits a day and reasonably anticipates a fair insurance payment of eighty percent of his already discounted two hundred dollar charge per visit, which is one hundred and sixty dollars. But the doctor only gets paid from ZeiiMed a mere fifty percent of one hundred sixty dollars, or eighty dollars. That is an eighty dollar per day reduction for each of the ten daily office visits, multiplied by seven hundred thousand doctors. You do the math."

"Wow," I said, "That's eight hundred dollars a day that ZeiiMed underpays each of the seven hundred thousand doctors. Multiply that by one hundred fifty work days a year and the damages caused by ZeiiMed's shenanigans are over eighty-four billion dollars. And it's been many years that ZeiiMed has been cheating the profession. Of course, a doctor in the low-country of South Carolina doesn't charge two hundred dollars for an office visit, but the percentage reductions are the same.

I quietly calculated the standard legal fee of one-third and quietly took a deep gasp of air. Dollar signs danced in my head. I think I was about to hyperventilate.

"By the way," I said. "A lawyer does not have to personally recruit all seven hundred thousand doctors to sign retainer agreements in order to be included in the Complaint and be part of the lawsuit. The procedure is simply to ask the Court to certify a nationwide class of doctors and then, after settlement or jury verdict, issue a notice to each doctor asking if he or she wants to participate or opt-out of the class. If the doctor elects to participate, he or she gets a proportionate share of the money being paid by ZeiiMed as restitution."

"Let's do it then," Dr. Brown proclaimed. "I have a lot of confidence in your ability to get this started and see it to a very successful conclusion. We did our research. We know of your many legal accomplishments, including your fine representation of Roy M. Cohn as was reported in several newspapers."

"Thank you. I'm confident I can meet your expectations. To start with, Mary and I will draft a Complaint setting forth our claims of wrongdoing against ZeiiMed. The Complaint will ask for money damages and an injunction forcing ZeiiMed to change the way it does business with the doctors."

"That sounds like a good start," Dr. Brown commented.

"Once ZeiiMed files an Answer responding to the Complaint, discovery will begin," I explained. "By that, I am referring to the Court Rules that permit us to compel ZeiiMed to produce all documents in its possession regarding ZeiiMed's procedures and practices in paying the doctors that performed medical services for patients with ZeiiMed insurance cards. The production is not just limited to paper documents. It encompasses all electronic communications, including emails sent and received by every employee of ZeiiMed that dealt with the paying of doctors' bills. Hopefully, this is how we will find a paper trail confirming what ZeiiMed's been doing. After that is completed, we get to conduct depositions to question ZeiiMed's employees and executives about the information revealed in the documents. And this all takes place before the trial starts."

"Well then, Dr. Hyman and I will not take up anymore of your time so you can get right to work," Dr. Brown said.

We exchanged cell phone numbers, said our goodbyes and shook hands.

Mary and I remained in the conference room after the doctors left.

"I will send a formal retention agreement to the doctors for them to sign, with a disclosure of our fee of thirty-three percent of any settlement or verdict," Mary stated.

"Okay," I responded, "and as soon as you get back from vacation, please draft the Complaint for my review. We will file the Complaint in the United States District Court for the Southern District of New York. Please allege in the Complaint that the wrongful acts of ZeiiMed constitute a breach of fiduciary duty and fraud, with a separate cause of action asserting violations of the Racketeer Influenced and Corrupt Organizations Act. You know, RICO. Also, add a count for violations of the Sherman Antitrust laws and a count alleging inadequate benefit payments in violation of the Employee Retirement Income Security Act, known as ERISA."

"No problem. I've got it all written down. Anything else?" Mary asked.

"Yes. Don't forget to add some other managed health care companies as defendants in addition to ZeiiMed," I continued. "ZeiiMed is the big fish target, but we need some other players to prove an illegal conspiracy under RICO. We will have to be vague on exactly what ZeiiMed did wrong, other than the fact it failed to pay the doctors the amounts due them for providing medical care to people insured with ZeiiMed. Then, once we get ZeiiMed's internal company documents we should learn how ZeiiMed actually made the mathematical reductions and ZeiiMed's rationale for making them, although I'm sure the only real reason is profit maximization."

"I thought Dr. Brown's comment about Roy M. Cohn to be strange," Mary stated, changing the topic. "I know you defended Cohn in a lawsuit and you got a good result, but that was many years ago. I'm guessing he died around 1986. The doctors want to file a massive suit on behalf of thousands of plaintiffs—that's got nothing to do with your defense of Cohn."

Mary's mention of Roy M. Cohn brought back memories. Mr. Cohn had been one of the prosecuting attorneys in the U.S. Government's espionage case against Julius and Ethel Rosenberg. The Rosenbergs were accused of conspiring to pass secrets to the Soviets regarding atomic bomb research at a government laboratory in New Mexico. The jury eventually found them guilty and both were executed in 1953 in the electric chair.

Later, Mr. Cohn became chief counsel to Senator Joseph McCarthy in connection with the Senate Subcommittee investigations of communists in the U.S. government. History refers to the investigations as a "witch hunt" because many of the accusations of communist leanings were unsubstantiated and without evidence.

I eventually met Mr. Cohn in the early 1980's when he was considered a prominent, yet combative, power broker and celebrity attorney. Although I was young and fairly inexperienced, my law firm gave me the opportunity to defend Mr. Cohn in a lawsuit against him in New York Supreme Court. It turned out to be a major piece of litigation that arose out of a high-profile matrimonial settlement between a billionaire couple living in Manhattan.

As a result, the litigation involving Mr. Cohn was in the newspapers, along with my name as his attorney. I was fortunate to obtain a very favorable resolution and Mr. Cohn never once complained that someone so famous shouldn't be stuck with a lawyer still learning his trade.

But Mary was right. It was odd that Dr. Brown mentioned Mr. Cohn. My representation of a flamboyant, newsworthy attorney many years ago certainly did not qualify me to handle a massive, billion-dollar class action lawsuit— especially when there are several well-known firms that specialize in bringing large, complex litigation, with teams of associates ready to spring into action.

But, being dazzled by the present opportunity, I elected to just disregard all doubts and embarked enthusiastically on this exciting new work that should turn out to be very rewarding, both professionally and monetarily. Why should I care why the doctors hired me? Why should I be wary of doctors bearing gifts? I am running full steam ahead and making the most of this opportunity of a lifetime.

"Mary," I said, finally responding to her question. "Let's not get too analytical here and just be thankful for the new work. I really don't care why they hired me. We'll meet after you get back from vacation and start on the Complaint. We'll show our new clients that their faith in us will pay off. End of discussion."

Next time, I won't be so naive and so short-sighted. More importantly, I will listen carefully when a bright young woman tries to instill a little healthy skepticism in me.

Chapter 5

I was sitting in my office on a bitterly cold day in December 2008. I could sense that change was in the air. The country was in the worst economic downturn since the Depression of the 1930s. President-elect Barack Obama was scheduled to be sworn in as President on January 20, 2009, with a promised revitalization plan to restart the economy.

In fact, the advisors to the President-elect already prepared a massive seven hundred billion dollars plus recovery plan intended to restore millions of jobs and reignite the flow of money through the nation's lending institutions.

On a personal level, I felt encouraged and energized by the new lawsuit that was fortuitously placed at my doorstep. While the prosecution of this massive litigation will be challenging and all consuming, I perceived the change in my life as reflective of a nationwide sense of optimism. Hope and new beginnings are being fueled by the incoming administration's "promise of change."

These uplifting emotions seemed to suddenly stream outward and convert into words and phrases as I sat at my desk and contemplated the change as promised over and over again by Mr. Obama. The change that was wholeheartedly embraced by those who elected him.

I felt a positive anticipation of a bright future on a personal level and on the national level. Everything was about to be different and would never be the same again.

Optimism and change were the key words of the moment. Although the world seemed to be on the brink of financial collapse, Mr. Obama was peddling a cure that was eagerly embraced by the voting public. Maybe things really were going to improve because everything we have will be redistributed for the better.

THE NEW

All that appeared true seems to be coming unglued;
All that was established is being questioned anew;
All that was in place is being quickly erased;
We are coming to a crossroad on a collision course
and the train is rapidly accelerating;
The winds of the New are howling and anxious to be
embraced;
The usual is blinding and needs to be replaced;

So, turn it around and rethink your thoughts;
The old ways are going and the cracks are showing;
Reshape the unchangeable and shake the unshakable;
Then face the new light with its brilliance absorbing
you;

Now you've left behind what shouldn't have been and
attained a new plateau to view the past;
When you arise the old will be left in the wake;
And you will go forward to a better place.

Don't worry. The moment passed and I quickly got hold of myself. I'm smart enough not to trust politicians and certainly smart enough not to trust strangers bearing gifts, except when the strangers are doctors with a multi-billion dollar lawsuit.

Within minutes, I had returned to reality and reverted back to the mundane routine of everyday life.

It's probably best not to get too excited about the future. Life can take a turn for the worse quickly.

Unfortunately, it was a lesson I learned the hard way.

Chapter 6

Shortly after returning from her Caribbean vacation, Mary came to my office with the newly drafted Complaint. Doctors Martin Brown and Stanley Hyman were the Lead Plaintiffs representing a nationwide class of doctors.

Although I was very interested in reviewing her work product, her tan got my attention.

"You look like you had a good time in the sun."

"Oh yes, I had a wonderful time and the weather was just perfect," Mary responded.

Mary wore a white short-sleeve top that certainly accentuated her skin tone. I wonder if all male office workers feel distracted in a similar situation, or am I some kind of a maladjusted, middle-aged man? Maybe I should get my mental condition checked out by a shrink. I could just see myself explaining, "Well, Dr. Shrink, it wasn't my fault. The thoughts just poured into my head. She's blond, tan, bright, engaging and terrifically proportioned—I'm only human, after all."

"You're wrong, Mr. Bradford. As your doctor, I'm telling you there is something wrong with you. I have evaluated hundreds of men and they were quite capable of controlling their prurient thoughts while conducting business in the workplace. Since you seem totally incapable of doing so, I am prescribing some pills that will straighten out your brain waves and extinguish your libido."

Having now decided never to see a doctor or tell anyone

my thoughts, I turned my attention back to Mary's conversation.

"The economy," Mary said, "is so bad that it was remarkable how empty the plane was. The hotel was only half-booked."

"I know," I responded. "It is incredible how the world can be so suddenly devastated by a massive recession. A few short months ago, mortgage money was easy to get, everyone could afford a home and credit was no problem. The government wanted a house for every person just like it once promised a chicken in every pot. The banks, financial institutions and brokerage firms were only too happy to lend the money with little or no background check on credit worthiness or employment history."

"I agree," Mary commented. "Then it got even more volatile when brokerage houses created pools of high-risk mortgages, essentially composed of sub-prime loans to borrowers with low credit scores and delinquent payment histories. Investors were then sold securities collateralized by the pools of high-risk mortgages, with little disclosure of the risks involved. The stage was set. The "subprime" borrowers started to default on the mortgages that never should have been approved. Real estate values plummeted worldwide. People could no longer refinance to remain liquid. The foreclosures began. As the defaults rose, the value of the mortgage-backed securities tumbled downward..."

"And that's when the house of cards really came down," I added. "Once the value of the mortgage-backed securities bottomed out, it caused the hedge funds, brokerage houses and banks with massive investments in these securities to take huge losses. The insurance industry was then required to put up billions of dollars of collateral payments to help cover the devaluation of the securities. The collateral was required as the result of the issuance of credit default swaps, the insurance-like contracts that provided protection against significant devaluation of the securities. The problem was that the insurance companies didn't have billions of dollars in cash necessary to make the collateral payments, requiring federal bailouts."

"Then panic set in," Mary astutely noted. "With the losses piling up everybody lost confidence and was seized with fear. Everyone wanted to withdraw their cash and the brokerage houses struggled to cover the cash calls. Next thing you know, Lehman Brothers is in bankruptcy. It couldn't survive the 'run on the bank' and the other brokerage houses and large banks wouldn't provide large cash infusion without a government guarantee of the funds.

"What a mess," I added.

"To make matters worse," Mary continued, "Lehman's competitors were shorting their stock, causing it to fall so dramatically that bankruptcy was unavoidable in the face of a credit downgrade by the rating agencies. It just went from bad to worse. I'm sure the federal government regrets its refusal to loan Lehman Brothers sufficient cash to stay afloat. It seems everybody failed to foresee that the Lehman bankruptcy would cause a worldwide credit freeze that almost resulted in a worldwide financial collapse."

"The huge government bailout to the private sector then began because everyone realized that further bankruptcies would cripple the economy beyond repair," I added.

"You know," Mary said, "It was like the scene from the 1947 film, 'It's a Wonderful Life.' In the movie, there was a 'run on the bank' because all the depositors at the old Bailey Savings and Loan wanted their money back at the same time. Jimmy Stewart, George Bailey in the movie, told his customers, as they crowded elbow-to-elbow into the bank, that their money wasn't sitting in the vault as cash. Rather, their deposits were invested in each of their homes as mortgage money. George Bailey explained that the bank needed time to get cash necessary to refund their deposits. The same thing essentially happened to Lehman Brothers. It had good value, but it needed cash immediately because everyone demanded it now by pulling their investments. At the same time, the financial industry had ceased doing business with Lehman. No one would loan it money and there was no time to sell its assets at fair value. With no cash or liquid assets, it was the end of the line for Lehman."

All this talk was starting to get depressing, so I decided to fall back on my newfound confidence in a bright and better tomorrow.

"I believe everything will work out fine," I responded to Mary. "The stock market will stabilize and the economy will rebound once the markets accept that the worst is over as a result of the government bailouts and the new economic plan of Obama. So, hand me the draft Complaint and let's get on with the business of doing what we are paid to do. I have great hope for the future so I'm not going to worry about the short term."

Mary decided not to pick up on my new message of cheerfulness and continued to debate the state of the economy.

"I agree that the real estate market, the banks and the stock market will eventually bounce back, but it won't be overnight. It will take years, maybe even a decade. Remember when Congress first approved the bailout money of seven hundred billion dollars, with three hundred fifty billion dollars to be distributed immediately to financial institutions under the Troubled Asset Relief Program known as TARP? Congress was told the money would be used by the federal government to purchase the bad bank assets such as mortgage-backed securities that were fueling the billion-dollar losses."

"Yes, I remember that was the purpose."

"Guess what happened," Mary asked, undoubtedly knowing the answer. "The Treasury Department instead invested the three hundred fifty billion dollars directly in the banks, leaving undisturbed the troubled assets that were continuing to grow red hot and burn up all available cash and liquid assets. No question that billions more will now have to be spent to buy the bad assets unless the Treasury Department purchases billions of dollars of preferred stock in the shaky banks. That being said, I do agree with your belief that eventually everything will turn around. The economy will stabilize and then move forward, assuming Europe doesn't crash and burn."

"I sure hope we're both right," I commented.

"And one final and very important point," Mary said, without catching a breath. "Who are these wizards of Wall Street that were so greedy and diabolical that they put the whole world in a deep recession? I'll tell you, but it is obvious—they were all 'MEN.' That's right—not a woman among this band of thieves. Women are not only hardworking, but 'Honest' with a capital 'H.'"

My goodness, I had no idea Mary was so well read on both the state of the economy and the battle of the sexes. Maybe this was her way of telling me she wanted a raise. If so, I was tempted to ask why that boyfriend she vacationed with doesn't throw in a few bucks for living expenses. But I am getting off the subject. The point is that Mary is very smart (and correct about the culpability of 'Men') and I was too stupid (and/or chauvinistic) to give Mary the credit she deserved for her accurate comments on the state of the world.

Whatever, I decided to keep to my theme of being upbeat and uplifting. I had only one last thought before returning to the Complaint and the lawsuit.

"So, in summary," I said, "we both believe the economy will start to recover, the government will stimulate change and everybody will eventually be fully employed with money in their pockets—but we disagree on how long it will take."

I guess I over simplified, because Mary responded with a sense of agitation. "You're being sarcastic about an important matter. And, by the way, no economic system will ever provide full employment or anything close, especially with the quickly increasing trillion-dollar deficit. However, I do firmly believe there will be better days ahead."

That said it all, so I finally conceded that she was right (a lesson learned, as we know, from marriage). I told her I would review the Complaint immediately and call her to discuss my revisions.

She left my office with a friendly good-bye.

Chapter 7

The Complaint was finally done. It had taken several weeks and many revisions, but it was finally ready for filing in the United States District Court for the Southern District of New York. Doctors Brown and Hyman reviewed it and confirmed it was accurate and truthful.

As the attorney in charge of the case, the Federal Rules of Civil Procedure require me to sign the Complaint. My signature certifies that to the best of my knowledge the legal claims are supported by existing law and the factual contentions were confirmed as accurate after reasonable inquiry.

The problem was that I didn't really know the exact procedure followed by ZeiiMed in calculating its underpayments to the doctors. Presumably, ZeiiMed had some massive computer program that contained enormous amounts of data regarding medical practices in each geographical area of the country, along with the amounts charged for each service and the amounts actually paid by ZeiiMed.

But I had no knowledge of how ZeiiMed went from having presumably reliable fee data from physicians and then leaping to the next level of issuing payment checks that vastly reduced the amount actually paid for the medical service provided. Also, my clients had no information that would provide these answers, other than to guess that old data was being dumped into its computers. Both Doctors Brown and Hyman seemed very credible and passionate about their cause, but certainly didn't know what actually went on behind closed doors at ZeiiMed.

As a lawyer, I have, however, successfully acquired the skills necessary to fudge it. Thank goodness. I did that by reciting the same allegations over and over, changing the wording slightly each time. These lengthy, repetitive, redundant recitals enabled me to complete a fifty-page Complaint that essentially said:

"ZeiiMed—you owe us big time because you have been underpaying (i.e., stealing) millions and millions of dollars from thousands of doctors for years and it has to stop—now!"

I can only hope that the judge assigned to the Complaint will refrain from immediately throwing me out of Court. If I dodge that bullet, I will have an opportunity to find and develop evidence against ZeiiMed through the discovery permitted by the Federal Rules of Civil Procedure.

At this point, all I could do was hope for the best and rely on my many years of experience in convincing judges, juries, and adversaries that I know what I'm talking about, although the truth was to the contrary.

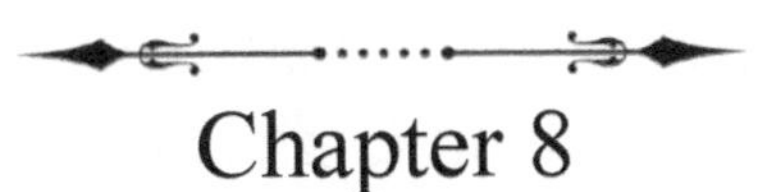

Chapter 8

After the Complaint was filed and served on ZeiiMed, I received a Notice from the Federal District Court to appear for a Pre-trial Conference.

The general purpose of the Conference was to discuss with the judge the issues in the case, including the claims asserted in our Complaint and ZeiiMed's defenses. Motions will be discussed, including the usual Motion to Dismiss filed by the Defendant.

Lastly, the Court will want to hear the attorneys' views on discovery. That is, what documents and depositions will be sought, as well as the agreed format for production of electronically stored information (ESI), such as emails. A Scheduling Order will then be issued by the Court, setting the trial date and the deadlines for completion of all pre-trial discovery and other pre-trial preparation.

I appeared at the courthouse for the Pre-trial Conference on January 11, 2009. The United States District Court for the Southern District of New York is located in lower Manhattan at 500 Pearl Street. The courthouse is dedicated to Daniel Patrick Moynihan, the United States Senator for New York from 1977 to 2001.

I entered the courtroom. I was astounded, as always, by how the design of the room emits an overwhelming expectation of justice with a compelling reverence of the law. The high ceiling contains an ornate gold leaf, with marble columns adorning the walls. The bench is an elevated wood platform with a high-backed leather chair for the judge.

The emblem of the United States is elevated on the wall behind the judge, just above the judicial entry door. The courtroom instills a humbling respect for the federal judiciary and a commanding sense of confidence that equal justice will be dispensed to all. At least, certainly, I hoped it worked that way today.

In front of the bench were two tables for the attorneys. There was a railing that separates the tables from the wooden pews for spectators.

I had asked Mary to meet me in the courtroom. I noticed she was already sitting at the counsel's table designated for the plaintiffs. At the second counsel's table (to my right as I faced the bench) were the attorneys for ZeiiMed. The law firm representing ZeiiMed was Tweed, Fox & Fortune. It is one of the oldest, biggest and most aggressive firms in New York City. The joke is that the attorneys at the firm wear tweed suits and are overwhelmingly skilled at "out-foxing" their opponents, all of which results in a fee payment of a "small fortune."

It was comical that Tweed, Fox & Fortune had an army of attorneys crowding around the small counsel's table (each charging five hundred fifty dollars an hour, at least), whereas it was just Mary and me at our table. Truth be told, I enjoyed the David versus Goliath stereotype of Mary and I against the white shoe legal establishment representing ZeiiMed. I hoped it gave us the appearance of righteous underdogs.

I sat next to Mary at our counsel's table. "Hello," I whispered to her, "isn't this exciting."

Appearing before a federal judge was an adrenaline rush and I hoped Mary would relish the professional opportunity and absorb the moment.

"How come all those lawyers at the other table look alike, dress alike and are all writing feverishly on identical yellow pads when the judge has not yet taken the Bench?" Mary exclaimed a little too loudly, apparently unhumbled by the surroundings.

"Good question," I responded quietly. "Aren't you being the sarcastic one today. But it's a good sign. It means you're relaxed and it's always important to appear comfortable and at ease when sitting in front of the Bench," I advised her.

"Thank you. I understand that," Mary responded. "But my point is why do ZeiiMed's lawyers all want to look like clones?"

"They think it makes them look very smart and very important. Actually, you should be very grateful that I don't make you dress up like my clone," I answered, with my usual impertinence.

We were interrupted by the sound of the Court Clerk banging his hand loudly three times on the door behind the Bench. Having gotten our attention, the Judge entered and all stood immediately. Once the Judge was seated, we took our chairs.

Judge Whitman Peter White is the oldest District Judge in the Southern District of New York. He is tall and thin, and appears fragile because of his drooping shoulders and shallow cheeks. His white hair is long and thinning, with isolated strands covering his ears. The deep wrinkles on his face, when combined with his other aging features, created a visual impression of meanness. His reputation is that of a taskmaster. He often spoke harshly to counsel and imposed difficult deadlines that were unchangeable. The courtroom was his world and he was the all-powerful master of it.

THE COURT: Come to order. Counsel for ZeiiMed,

please tell me what this case is about and your proposed discovery schedule.

This comment by the Judge was unusual and took me by surprise. It's my case, I'm counsel for the Plaintiffs, I filed the Complaint. I should be the one explaining what it's all about, not the counsel for ZeiiMed.

The lead attorney for ZeiiMed stood. His name is Charles Wadsworth and he is known as the Count of Confrontation. By all accounts, he was unrelenting, compulsive and uncompromising. Physically, he had a very good appearance. His hair was dark, thick and slicked back. His tan face was handsome and athletic, with sparkling white teeth. I wanted a "do-over." How could my luck be so bad that I'm stuck with the impressive-looking Mr. Wadsworth and his unpleasant personality as my adversary.

Since ZeiiMed was always saving money by underpaying the doctors, how come it overpaid when it comes to hiring a lawyer? Well, I guess I'm forced to play the hand I'm dealt.

MR. WADSWORTH: Good morning, Your Honor, it is always a privilege and an honor to appear before you. I've read the Complaint and I am at a loss to tell you exactly what the Plaintiffs' case is. As far as ZeiiMed is concerned, we would like to make a Motion to Dismiss the Complaint as factually and legally insufficient to support a claim for money damages. There just aren't sufficient particulars to make out a cause of action and I don't even know what the cause of action is. Fraud? Negligence? Breach of Contract? He makes many references to RICO, ERISA and the antitrust statute, but doesn't say exactly how and when ZeiiMed violated these laws.

Also, in the unlikely event this Court decides not to dismiss the Complaint, ZeiiMed would request an expedited trial date. We want this matter resolved quickly because the scandalous allegations, although farcical, have damaged the reputation of ZeiiMed and will continue to do so until Your Honor throws this Complaint into the corridor. We can produce over 100 million written documents and ESI in a month and complete all depositions six months after we get the Plaintiffs' documents.

THE COURT: "Mr. Bradford, what do you have to say? I'd like you to start by telling me what your case is about. I already understand that your clients want more money for medical services they already got paid for. You know, every Plaintiff that comes before me feels underpaid or cheated. However, that doesn't mean a legally sufficient Complaint has been filed with the necessary specificity.

MR. BRADFORD: Good morning, Your Honor. I will try to be succinct, but it is necessary to provide some background information that may appear overly simplistic and duplicative. I represent doctors throughout the country that have at least one major similarity. For years they were systematically underpaid by the defendant for the medical services they were asked to render. Moreover, they received the same ridiculous explanation from ZeiiMed when the payments were questioned. ZeiiMed told my clients that the Company puts all the billing data it has collected for many years into its computers and then produces a reasonable payment schedule that pays each doctor in the same area the same amount of money for the same service. This explanation is simply not true and we intend to prove it at trial. If the doctors had been paid a fair compensation we simply wouldn't be here.

I am here and the Complaint has been filed because the underpayments are extreme, the rationales untenable and the explanations unacceptable. Plus, ZeiiMed's only defense is to say 'we didn't do it' a thousand times over, like fifth grade boys denying they put the girls' braids in the inkwell.

THE COURT: But you have not given the Court a detailed explanation as to how the payment calculations made by the defendant are unfair or unreasonable, other than the fact that you simply don't like the actual amounts paid. What are the wrongful acts committed by ZeiiMed, who on behalf of the defendant committed them and when?

MR. BRADFORD: At this early stage of the case, I haven't yet located a 'deep-throat' confidential witness or obtained confidential ZeiiMed documents revealing who planned the wrongful acts, who executed the plan, the precise individuals who committed the wrongful acts and how the entire scheme was implemented. But I can state one thing for sure. ZeiiMed did what we allege and it wasn't done without important people at ZeiiMed planning and orchestrating it as part of a massive computer-driven scheme. And, once discovery begins, I'll get the rest of the answers. If I can get the computer data that's behind this whole mess we will eventually learn how ZeiiMed planned, executed and accomplished its unlawful operation, with the names of the ZeiiMed people who implemented it.

At this point, Mr. Wadsworth couldn't resist interrupting me with a negative comment. Up to now, he had been doing his best to appear courteous and civil. Of course, politeness was an unnatural act for him.

> MR. WADSWORTH: It has been my experience that you are supposed to have the evidence before you file a lawsuit and start spreading lies about a Defendant. He has no evidence and has now admitted as much to the Court. All he has is a couple of doctors complaining about how underpaid they are. Big deal. Lawyers gripe about the same thing, but usually don't make a federal case out of it.
>
> THE COURT: I'm inclined to agree with Mr. Wadsworth, but the Court will give the Plaintiffs six months to exchange documents and take depositions. After that, I will hear ZeiiMed's Motion to Dismiss. By then, Mr. Bradford, you had better put an awful lot of meat on your bare bone allegations or I'm throwing the Complaint out and you along with it. Clerk, call the next case.
>
> MR. BRADFORD: I will proceed accordingly. Good day, Your Honor.

As we left the courthouse, I mentioned to Mary an observation so obvious it didn't need to be spoken.

"We were lucky to get out of there alive. The Judge came pretty close to throwing us out on the street. Plus, I made some pretty strong promises to the Court and I'll be in big trouble if I don't deliver."

"It could get worse," Mary noted. "Judge White and Mr. Wadsworth both went to Harvard and the Judge started his legal career at Tweed, Fox & Fortune. And I am curious, do you always have such a good rapport with the Judge you appear before?"

"Very funny," I responded. "Yes, the deck is stacked against us. The Judge should have disqualified himself, but didn't. Our adversary is formidable and getting the evidence we need will be difficult. But we promised our clients that we would proceed zealously and apply ourselves completely. When we get back to the office, let's draft a demand for every conceivable letter and email ever created by ZeiiMed that pertains to the calculation of every payment made to each doctor for the last ten years."

"Sounds like we've got a ton of work ahead of us and I don't mean that sarcastically," Mary said. "A lot of late nights and weekends."

"I guess neither one of use will be taking a vacation to the Caribbean for a while," I said, as we walked back to the office.

"That's true for more than one reason," she said. "I broke up with my boyfriend last night so I have no one to travel with, even if we didn't have all this work."

I wasn't going to touch the subject of her social life, especially since we would be spending a lot of time together on this case. Besides, she just broke my "Don't Ask, Don't Tell" Rule of workplace decorum. But since I haven't yet explained the Rule to Mary, I guess she can't be blamed for the violation.

I changed the subject and made sure we talked about the weather the rest of the way back to the office.

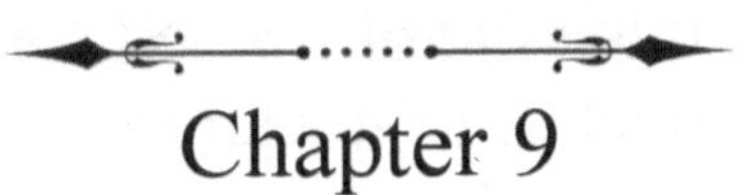

Chapter 9

The Federal Rules of Civil Procedure permit my clients to request all forms of Electronically Stored Information from ZeiiMed. ESI includes all emails sent and received on a desktop computer, notebook or laptop, as well as all current forms of digital communications conducted on phones with access to cyberspace, such as BlackBerrys, iPhones and other smart phones. Also, it includes all letters, contracts, memoranda and court filings sent or received electronically.

ZeiiMed is required to search for documents on each employee's specific work computer. In addition, there must also be a search for relevant emails on the network servers and hard drives that contain all active data, as well as a search of back-up systems, back-up tapes, disaster recovery tapes and cloud service data archiving.

The computer search is conducted by inputting mutually agreed "key words." On my list of "key words" are the names of ZeiiMed executives, as well as selected topics such as "payment data," "formula for reimbursement," "calculation of payments to doctors," "underpayment of doctors," "profit maximizing" and "cheating the doctors so ZeiiMed can make more money." Well, not the last topic because ZeiiMed would object, but you get the idea. In the search, any document that contains one or more of the key words will be flagged for possible production. Since the key words I submitted are directly relevant to the allegations asserted in my Complaint, ZeiiMed will have no grounds to assert any opposition, unless it's a privileged communication with ZeiiMed's lawyers.

Finally, there is the issue of the ESI format to be utilized in collecting the electronic documentation. A production can take place in "native format" or, alternatively, a format referred to as PDF or TIFF. The production in native format will consist of all ESI exactly as it was created and maintained on ZeiiMed's computer systems. The TIFF or PDF format means that a photo image of the ESI is taken and the snapshot of the document then produced. So, what is the difference? The difference is critical. Documents in their native format contain metadata, whereas the other format, being essentially copies of original communications, does not contain or reveal metadata.

This, of course, leads to the next question: What is metadata? Metadata refers to the universe of information that is embedded but retrievable from an electronically stored document. Metadata is usually hidden in the sense that it is not revealed by looking at the front of the document itself. It includes information such as the create date, revisions and drafts of the document, changes to particular words and phrases, comments made about the document, the identity of all persons copied on the document, as well as all attached emails that are part of a stream of emails created both before and after the document being reviewed. A double-click to various parts of the document will usually reveal the metadata.

Obviously, a lawyer looking to examine an opponent's records wants all ESI in native format with metadata attached.

ESI with metadata attached often discloses revealing information about an employee and their employer that cannot be otherwise obtained. People send and receive emails all day long on their work computers, BlackBerrys, iPhones, and other smart phones. The frequency and ease of use makes email a casual, informal form of communication that tends to reveal candid thoughts and true emotions. Many people view emails as some sort of private and protected form of speech for which they will never be held accountable. Emails are often quickly typed out in a candid, conversational, chatty tone for co-employees, bosses, children, spouses and friends, without giving the actual content of the email much thought. A review of months of such communications provides the building blocks to put together a picture of the personality traits of the cyberspace user. Add to the profile a history of frequent hits to certain websites (shopping, travel, entertainment, hobbies, porn) and many aspects of the person are revealed.

From 1959 to 1967, there was a TV game show called "What's My Line" in which a panel of celebrities would ask questions of a guest until the panel could determine his or her occupation. Today, there could be a show, "What's My Personality," in which a panel of psychologists could study the guest's electronic communications for a certain period of time and then give their professional opinions about the good and bad personality traits of the guest.

Equally overlooked and/or ignored by users of digital communications is the permanent nature of the records created. While email is easily deleted from the "in-box," it is nonetheless stored on the computer's hard-drive. It can only be permanently erased by having the computer "wiped" by a forensic engineer or by filling the hard-drive with enormous volumes of new data that "write over" (and obliterate) pre-existing emails. Neither is usually done. Plus, the "write over" technique is unreliable because the deleted data is often merely moved to a new unused space in the hard drive disk that cannot be seen by the computer's everyday user. Moreover, deleted documents and files are routinely retained on the back-up tapes and/or third-party cloud servers in case of some unforeseen computer disaster.

It is not surprising that an experienced trial attorney will review in detail every electronic communication that can be obtained from the adversary in the hope of finding hastily and poorly written emails that can be used on cross-examination to twist the truth and distort reality. As a result, I looked forward with great anticipation to a review of the millions of pages of emails and other ZeiiMed documents to be delivered to my firm from Tweed, Fox & Fortune.

It took about six weeks from the Court Conference before I received 50 compact disks, each containing approximately 35,000 pages of data, for a total of 1,750,000 pages in all. Most of it consisted of ESI, as I had specifically demanded from ZeiiMed.

I guess I should be more careful about what I wish for.

Chapter 10

After receiving the CD's from ZeiiMed, I immediately called a document management service that specializes in electronic discovery in order to set up an online depository. The service placed all 1,750,000 pages of documents in a digital database so they can be reviewed on large computer screens that look like flat screen televisions. Each document was logged into the system and numbered. The documents will be reviewed in the sequence they were produced and then batched into files based on categories such as author, recipient, document type and/or date.

Once the document management service completed its magic, I had two work stations set up in the conference room so Mary and I could review the documents on line. Long hours and long days were spent reviewing each document and electronically memorizing any important part of each document.

Periodically, Mary and I would discuss our thoughts about the contents of the documents. It was tedious work, and we encountered our first major problem early in our review.

One evening during the first week of our document review project, Mary commented with frustration, "I have looked at hundreds of documents and it is clear that ZeiiMed scrubbed the metadata from all of them. ZeiiMed must have gotten a special software and a forensic engineer to make sure that no metadata could be found when double-clicking any part of the document."

"I agree. It's obvious that ZeiiMed purposefully restricted our ability to go behind each email to find out the changes made after it was created, as well as the identity of everyone who saw it and then forwarded it to others. ZeiiMed knows exactly what the documents say and has made sure we wouldn't come across a single damaging document or metadata."

Mary stood up and walked closer to me. She sat on the conference room table next to my work station. We were now facing each other, while I remained in my seat. Mary crossed her long legs, her skirt rising, and resumed our conversation.

"I can draft a Motion for filing with the Court demanding that ZeiiMed produce the metadata as required by the Court's rules, at least with respect to the ESI that was retrieved from any source other than the back-up tapes."

"No, I don't want to do that because then ZeiiMed will know what we are doing," I responded. "We have to beat them at their own game without telling them what we know and without ZeiiMed being aware of what we've found. From my experience, metadata scrubbing is never perfect. Mistakes are always made. Metadata can be found that wasn't intended to be available. If we make a Motion, ZeiiMed will argue to the Court that the scrubbed metadata consisted of privileged communications with its lawyers that are protected from disclosure. ZeiiMed will then offer to make a log of the attorney-client communications that were withheld and we won't get the log for another six months."

"That's a lot of wasted time under the bridge," Mary commented.

"Most importantly, ZeiiMed will never voluntarily

produce the metadata to us. What we need to do is find the few instances where mistakes were made during the scrubbing of the metadata and find the confidential communications that were not deleted."

"I'm willing to stay late with you, Brian," Mary said. "I've got nothing going on in my life that's pressing."

What happened to "Mr." and who mentioned Mary's social life? Ignoring her comment, I went on, "Putting in the time is imperative but we can increase our chances of success by focusing on the ESI that was produced from ZeiiMed's back-up tapes and cloud servers. Retrieving ESI from these back-up systems is difficult because of the random manner in which the communications are bundled and stored. Most of the emails were archived on magnetic tapes rather than using modern cloud data storage. This works to our advantage. Tape drives are often used to hide possibly explosive emails because it can only be accessed by reading tons of preceding electronic data. As a result, ZeiiMed may have encountered problems in finding and scrubbing all sensitive ESI. The tapes provide our best chance to find a mistake by ZeiiMed in the deletion of the metadata. Thank goodness ZeiiMed is still in the dark ages when it comes to moving data to a cloud service provider."

I guess my conversation was pretty boring because Mary suddenly put her hand on top of mine as I was hitting some letters on the keyboard. I quickly looked at her eyes to try to assess her thoughts. As our eyes met, she said, "I'm here for you and for this project. Just tell me your timetable for getting it done and I'm all in."

Although the conversation seemed borderline professional, the touching was another matter altogether and clearly over the line. Did I mention that the door to the conference room was closed and it was about 6:30 p.m. so most of the staff had left?

While trying to quickly think of a comical comment as I gently pulled my hand back from her touch, someone knocked on the door. Mary immediately withdrew her hand, but communicated affection by pleasantly smiling at me without turning towards the slowly opening door.

"Mr. Bradford, your wife is on the line. I was working late so I answered your phone," my secretary said.

Thank goodness the interruption was so perfectly timed. I mean, what did Mary expect me to say? The choices were limited: (1) "I've always been very fond of you too," (2) "I'm really hot for you so let's leave together now," or (3) "Guess what? I was just about to mention that tomorrow I am dumping my wife after decades of marriage."

Of course, I didn't say anything and was quite happy to answer the phone in my office.

"I'll wait here for you," I heard Mary say, as I was leaving the conference room.

After my telephone call, I did some very quick thinking as I returned to the conference room.

"My wife is such a lovely person. I am so fortunate that we have been together for so long," I said loudly, upon returning to the conference room.

Hopefully, she got the message.

Mary just nodded.

I went on, "I've decided to add another associate to this project. I'll set up another computer work station in this room and ask Herb to join us."

Now I was sure she got the message—no more alone time for us. We are moving forward as a threesome. Maybe the increased staffing will allow more time for her to meet a nice new boyfriend that isn't married and isn't old enough to be her father.

The next day, Mary and I were at our computer work stations in the conference room, this time with Herb joining us. Herb is a jovial, slightly overweight young man about 5'8", with thick glasses. He is very young, but helps out the IT Department and he's a genius in computer science. He started college at fifteen and graduated in two years. He'll probably finish law school before he turns twenty years old. I probably should have brought him on board from the beginning. If I had, maybe I could have avoided my uncomfortable moment with Mary.

Before everyone got started, Mary asked to speak to me privately. We walked to my office to talk, with the door open.

"Mr. Bradford, I'd like to apologize for my behavior last night. I didn't really mean anything by it. There's been a lot of stress at work and I so admire your skills as a lawyer and appreciate the time you have taken to teach me the ropes. I momentarily lost track of priorities and proprieties."

"Let's just forget it happened and get on with the litigation work."

Of course, I was flattered to have captured her attention and I momentarily fantasized that maybe it would be fun to spend time with her outside of the office. No, not really. It would eventually end badly and subject her to ridicule and gossip in the firm. I would be labeled the one responsible, i.e., the sexual predator and "woman chaser." Our work relationship would end and one or both of us would lose our jobs. It would probably be me. I made the decision to pass up what will probably be the last time (only time) in my middle-aged life that a young, smart and pretty woman found me irresistibly attractive (for a fleeting moment anyway).

For the next several weeks, Herb applied his computer

genius to the ESI retrieved from the magnetic tape drives maintained by ZeiiMed. He provided me with his evaluation as we sat together in the conference room one morning before Mary arrived at the office.

"I've gone through over a million documents and the metadata has been thoroughly scrubbed and deleted by ZeiiMed from every page. I am good at what I do, but they are even better. There is no way to access the email stream created before and after a particular email was created and no way to find the changes, revisions and amendments to the email. By the way, do you mind if we call out for pizza? I know its early, but I need some fuel."

"I appreciate that you have applied yourself to the task," I said. "But I find it very hard to believe we can't discover a few elusive documents that we know ZeiiMed didn't intend to produce and accidentally did. Without a trail of damaging emails the Judge will eventually throw the Complaint out of Court. A mistake in the scrubbing had to have happened. Our luck can't be that bad."

Herb thought a moment and commented, "I'm telling you I searched every inch of the ESI produced from ZeiiMed's desktop computers, the servers, the back-up tapes, and the limited cloud data, other than the cyberspace junk. There is nothing there."

"Herb? Herb? What is that? What the hell is cyberspace junk?" I said, raising my voice in obvious annoyance.

"It's about fifty pages of documents with nonsensical gibberish. It's basically a continuous flow of sentences that just run on for pages without capitalization or periods. Most of the run-on sentences are simply a constant stream of words put together from the contents of hundreds of emails we have already seen, combined together with unpredictable groups of random alphabetical letters that spell nothing. The lack of punctuation, the spelling errors and the nonexistent spacing between words makes it cyberspace junk because it's practically impossible to make sense of."

"What are you telling me, Herb? That you skipped over a bunch of documents because they looked hard to decipher? Maybe some computer genius at ZeiiMed thought the same thing and didn't bother to look for metadata or apply the scrubber software. Let's get working on this cyberspace junk now—and by that I mean 'YOU.' I'll call for the pizza."

I don't profess to be the smartest lawyer in town. In fact, I may not be any brighter than the average lawyer, whatever that is. But sometimes I do have a hunch about things and I had a very encouraging premonition about this.

Herb isolated the cyberspace junk and started posting it on the computer screen after eating his five slices of pizza. I only had one slice, which my wife always says is strange. Kim said no one ever heard of anyone eating just one slice of pizza. Same deal as potato chips, I guess.

Herb applied his magical touch to all aspects of the cyberspace junk, including several metadata mining techniques contained in some brand new, cutting-edge extraction applications. Of course, I didn't really understand any of the fine details. All I knew was that the implementation of the advanced extraction techniques was time consuming and meticulous work, but was also our best and only opportunity to hit pay dirt.

"I've got something," Herb finally exclaimed.

"What do you mean? What have you got?" I asked.

"Someone tried to embed a whole series of emails in this one section of the cyberspace junk. Fortunately, the programmer unintentionally left a signature in the data that

I can follow in order to retrieve the hidden electronic images in a readable form," Herb explained.

"You're kidding—that's great! I don't really understand what you said, but post whatever you have on the screen so we can see it." Herb hit a bunch of computer keys in rapid succession.

We were hunched over in front of the computer as several emails suddenly popped on the screen. It was a peak moment.

"February 6, 2001

> From: John Edison
> ZeiiMed National Accounts
> Executive VP, New York
>
> To: Robert Finley
> Assistant Finance Director and
> Regional VP of Computer Operations
> New Jersey
>
> Re: Modification of Fee Calibration

No need to continue to rehash our tiresome discussions of the last several days. Like it or not, the big money simply cannot continue to fly out the front door. What goes out is dictated by what we put in the computers to calculate the payments to the doctors. So, go to the source of the problem and fix it. Input the oldest data you can find to establish the lowest possible rates for payments to physicians in each region of the country. Simply delete the high-end rates. When putting the info in our computers, be sure to delete whatever is currently there. Don't tell anyone without my

approval. End of discussion.
   Regards,
   John"

"March 2, 2001

   From: Kevin Long
   Chief Financial Officer, New York

   To: Robert Finley
   Assistant Finance Director and Regional VP,
   Computer Operations—New Jersey

   CC: John Edison—New York
   Re: New Rate Implementation

John told me about the modifications you implemented with regard to our rate calculations for payments to the medical profession. The data is the key. The older the better. We are under immense pressure to deflate and depress the balances due to the docs. The savings for the next three quarters and thereafter will be substantial. Make sure the newly inputted data in our computers remains in place until notified otherwise. Keep up the good work and don't discuss with anyone. I've spoken with our lawyers about this and they are on board. Legal understands that we can't keep paying these doctors big dollars. If there are any questions, I've been told we simply say there was a programming error.
   See you when I'm in New Jersey.
   Kevin"

"April 12, 2001

From: Linda Santini
Assistant Supervisor—Computer Operations
New Jersey

To: Robert Finley
New Jersey

Re: New Rate Data

Bob,

Sorry to bother you about this, but I noticed a dramatic drop in amounts paid out to the medical doctors. I did some looking around and found the servers reprogrammed with old data reflecting payments schedules and payment histories not used in a decade. I don't know how it happened, but it would be devastating if discovered and made public. Am I authorized to correct this mess before it explodes on us?
Please let me know as soon as possible.
Have a nice day.
Linda"

"April 13, 2001

From: Robert Finley
New Jersey

To: John Edison
New York

Re: Forwarding Santini Email

FYI.

Santini is one of the supervisors that I hired in the Computer Network Ops. Do you have any suggestions as to a response?

I assume we need to shut her down before she learns anything else. We can't afford a loose cannon.

Thanks,
Bob"

"April 16, 2001

From: John Edison
New York

To: Robert Finley
New Jersey

Re: Santini Email

Hope you enjoyed the weekend. Just tell Santini the adjustments were on the instructions of upper management and are just temporary. Say that docs will get all that is due shortly. Also, tell her we talked to Legal and got the okay. And see if there are any openings in sales in the Midwest that we can transfer her to. If she keeps asking questions, let me know immediately.

Regards,
John"

I saw Mary in the hallway and called her in. I wanted to show her our newly discovered emails and discuss their implications.

"Certainly, these emails will get the Judge off our backs about dismissing the Complaint," Mary noted. "Can I be at the deposition when you show these documents to Tweed, Fox & Fortune? It should be a lot of fun watching their glib faces change expression. I am shocked by the contents of these emails."

"Yes, of course I want you at the depositions. You've earned the opportunity. But don't be surprised by ZeiiMed's litigation tactics and remember this doesn't win our case for us. Most importantly, the emails should help to convince ZeiiMed it is better to settle now because the case is alive and moving forward and will only get worse for ZeiiMed as the trial approaches. ZeiiMed's concern over public disclosure of negative information will certainly enhance our settlement position. But the documents have to be sprung on ZeiiMed by surprise during sworn deposition testimony in order to get the damaging first reaction of the witnesses on the record. Hopefully, I'll be able to do this during the depositions of the ZeiiMed executives, which we should schedule as soon as possible."

I turned to Herb. "Herb, I can't thank you enough. Your efforts have changed the whole complexion of this litigation by discovering critical evidence in support of the Complaint. Well done."

Mary, having now done a review of the rules of ESI discovery, threw a little cold water on my excitement.

"Under the ethical and disciplinary rules of several states, we are required to notify ZeiiMed immediately upon finding metadata that was unintentionally produced and may be protected by privilege."

"You're right on your interpretation of the rules, but I have no intention of giving ZeiiMed advanced warning of these emails," I said. "We're at war with Tweed, Fox & Fortune and I will not give up my tactical advantage. Besides, there is no way these emails were prepared in consultation with counsel and, therefore, are not privileged. The reference in the emails about approval by ZeiiMed's lawyers is just crap. It never happened. Any lawyer giving approval to this would be disbarred. Let's get ZeiiMed to give us a date for the deposition of one of their executives and we will hopefully get the real story."

Don't get me wrong, Mary's comments about the disciplinary rules were a concern to me. But, just as importantly, the emails we found should not have been purposefully hidden in the cyberspace junk, as Herb called it. And let's not forget my egotistical side. I admit to salivating at the thought of springing these damaging emails on my unsuspecting esteemed legal adversary, Mr. Wadsworth. It's the least I can do after he so enjoyed embarrassing me in court.

I know it may be juvenile and possibly vengeful, but I couldn't be more pleased with my plan. If it is necessary to bend a few rules to avoid dismissal of the Complaint, then I fully intend to do so.

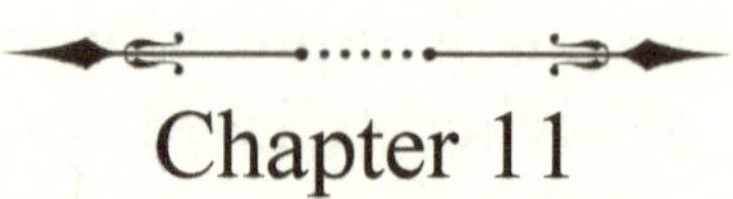

Chapter 11

About a month later, in early spring, with the cherry trees in bloom, the deposition of a representative of ZeiiMed was scheduled to proceed at my law office. The procedural rules of the Court require a party such as ZeiiMed to produce for the deposition the person with the most knowledge of the issues in the litigation.

ZeiiMed has the discretion to produce whomever it wants, but I had told ZeiiMed's lawyers that Robert Finley seemed to play a central role in the computation of the payments to the doctors based on my review of the documents. Of course, I never mentioned the "smoking gun" emails to ZeiiMed's attorneys. I had no idea if Tweed, Fox & Fortune was aware of them or not. ZeiiMed wouldn't be the first client to keep its lawyers in the dark.

Eventually, ZeiiMed's attorneys agreed to produce Mr. Finley for the deposition, so our litigation strategy remained on course. Maybe the Tweed lawyers knew of all the emails, but correctly concluded that the Court would eventually require Mr. Finley's testimony sooner or later. Why fight a losing battle?

There was a large conference room on the 45th floor that I scheduled for the deposition. It consisted of a long conference table surrounded by about twenty leather chairs. It was a much larger room then the one I used to first meet my doctor clients. The side of the room facing north was essentially a glass wall providing a mesmerizing view of midtown.

The deposition, by agreement, was to be videotaped. A video camera is set up and pointed at the witness so the witness is continually filmed while testifying. This provides a permanent record not only of testimony itself, but also a visual tape recording of the witness while giving the testimony. If, for some reason, the witness is unavailable to appear at the trial, the videotape of his or her testimony can be shown to the jury. It is a much more compelling presentation of the witness testimony when compared to the mere reading of a transcript of a witness's former testimony without the visual. I wasn't taking any chances. If something happened down the road to Mr. Finley, I was going to make darn sure I had his entire testimony on a videotape for everyone to see.

The deposition was scheduled to begin at 10:00 in the morning. The video camera operator and the stenographer got to the conference room at 9:00 to set up their equipment. The stenographer records the testimony of the witness and eventually prints the entire testimony in a transcript that is then signed by the witness, confirming its truthfulness. The transcript is a word-for-word reproduction of every question and answer during the course of the entire deposition, along with whatever "on the record" comments are made by the attorneys during the deposition.

The stenographer was a smiling and bubbly young woman named Judy Connolly. She had a slim face with straight, light brown hair that fell below her shoulders and hid the sides of her face. She was wearing slacks with a blue matching top. In the past, I had used other stenographers from her agency, but had never met her.

The same was true of the video operator, Sam Jenkins. Sam was a short, dark-haired man with a thick beard. He was casually dressed in a short-sleeved shirt that exposed his bulging arm muscles. He seemed to know what he was doing, but was bored by his tedious job of spending his entire day pointing a video camera at the witness and turning it off and on at the request of counsel.

I shook hands with Judy and Sam and mentioned that I had used their agencies many times in the past.

"Sam, let's take a moment to go over the procedure for turning off the video camera when requested by one of the attorneys."

"Well, Mr. Bradford," Sam said, "as you know, the usual procedure is to turn off the camera when anyone in the room says 'off the record.'"

"That's just what I want to talk to you about, Sam. I would like to change the usual procedure. I want you to keep the camera running until the attorneys for both parties agree to go 'off the record.' So, if only counsel for the witness says 'off the record,' you will keep the camera rolling until you hear me also say that I agree to go 'off the record.'"

"I guess I can do that, Mr. Bradford, even though that's not usually how it's done. I'm not going to get into trouble, am I?"

"No, and thank you, Sam, because that's how I want it done today. Plus, I know your usual procedure is to point the camera directly at the witness's face and not move it. I also want to change that slightly today. If the attorneys are arguing on the record over the propriety of a question or a document, I may ask you to focus your camera on the face of counsel for the witness and video tape the attorney as he makes his remarks on the record. In other words, I want the attorney for the witness also filmed as he speaks, when I ask you to."

"Mr. Bradford, I've never done that before so I don't know if I can," Sam responded.

"Sure you can, Sam. If the witness is not giving testimony because the attorneys are arguing on the record, there is no reason you can't point the camera at the adversary attorney when I ask you to do so. I know it's very unusual, but there is no rule or regulation against it."

"Alright, but I sure hope the lawyer I'm filming doesn't complain to my agency."

"Don't worry, Sam, I'll tell your boss I instructed you to do it and told you it was totally permissible," I said.

"And Judy, I want you to continue to type all the words spoken by the attorney or the witness no matter how many times my adversary screams, 'off the record.' We only go off the record if everyone agrees, so keep recording every word until I agree," I instructed Judy.

"Okay, Mr. Bradford, I'll just keep typing into the computer everything that is said until both attorneys agree to stop. But I can only record the words of one person at a time. So, if you and the attorney for the witness start talking over each other, I can't get it down. You have to take turns talking," Judy responded.

"I'll do the best I can and hopefully the attorneys wouldn't get so worked up that they're yelling at each other at the same time," I said, knowing that there was a pretty good chance that the deposition would become emotional and highly agitated once I started asking questions about the damaging Finley emails.

Now that I had set the ground rules for the deposition—presumably in my favor and at my command—I was ready to meet Mr. Finley and his attorney.

There was a knock on the conference room door and in walked Attorney Charles Wadsworth of the esteemed, white shoe law firm of Tweed, Fox & Fortune.

"Good morning, Brian, nice to see you again," said

Charles, in his usual insincere tone.

But he did look good—handsome, dashing and slim, with every hair in place and combed back with a healthy shine created by some kind of hair lotion. His tweed suit was perfectly tailored, with a white hanky protruding neatly from the front pocket of his suit jacket.

I better settle this case because if it goes to trial, this guy will charm the pants off every member of the jury, as well as the judge. It was like trying a case against Cary Grant. My only solace was that I am a couple of inches taller than him. I made sure I stood as straight as I could for maximum height.

"Hi, Charles, hope all is well with you," I said, as politely as I could.

"We haven't talked since the Court Conference," Charles said. "But I hope you didn't take my critical comments to the Judge regarding the Complaint personally. You know how it is, all is fair in love, war and litigation. By the way, Mr. Finley doesn't have as much knowledge of the issues and facts as you may think, so I really hope we can get out of here early and not drag out this deposition all day."

I bit my tongue, held back my Irish temper and sweetly responded, "I'll do my best to get through all my questions as quickly as I can."

"Here is Mr. Robert Finley of ZeiiMed, the witness for today," Charles said, as Mr. Finley followed him into the room.

I said hello and introduced Charles and Robert to Judy and Sam.

Mr. Robert Finley was an odd-looking person. Although his face was not bloated or puffy, his belly protruded from his body in such an extreme fashion that he looked to be in the later stages of pregnancy. His cheeks were red either from booze, medication or both. His knees buckled outward from the weight of his upper torso. He had a full head of short brown hair and his small eyes were actually clear and attentive (despite the booze), with a smile that expressed sincerity and an eagerness to please.

I shook Finley's hand. His grip was weak and tentative. He was clearly nervous and would rather be anywhere but here giving testimony. I'd bet he didn't sleep too well last night.

Judy, the stenographer, was at the end of the table and I sat Mr. Finley next to her with Charles to his other side. I sat directly across the table from Finley so we were face-to-face, with only the width of the table separating us. Mary and Herb joined me on my side of the table. The video camera was on a large tripod behind me staring directly at Mr. Finley, who was slightly pushed back from the table by the size of his stomach. I started to feel sympathetic towards him, but quickly caught myself. I had a job to do.

We were ready to begin. The camera started to roll. We were on the record.

Judy started the deposition by asking Mr. Finley to raise his right hand and agree to swear under oath to tell the truth, the whole truth and nothing but the truth. He agreed. I then started my questions.

EXAMINATION BY MR. BRADFORD:

Q. Good morning, Mr. Finley. My name is Brian Bradford and I am the attorney representing the doctors that filed the Complaint against ZeiiMed. Please state your name for the record.

A. Robert Finley.

Q. We are here today to ask you questions about the

factual matters discussed in the Complaint and I want you to answer to the best of your knowledge. Do you understand?

A. Yes, I will answer as best I can.

Q. You have been sworn to tell the truth and it's my job to remind you that if you fail to tell the truth, you may be subject to perjury charges. Do you understand?

A. Yes, I do.

Q. If you do not understand my question or you find my question confusing, please tell me. If you answer the question, I will assume you fully understood the question.

A. Okay.

Q. If you realize during the deposition that an earlier response you gave was incomplete or inaccurate, just let me know so you can fix it. Is that satisfactory?

A. Yes, it is.

Q. Because Judy can only record the spoken word, you need to give audible responses rather than the shaking of your head or a nod. Is that clear?

A. Understood.

Q. Lastly, please wait for me to finish my question before answering so we won't both be speaking at the same time. Do you have any questions regarding the deposition rules that we have discussed?

A. No, it all seems pretty straightforward.

Q. Please provide a description of your educational background.

A. I attended grade school at Infant Jesus of Prague in Chicago. Then my father's job was transferred to New York. The family moved to Long Island and I went to Schreiber High School in Port Washington. I attended the University of Rochester with a major in accounting.

Q. Please describe your work history.

A. I was first hired as an assistant bookkeeper at a small printing company in Huntington. After two years, my boss retired and I became head bookkeeper for three years.

Q. Where did you go after that?

A. I was fortunate enough to land an entry-level job with ZeiiMed in their Accounting Department. I was there for fifteen years, getting various promotions to Finance Director and Regional VP of Computer Operations.

Q. How did you go from an accounting and finance background to specialize in computer operations?

A. That just happened gradually as computers over time became the life blood of every major corporation. I learned on the job as a matter of necessity because all our communications with the medical industry are based on information we have programmed into our computers. ZeiiMed's computers generate all letters, emails, checks and invoices sent out to the medical profession.

Q. Did you discuss your testimony with your lawyer prior to appearing here today?

MR. WADSWORTH: You may tell Mr. Bradford that you met with me—just don't reveal what we said to each other, that is privileged.

A. Well, Mr. Wadsworth and I met at his office yesterday and we talked about my testimony for about three hours. There were three associate lawyers also present and each had an outline of proposed questions I might be asked today. We sort of practiced answering questions just like we are doing now.

Q. Did Mr. Wadsworth show you any documents?

A. Yes, some.

Q. Please identify the documents shown to you by Mr. Wadsworth.

MR. WADSWORTH: Objection. Identifying which documents I selected for his review is privileged information—but I will confirm that any document I showed him has already been produced by ZeiiMed.

MR. BRADFORD: ZeiiMed has produced millions of documents. How can I possibly identify the documents you gave him to look at without spending the next two weeks showing him every piece of paper produced by ZeiiMed?

MR. WADSWORTH: Do what you like, but I am not going to show you which documents I picked out as the most important and reviewed with the witness.

MR. BRADFORD: Note my objection and I'll bring the issue up with the Judge at the next Conference.

Q. Have you read the Complaint?

A. Yes.

Q. When?

A. When I met with Mr. Wadsworth yesterday.

Q. Is there anything in the Complaint that is not true?

A. Uh. I don't know... I guess so.

MR. WADSWORTH: Objection, it's the jury's job to decide if the allegations in the Complaint are true, not this witness.

MR. BRADFORD: I'm asking Mr. Finley and I want an answer. He's been with the Company for years so he certainly must know if the allegations against ZeiiMed are correct. And I want it noted for the record that Mr. Wadsworth is quietly whispering in Mr. Finley's ear while the question remains unanswered. That's a breach of the local rules of the Court regarding attorney conduct at depositions. I want it stopped.

MR. WADSWORTH: I was not coaching him so refrain from making your gratuitous accusations.

MR. BRADFORD: I want an answer to my question.

A. Some of the things alleged in the Complaint are true. For example, it accurately describes the business of ZeiiMed and the fact that we sell health insurance and then pay the doctors a scheduled rate for medical services performed for a patient. But the paragraphs that claim we underpay the doctors based on computers that are rigged to make inadequate payments couldn't be further from the truth.

Q. Don't you regularly get complaints from doctors who provide medical services to patients insured by ZeiiMed?

MR. WADSWORTH: Objection. That is a ridiculously broad and irrelevant question.

A. What kind of complaints?

Q. That ZeiiMed pays less than 50 percent of the fee that is charged by the doctor performing a medical service.

A. That's true, we do get some complaints, but that is to be expected. And the complaints are fairly isolated incidents that make up a very small percentage of the correspondence we get each day.

Q. What do you tell the doctors, generally, when they inform ZeiiMed that substantial underpayments have been made?

MR. WADSWORTH: Objection. Mr. Finley didn't use the word 'substantial.'

A. Well, we explain that we conduct regular and systematic surveys of doctors in each geographical area in order to determine a fair and reasonable charge for each particular medical service administered in a given specialty or general practice.

Q. How do you know that ZeiiMed actually takes the up-to-date information from the surveys and inputs the information into its computer in calculating the rates?

A. Because I am in charge of reviewing the results of the surveys, orchestrating the administration of the surveys and properly programming our computer databases to input the information in calculating rates.

Q. Is there a particular name for the information in this database?

A. Well, there are technical names, but inside ZeiiMed we just refer to the 'Depressor Data.'

Q. Where did the term 'Depressor Data' come from?

A. It's slang. You've heard of a doctor referred to outside of the medical profession as a 'tongue depressor,' just like a lawyer might be called an 'ambulance chaser.' You probably remember when doctors would press a flat wooden blade on your tongue while examining your throat. We eventually started using our own derisive jargon—referring to a doctor as a 'depressor.' So, it really means 'Doctors' Data.'

Q. Is that all the term 'Depressor Data' refers to?

A. Yes, as far as I know.

Q. Who is John Edison and what position does he hold?

A. He is one of the top bosses in the New York area. He is an executive vice president in charge of national accounts. For example, if IBM decided to use ZeiiMed to provide health insurance to all its employees, John would be in charge of the account.

Q. Have you ever had a discussion with Mr. Edison wherein you discussed the inputting of outdated

'Depressor Data' so that the current reimbursements to doctors would be reduced?

MR. WADSWORTH: Objection. Leading, argumentative and lacking any foundation. You have no factual record to support any belief that there were such conversations.

MR. BRADFORD: Your objection is noted. I want an answer from Mr. Finley.

A. I don't know—I don't remember—maybe, maybe not.

MR. WADSWORTH (interrupting the witness): Don't guess, Mr. Finley, if you don't remember any such conversations, just say so.

MR. BRADFORD: I warned you to stop coaching the witness. One more time and I'm going to call the Judge's Chambers and read the record to the Judge. The rules say you can object, but not make speeches to the witness or suggest an answer.

MR. WADSWORTH: I'm not coaching the witness and I have a right to object.

Q. Please complete your answer—What do you mean when you say you 'maybe' had such conversations with Mr. Edison regarding the use of old Depressor Data?

A. Well, what I mean is...

Mr. Wadsworth interrupted Mr. Finley again. This time, he grabbed Finley's arm and pulled him closer, positioning him outside of the video camera's stationery view. Covering his microphone with his hand, Wadsworth talked quietly into Finley's ear.

MR. BRADFORD: Sam, turn the video camera on Mr. Wadsworth now as he is speaking to Mr. Finley.

Sam slowly turned the camera on Mr. Wadsworth and recorded him for several moments.

Mr. Wadsworth then realized that he was caught on camera coaching the witness by impermissibly whispering in his ear while a question was pending.

> MR. WADSWORTH: How dare you. Go 'off the record'—that was a dirty trick. I'll screw you every chance I can get in this litigation as payback. Damn it! — The camera is still on. Shut it off and Mr. Connolly stop recording what is said. I clearly stated 'off the record'—are you idiots deaf? You are required to go 'off the record' and stop recording everything when I say so.

> MR. BRADFORD: All your insulting comments have been recorded because I did not agree to go 'off the record' and I don't plan to do so unless the witness tells me he needs a break.

> Q.   I want an answer to my question Mr. Finley and I am prepared to keep asking it until I get one. I don't care how long it takes.

> A.   I don't really remember very clearly, but I guess it's possible that we had such a conversation. I just find it hard to remember.

> Q.   I am now showing you Finley Exhibit #7, which is an email dated February 6, 2001 from Mr. Edison to you regarding 'Modification of Fee Calibration.' Have you ever seen this document before?

Mr. Wadsworth read the email along with Mr. Finley. Mr. Wadsworth's face quickly turned a bright red.

MR. WADSWORTH: Where did you get this email? ZeiiMed never produced it. It wasn't part of the electronic discovery we produced to you. I've never seen this document before and wasn't aware of its existence.

MR. BRADFORD: I represent for the record that this email was part of the electronic communications produced to my office by ZeiiMed.

A.   I think I remember this email now that I have read it. I'm not sure, but I seem to recall it.

Q.   Does it refresh your recollection that you had discussions with Mr. Edison regarding a programming of the computers with outdated Depressor Data to lower rates paid to the doctors?

A.   Sorry I hesitated. I'm not sure. It does seem to ring a bell to me, sort of anyway.

MR. WADSWORTH: I want to take a break for a few minutes.

MR. BRADFORD: In a few minutes. I want to finish this line of questioning.

MR. WADSWORTH: I need to use the men's room. I need to break now.

MR. BRADFORD: In a minute. I'm getting an answer to my question.

Q.   Did you or did you not have discussions with Mr. Edison regarding the utilization of the oldest Depressor Data available to lower the rate of payments to doctors that perform medical services for patients with medical plans with ZeiiMed? A manipulation of the data to depress the reimbursement rate, so to speak?

MR. WADSWORTH: Objection to the question. You are putting words in his mouth. Also, the question is compound and confusing.

A.   Yes. But I didn't like the idea at all and I told exactly that to Mr. Edison in several conversations. However, I felt my job was at stake if I didn't go along. Plus, the doctors have ways of getting back at ZeiiMed when underpayments are made, so I didn't feel very guilty. The doctors routinely list multiple medical procedures on the billing forms using multiple medical codes for one office or hospital visit to dramatically increase the total fee. That way, the eventual reductions by ZeiiMed don't hurt as much. Of course, ZeiiMed catches on sooner or later and pays an even smaller percentage of the normal rate for multiple surgical or medical procedures performed on the same date. It's a back and forth cat and mouse game played by the doctors and ZeiiMed.

Q.   In your own words, what did Mr. Edison instruct you to do?

MR. WADSWORTH: Objection, you are asking him about an email document that ZeiiMed has not authenticated as real and did not produce from its files to the best of my knowledge. Plus, you are putting words in his mouth and trying to mislead him.

MR. BRADFORD: Object all you want, but I want an answer to my question. ZeiiMed produced the document and its not my problem if ZeiiMed didn't tell you about it.

A.   It happened just like you said. We took obsolete and outdated Depressor Data, manipulated it a bit and then plugged it in the computer. That's what I was told to do. Out came rate payment schedules significantly below the usual and reasonable rate at the time. Oh, I forgot to tell you before—that is also how the term 'Depressor Data' came about. The term refers to the old data that reduced or depressed the payments to the doctors. In other words, the data that deflated or depressed the payments to the medical professionals. That's what the slang 'Depressor Data' really meant within ZeiiMed.

Q.   What happened next?

A.   The doctors yelled and screamed, but we told them the computers don't lie. We told them ZeiiMed uses up-to-date rates based on the most recent surveys and other market data submitted to ZeiiMed by their peers.

Q.   So, Depressor Data actually refers to the inaccurate data—the outdated data—that you fed into your computers to depress payment to the doctors?

MR. WADSWORTH: Don't answer that Mr. Finley. He's trying to get you to incriminate yourself. Mr. Bradford is twisting your testimony and asking you to agree with his summary of your testimony.

MR. BRADFORD: You swore to tell the truth. Tell me the truth now.

A.   Yes, that's right. The answer to your question is 'yes.'

Q.   So, the record is clear, the term 'Depressor' doesn't refer to a doctor, it refers to the distorted, manipulated and outdated payment information put in the computers to depress the reimbursements?

A.   Yes, that is correct. I guess I was confused before.

Q.   You didn't tell the truth when I first asked you about the term Depressor Data, isn't that correct?

MR. WADSWORTH: That's it. I'm stopping you right there. The witness is instructed not to answer.

You're asking him whether he committed perjury by lying under oath. I will not permit him to admit to a crime and you know the question is out of bounds.

MR. BRADFORD: Is your witness invoking the Fifth Amendment?

MR. WADSWORTH: No, we are just not answering the question. His testimony speaks for itself. Next question, please.

A.   I want to explain myself. I don't want anyone to say I lied under oath. So I am going to answer the question the best I can. I first said what I did about the Depressor Data because Mr. Edison said I needed to make up a story about what the term 'Depressor Data' meant.

MR. WADSWORTH: I told you not to answer, Mr. Finley. Now listen to me and shut up when I object or get yourself another attorney. No one will ever accuse you of perjury in a deposition in a civil lawsuit. Every witness stretches the truth in a deposition. Do what I tell you.

A.   Okay. Okay. I'm sorry, Mr. Wadsworth. But what am I supposed to do? He's got the email, he's got the proof.

MR. WADSWORTH: As I said, next question please. Also, I move to strike the last answer of Mr. Finley based on his accidental disregard of the instruction of his lawyer not to answer.

MR. BRADFORD: You're stuck with the answer. The truth is the truth. You can't strike a response just because you didn't like what he said.

Q.   Didn't anyone at ZeiiMed notice the use of the Depressor Data and investigate?

A.   Yes. Ms. Linda Santini did, but it wasn't before

long she was working in ZeiiMed's office in Kansas somewhere. People heard the story and no one else poked their nose around again.

MR. WADSWORTH: Mr. Finley and I are taking a break. We have been going for about two hours now.

MR. BRADFORD: Okay. Let's take a break and be back in fifteen minutes. Both counsels agree that we are now off the record.

Everyone returned to the conference room after the break and the deposition continued.

MR. JENKINS: We are now back on the record. The video camera is on. The stenographer is ready.

MR. WADSWORTH: Before you ask your next question, I have a statement to make on the record. I spoke with Mr. Finley during the break and I'm afraid he will not continue because he is ill. He told me he felt he was getting the flu before we started today, but he decided to proceed anyway. However, I'm afraid his flu symptoms have gotten worse and he simply cannot go on.

MR. BRADFORD: This is simply beyond belief. I sat across from him for two hours asking him questions and he clearly had no immediate health issues. The only thing that happened here is that Mr. Wadsworth realized that Mr. Finley's truthful testimony just destroyed ZeiiMed's defense to our Complaint and lost the case for ZeiiMed. Plus, I have additional emails that Mr. Finley received that implicate high-level executives at ZeiiMed, including the CFO.

MR. WADSWORTH: I'm sorry you feel that way, but it's simply not true. Mr. Finley is sick and I told him to go home. We will continue where we left off at a later time. We are 'off the record.'

MR. BRADFORD: No, we're not. You know the procedure. Please tell Mr. Finley not to leave. I intend to call the Judge's Chambers and get a ruling as to whether you can leave or not. The court reporter and video operator will continue to keep all statements on the record.

MR. WADSWORTH: Go ahead, dial the Judge, I'm sure the Court will find you just as unreasonable as I do.

Mr. Bradford dialed the Judge's Chambers on the phone in the conference room with the speaker phone turned on.

CLERK OF THE COURT: This is the Chambers of the Honorable Whitman Peter White. Mr. Timothy Garcia speaking. Can I help you?

MR. BRADFORD: I am counsel for the Plaintiffs in the class action styled Martin Brown et al v. ZeiiMed, pending before the Judge. Mr. Charles Wadsworth, Counsel for ZeiiMed is here. We have a dispute that arose during a deposition and we would like a ruling from the Judge.

MR. WADSWORTH: Hi, Tim, how's the family? Sorry to bother you, but Mr. Bradford insisted we involve the Judge.

CLERK OF THE COURT: Nice to hear from you again, Charles—I mean Mr. Wadsworth. I haven't seen you around the courthouse lately. Everything is good with the family. As to your request, I will speak with the Judge now. Please remain on the line.

The Clerk returned to the conference call five minutes later.

CLERK OF THE COURT: The Judge was very busy. It was hard to get a moment with him. However, the Judge will speak with you now, I am transferring the call to Chambers.

JUDGE WHITE: Counselors, this better be good. I have to charge the jury in a murder case, so I don't have time for lawyers that can't professionally and respectfully arrive at solutions to their disagreements. So, proceed. I remember the case from the initial conference. Mr. Wadsworth was at his eloquent best and had almost persuaded me to dismiss the Complaint without any discovery.

MR. BRADFORD: Yes, Your Honor, your memory is accurate. Let me start by apologizing to the Court for this interruption. I believe the gravity of the problem warrants your intervention. A ZeiiMed witness was testifying in response to my questions for about two hours or so. After the witness, a Mr. Finley, gave revealing testimony that clearly supports the allegations in the Complaint, Mr. Wadsworth took a break. After the break, Mr. Wadsworth informed me that Mr. Finley was too ill to proceed. I've been with Mr. Finley in the conference room all morning and he was perfectly fine. His voice was clear and he was in no discernible pain. He didn't appear totally comfortable, but that may be due to his very large physical frame and his candid responses to difficult questions he knows his employer will not be happy with.

JUDGE WHITE: I need more details—give me a quick example without going on too long.

MR. BRADFORD: I received, as part of its electronic document production, a series of emails from ZeiiMed that I contend are a 'smoking gun' that will prove beyond any reasonable dispute that ZeiiMed used outdated and antiquated fee data—called 'Depressor Data' by the witness—to calculate inadequate, unreasonable and extraordinarily low payments to doctors nationwide. That is the simplified essence of what I alleged in the Complaint and now I have the evidence to support it. I just need to continue a particular line of questioning in this area and I will then agree to adjourn to another day.

MR. WADSWORTH: I don't think it's necessary to discuss the testimony given today because that is not the issue. The issue is that Mr. Finley is ill and cannot continue. Mr. Finley will be happy to come back as early as next week to finish his testimony.

JUDGE WHITE: What are his physical discomforts? Fever, stomachache, what?

MR. WADSWORTH: The witness is out of breath, red in the face with swelling in his legs and arms. In addition, he is experiencing a general feeling of weakness and anxiousness.

MR. BRADFORD: That's because Mr. Finley is overweight and unhealthy, with high blood pressure for certain, but he is not ill. His lawyer doesn't want him to continue to testify because the witness clearly was not prepared by his counsel to answer the type of questions I've asked him.

JUDGE WHITE: I'm going to rule that the witness should continue for another hour. If Mr. Finley continues to be sick, you are to adjourn to the next available date. I'll see you both at the next conference in my courtroom.

MR. BRADFORD: Thank you for your time.

MR. WADSWORTH: Judge, I'll see you next week at the Waldorf Astoria. We have the black-tie dinner for the Bar Association of the City of New York. I think we're at the same table. Talk to you then.

JUDGE WHITE: Good day.

MR. JENKINS: We are back on the record and the video camera is on.

MR. WADSWORTH: Mr. Finley has returned to his seat and is prepared to continue the deposition.

MR. BRADFORD: How are you feeling?

A.   Okay. Not great, but let's continue so I can go home.

Q.   Do you know a Mr. Kevin Long?

A.   Yes, he is the Chief Financial Officer of ZeiiMed. I have a lot of bosses, but he is my top boss, you could say.

Q.   Did you ever talk with Mr. Long about the Depressor Data being programmed into the computers for the calculation of smaller reimbursement payments to the medical profession?

MR. WADSWORTH: Again, you are assuming facts not in evidence and asking leading questions. I object and I expect you to ask a proper question.

MR. BRADFORD: The question is entirely proper. The reason you're objecting is not because the question is improper. It's because you're afraid of the answer the witness is about to provide. Please respond to the question, Mr. Finley.

A.   Give me a minute. I really have to think about this. I mean, maybe I did have such conversations with Mr. Long, but they were very general in nature.

Q.   Are you telling me you can't specifically recall whether you had such conversations or not?

A.   Yes, I think that is what I mean.

Q.   In order to refresh your recollection, I am now showing you an email dated March 2, 2001 from Kevin Long to you regarding 'New Rate Implementation.'

Q.   Does this email refresh your recollection of conversations with Mr. Long regarding what you have called here today the 'Depressor Data'?

A.   Yes, I guess so. Apparently, Mr. Long was aware of the programming instructions I had received from Mr. Edison. Mr. Long brought it up to me on several occasions and sent me this email. Mr. Wadsworth, please stop tapping my arm. There is nothing I can do. How can I say I never saw the document and never discussed it? The damn email is addressed to me.

Q.   So, Mr. Long knew you were putting old Depressor Data in the computer so ZeiiMed could save money on what it paid to the doctors that treated patients insured by ZeiiMed? Don't look at Mr. Wadsworth. Please answer the question. Mr. Wadsworth will object if he thinks it's appropriate, without bullying you or me.

A.   Basically, yes. I tried to duck Mr. Long once I realized he knew, but I kept running into him and he would always bring it up.

Q.   What would he say to you?

A.   Just what's stated in the email. Kevin knew about the Depressor Data. He would tell me I'm doing a good job with the 'modifications,' as he would call them, and instructed me to continue with my fine work.

Q.   So, is it fair to say you did just that? You kept

the modifications, the Depressor Data, in place and didn't mention it to anybody else?

A.   Yes, I think that pretty well describes how things went down.

MR. WADSWORTH: Don't say another word, Mr. Finley. We're finished here today. I'm adjourning this deposition now. We have stayed and answered your questions as instructed by the Court, but the witness has gotten sicker and must leave.

MR. BRADFORD: You haven't even asked Mr. Finley how he is feeling. How do you know that his condition has worsened? Nonetheless, I will note for the record that it appears to me that Mr. Wadsworth has become ill from today's testimony, not Mr. Finley. As a result, I agree to adjourn now and end for today, subject to a continuing of the deposition in the near future.

MR. WADSWORTH: So agreed, as ordered by the Court.

Mr. Finley left the conference room quickly and headed to the elevator. I'm sure he was worried about the stability of his job once his bosses at ZeiiMed learned about his testimony. Clearly, Wadsworth did not know that Finley had such damaging information and wasn't aware of the emails confirming it. If Wadsworth had known, he never would have made Finley available for a deposition, unless ordered by the Judge to do so.

I thanked Sam and Judy for their work and left the conference room. I ran into Wadsworth by the elevator bank as he was leaving. He was steaming.

"Where did you get those emails? I didn't produce them

to you and ZeiiMed didn't give them to you. In fact, I never saw them before. You either have a mole at ZeiiMed that stole them or you bribed an employee. Then again, maybe you hacked into the ZeiiMed computers and committed a felony. No matter which, you acted unethically and I'm not going to just drop it," Wadsworth said, in his usual style of accusing first and asking questions later. Plus, I should mention that he really loses his good looks when he grinds his teeth, narrows his eyes and starts pointing his finger.

I quickly defended myself.

"ZeiiMed produced the emails as part of the millions and millions of electronic documents you dumped on me and now you're just going to have to live with it. Your threats are ridiculous and your ethical accusations absurd."

Wadsworth stepped closer to me.

He was inches away.

Wadsworth's face looked menacing and yet cautious at the same time, as if he was uncomfortable with physical aggression.

His white shoe, upper crust demeanor then vanished, as if it had been peeled off like old wallpaper.

He spoke in a deep yet whispering voice, "I report to some very high and influential people at ZeiiMed. They aren't pleasant and they don't play nice. They're maniacal, driven to win at any cost. Once I tell them about your knowledge of these emails, I can't say for sure what will happen, but it's well beyond the usual lawyer-like gamesmanship and maneuvering. I don't know exactly what will be done to you, but I know the reaction from ZeiiMed will be forceful and distasteful. My client won't tell me what it intends to do and will deny it when it's done, but I'll warn you that everything is in play in ZeiiMed's world. Your physical discomfort or harm is of no consequence if it accomplishes the corporate purpose."

I had enough Charles Wadsworth. I forcefully chest-bumped him. It knocked him back several steps. The wimp didn't have the moxie to push back or take a swing at me. He's lucky I didn't knock him out. Unfortunately, he was too meek to make it any fun.

"You will never threaten me again or I will break you in two," I said. "I won't report you to the Bar Association or inform the Court. I'll just take care of you myself. Now get the hell out of here while I still have my composure."

My Irish temper flared again. But Wadsworth had it coming because of his behavior today and every day since he first learned to talk.

Wadsworth turned and stepped into the elevator. He was breathing heavily and rubbing his chest. I continued to glare at him as he left.

Back in my office, I thought about what happened at the deposition and especially Wadsworth's remarks at the elevator bank before he left. During trials, depositions and mediations, attorneys will often get agitated and upset, with derogatory comments hurled back and forth. It is common for curt, sarcastic statements to be made by both counsels, but not profanity and certainly not physical intimidation or contact.

What happened here was different. Much different. Wadsworth wanted me to know that ZeiiMed's capable of resorting to physical harm. How could that be? This is the American judicial system and lawyers don't go around beating each other up (my chest-bump being the exception rather than the rule).

But something told me this was different. I had no idea what might happen, but I had an overwhelming sense of anxiousness and dread. It seemed like I was a little player in a massive scheme and the little player just became intolerably inconvenient. Was ZeiiMed truly capable of taking an everyday class action Complaint seeking money—just money—and escalating the dispute into a felonious, criminal assault on counsel that commenced the lawsuit?

I don't know, but it was eating at me and I couldn't seem to shake it. I didn't want to admit it to myself, but I knew deep down this legal dispute had just morphed into a dangerous and possibly life-endangering pursuit.

These thoughts were disturbing, so I decided to temporarily suspend my ranting because it was Friday afternoon and the spring weekend was forecast to be warm and pleasant.

Little did I know that while I was momentarily distracting myself from concern about ZeiiMed, ZeiiMed had no intention of forgetting about me for one moment.

Chapter 12

I collected my papers from the conference room where the deposition had been conducted and returned to my office to make a few phone calls before leaving for the weekend.

I called my wife to confirm that we would drive out to Baiting Hollow on Saturday, a small hamlet on the North Fork of Long Island. We have a condominium located on a 150-foot bluff overlooking Long Island Sound. I told Kim that the deposition was acrimonious, but I didn't tell her about the "red-hot," incriminating emails that Finley testified about. If there was any chance whatsoever that the threats by Wadsworth were real, she was better served not knowing and not being involved. I've heard the Mafia doesn't harm innocent family members when violence erupts, but I didn't know ZeiiMed's policy on that.

My thoughts were interrupted by a knock at the door. It was Mary. She looked worried. "Mr. Bradford…"

Ever since our uncomfortable and hopefully forgotten misstep in the conference room, Mary no longer addresses me by my first name. It's best that we keep an emotional distance between us while working in our professional capacities. That's the plan, anyway.

"Mr. Bradford, the animosity at that deposition was alarming enough, but I was shocked at the encounter between you and Mr. Wadsworth by the elevators."

"You were there? You saw that?" I asked.

"Yes, I was a few feet behind you, but I tried to make sure

Mr. Wadsworth didn't see me. I really don't know if he did or not. I was startled when you made contact with him and then became downright scared when he made those awful threats."

"As you can probably guess, lawyers at depositions don't usually hurl death threats at one another. When someone of Mr. Wadsworth's stature and background promises physical harm, it is extreme behavior, criminal in fact. It can't be disregarded and must be treated as real. I don't know what will happen next or what the top people at ZeiiMed might do, but I'm perceiving shades of evil that cannot be ignored."

"Well, I heard what you heard and I totally agree that it's real and not going away. I'd call the police if I were you. Tell the cops to question Wadsworth about his remarks."

"No, the police aren't the answer. Even though you were a witness to Wadsworth's threats, I wouldn't want to involve you with the authorities. Wadsworth will just deny everything and our firm would end up in the gossip column on Page Six of the New York Press."

"Alright, no police then, but I'm scared. I've decided to take a vacation for two weeks. In fact, you should think about a vacation yourself. Of course, to a different destination."

I think she winked at me when she said that—yes, she winked. Is it possible she has a subtle sense of humor that I've not appreciated?

Mary continued, "All kidding aside, I'm out of here for two weeks and no one will know where I'm going. Wadsworth saw me at the deposition, so he knows I'm involved and I'm not taking any chances."

"Yes, he knows you're on the case, but it's me he's angry at, not you. Wadsworth's venom is directed exclusively at me. You are not a target. But I want you to be comfortable, so please feel free to take the time off."

"I'm leaving tonight on a plane and I'm not telling the firm where or how to reach me. Also, I'm not taking a cell phone," Mary said.

"Alright then, see you when you get back and hopefully I'm still around," I joked, only half in jest.

"Now, don't say that. But be careful and buy a gun just in case," Mary said.

"A gun? No way. I'd end up missing the bad guys and shooting myself in the leg."

Mary started to leave, but stopped in the doorway, apparently with something else still on her mind.

"To quickly change the subject and get my departure off on a less violent subject, I've been meaning to finish our discussion on the financial crisis," Mary remarked.

"Feel free to get it off your chest," I said, thinking I could have worded that better.

"As you probably read, the Treasury, the Federal Reserve and the FDIC collectively instituted programs several weeks ago, in late March, to purchase the toxic assets and toxic securities held by banks, brokerage houses and insurance companies. Remember, that is essentially what I told you had to be done when we spoke in December of last year," Mary said.

"Yes, I recall that you believed such action by the Feds was mandatory if we are to get out of this financial mess," I responded.

"It's called the Public-Private Investment Program," Mary continued. "It has two parts, the Legacy Loans Program and the Legacy Securities Program. It seems the Feds like the word "legacy" better than toxic, but they essentially mean the same thing. The Program will use seventy to one hundred-billion dollars in TARP funds from the Treasury, with co-investments from the private sector," Mary continued, with surprising excitement in her voice.

"So, tell me again how is all this money going to be used?" I asked, not wanting to appear rude by telling her I simply didn't care.

"The Legacy Loans Program is designed to remove from the balance sheets of banks the toxic real estate loans that were created by the sudden depression of real estate prices coupled with poor underwriting guidelines that granted mortgage loans to everyone, job or no job," Mary explained.

"Sounds great," I commented. "Now tell me when the recession will end and good times will roll again—new houses, new cars, vacations and plenty of beer money."

"Very funny. Of course, it will still take time, maybe even many years. But it has to start with the financial institutions being strengthened, then positive earnings will be generated and confidence restored in the equity markets. Basically, we should go from a downward spiral to a slowly expanding and ascending economic marketplace."

"Just let me know when Las Vegas Sands will jump back to one hundred dollars a share from its current price of three dollars a share."

I was probably starting to wear on her nerves, but it really was a very dry topic of conversation.

"Your sarcastic comments make it very difficult to have a serious conversation about an important topic that impacts all of us. Did anyone ever tell you that?" Mary asked.

"Just my wife, a thousand times," I responded.

"I know you're under a lot of pressure and anxiety from today's deposition," Mary went on. "So, I'll just say good-bye and be off to the airport after a quick stop at my apartment."

"Be safe and enjoy your time off without thinking about the Complaint, ZeiiMed, or our dear friend, Mr. Wadsworth," I said. "And remember, the good news to come out of this massive economic downturn is that it wasn't the fault of the lawyers—for once. John Q. Public can't blame this on the legal profession. It was the movers and shakers of the corporate world that made incredibly risky investments in securities backed by questionable mortgages, with the securities losing their value once the booming real estate market collapsed. Stock markets around the world nose-dived, causing hard-working Americans to lose jobs, health benefits, pensions and personal investments. It's a horrible situation when wealthy corporate executives inflict such extreme pain on millions of everyday nine-to-five workers. But as I said, thank goodness it wasn't the fault of the lawyers for once."

"Yes," Mary agreed. "That is true. It is comforting that our profession isn't responsible for this economic disaster. Oh, and as I said before, it wasn't the fault of women either. A few days ago, the front page of the *New York Times* showed a line of top bank executives leaving the White House after a meeting with the President? It looked like a line-up of the usual suspects being called to the principal's office and, once again, not a woman among them. Got to run now, it's getting late."

Mary quickly turned and left, the discussion of the economy ending as abruptly as it began.

I looked at my LIRR train schedule to double-check the time for the next train home for the weekend.

Chapter 13

Saturday morning in early May and the sky was brilliantly blue and the temperature warm. Kim and I planned to drive from Port Jefferson to Baiting Hollow on the North Fork to spend the weekend at our two-bedroom condo.

About 78 miles from Manhattan, Long Island splits into the North Fork and the South Fork at the town of Riverhead. The North Fork extends about 35 miles to the last town of Orient. The North Fork is bordered on the north side by the Long Island Sound and on the south side by the Peconic Bay and further out, Gardiner's Bay.

We started our drive east on Route 25A until we reached Sound Avenue in Wading River. In Wading River, I exited off 25A by turning left onto Sound Avenue. After several miles of farms, the road winds down a steep hill, past a Boy Scout camp, and then a winding climb up the other side. Once on level ground again, you're in the totally enchanting North Fork. A unique setting of relaxed country landscape filled with golf courses, cottages, farms and wineries. You first drive past Fritz Lewin Farms where roosters, chickens and other farm animals often wander to the shoulder of the road without an apparent care in the world.

Further east on Sound Avenue, you cross Edwards Avenue and reach the Baiting Hollow Farm Vineyard, a picturesque colonial tasting house (original house circa 1861), with a small bar and acres of grape vines. The atmosphere is warm and friendly, with live music in the backyard to accompany the wine and cheese, as well as several horse stables and pony rides. The local lore is that the climate on this part of the North Fork is essentially the same as in the wine growing region in the South of France.

Next to the Baiting Hollow Farm Vineyard is the LiV Vodka Distillery situated on an 80-acre potato farm with a barn. LiV Vodka is advertised as an ultra-premium vodka distilled totally from potatoes. Potatoes are what Long Island traditionally grew best and most, although grape vines have displaced the potato as the predominate crop on the North Fork. Today, there are thousands of acres of wineries on the North Fork.

To the east of the LiV Vodka Distillery is the Cooperage Inn, a wonderfully warm and welcoming casual country restaurant. You can't miss it. It has a white picket fence in front of a white building with purple trim, a blue sign and lovely gardens. Although there is an eye-catching triangular roof above the front door, the main entrance is located in the rear of the building. Personally, my favorite part of the restaurant is the cozy tap room, with a copper-surfaced bar that runs the length of the room, dark wood trim and a mural of a wine cellar behind the bar. But it is the people that make the bar particularly entertaining. Although mostly populated by local folks who live on the North Fork, there is also a mix of out-of-towners who traveled far to get there.

Sitting at the bar in the Cooperage Inn, the conversation is friendly and engaging with everyone talking with each other, strangers or not. Sitting on the bar stool next to you may be a local farmer, a business man from Manhattan, a fisherman or the owner of the Pindar Winery. It doesn't matter, everybody mingles. And everyone at the bar gets an enthusiastic greeting from Darlene, the engaging, informative and very popular bartender with wit and charm.

She is a North Fork icon who makes everyone feel they belong. The draft beer is the coldest on the North Fork and her martinis are always the perfect pour. She knows most of the customers because most of the customers are regulars because of her. She enjoys hearing about your life and offers insight on any topic. Her interests are many and she loves all animals, but her passion is horses.

The Cooperage has been open since 1994, when it took over Bernie's, a small tavern that was known for its famous potato salad. When Bernie's first opened in 1960, its draft beer was 15¢. The Cooperage is now much larger than the original Bernie's, with several large rooms for dining and a spacious outdoor area. The place is especially popular in September and October when it seems everyone who owns a car is collecting pumpkins on the North Fork and drinking pumpkin-flavored beer at the same time.

Continuing east on Sound Avenue is Rottkamp's Fox Hollow Farm on the right, with "You Pick" acreage that is seasonally stocked with strawberries, pumpkins and corn.

A short distance further, my wife and I take a left-hand turn onto Oakleigh Avenue.

I continued my drive on Oakleigh north towards the Long Island Sound. Oakleigh Avenue, in fact, ends at the Sound. Before reaching the end, we turn off Oakleigh at the security booth that forms the entrance to my condo project, called the "Bluffs." Our unit is a second story, two-bedroom condo in one of several dark wood buildings. The Bluffs are aptly named, since the units sit atop enormous bluffs that hug the coastline, providing awe-inspiring views of Long Island Sound.

Just past the security booth on Oakleigh Avenue is a bronze figurehead of a fox, of course. After passing the security booth, the road changes to Fox Hill Drive and continues up a hill past the pool on the left.

Directly behind the Bluffs is Giorgio's Restaurant and Caterers, an elegant and well-run brunch and catering house that specializes in picture-perfect weddings and other affairs. Adjoining Giorgio's is a 6,920-yard championship golf course designed by Robert Trent Jones, Sr. The golf course was formerly known as Fox Hill Golf and Country Club. The name was recently changed to the Baiting Hollow Club and several holes were reconfigured with the building of a huge, colonial-style clubhouse that can be seen from Sound Avenue.

Our unit is the first building to the left as you pass the pool and reach the stop sign at the top of the hill. We have a third-story unit with a large wrap-around deck that faces north with a view of the water, but also extends along the side of the condo to provide a view to the west.

To the west of our building is a beautiful area of freshly cut grass that referred to as the "grassy knoll." It is a well-maintained area of grass approximately 75-feet wide and extends 200 feet from the large bushes at the base of our building all the way to the end of the bluffs, where the cliff drops down precipitously to the beach over 150 feet below. Looking up from the grassy knoll provides a clear view of our deck and the inside of our condo, easily visible through the continuous glass sliding doors.

As we drove to the condo that day, Kim and I had talked about the usual day-to-day topics discussed between husband and wife, i.e., the repairs that needed to be made in the house, our two grown daughters' progress in law school, the ill-health of elderly family members and upcoming family social functions. I was also doing my best to avoid any discussion of the litigation against ZeiiMed. Kim knew I had conducted the Finley deposition, but I didn't want to get into the details, especially Wadsworth's post-deposition threats.

Well, my plan didn't work out as planned. As we approached the parking area at the condo, Kim switched topics.

"By the way, you didn't tell me how the deposition went in the ZeiiMed matter. Did you get any juicy testimony Perry Mason-style after grilling the witness into submission?"

"No, not really. Remember, we've discussed that depositions are usually mundane, predictable sessions where the witness says just what needs to be said to prove their position, regardless of whether it's the truth or not. Experienced litigators know that a witness in a civil case, as opposed to a criminal case, almost never gets prosecuted for perjury based on false testimony during a deposition. I don't engage in such tactics, but other attorneys let their clients testify to any untruth they want during a deposition in the hope it will force the other side to settle. So, it's very rare to get a damaging confession or revealing admission during a deposition in a civil lawsuit."

We had parked the car and were climbing the stairs to the second story as we continued the discussion, but it was clear she wasn't buying my response.

"What do you mean the deposition was mundane and uneventful? What happened when you asked for details about the data used to calculate reimbursement rates to the doctors?" Kim asked. "I thought you wanted to know when the data had first been collected, the geographical location of the doctors surveyed and the skill level and specialties of the physicians who were polled?"

As I unlocked the front door of the condo, I realized there was no chance Kim was going to let the topic drop or get distracted by something else. I tried my best to downplay the deposition. In fact, I lied.

"The witness did provide some interesting testimony regarding ZeiiMed's sampling procedures, but it was articulated in a very scientific manner based on proven mathematical and statistical models that have stood the test of time."

"Oh, come on," Kim countered, "did the ZeiiMed guy say that ZeiiMed underpaid doctors on a consistent basis or not?"

"Yes, he did, but not in straightforward language. He hid his cards as best he could."

I was making it up, of course. However, I wasn't going to reveal the true story of what occurred because she did not need to know about Wadsworth's comments regarding ZeiiMed's revenge. Kim could end up on ZeiiMed's "hit-list," if Wadsworth is to be believed.

"I guess you're losing your edge. In your younger days, you were always able to go for the jugular vein and get the witness to either tell you what you wanted or, at least, make inconsistent statements. Maybe you should have been better prepared."

At that point, we were in the living room of the condo and my sole agenda was to change the subject as best I could.

"Honey, let's go out on the deck. The Sound looks beautiful."

We stepped out on the deck. It was a crystal-clear day that permitted a vivid view of the Connecticut coastline twenty miles away. There were white, shimmering slivers of sunlight dotting the water's surface. From a distance, it looked like hundreds of white diamond doves floating on the surface just as the rolling tide curled into waves.

The Sound is approximately 110 miles in length and

consists of salt water from the Atlantic Ocean, combined with fresh water from a number of rivers in Connecticut. Looking down at the waves breaking on the shore, you can hear even the slightest ruffle of the water caused by the flap of a sea gull's wings as it drifts on the water. By the shore, there are large boulders protruding from the clear green water. As you extend your vision forty or fifty feet from shore, the water abruptly changes to a crisp blue.

This aquatic experience, when coupled with salt air breezes, created amorous sensations as I stood with my wife on the deck. My mind shifted to the manner of best approaching the subject with the highest likelihood of success. I've found that after twenty years of marriage, you can never be positively sure of anything when it comes to marital relations.

When you were first married, it was, of course, a different matter altogether. Sex was all the two of you thought about. Then came the pre-conception period when sex became a more mechanical endeavor, to be performed on demand at optimum conceiving conditions. I actually thought that stage was very interesting. I would be cutting the lawn, washing the car or trimming the bushes when the urgent "call for conception" would be made by Kim out the second-story bedroom window, meaning that temperature, ovulation and hormonal balance were most inclined to create conception. Kind of like the perfect storm of life. In response, I would drop everything (literally) and head for the bedroom where Kim was already prepared for the moment. Forget foreplay, this conception stuff was pure business and I was always happy to play my part, however robotic it might be. Those were the good old days.

As everyone with a family knows, the next major stage in marital relations is the drought years due to the exhausting task of child-rearing.

Now after more than twenty years of marriage, it is very challenging to sense the mood of one's life mate on the subject of sex. A quick sideways glance, a stretch, a momentarily soft touch on the arm might be the signal to proceed you were hoping for. Then again, maybe not.

We left the deck and went inside to get a beverage. If my prurient impulse wasn't mutually reciprocated, an ice-cold beer would be the second great pleasure in life. As we walked, I touched her hand. She stopped and turned towards me. "You look lovely today," I said and leaned towards her to gently kiss her lips. She seemed receptive. She placed her hand on my stomach as we held the kiss. I pulled her closer until our bodies touched, as my hands massaged her lower back in a circular motion that extended below her waist.

"That's pleasant," I think I heard Kim say, in a whispering tone.

I momentarily opened my eyes to zero in on a second kiss. I instinctively noticed an unfamiliar sight as I looked over Kim's shoulder. Just outside the windows providing the view west is a support beam in a decorative white encasement. The beam that has a diameter of twelve inches and runs north to south the entire length of the window. My sight immediately focused on an object attached to the beam. It was a rectangular block of a putty-like substance about ten inches long and three inches wide. It had an adhesive coating that held it to the beam and was connected to a smaller object that clearly was a cell phone detonator. After a split-second mental evaluation, there was no doubt that the rectangular block was C-4 plastic explosive. The C-4 was about a pound and a quarter, containing enough chemicals to rip apart a medium-sized truck. It had the power to release an instantaneous and unyielding expansion of compressed gases that would collapse most of the second-floor condo. Usually C-4 is difficult to ignite, but the cell phone detonator wired to the explosive will trigger the blast by a single ring.

I dropped my arms and grabbed Kim's hand while uttering in restrained panic, "Come on, we have to get out of here now. Don't talk, don't hesitate, just move now—quickly."

We had about thirty feet to cover before we got to the front door. The explosion could take place any second and would happen so fast we wouldn't even know the Grim Reaper was upon us. Also, I was concerned about Kim being severely injured, even if she did survive. Often the C-4 is embedded with ball bearings that saturate the area with piercing metal fragments traveling faster than bullets from a shotgun.

Kim pulled back, "What are you doing? What is wrong with you?"

While dragging her by her arm as best I could, I spoke urgently in a firm voice, "There is going to be a massive explosion. We've got to run now. Just follow me."

She got the message. We made it to the front door. I stepped out first to hurry Kim out the door and down the wooden stairs. Somehow, my foot missed the first step. I lost my balance and fell against the railing. I landed on my rear-end at the top of the stairs with a badly twisted ankle. I wasn't sure I could regain my balance and walk down the stairs.

Kim, a slim and naturally athletic person, bent down to help me get up. She put her shoulder under my armpit, extended her arms around my back and pushed me forward until I was able to straighten my legs and resume a standing position. Slowly, we started down the stairs, moving steadily one step at a time, with Kim's arms firmly around my waist as I descended on one able leg.

I was worried beyond belief, but Kim was cool and deliberate in her forceful and decisive command of the situation. She helped me down the stairs to ground level and even uttered some sarcastic comment that I should repeat my fantasy story about how the ZeiiMed deposition had been so uneventful. I guess she somehow connected this current predicament with my lawsuit against ZeiiMed. She's smart in addition to being very strong.

Just as we finished going down the stairs, I heard a cell phone ring and felt a massive wave of force that pushed us to the ground. There was an ear-shattering blast of wood and concrete splitting, crumbling and separating in all directions. We kept our faces in the dirt while burning debris started falling to the ground. We were lucky that the concrete blocks and red-hot wood beams didn't land on us.

An eerie silence suddenly developed. I turned my head to see that the entire roof had been blown off and the walls essentially incinerated, with our clothing and other possessions dangling down the side of the building in bits and pieces.

"Are you all right?" Kim asked, with a surprising calmness.

"Yes, thanks to you for getting us out. You were very brave and I certainly wasn't any help," I said.

I leaned toward her and kissed her dirt-crusted face. We were alive and the elation of the moment created an out-of-body sensation of euphoria. It didn't last. Kim gazed at the destruction and started to cry. Reality had now set in. The closeness to death coupled with the destruction of cherished personal items overwhelmed her emotionally.

"It's gone—it's all gone—why would anyone do this to

us?"

As I was about to console her, we heard two people running from the large bushes at the base of our building. They were quickly heading for a waiting car and were soon gone before we even got to our feet.

"Come on, help me walk over to those bushes away from this smoldering mess," I said.

As we approached the bushes, I saw something on the ground. I got closer. It was a phone, a powerful Iridium 9555 satellite phone. The bad guys must have accidentally dropped it as they were running to their getaway car.

"Kim, these guys left a phone. It's right there on the ground. They were smart enough to get a global satellite device because somehow they knew that the Bluffs has no cell phone communications so close to the water. I guess they have been following me for several weekends."

"Brian, that's the key. Use the keypad to access the address book feature and find out the telephone numbers of the last several calls. Maybe we can find something the police can use," Kim astutely noted.

"You're right. It's here. The last call must have detonated the bomb, but the second number is—this can't be right—it's Dr. Brown's number. I know his cell phone number by heart. He left it with me when we first met on his case. I've called him several times as the case progressed."

Kim looked more afraid than ever.

"Brian, this is totally beyond our grasp. Whatever is happening here involves people of such great evil we can't even comprehend it, no less attempt to fight it. Dr. Brown is talking to these terrorists as they rig a bomb? Your client tried to kill us? We've got to get protection of some sort. Let's check to make sure no one was hurt in the explosion and then tell the police everything we know. I'm sure every fire engine and police car on the North Fork will be here soon."

We went back towards the building and saw there had been no one downstairs on the floors below us at the time of the explosion. The structure of the building next to us appeared unharmed, but a few residents were leaving the building looking fairly hysterical.

As I limped over to one of the neighbors, I remembered to look for the cat that lives under our building. The cat usually answers to the name Michelangelo. I tossed aside some wood wall panels and, sure enough, I heard her purring as she emerged from the rubble. Michelangelo seemed fine and had the usual "dinner-time" look in her piercing yellow eyes with vertical black pupils. I picked her up and gave her to Kim to help calm them both.

Harry, a retired newspaper reporter who lives next to us, approached me and asked in a loud, accusing tone, "What the hell did you do? Ignite the natural gas line to your condo? You've ruined our entire complex—everything has to be rebuilt and replaced."

I did my best to remain calm, but I was agitated that he failed to mention the extraordinarily happy event that Kim and I had survived.

"Listen, I didn't cause it," I said, with exasperation. "The explosion was planned and detonated by outsiders for reasons that I can't be sure of and can't explain."

"Don't you read the local newspaper?" Harry asked. "The Iranian Ambassador and Representative to the United Nations was vacationing here for a couple of days between sessions at the U.N. in New York. Someone wanted him dead, but whatever idiot set off the bomb not only had the wrong day, but also had the wrong building. The Iranian Ambassador left two days ago, and didn't stay in your building. And now we're stuck with the carnage."

"That explains it then, Harry." I certainly wasn't going to divulge the true story, especially since I was set on leaving immediately to head back to my office in New York.

"Well, I've got to go now. I'm glad no one is hurt," I said.

"You can't go," Harry responded. "The police are coming. They're going to want to question you and fill out reports. If you leave, I'm going to be required to tell them you left the scene of a crime."

"Do what you have to do, but I'm going and, by the way, I'm glad you weren't hurt."

As I walked away, Harry yelled, "The police are going to have your name, address and license plate, so expect a call."

I reminded myself to never talk to a newspaper reporter again.

I walked over to Kim. "Honey, we need to go now. The bad guys were unsuccessful today, but are unrelenting. They will come after us again and maybe soon. I've got to get to my office, scan the critical ZeiiMed emails that probably caused this mess and email them immediately to the Attorney General. We have no choice. It's the only way to go."

"So, you lied to me when you said nothing important happened during the deposition. Thanks a lot for your honesty and consideration. Look at all you caused by pursuing that stupid Complaint against ZeiiMed," Kim said, in a mocking tone of hysteria and betrayal.

"I didn't want you to know what was happening because I didn't want you in harm's way," I said, realizing how silly I sounded.

"What are you…crazy? I'd say I'm deep into harm's way already. Your selfish plan was ineffectual and misdirected."

"I agree with you. To say I apologize and admit it was a

mistake is a gross understatement. But right now, we have a much bigger problem than our marital miscommunications. We've got to fight back and protect ourselves. We can't spend hours talking to the police or waiting until I get to the office on Monday. These killers know what they're doing and they are not going to stop. Murder is apparently what they do and they will keep doing it until successful."

"I think that's become fairly obvious," Kim remarked.

"We need to immediately get in the car, drive to my office and get the important ZeiiMed documents to the Attorney General's desk. It's the only way to stop them from pursuing us. After the Attorney General gets the documents, no one will touch us since the emails reveal the ZeiiMed people at the core of this mess. The AG will know who the bad guys are. We can't trust anyone until then because it's clear my clients are in bed with ZeiiMed and the entire Complaint was a secret scam orchestrated by Dr. Brown and ZeiiMed. I was their unsuspecting pawn. I don't know all the reasons as of yet, but I will get the answers eventually."

Kim exhaled. "Okay, I'll go with you. We have no choice."

We quickly jumped in our car and raced past the Bluffs just as a string of police, fire and emergency vehicles were entering. One of the police officers started waving, motioning for us to pull over. I ignored the gesture and drove on.

"We're on our own now. Everyone will be after us, including the police."

"Just keep going and don't stop for anything," Kim stated. "By the way, how did you know that an explosive was about to detonate in the condo?"

"Well, we hang out at the bar at the American Legion Hall almost every week. The Legion has lots of available military books I borrow from the back room. Several of the books have chapters on military-type explosives, especially the type used by the Taliban in Iraq and Afghanistan. The device used today was very similar and I immediately recognized it."

"Thank God, or else we would have died a horrible death while being ripped apart and scattered all over," Kim said grimly.

"Let's not think about it and just focus on getting to the City and exposing the people who caused this."

With two hands on the wheel, I stepped on the gas and started up the entrance ramp heading west to New York City on the Long Island Expressway.

I hoped to maintain a speed of about 80 mph in the HOV lane. At that speed, we would arrive at my office in ninety minutes without congested traffic, a police blockade or the bad guys crashing their car into my vehicle. Of course, only one of the three possibilities had any realistic chance of occurring—and already I could see the traffic volume starting to spike.

Chapter 14

The drive to New York City turned out to be congested, but uneventful. We passed several police cars by the side of the highway, but no one pursued us. I guess my neighbor Harry told his assassination theory so persuasively that the police considered us secondary witnesses.

However, the conversation with Kim on the ride to New York City continued her inquisition of me.

"So what exactly happened during the deposition of Finley that has us running for our lives," she asked several times.

"In a nutshell," I finally explained, "it was fortunate— very fortunate that Herb located an email trail that revealed the scheme of ZeiiMed to intentionally underpay the doctors on a massive scale. It was a million to one chance we would get our hands on such damaging evidence and probably only a handful of top executives are actually involved, but we got lucky and it worked out in our favor. Then, during the deposition, Finley explained how the computers were programmed with outdated data to depress the reimbursement to doctors by millions and millions of dollars for many years. ZeiiMed's lawyer, Charles Wadsworth, a pompous snob, expects to win all the time and just couldn't control himself as his defense of ZeiiMed crumbled before his eyes."

"Tell me, what did he do?"

After hesitating, I responded. "Essentially, he threatened

me with bodily harm once the higher-ups at ZeiiMed found out what Finley testified to."

"That is shocking," Kim replied. "And you're telling me Wadsworth had no idea that his law office turned over to you, along with millions of pieces of other electronic information, some emails so damaging to his client that murder is the only recourse?"

"I am certain that Wadsworth was not aware that the 'hot' emails were disclosed to us, or that they ever existed. The production of the electronically stored information was probably arranged and organized by ZeiiMed. The emails I showed to Finley were embedded in a massive mound of cyberspace junk that ZeiiMed was convinced my law firm had neither the talent nor the time to find."

"Why didn't ZeiiMed just delete the emails and pretend they never existed?" Kim asked.

"The problem is that the deletion would leave a trail that can't be eradicated. An astute computer geek could not only detect the deletion, but could also eventually find the emails in some back-up storage space in the recesses of ZeiiMed's computer system. Consequently, the deletion would be like placing a 'red-flag' alert where the deleted email should have been sequentially located in its native format. Quite simply, deleting electronic mail in the computer age doesn't get rid of it and the 'space' in the electronic stream is apparent."

"Well, I'm still mad you lied to me about all this. Especially after I cautioned you that no good would come from representing a bunch of doctors that drive fancy cars to work while crying about not getting paid enough for administering their godlike ability to prolong life and cure sickness."

Kim does seem to have a way of looking at the Complaint

and the lawsuit against ZeiiMed in the worst possible light. Of course, she is right. Thank goodness she isn't the lawyer representing ZeiiMed. I wouldn't have a chance.

"I'm not saying you're wrong, Kim. But there is another side to this story. Remember when I went to the dermatologist in New York City for two visits last month? The doctor diagnosed a pre-cancerous spot on my arm, cut a piece of flesh out of the spot for a biopsy and eventually applied a nitrogen spray to kill what was left of the growth. The bill for the surgery, office visits, lab results and the nitrogen spray was about seven hundred fifty dollars, of which ZeiiMed paid about one hundred fifty dollars. In my opinion, that was an outrageous slashing of the fee that will jeopardize the availability of talented doctors since the payment barely covers the cost of doing business. Worse yet, the most accomplished doctors will simply refuse to accept the insurance ZeiiMed is peddling and demand cash only from all their patients."

"I know what you mean," Kim said. "The rich can and will buy the best doctors, with the rest of America being left with the unhappy, underpaid doctors. In turn, the patients of the underpaid doctors are displeased because the out-of-network doctors often make the patients pick up the tab when ZeiiMed refuses to do so. It's a double hit on the patients. The best doctors won't deal with ZeiiMed and most of the remaining doctors require the patient to pay more when ZeiiMed pays less."

We were now in the City approaching Wall Street, which was totally torn up with the construction of underground improvements. We switched seats and Kim dropped me off on a side street. I ran to the front door of my office building at 40 Wall Street. She parked the car.

All my thoughts were focused on getting the evidence

against ZeiiMed to the Attorney General. Not only would ZeiiMed be exposed but, more importantly, my involvement would be documented. Any harm to the whistleblower would result in a criminal investigation and indictment of ZeiiMed and the executives involved. I anticipated that I only needed a few minutes alone in my office to send the critical document to the authorities and get this nightmare behind me.

Anyway, that's what I thought at the time.

Chapter 15

As I entered my office building at 40 Wall Street, I was met by three security guards surprised to see me on a Saturday. I signed in and used my ID card to get through the turnstile leading to the elevator banks. As I headed up to my floor, I finally felt safe and insulated from Dr. Martin Brown and his maniacal bombers.

It seemed beyond belief that Dr. Brown was actually behind a plot to kill his lawyer. But there could be no other explanation for his cell phone number on the satellite phone. Who would believe that Dr. Brown created a scheme where he would convince me to file a Complaint against ZeiiMed while really conspiring with ZeiiMed against me? How could this be?

Once I arrived on my floor, I exited the elevator and searched for the light switch. I guess no one else came to work this Saturday. I quickly went to my office, grabbed a hard copy of the emails that Finley had testified about and headed to the scanner down the hall. I scanned them and sent the electronic images of the documents to my computer. I then walked back to my office and sat in front of my desktop computer.

My office is arranged with my desk in the middle of the room, facing the doorway. My computer is on a separate perpendicular table. Sitting at my desk, my line of vision includes any activity in the hallway outside my office.

Immediately inside the doorway to my office is a six-foot credenza against the wall across from my desk. It fits along the same wall as the doorway because the doorway is not in the middle of the room, leaving enough continuous wall space. There are various personal items on top of the credenza, mostly travel memorabilia, family pictures and office gifts from family members, such as the new glass globe from Kim.

At my computer, I searched for the email address of a fairly high-profile attorney with the Office of the New York Attorney General. A year ago, I had met a Deputy Attorney General at a deposition of an insurance company executive who paid "under the table" kickbacks to insurance brokers. I found the address and typed a short explanation of what had occurred at the Finley deposition and how the attached emails reflected a secret cost containment conspiracy created by manipulation of computer data, the Depressor Data, to underpay the medical professionals.

As I was finishing, my attention was alarmingly turned to the door of my office as someone hurriedly entered my office. Dr. Brown suddenly stood in front of me with a wry smirk, perspiring face and a gun in his right hand. The gun was pointed directly at me. He was wearing a tight grey tee shirt that highlighted his muscles and a black medical bag in his other hand.

"How the hell did you get in here?" I said, with a stunned blankness of thought.

"Shut up, you fool. What are you surprised about? I guess you still don't understand what you are up against. ZeiiMed employs one of the largest private security forces in the world other than defense contractors. ZeiiMed's security team makes a call to this building's security and I'm cleared right through. The global positioning device attached to your car told us right where you were headed after the explosion. You have no idea of the contacts and influence we have," Dr. Brown stated.

"I do know one thing. You almost blew me to pieces with your C-4 bomb trick. Don't you think the C-4 explosion was a little bit over the top? You took out practically the entire building," I commented, although it was probably not the best time to be a wise guy.

"It was a great plan. The police think it was some kind of terrorist attack on the Ambassador gone awry. Just to make sure, ZeiiMed has a newspaper guy who resides there to make sure the story sticks."

"Harry? Harry's one of your people? You've got to be kidding."

"There's a lot you don't know, including what's going to happen to you next. But I'll let you know as we go along." Dr. Brown laughed out loud, with a perverse facial expression.

I realized Dr. Brown was a formidable and resourceful enemy focused only on my demise. Panic started to overcome me as a sense of imminent defeat set in. I had to be very lucky to get out of this and needed to just keep talking until I figured out how to change the odds in my favor.

I tried to stand.

"Sit the fuck down, now!" he screamed.

"Someone is going to hear if you discharge that weapon. It will be noticed," I said.

"I don't intend to shoot you unless you try to stand up again. The plan is to handcuff your wrists, tie you to the chair with gaffer tape, seal your mouth and stick a syringe from my medical bag in your inner ear. The induced heart failure will make it look like just another heart attack for an over-worked, stressed-out, middle-aged attorney. The tape comes off after you're dead. It will all happen quickly. But if you don't cooperate, I have no reservations about going to Plan B and simply shooting you in the forehead. I care about the technique, but my bosses are concerned only with the result."

"You can't possibly believe that killing me is going to solve all your problems. Numerous people at this office know about the emails identified in the Finley deposition and the authorities will eventually find out about them, even if I'm not around to tell them."

"When are you going to finally appreciate the enormous capabilities of ZeiiMed?" Dr. Brown responded.

"ZeiiMed can't be stopped and we always get our way," Dr. Brown continued. "Your pal Herb has already been talked to. He knows you're a dead man and fully understands he will get the same unless he shuts up and takes an immediate sabbatical from the firm, claiming extreme emotional distress from your death. We are going to make contact with Mary tomorrow. We know where she went and I think she will decide to stay on vacation for a long time."

"But you still have a bigger problem—the Court is generally aware of the existence of the 'hot' emails and good old Wadsworth will probably decide he didn't sign on for a murder conspiracy. He's a wimp, like most lawyers. He'll talk."

I didn't want to mention Kim. If Dr. Brown doesn't know Kim is involved, then maybe she'll be left alone, or so I thought.

"Wadsworth doesn't know anything other than what he was spoon fed by ZeiiMed's upper management," Dr. Brown said. "He didn't know of the emails until he saw them for the first time at the deposition. He has no idea that ZeiiMed purposefully buried the emails in the cyberspace junk to throw you off the track. After your untimely death, Wadsworth will be instructed to destroy all evidence of the incriminating emails at both ZeiiMed and his law firm and then settle the case at a reasonable figure in a settlement range set by ZeiiMed."

"Sounds like you've got it all worked out," I commented.

"Your office," Dr. Brown continued, "will be more than happy to settle rather than get a new partner up and running on a complex case. Just return or destroy all documents in order to get the settlement check. Since I'm the client, I will insist that ZeiiMed's settlement offer be accepted. The Judge will be overjoyed to get the case off his calendar rather than read hundreds of pages of trial briefs and motions to dismiss. As you know, Wadsworth and the Judge have a very tight relationship."

Dr. Brown was clearly on a roll and couldn't help but extol the virtues of the Great American ZeiiMed Caper. Of course, the more he talked the more time I had to figure out how to survive this mess.

"And don't think your wife is out of the woods," Dr. Brown rambled on, with obvious pleasure. "In a couple of days, your wife will be taken from your house and brought to an isolated, abandoned warehouse in the New Jersey swamps outside Newark. She will be tortured mercilessly after being stripped and tied spread-eagle on a metal frame. She will scream and moan as ancient medieval torture techniques are skillfully applied by two salivating misfits in head masks. They will find out what you told her about ZeiiMed and, if she knows nothing, she will be let go with a warning that if she ever talks about the torture we will do the same thing again—this time to your daughters. If she does know anything, she will regret the day she ever met you."

His disgusting comments made me sick to my stomach. But I had much bigger problems. This confrontation will not end without bloodshed. It was a fight to the end and one of us was going to be dead very shortly. My desperation was growing as a wave of extreme and uncontrollable rage quickly engulfed me. Every inch of my body prepared to lunge into battle with my tormentor on the other side of my desk. The plan was to keep asking questions until the best opportunity for a head first charge over my desk.

"Why me?" I asked. "You obviously had hundreds of New York City attorneys to choose from. But you came to me."

"Isn't it obvious? You were chosen because of your presumed incompetence in prosecuting a high-profile class action Complaint. You are a typical, run-of-the-mill, insurance defense lawyer. ZeiiMed knew you would blindly accept our case with a salivating tongue and dreams of a monster payday. It would provide you with the opportunity to handle an exciting, once in a lifetime, lawsuit as plaintiffs' counsel for hundreds of doctors. Once we reeled you in, the plan was to produce the damaging internal ZeiiMed documents as part of millions of other documents, with the additional safeguard being that the inculpatory emails were embedded in a group of run-on, nonsensical documents containing repetitive gibberish without syntax or punctuation. Knowing your lack of professional experience in handling a lawsuit against a large multi-national corporation, it was a no brainer to conclude you wouldn't find the incriminating emails."

"You were convinced my incompetence would guarantee your plan's success."

"That's right. ZeiiMed would settle fast, with an agreement that all documents be returned or destroyed. No lawyer could ever again file the same Complaint alleging the same allegations against ZeiiMed. Since ZeiiMed did not hide, withhold or destroy any documents before settling, the law will stop any lawyer from ever bringing the same case against ZeiiMed again. That's why we produced the incriminating emails. So long as ZeiiMed produced them and then settled, no shark attorney could bring the same lawsuit against ZeiiMed again. Plus, we were sure that your lack of effort, questionable thoroughness and inexperience would guarantee the hidden emails would never be found in the documents we produced. The documents were produced but that didn't mean they could be found."

"I guess it was just good luck on my end," I added, to aggravate the doctor.

"Yes, you got lucky, or should I say unlucky, and stumbled upon the emails. It doesn't matter though, the result is the same," the doctor went on. "ZeiiMed settles and ends all inquiries into its business practices forever. As part of any settlement, a class of doctors is certified to include every doctor nationwide, precluding any possibility of any future lawsuits. The file will be closed, sealed and sent to the warehouse. Every doctor across the country will be forever released from any and all claims of wrongdoing against ZeiiMed in return for ZeiiMed's settlement payment. The only change of plan was your discovery of the guilty emails, but I'm taking care of that now."

"And ZeiiMed doesn't care how much it has to pay to settle so long as its executives never have to answer the types of questions I asked Finley about the 'hot emails,'" I responded. "The business of ZeiiMed is preserved and continued. The flow of millions of dollars of corporate revenue is unabated and uninterrupted. I get the big picture now."

"And you were the one who almost screwed up this flawless plan."

My mind was racing. Almost? What does he mean by 'almost'? I fully intend to show the whole world all the flaws in his so-called perfect scam. I needed only a few more moments, since his hand holding the gun was starting to lower as his arm tired.

"How can you betray your fellow doctors who trusted you to prosecute the Complaint on their behalf?" I asked, while placing my arms under my desk to turn it towards him as I lunged forward.

"Don't be such a buffoon. Do you really think I care about any other doctor? They will survive. They have learned how to play the game with ZeiiMed. They take one simple office visit and bill ZeiiMed for multiple different procedures and treatments supposedly performed during the appointment. It's kind of like a lawyer padding a bill so when the client demands a discount, the lawyer still ends up getting more money than he actually earned. The doctors and lawyers know their bills will be cut, so they just inflate them and hope to beat the system."

"So, everybody is crooked... the lawyers, the doctors and ZeiiMed. What a mess," I added.

"You know," Dr. Brown babbled on, his glasses slipping down his large nose and his little eyes narrowing to slits, "the whole system is about to end anyway, including ZeiiMed. Once the President signs the legislation to provide health care to everyone, ZeiiMed is out of business. The nationalization of health care insurance to 35 million uninsured people cannot happen without much lower reimbursement payments to both doctors and hospitals, much lower than even ZeiiMed pays with its rigged computer models and manipulated data. Whether it's an

Insurance Exchange or the government itself selling insurance, ZeiiMed will not be able to compete."

"What a shame—ZeiiMed may be out of business—you'll need to find another illegal scheme," I noted, to buy a little more time.

"It's not funny. Without a profit motive, the premiums charged by the government or the Exchanges will be so low all Americans will join up with Uncle Sam's program and drop private companies like ZeiiMed in a heartbeat. But politics will delay this result awhile and ZeiiMed doesn't want a whistleblower like you exposing its cash machine and shutting down its operations sooner than expected."

I was ready. I was hoping that Dr. Brown would step a little further into my office and out of the doorway so he was closer when I flipped the desk. My eyes must have glanced down at the desk because he seemed to sense my plan.

"If you don't slowly raise your arms from under the desk right now, I will make the insertion of the syringe as painful as possible as it pierces the deep recesses of your ear membrane."

I lifted my arms and put them on top of the desk. Dr. Brown put down his medical bag and reached for something.

"Good. Now put these handcuffs on. Then comes the tape to keep you still for the injection. It will be over quickly. And don't squirm too much, I don't want the police to notice any marks on your wrists. ZeiiMed certainly doesn't want a murder investigation if I can avoid it. In case you're wondering, the gaffer tape doesn't leave a sticky trail once it's removed. In fact, I'm going to put your body by the doorway to make it look like you were seeking help as your heart failed."

As I picked up the handcuffs he had thrown on the desk,

I saw in the darkened hallway outside my office the shadow of a figure behind Dr. Brown. It was a woman. She stepped into the doorway. Her hand quickly and quietly reached into my office and grabbed the softball-sized, solid glass globe on top of my credenza. Just as Dr. Brown sensed the motion behind him, the woman lifted the globe up above her head and brought it crashing down with lethal force, smashing the globe into Dr. Brown's skull. The sound of crushing bone was audible. Dr. Brown, dazed and bleeding, started to fall forward towards me. My hatred for this man instantly overcame me as I punched him right between his two little eyes, breaking his big nose and shattering his glasses. His body changed direction in midair and he fell against the side wall, out cold.

"Mary, Mary, where did you come from? I can't believe what you just did! I think you fractured his skull, thank goodness!"

"Thank goodness all you want, but I'm the one who just saved your skin," Mary replied, in a remarkably stable tone of voice.

"Yes, I mean thank you, a thousand times over. And what are you doing here? You're supposed to be flying off to your secret vacation spot by now."

Mary didn't answer. She looked pale and appeared wobbly on her feet. I stepped over the unconscious Dr. Brown and grabbed her by the arm.

"Here, sit down. You don't seem okay," I said.

Mary sat and looked up at me.

"My neighbor decided at the last minute yesterday that she couldn't take my dog for the week. I had to call a kennel and make arrangements to bring the dog there today. So, I changed my flight to depart tonight and decided to do some last-minute, catch-up work at the office before leaving.

Once I got on the floor, I could hear our very sick client threatening you and I quickly assessed the danger you were in."

"You were very brave, to say the least," I said.

"Hey, I'm proud of myself," Mary responded, as she stood up from the chair, obviously feeling better. "I did what had to be done and I found the strength within myself to do what was necessary," she continued.

Facing me now, Mary quickly kissed me on the cheek and said, "I have to go. If I stick around for the police, I will never get out of here. I'll make a written statement and get it to you, with my phone number at the hotel so the police can call. So long and don't expect me to ever apologize for the kiss. I am what I am and I have no regrets. Either you like me as I am or not."

She then briskly walked out of my office and down the hall, without hesitation or a look back.

"Well, I do think you are very special," I awkwardly called to her, as her elevator arrived. I quickly realized how stupid I sounded.

"Don't leave now," I implored. "We need to talk. I can't believe what just happened here. What am I going to do with this guy?"

Mary didn't respond.

She entered the elevator and the doors closed.

I guess I'm in charge of Dr. Brown's fate now.

Dr. Brown was still unconscious. I went through his medical bag and found a syringe with fluid in it. I bent down and slapped his face as hard as I could. His face jerked to the side, as he was sitting on the floor, his back leaning against the side wall. He opened his eyes. They were cloudy and red. He was squinting since his broken glasses were in pieces next to him. I grabbed him by the throat.

"Now you are going to answer my questions or I'm going to stab you in the heart with this syringe. If the seizure-inducing chemical couldn't have been traced in my body, it won't be discovered in yours either. I'll hide the syringe and everyone will just assume the blow to your head induced heart failure."

I had no sense of pity for this man. He had been quite willing to kill me and my wife without a second thought. He was a diabolical, ruthless and manipulative killer, without sympathy, compassion or moral compass.

More importantly, it seems that evil of this magnitude can cancel out and neutralize the moral balance of any human in its path. All I knew for sure was that his violence had created a rage within my soul that was driving me to a previously unknown, instinctive compulsion to counter evil with evil. I was prepared to kill Dr. Brown and the realization of how easy it would be for me to do so was surprising, but not restricting.

"I will say again, I am going to puncture your heart with the syringe unless you tell me the person at ZeiiMed responsible for all of this."

Dr. Brown lifted his head, his blood running down the wall behind his head.

"You stupid ass," he said.

I guess Mary didn't hit him hard enough with the glass globe. He still had his nasty attitude.

"Who do you think?" he continued. "Everyone in upper management at ZeiiMed. The emails you discovered refer to the Chief Financial Officer Kevin Long and the Executive Vice President Edison, but the scheme is known and sustained by at least 15 to 20 executives that include the CEO and his band of enablers. This isn't over and ZeiiMed is not done with you."

"Tell me again about Charles Wadsworth's involvement. What does he know and when did he become part of this?" I asked.

"He's a lawyer. Do you think for one second we were going to let some Ivy League mouthpiece in on our secrets? As I said, he does what he is told and he knows the punishment that will be inflicted if he deviates from instructions."

I'd had enough of this cockroach. I slammed his head against the wall and knocked him back into unconsciousness. I hoped his skull was cracked in two. But no such luck, he seemed to be still breathing.

I fought back the impulse to finish him off. Suddenly, I realized I was no longer on the same amoral level as this bastard. Thank God. There is hope for all of us. The confrontation with evil created only a brief, temporary compulsion to counter with equal savagery. It passes and some level of sanity is restored.

Now I had to decide what to do with this bloody mess of a human being slowly bleeding to death on the floor of my office.

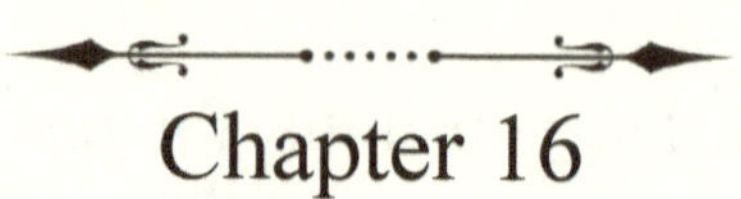

Chapter 16

I called the police. They took one look at Dr. Brown and called an ambulance. I guess I forgot to do that—not all my pernicious impulses evaporated after the heat of battle.

The medics tended to him and brought him out on a stretcher. I was told he would probably survive, but had lost a lot of blood. Forensic investigators turned my office upside down and a few cops asked me some preliminary questions in the conference room. I tried to be vague because I wanted to make sure that Mary had time to get on her plane and get out of town. Sooner or later I would be required to explain her role to the police, but I figured I could stall awhile.

I complained to the police officers that I felt ill, with dizzy spells and a splitting headache (although certainly not as bad as the headache Dr. Brown was going to have when he regained consciousness). I guess the officers eventually concluded that I was being purposely evasive. A new detective arrived and took over the questioning in the conference room as everyone else seemed to fade into the background.

"Hello, Mr. Bradford, I'm Detective John Jarrett. You can call me 'Jack,' everybody does."

Jack was in his mid-forties, pleasant looking with thick, wavy, black hair cut above the ears. His sparkling blue eyes had surely relaxed many a nervous suspect. He was quite a few inches shorter than me, wearing an ordinary dark suit and a bland tie, with his shirt opened at the neck. His pale complexion was probably from long hours of work and unsolved homicides.

"Hi, Jack. You can call me Brian."

"I've been waiting for the opportunity to speak with you ever since I received word of the bombing out in Baiting Hollow. The cops weren't sure where you went after leaving the scene of the crime. My guess was either you went to your home in Port Jeff or your office in the City. Lucky me, you went to your office and fell into my jurisdiction. Now I'm stuck with a possible homicide if the doctor dies, unless he was injured by you in self-defense. I can't wait to hear this story. Maybe you can start by you telling me what happened here, with special emphasis on how you won a face-to-face confrontation with an assailant carrying a loaded gun and a lethal syringe."

I immediately realized that this cop's personality was aggressive and clever.

"I'll start by saying that the guy you saw going out on the stretcher, Dr. Brown, was doing everything possible to kill me. He probably would have succeeded except I was very lucky on two occasions. First, I was at the condo in Baiting Hollow when I was fortunate enough to spot the explosive device. My wife helped me to safety after I fell on the stairs, just before the explosion. I would never have made it on my own. Second, my life was saved later in the day by a female colleague here at the firm. She smashed Dr. Brown on the head with a heavy glass globe before he was able to inject me with a deadly chemical and/or shoot me. After his skull was smashed..."

Detective Jarrett interrupted me. "The police ran into your wife downstairs and we are questioning her now. Can you give me the name and address of the woman that helped you disarm Dr. Brown?"

"Her name is Mary, but she is now on an airplane headed out of town. She said she will provide a written statement and a phone number when she arrives at her hotel."

"I am going to need a lot more information than that. She could be in danger. Your enemies went to great lengths to kill you, and now she is involved and also a target. I need to know where she is exactly so I can contact the local authorities to protect her."

"That's fine, Jack. I'll get that information to you as soon as I get it. Right now, I need to send an email to the New York Attorney General with some documents I've scanned and a short explanation of how this all started with the filing of my Complaint against ZeiiMed, a giant managed health care company. I will give you a copy of everything I send to the New York AG so you will have all the background information."

"Okay," Jack said. "I hope you don't mind if I come with you to the computer and watch what you do."

"No problem," I responded.

We stood in front of my computer as I sent the critical email documents to the professional acquaintance I had at the Attorney General's office, along with the explanatory email I was composing when so rudely interrupted by Dr. Brown. A copy of everything was also sent directly to the Attorney General himself.

That done, I provided Jack a copy of everything. I then told him most of what had occurred since Dr. Brown first appeared in my office looking to hire a lawyer. I did my best to emphasize the heroics of Mary, without which the police would be picking up my body rather than the bloodied Dr. Brown.

Somehow, I forgot to tell Detective Jack that I tried to split Dr. Brown's skull open while he sat defenseless on the floor of my office. My memory just isn't what it once was.

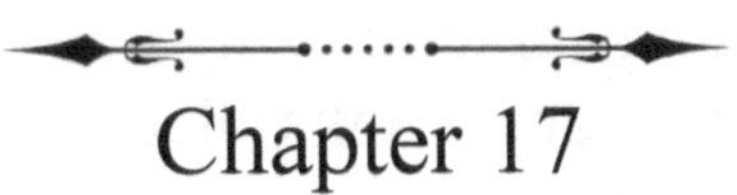

Chapter 17

"When Dr. Brown is able to leave the hospital, I will have my men arrest him for attempted murder and other charges. You won't have to worry about him again. But it's up to either the New York Attorney General or the U.S. Attorney to criminally charge the executives at ZeiiMed who created this alleged scheme for underpaying the doctors. It will take some time to build the evidence against them—probably it will start with the New York Attorney General serving subpoenas on all ZeiiMed's top executives," Detective Jarrett told me as my meeting with him in the conference room was ending.

"Thank you for your help, Jack. I'm going to go find my wife now and head home."

"That's fine. But like I said, be careful. From what I've seen so far, the bad guys at ZeiiMed are ruthless and vengeful. I find it hard to believe they will just forget about you now that Dr. Brown is out of the picture. I will keep in touch," Jack said, as we shook hands. Jack had slowly lost his edgy demeanor and turned out to be a considerate and likeable human being.

I found Kim. We left the building and headed home to Port Jefferson. As we drove home, I couldn't help but rehash in my mind my selfish motivation for agreeing to file the Complaint after the first meeting with the doctors. I had been manipulated, but the manipulation would not have succeeded without a target that had weaknesses susceptible to manipulation.

A quick research of my professional career immediately revealed to ZeiiMed a very ordinary defense attorney in a dull and unexciting practice of doing paperwork for insurance companies and banks at minimum lawyer pay. The boredom must have been dripping off me in an all too obvious manner when I first met Drs. Brown and Hyman in my office.

In order to lure me into the ZeiiMed web, they had complimented me about my defense of Roy M. Cohn when that legal work was ancient history. But my ego so needed an infusion of flattery that I suspended my instinct for sensing insincerity and deceit.

I had the delusion of litigating a multi-million-dollar lawsuit as lead counsel, with all the publicity and notoriety that would accompany the position. I had a fantasy vision of high-priced, white shoe counsel for ZeiiMed pleading with me to settle the case for buckets of cash.

I had the foolhardy dream of sitting with arms folded across the conference room table telling ZeiiMed's lawyers, "Sorry, fellas, your offer of fifty million dollars just won't work. I'm now going to the men's room and when I return your new offer better be nine figures or we're going to trial." I seduced myself with projections of money, fame, excitement and prestige. How pathetic.

The only good news is that the worst may now be over, despite Detective Jack's warning to the contrary. The man who wanted to kill me was in custody and the New York Attorney General's office was aware of ZeiiMed's business practices. There was no longer any reason for ZeiiMed to pursue my family. The cat was out of the bag.

In fact, I suspected that ZeiiMed might want to limit the damage as much as possible and make every effort to settle with the large class of doctors that filed the Complaint, minus Dr. Brown. A settlement would seem to be a satisfactory conclusion to this very unpleasant situation. So I decided at that moment to focus all my energy on achieving a negotiated resolution of the litigation that started with the filing of the Complaint.

But first, I am going to take a short vacation with Kim to get away from all this madness for at least a few days.

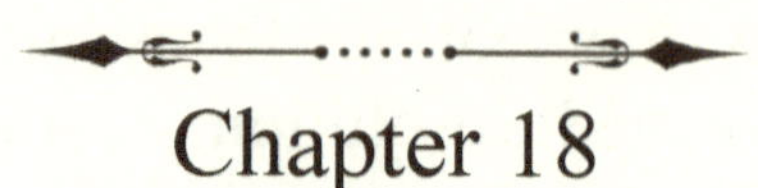

Chapter 18

On the Monday after the weekend from hell, I needed to address some loose ends before planning our vacation. I couldn't possibly face going to the office, so I made the necessary calls from home.

I couldn't wait to hear the "spin" that ZeiiMed's counsel, Charles Wadsworth, would put on all this. He answered the phone pretending to be glad to hear from me.

"Brian, I'm so happy you called. Some people at ZeiiMed told me about Saturday. It's unbelievable what you went through, old buddy. I had no idea your client was so insane. You really need to rethink your client screening procedures at the firm. Putting all that aside, I've got important matters to discuss with you about resolving the Complaint."

This idiot irritated me as soon as I heard his voice.

"Listen, you creep, cut the crap. The only reason I'm not in your face with my hands on your throat is because my former client, Dr. Brown, now in surgery, told me you were not involved in the attempted murder. And maybe you wonder why I believed his ranting about how ZeiiMed would never tell its stupid mouthpiece about its diabolical plans. Well, the answer is that Dr. Brown's excited utterances have a special credibility when he is about to kill me either by gunshot or lethal injection, depending on my degree of cooperation. But I still think you had a pretty good hunch about what ZeiiMed was up to. If I'm ever able to prove it, I will take my revenge on you personally without going to the police."

Charles decided to respond like the idiot he is.

"Brian, I don't know what you mean. That crazy Dr. Brown was your client—he's got nothing to do with ZeiiMed and certainly nothing to do with me."

"Shut up and listen. Brown told me he works for ZeiiMed and takes his orders from ZeiiMed. ZeiiMed created the plan to blow up my condo, with me in it, and he implemented it. Once it failed, Brown followed me to my office and tried to finish matters there. The Attorney General now knows all of this, the NYPD also knows and both will be visiting you shortly."

"I understand that," he said. "I already have a team of lawyers, paid by ZeiiMed, retained to represent me during any questioning. I'm telling them I'm just a lawyer and I don't know anything other than what ZeiiMed told me about their corporate operations. ZeiiMed said all your doctor clients were paid by a fully-disclosed computer model programmed to calculate the payments in accordance with the usual and customary rates in each geographical area. If the doctors had a pre-existing contract with ZeiiMed, in accordance with the terms of the contract. That's what I was told and that's all I know."

"However," Charles continued, "none of that matters now because ZeiiMed wants to settle and it's willing to pay a premium in order to get it done expeditiously. Subject to approval by the Court, ZeiiMed is prepared to pay five hundred million dollars to settle the case quickly. However, there are certain non-negotiable terms: The Court's records must be sealed by Order of the Judge and all documents that were produced to you, electronic or otherwise, must be returned with no copies retained by anyone. The emails must be scrubbed from the servers and back-up tapes. Of course, your one-third fee will be paid out of the five hundred million dollars."

"Your client is such slime," I responded. "I know exactly what you are up to. The New York Attorney General will be going through every one of ZeiiMed's files shortly and your upper management knows that the search will lead to a referral to the U.S. Attorney's Office for possible criminal indictments. ZeiiMed's only way out is to settle quickly with the NYAG, but you know the NYAG won't settle until you pay the doctors all the money ZeiiMed secretly refused to pay them for the last decade or so. You are in full cover-up mode and the first order of business for ZeiiMed is to settle the Complaint fast."

"This is a sincere and generous offer of settlement. I think you should consult with your clients," Charles suggested.

"Regardless of your disingenuousness," I explained, "I have an ethical duty to tell my client of the five hundred-million-dollar settlement offer. My problem is that my main client contact, Martin Brown, tried to kill me and ended up with a smashed skull when he failed. So, I've got to call Dr. Stanley Hyman, the second named plaintiff in the Complaint, and discuss the offer with him. But I can no longer represent the hundreds of other doctors on whose behalf I filed the Complaint. I am withdrawing as their counsel. There is no specific Disciplinary Rule directly on point, but I bet an attorney has a legal obligation to terminate the professional relationship when the client unsuccessfully attempts to murder him. I will tell Dr. Hyman to find a new lawyer to continue the settlement discussions with you."

"Are you crazy? Just take the money and end this," Charles stated.

"I don't want any of your money. I'll take a referral fee from the new counsel to cover my expenses and a reasonable hourly rate for my time in drafting the

Complaint. As far as the usual one-third fee goes, give it to charity after the new attorneys take their cut. This conversation is now over and I hope to never run into you again. I don't think I could restrain myself from making you the second person I have put in the hospital. Good-bye."

I hung up quickly. I didn't want to hear one more word from him. Now that I've decided to withdraw from my representation of the doctors, the new counsel can deal with Wadsworth and ZeiiMed's settlement offer.

The funny thing is that I'm sure the doctors' new lawyer will eventually agree to the settlement, after trying to squeeze a few million more dollars above five hundred million dollars. The Court will approve the settlement because everyone will agree that it was a generous resolution, coupled with an admission by ZeiiMed that there were some flaws in its reimbursement computer programs, probably caused by a doctor who submitted some low-ball payment data that contained accidental misinformation. The lies will be memorialized by a court reporter and the record then sealed forever in the bowels of the courthouse's basement. Maybe I should have smashed Dr. Brown's skull one more time when I had the chance. It looks like that's the only gratification I'm going to get.

I called Dr. Hyman.

He wasn't at his office.

I left a message.

"Dr. Hyman, this is your attorney, Brian Bradford. We met in my office with Dr. Brown. In case you don't know, Dr. Brown is in the hospital and will be arrested once he is discharged. He tried to physically harm my wife and me, so I can no longer serve as counsel for the nationwide class of doctors described in the Complaint. I will explain further when you call back. You need to get another attorney expeditiously because a significant settlement offer has been made by ZeiiMed. I am planning on taking a short vacation to the Turks and Caicos Islands. I will probably leave next week and that will give you some time to find a new lawyer. I'll call you as soon as I get back, if I don't hear from you before I leave. Thank you."

As soon as I hung up, the phone rang. I picked it up.

"Hi, this is Detective Jack Jarrett. I just called to see how you're doing. I noticed you didn't go to the office today."

"Thank you for calling," I replied. "I feel fine. I'm planning a vacation for next week and didn't want to commute all the way into New York City to see blood stains on the carpet in my office."

"It's going to take a while for the memories to fade. Vacation? Where do you think you'll go?"

"If you must know, Detective, the Turks and Caicos Islands, but I don't think you called to chat about that."

"You're right, but I would like to be kept posted on your whereabouts. I'm very suspicious of the people at ZeiiMed and my police instincts tell me you have not heard the last of them. Since Dr. Brown was brazen enough to try to kill you in your own office after blowing up your entire condo building, I think you better remain alert and very careful. Please call me each day to let me know whether you will be staying home or going to work. If you do go on vacation, I'd like a copy of your itinerary. That way, I can have one of my men check in on you periodically. Don't worry. You won't even know they're close by."

"I do appreciate your concern for my well-being, but that won't be necessary. And I certainly don't want some cop sitting in a squad car across from my house. But I will call if I think something is suspicious."

"I'm not trying to scare you, but by the time you realize

something is suspicious, you probably won't have time to call before the bad guys pounce. By the way, which island in Turks and Caicos are you going to stay on? I used to go diving down there years ago. Beautiful place."

"I'll be staying in Providenciales and hopefully leaving next week. I promise to call you as soon as I get back."

"Okay. Have nice trip. Keep your eyes open and bring plenty of sun tan lotion. The sun down there can really burn your skin up."

"Yes, I know. I've been to Providenciales many times and thanks again for your concern."

Now the friendly and persistent Detective Jack had me worried. The odds were that I wouldn't survive a third attack on my life. But what are my alternatives? I can't stay locked up in my house. Even if I agreed to police protection of some sort, it wouldn't be twenty-four hours a day and it wouldn't last forever. Sooner or later, ZeiiMed would have an opportunity if so inclined. I had to just live my life and hope for the best. Plus, now that the authorities were investigating ZeiiMed and digging through its dirty laundry, there was no reason for ZeiiMed to bother me anymore. I hoped, anyway.

With that thought in mind, I felt better and picked up the phone to call the International Reservations Desk at National Airlines.

After booking our vacation for the next week, I started to think more about Detective Jack's concerns about my safety. He was only trying to be helpful and do his best to make sure ZeiiMed keeps its hands off me. I called him back and asked to meet him for lunch. He agreed.

We decided to go to Louie's Oyster Bar and Grille on Manhasset Bay in Port Washington, Long Island. Jack took the very short train ride from Penn Station to Port

Washington and I picked him up at the train station. Jack looked more relaxed in his slacks and golf shirt.

Louie's has been in business since 1905 and was completely renovated in 2002. It's located on the waterfront on Main Street in nautical Port Washington.

Jack and I decided to sit at a table outside on the deck directly in front of the marina. The marina has two long wooden docks with moored sailboats that extend into Manhasset Bay. In the distance, there is the Long Island Sound and an outline of the City's skyscrapers. The sun was shining and our view magnificent.

Our beers came out in chilled mugs with the foam overflowing. We ordered steamers and fried butterfly shrimp with plenty of creamy tartar sauce.

"This is great. I'm so glad you could find time to meet me here," I said.

The sun was shining directly on Jack's face. He didn't have sunglasses, but the sun definitely gave him some much-needed color in his cheeks.

"I was surprised that I had the time myself, but a couple of things resolved and my schedule temporarily cleared," Jack responded.

"I guess the murder, mayhem and mugging business is booming as usual."

"Yes, it is. You become hardened to it all, but it's impossible to disconnect all emotional responses. Plus, the hours are long and the open files are piled high. I always intend to spend more time at home, but it never happens and suddenly my daughter is grown and will soon have her own life. I've been spending as much time as possible with her, kind of making up for lost time. But enough negativity. All my work over many years has gotten me pretty good at what I do, so let's talk about your situation."

"Well, I did speak with ZeiiMed's lawyer about settlement and a very large offer of money was made. Plus, I don't think ZeiiMed is watching my every move. Also, I'm convinced ZeiiMed's lawyers knew nothing about their client's dirty laundry."

"Like I said before, you won't see the bad guys until it's too late, so don't get too comfortable. I'm very concerned about your safety. If ZeiiMed can recruit an esteemed physician such as Dr. Brown and motivate him to carry out ZeiiMed's plan for murder, then anything is possible. What's next, your neighbor or law partner will suddenly become a ZeiiMed robot programmed to eradicate the Bradfords? We are dealing with an evil organization that apparently can find people's weakest link and use it to force them to do the Company's business."

"Now I'm more worried than ever. I think I'll have a shot of tequila with my next cold beer. Other than drink alcohol, what else am I supposed to do?"

"You don't really have to do anything, other than stay alert for obvious signs of danger and make an effort to never be alone, as best you can. My men are watching and you will have full protection as long as I'm in charge. The last thing we need is ZeiiMed setting off other explosive devices, so my department is on double duty."

"Well, thank you. I hope I don't spend too much of the taxpayers' money and hog all the City's resources."

"You let me worry about that. There is no way a lawyer and his wife are being taken out on my watch. Plus, I like you and want you to be safe. It's pretty rare that the first two attempts fail and we get a chance to prevent the third attempt. Usually, the criminals I know have a better success rate than that."

"Are you sure there will be a third attempt? I mean, isn't

there a chance that ZeiiMed realizes the authorities are investigating and watching, so restraint is now the order of the day?" I asked.

"No. No chance at all. This is only the beginning. The worst is yet to come. But that doesn't mean we won't be successful in protecting you. It only means we have to be vigilant and not let our guard down for a moment," Detective Jack responded.

"Okay. Enough said. We have a bond, a commitment and a mutual agenda. We're in this together. Let's drink to our success and may no harm come to us while defeating the enemy," I said, with a surprising jolt of emotion. Maybe it was the tequila.

"Amen," Jack responded, and we clinked glasses.

"By the way," Detective Jack added, "We still can't figure out how Doctor Brown broke his nose when Mary's blow was to the back of his head. Can you help me out on this?"

"No, I have no idea, I never touched him. He must have injured himself when he fell to the ground."

"Of course, that's it. You see, what you're forgetting is now that we have this bond, I know you're lying. Cops are good at figuring this stuff out. Guess what, I don't care. Dr. Brown deserved what you and Mary dished out to him. But, in the future, please let my department be in charge of physical injury to perpetrators. We've done it before and know how to do it properly."

"I put my fate in your hands. You are in charge," I responded.

It was a very pleasant, seaside lunch. We actually became pretty good friends. We later talked more about our wives, children, careers, retirement and the many dangers of being a law enforcement officer in the City. Away from the crime scene where we first met, Detective Jack was engaging and interesting. We had our bond and I am very thankful to have him in charge of my protection. I agreed to keep him posted regarding my daily schedule and call him at least once a day.

I paid the check and we decided to have lunch together whenever our schedules permitted.

Chapter 19

Arriving back home after lunch, I heard my fax machine printing furiously. It was a copy of the subpoena being served on ZeiiMed by the New York Attorney General. My secretary knew I wasn't going into work, so she faxed it to my home as soon as she received a courtesy copy from the New York AG's Office.

The subpoena demanded that ZeiiMed produce all its computer records and hard copy documents reflecting the manner in which ZeiiMed calculated the payments to doctors. All the billing data was requested, as well as the database information programmed into the computers to calculate the payments. Plus, ZeiiMed was also required to turn over everything discussing a pattern of delaying, depressing or downwardly manipulating the rates used in calculating the payments.

Mostly, the subpoena focused on out-of-network doctors. This refers to the situation where the patient pays a higher premium to ZeiiMed to obtain medical services from a doctor who is not in ZeiiMed's medical network. In return, ZeiiMed agrees that the out-of-network doctor will be paid eighty percent of the usual customary and reasonable rate for doctors practicing the same specialty in the same geographical area. The out-of-network doctors have no contract directly with ZeiiMed, but understand and agree to accept payment under the eighty percent formula. Of course, the Complaint alleges that ZeiiMed didn't keep up its end of the deal.

The subpoena demanded all the records of ZeiiMed regarding the calculation of payments to out-of-network doctors. All documents reflecting a manipulation of data must be revealed, along with corporate revenue documentation demonstrating the millions of dollars of additional profits generated as a result of the underpayments. Lastly, the New York AG requested all records reflecting each and every instance wherein ZeiiMed "scrubbed" the data being inserted into the computer models so that the medical rates of the highest paid doctors were deleted, automatically reducing the average reimbursements rates to all doctors.

I found it curious that the New York AG was not focusing at the present time on the in-network doctors. Dr. Brown had told me at our first meeting that ZeiiMed also programmed its computers to make sure the in-network doctors were likewise underpaid. This seemed to me to be a more daunting task for ZeiiMed since in-network doctors have a payment contract with ZeiiMed wherein both the doctors and ZeiiMed agree on a formula for calculating a payment for a specific medical treatment.

However, I also remembered Dr. Brown telling me that in-network doctors never really understood the complicated formula for payment because it was purposefully made impossibly vague and ambiguous by ZeiiMed. But the doctors need the patients and most people have their managed health care insurance with ZeiiMed because ZeiiMed has the cheapest premiums in the marketplace. As a result, what option does a doctor have once he gets a thirty dollar payment for an office visit that he charges one hundred fifty dollars? The doctor can appeal and insist that his contract with ZeiiMed entitles him or her to more. Guess what? The appeal process and all the rules of the appeal process are dictated by ZeiiMed. Good luck with the appeal.

Dr. Brown had also explained that ZeiiMed simply "down codes" the payment requests of the in-network doctors. That is, once the doctor performs a specific medical treatment, he sends a bill to ZeiiMed by submitting the designated "code" for the treatment rendered. When ZeiiMed gets the bill, it simply assigns a code to the treatment that provides a lesser payment than the code submitted by the doctor. If the doctor doesn't like the underpayment, you're back to the mandatory appeal process. Plus, the in-network doctors are forbidden by their contracts with ZeiiMed to demand money from patients to compensate for the underpayments.

On the other hand, maybe everything Dr. Brown told me was a lie. Maybe he didn't have any knowledge of anything. Maybe everything he told me about ZeiiMed was false. The 'hot' emails I used at Finley's deposition were real, but maybe ZeiiMed didn't actually have this massive, worldwide scheme to cheat and deceive. Maybe it was restricted to a limited period of time when some faulty data accidentally resulted in some minor underpayments to a small number of doctors. Maybe ZeiiMed realized its accidental mistake and now wants to pay what it owes. I know—we're talking about a one-in-a-million chance.

Of course, we will never know the truth. The public will never know the truth. Settlement money will be paid by ZeiiMed, whether it's guilty as charged or not. All ZeiiMed's accusers will take the money, shut up and go away. ZeiiMed will be free to continue its business with no admission of wrongdoing and some cosmetic changes in its computer model to demonstrate to the Court its sincere remorse for any injury it caused. Everything will be quickly restored to how it was. What a world we live in.

But the good news is that the subpoena will shake up

management at ZeiiMed. ZeiiMed knows what its documents reveal and knows the documents cannot be made public. ZeiiMed also is aware that the New York AG will start taking depositions of every executive once it gets the documents sought by the subpoena. ZeiiMed is cornered and something will have to give. I'm sure that's the reason that ZeiiMed is working double time on a solution that involves the payment of a lot of money to settle the Complaint.

As it turned out, money was only one of ZeiiMed's solutions to its problems.

Chapter 20

K im was delighted when I told her that we leave next Monday for Providenciales in the Turks and Caicos Islands.

Providenciales is only 37.5 square miles, but it is the primary tourist destination in Turks and Caicos. It has numerous ocean front accommodations on twelve miles of soft, brilliantly white sandy beaches along Grace Bay.

The Turks and Caicos Islands are considered an archipelago located in the British West Indies consisting of eight major islands and five times as many much smaller islands referred to as "cays." The non-stop flight is only 3 hours and 20 minutes gate to gate from Kennedy Airport, although the Turks and Caicos Islands are actually 575 to 600 miles southeast of Miami.

At the approach to Providenciales International Airport, the jets fly directly over a large cove of calm, milky blue water known as Chalk Sound National Park. The water in the Sound is unique in texture and color because of its creamy turquoise blend, yet equally endearing as the crystal-clear water at the beaches over the rest of the Turks and Caicos Islands.

From the airport, Leeward Highway is the main thoroughfare east towards the major hotels. Fifteen minutes from the airport is a left turn towards Turtle Cove on the "lower road." Continuing east on the "lower road" leads to the hotels directly on Grace Bay. The turquoise waters of Grace Bay are a breathtaking, crystal clear, light shade of blue that sparkle with astounding visibility. As the water deepens offshore, it takes on a richer shade of blue that creates a stunning contrast with the nearshore water, while retaining its striking clarity.

The Palms, the Somerset, the Sands, the Ocean Club, the Alexandra and several other resorts all offer friendly, first class accommodations right on the beach, with magnificent sunsets included at no additional charge. One of the newer "glamor" beach hotels is the elegant Ritz-Carlton. It has resort pools, beachfront bar with an unobstructed, close-up view of Grace Bay, vibrant music, sophisticated styling and a young, modern clientele that enjoys life and wants to live it to the fullest. Quite simply, it is a fun place to hang out and watch people.

Kim and I have been coming to Providenciales since 1995. It was essentially undeveloped at that time, with only two or three hotels in addition to Club Med Turquoise. Back then, we stayed at the Turquoise Reef Resort and Casino that included the island's main social meeting place, Buddy's Beach Bar and Grill. Everyone we know on the island today can be traced back to friends we first met at Buddy's Beach Bar.

The "Dive Provo" dive shop used to be located thirty feet down the beach from Buddy's Beach Bar, also in front of the Turquoise Reef. In fact, it was at this dive shop that we first met our longtime friend and master dive instructor, Wayne Hall. Over the years, he has taken us on many dives and introduced us to spectacular underwater sea life, coral reefs, caves and walls that seemed to extend forever towards the center of the earth. Wayne's vast array of underwater skills and engaging smile have found him in much demand over the years. He now owns his own dive shop called "Ocean Vibes" and provides the best dive experience available in the Caribbean.

After the Turquoise Reef was closed, the property was purchased by various resort developers that didn't last long, until the recent completion of Seven Stars. Seven Stars is a gated resort of multi-million-dollar oceanfront luxury residences that can be booked for the short term by the vacationing public. The room rates are very expensive, but the resort adjoins one of the most beautiful stretches of beach on Grace Bay.

Once the Turquoise Reef was no longer operational, we stayed with the children at the Ocean Club until the opening of the Alexandra, which is now our vacation home away from home. The Chelsea Building at the Alexandra is right on the beach with unobstructed views of the enchanting waters of Grace Bay from spacious balconies. It is truly a stunning slice of heaven on earth.

I couldn't be more excited about leaving for paradise next week.

Chapter 21

It was early in the day at Kennedy Airport. Around 5:30 a.m.

There weren't many people in the recently opened, massive 2.2 million square foot National Airlines Terminal.

From curbside, Kim and I proceeded inside the terminal's front doors to the ticket counters. The sleek, open look of the terminal was created by the high ceilings above an unencumbered, huge open area where all classes of passengers check their bags at a countless number of counters dotting the perimeter.

The security screening was at the far end of the terminal.

After checking our bags and passing through security, we walked past many high-end shops and eateries on our way to the gate. We stepped into a sharply inclined escalator that descended sixty feet to a moving sidewalk bordered by a continuous wall of large, brilliant flat screen LCDs coordinated to provide a dazzling display of lights and sounds.

At the end of the moving sidewalk was a second steep escalator, this one ascending to the international gates, including the departure gate for Providenciales.

Chapter 22

The Janitor pushed his wheeled garbage pail slowly towards the men's room, not far from the departure gate for the flight to Providenciales. His broom and cleaning materials were attached to the side of the mobile garbage pail. Since it was just 5:30 a.m., there were very few people gathered at the sitting area near the departure gate for the scheduled 7:15 a.m. non-stop flight to Providenciales.

The Janitor felt uncomfortable disguised as a custodian. He wasn't used to such a seemingly low stature in the pecking order of society and certainly wasn't comfortable in the shabby blue uniform of the airport sanitation staff. But it served his plan perfectly.

No one seemed to take notice of the Janitor. The public hardly looked at him as they passed frantically searching for their gates. While milling near or in the bathrooms, the Janitor fit in naturally and no one asked for him unless the dispenser had run out of paper towels.

Passing through the security devices at the National Airlines Terminal had been uneventful. Of course, he was not dressed as the Janitor at the time. He had worn a suit and had a boarding pass for a flight that day. The Janitor had been worried about getting the needle and the small vials of liquid through without detection, but the needle didn't register on the metal detector and the drugs were in four vials, each less than the maximum weight for liquid carry-on items. He thought his hand-made belt was a brilliant idea and would never be mistaken by security as anything other than a common clothing accessory necessary to hold up one's pants.

The day before, the Janitor had taken three slim strips of durable, heavy strength leather similar to the leather straps of a whip used by a lion tamer at the circus. Each piece of leather was long enough to fit around his waist and he had manually intertwined and twisted them to form one continuous piece. The Janitor then attached an interlocking belt buckle apparatus to the interwoven long straps of leather to create a simulated belt. Once past the security gates, the belt could be easily disassembled back into three individual leather strips perfectly suited to accomplish his deadly plan.

The Janitor had several close friends in the Security Department at ZeiiMed. His personal "off-the-books" request to make available to him a standard blue janitor's uniform and essential cleaning equipment used by National Airlines was not difficult to accomplish. The Janitor was told the exact location of a small locked closet near the departure gates that contained a wheeled, standard issue garbage pail and uniform with sufficient room for him to change out of his suit. He was given the key to the closet. Everything had gone as planned as he quickly and without notice changed clothes and transformed himself into the Janitor after he passed through security.

It was necessary to become the Janitor because his friend in the ZeiiMed Security Department had tipped him off that Brian Bradford was being closely watched by the police, essentially monitoring him at all times when he left his house. The Janitor didn't know whether Bradford was aware of the police surveillance, but it was necessary to deal with it if he hoped to accomplish his master plan.

It was easy to spot the plainclothes detective in the airport terminal near the departure gate for the flight to Providenciales. Cops usually stick out like sore thumbs, if you know what to look for. Bradford wasn't even at the gate yet, but the detective assigned to him certainly was. The Janitor simply couldn't take the chance that the detective would board the plane to Turks and Caicos that morning.

Detective John Jarrett was not happy about being up so early. He had arrived at the National Airlines Terminal at 5:30 in the morning. Everyone on his staff had come up with a reason why they were unavailable for airport duty. As usual, if you want something done right, you have to do it yourself. Detective Jarrett had thought about obtaining authorization to actually board the flight to Providenciales and "watch over" Bradford while he was away, but the detective knew that his superiors would never approve what they surely would view as nothing more than an unnecessary "boondoggle."

He decided instead to just make sure Bradford safely got on the jet. Of course, he would also notify the local authorities in Providenciales to keep an eye out for him as a possible target of violence or kidnapping.

So here he was, sipping his third cup of coffee while walking quickly through the airport terminal before the sun had risen. Just over an hour and half from now, Bradford would depart and he could head back to the police precinct in Manhattan. Once he got to the international departure gate, he decided to kill time by making a bunch of cell phone calls regarding several unsolved murder files that he was still investigating. The detective had long ago mastered the art of pacing, drinking coffee and talking on the phone at the same time.

Distracted by his police work, Detective Jarrett didn't notice the Janitor who glanced at him momentarily as he walked past about ten feet from where the detective was pacing and talking on his cell phone.

The Janitor kept a distant yet close eye on Detective Jarrett. With all that coffee he was drinking, the Janitor knew the detective would head to the men's room soon. The Janitor was now standing near the front entrance of the men's room with the "Cleaning in Progress" sign posted to keep customers away. But the Janitor was ready to remove the sign quickly, once he noticed the detective looking for the closest bathroom.

The moment came.

The Janitor saw the detective put away his cell phone and turn to look for a men's room in the main corridor that connected all the gates. The Janitor took away the "Cleaning in Progress" sign and put it next to his garbage pail. As Detective Jarrett entered the bathroom and headed for a stall, the Janitor quickly returned the "Cleaning in Progress" sign to the front of the bathroom entrance.

The Janitor had put duct tape in an "x" shape in front of each of the four urinals, leaving the detective no alternative but to use one of the stalls to urinate.

The plan worked.

The Detective entered the stall and started to relieve himself with his back to the partially opened door of the stall. The Janitor moved quickly. He entered the same stall standing directly behind the Detective, facing his back. He forcefully placed his left hand over Jack's mouth and jerked his head to the side while keeping his grip firm. In his right hand, the Janitor held a syringe containing a megadose of sodium thiopental, a barbiturate that would induce unconsciousness in less than 10 seconds. The Janitor immediately brought his right hand around the front of the Detective's body and firmly stabbed the syringe directly into his testicles through the unzipped front of his pants. The Detective's body immediately jerked backward as the pain of the forceful injection created the urge to scream. The Janitor subdued his defensive movement and muffled the sound of his pain. The Janitor used all his strength to firmly hold the Detective motionless and soundless while his precious last ten seconds lapsed before paralysis and coma consumed him.

The Detective knew he was done as he fought to stay conscious. He shouldn't have been such an easy prey and he shouldn't have been so easily distracted. Most importantly, he should have made sure that he would be alive when his daughter's wedding day came shortly. Darkness engulfed him as his brain went blank.

The Detective collapsed in the Janitor's arms. He was still breathing. The megadose that had been injected does not cause respiratory collapse. The Janitor had one of the leather straps from his belt in his pocket. He quickly put it around the Detective's neck and started to strangle him. The Janitor could feel his victim's windpipe cracking as the rings of cartilage on the trachea snapped from the power of the chokehold. It wasn't long before his breathing stopped completely.

The Janitor turned the Detective around and sat his slumping body on the toilet seat, using his broom to keep the body from falling to the side. As the Janitor tried to lift the Detective's lifeless head up, he noticed tears coming down his cheeks. "You shouldn't have gotten in the way," the Janitor mumbled quietly. "You weren't the one I am after."

The Janitor couldn't wait to get out of his blue uniform and back into his expensive suit.

He closed and taped the door to the stall and left the men's room with the "Cleaning in Progress" sign still in place. He wheeled the garbage pail at a leisurely pace to the closet where his suit was.

Chapter 23

Kim and I arrived at the departure gate of the National Airlines Terminal around 6:15 a.m. for the 7:15 a.m. flight that day to Providenciales. There were only a few people in the waiting area around the gate. I guess it was just too early.

Since our daughters were home from college for the summer, they were able to join us for what was now a real family vacation. One is a senior and the other a sophomore at the College of the Holy Cross, a small liberal arts college in Worcester, Massachusetts. It was great to have them join us. Such precious moments are to be cherished since the opportunities will quickly diminish in time.

Suddenly there was a commotion at the men's room, not far from the gate. Medical personnel were running into the bathroom and the airport police were blocking the area. Probably, some old guy had a heart attack on the toilet and wasn't going to make his flight that day. I said a quiet prayer for a quick recovery from whatever had stricken the passenger.

We were able to board early because we fortunately had received a free upgrade to first class. Because I have flown National Airlines on business trips most of my professional life, I have accumulated over one million miles of air time. The million-mile status entitles you to special perks and one of the perks was paying off handsomely today. Our daughters had their seats in the main cabin and were probably glad they didn't have to sit anywhere near their parents on the flight.

Kim and I were assigned seats "D" and "F" in the first row of the first-class section on the right-hand side of the Boeing 757. The galley was in front of us, just past the bulkhead that separated our seats from the galley.

Across the aisle from the galley, on the left side of the jet, was the bathroom. The bathroom was no more than three large steps in front of our seats. Two steps past the bathroom was the door to the cockpit.

I was reading the newspaper as the rest of the passengers walked past us heading into the body of the plane. It seemed everyone must have shown up at once because the boarding line suddenly seemed endless.

I went back to my reading. I didn't notice the short man in a suit walking pass me with a small, black leather carry-on bag. He took a seat in the fourth row of the first-class section directly behind us on the right-hand side of the jet.

The flight attendant closed and sealed the cabin door in preparation for take-off. We were ready to go. I looked around and noticed there was no one else in first class other than another couple in the last row across the aisle and a man in row four directly behind me. He was apparently short and leaning forward because I couldn't see his face over the high-backed seats between us. I only knew the person was a male because I could briefly see the short, thinning hair on the top of his head.

Once at cruising altitude, a courteous and professional flight attendant asked us our choice of beverages. She was in her early fifties, about five feet, eight inches tall, with the muscle tone of one who had lifted and moved heavy carry-on luggage for many years. Her light brown hair was very short and combed back, and she had a petite nose and dark-framed glasses. She wore very little make-up, but didn't need to. She was plain, yet attractive, and smiled easily. Experience and confidence just seemed to emanate from her. She knew what she was doing and I knew not to question anything she did.

"Mr. and Mrs. Bradford, would you care for a beverage? Coffee? Water? Juice or a cocktail?" the flight attendant asked, while looking at a chart she was carrying.

"Hi, thanks for asking. My name is Brian and this is my wife Kim."

"I'm Kathleen Ferris," she responded with a slight Texas accent.

"Since the vacation has now begun, we would like two Bloody Marys. It's always nice to have a little alcohol in the morning before your eggs," I said, eliciting a very slight grin from Kathleen. Or was it a grimace? I guess it was too early for stupid comments.

Kathleen returned with the drinks and took our breakfast order.

"You have a lovely accent, where are you based?" Kim asked.

"I'm from Austin, Texas. I'm looking forward to getting back home to see my family. I've been on the road for a while now. This is my last round trip to Provo before I head home."

"We have two daughters in Row 23. They're in college, but I still think of them as kids. This is our one family vacation of the year. We're from Port Jefferson, Long Island."

"I'll keep an eye out for your girls when I'm in the back. I have two daughters myself, but they are both grown up with husbands and children themselves. But they live close to Austin, so I get to see them often."

"You're blessed that your daughters live so close to you,"

Kim said.

"Thanks. I do know how fortunate I am. I'll be back with your breakfast in a few minutes. I need to take the order of the gentleman a few rows behind you. He's perspiring profusely, so I'm sure he must need a beverage of some kind."

Breakfast came. I decided a nice cold beer was in order and asked for one.

"No problem," was the response. Kathleen was just great. She was not only looking out for my safety, but also providing wonderful things to eat and drink. Life doesn't get any better than this.

On the breakfast tray she delivered, I was very surprised to see a metal knife and fork. The blade on the knife was about two inches and the tip slightly rounded, but it was a real knife. This was the first time since 9/11 that I had noticed plastic utensils were no longer uniformly provided on airplanes. Metal knives are still prohibited from being carried onto the plane and have been ever since it was learned that the 9/11 hijackers had box cutter utility knives. Nonetheless, metal knives were now being dispensed in the first-class cabin. Apparently, memories fade and everything changes with the passage of time.

Maybe it was the alcohol so early in the morning, but I decided to bore Kim with my views on current world events while eating breakfast.

"I found it fascinating to read about the conversations between Henry Paulson, the Treasury Secretary, and Kenneth D. Lewis, Bank of America's chief executive, regarding the events that occurred after BofA agreed to pay about fifty-billion dollars to buy the financially distressed Merrill Lynch during the financial crisis in mid-September 2008."

"Okay, I'll bite. Tell me your thoughts on the issue and I promise to listen to every word," my dear wife invited. But I didn't care about her sarcasm because she just gave me the green light to pour out my soul on a series of events that I found absolutely fascinating.

"So, in early December 2008, around the 5th, the shareholders of BofA approved the purchase of Merrill Lynch with a closing projected for January 1, 2009. Then, on or about December 14th, Lewis allegedly learned from his CFO that there were billions of previously undisclosed losses at Merrill Lynch. Plus, the losses were deteriorating at a staggering pace, reaching approximately twelve billion dollars by the middle of December. As a result, Mr. Lewis started a series of conversations with Paulson about possibly not closing on the deal. That's when all hell broke loose."

Kim interrupted my slowly building story and correctly noted an important issue.

"It seems to me that a fundamental aspect of the transaction had not been disclosed," she said. "Such a material adverse change should permit Bank of America to step back from the deal."

"You would think so, and maybe BofA had the contractual right to terminate. But Mr. Lewis testified that he was told by Paulson that a failure to proceed would show a 'colossal lack of judgment' that might justify a removal of management at the bank. Additionally, Lewis was allegedly told that the federal government did not want a public disclosure of the new adverse financial data. By the way, Paulson disputed that in a statement he submitted to Congress. Paulson's position was that neither he, the Federal Reserve, nor anyone at the Treasury ever told Lewis not to disclose any information to the public markets that BofA believed was legally required to be disclosed.

"So, it looks like Paulson and Lewis each have different recollections on some very important points," Kim noted.

"That's true, but the most interesting aspect is Mr. Paulson's comments regarding what could have happened to life as we know it if he hadn't acted quickly to avert a collapse of the financial system by saving Merrill Lynch, AIG, Bear Sterns and others from bankruptcy. Apparently, Paulson believed that the banking system could have frozen, causing greater unemployment with people in the streets all around the world... and a meltdown of the financial system that could lead to chaos and a failure of the country's entire economic system."

I continued, "It appears that Paulson had a doomsday vision of people rioting in the streets of America, tossing rocks at the windows of locked up banks and smashing battering rams into the barricaded doors of the New York Stock Exchange. I think Paulson was convinced that America was about to crumble to its knees, yet America was not told. This was history occurring right in front of us and we, the public, had no idea what was truly unfolding and the harsh consequences possibly to come. I'm guessing he believed we couldn't be trusted to act rationally with the truth. In other words, it was like parents sparing the kids bad news so they wouldn't be traumatized. Meanwhile, we were all glued to the television watching the stock market take a nose dive and fearing the worst."

"Well, that was some speech. Would you like another drink?"

"Very funny, Kim. But I do get a little worked up when I start thinking about all this," I responded.

"It makes you wonder how these people can sleep at night knowing what their financial manipulations did to the American workforce and retirees. It is an endless and constantly repeated theme of shameless and irresponsible behavior."

Luckily, the moment was broken when Kathleen came back to pick up our breakfast trays. "Need any more drinks to douse all that dry talk?" she asked. I guess I was talking too loudly.

"No thanks. I'm done both drinking and pontificating," was my only additional comment.

"I was back in coach and saw your daughters—they are doing fine and seem to be enjoying the ride," Kathleen mentioned.

"Thanks," Kim said. "I'm going back to see them right now and say hi."

Kim got out of her seat and left. I noticed the lavatory was vacant. I walked a few steps to the kitchen and turned to my left to open the outwardly swinging door to the lavatory.

It was dark in the bathroom. No light was on. I entered the cramped area inside, pulled the door closed and started to slide the small latch on the lock mechanism. This automatically turned the lights on once in the locked position.

Before I had completed the sliding motion of the lock mechanism, the door was suddenly yanked open. A short, quick figure of a man placed his open palm against my face and pushed my head against the back wall of the lavatory and its downwardly sloping ceiling. He swiftly entered the lavatory and closed the door while sliding the latch into the locked position. The light went on.

Dr. Stanley Hyman stood in front of me, his face twelve inches from mine in the confined space. I could smell his stale, sickly breath as I stared at his perspiring, slimy face. His thin hair was disheveled and his glasses were off. The veins in his large forehead were quivering grossly.

"What the hell is wrong with you? Get out of here and don't touch me again," was all I could think to say in this absurd situation. That's when I saw the airline knife from the breakfast tray in his hand and realized the situation was desperate.

"I've been anxiously awaiting this encounter. You're not easy to get close to, especially with the former detective and his merry men always watching. But this will do. Don't move and don't make any noise or I swear I'll open this door and stab your wife before anybody can react," he stated very quickly, in a low tone of voice.

"Tell me what you want and go away," I responded, as I inhaled the rancid odor of his sweating body and the repulsive smell of his stale, cigar-tainted breath.

"I'm going to do to you what ZeiiMed will shortly do to both Martin Brown and myself. Martin failed to kill you and his death penalty will be inflicted shortly by ZeiiMed. He will never leave his hospital bed alive... I don't care how many cops are watching him. Then ZeiiMed will take me out just because I was his teammate in our doomed assignment. We were unable to persuade you into settling before you discovered the damaging emails and used them against ZeiiMed. Then, we failed to take you out in Baiting Hollow after you used the emails at the deposition.

Hyman took a deep breath and continued. "But, before the inevitable occurs, I have one important matter to attend to and that is watching you bleed to death. I don't care what the authorities do to me—my incarceration will just make it harder for ZeiiMed to get to me. Martin was my friend and colleague for many years. I cared for him and you put him in the hospital. Then you signed his death warrant by going to the authorities. Now I'm going to slice your throat so I can watch your face turn white as the blood drips down your chest. And if this dull airline knife doesn't work, I have FAA-approved, three-inch metal scissors that will make a precise and fatal puncture in your throat. So even though I'm a doctor, it might take two tries to impose the precise fatal incision."

"You're a sick puppy and a smelly son-of-a-bitch to boot," I said, as I tried to push him backward against the door. It didn't work. He was stocky and well-balanced. His hand with the knife lunged at me and cut into the skin on the side of my neck as I jerked my head to the side.

Blood spurted out as he pulled the knife out of my flesh. My vision became hazy. I felt weak and helpless.

Hyman started to thrust his arm forward for a second cut, aiming directly for my throat. There was no room for me to deflect his arm to avoid a possibly fatal cut into my windpipe. The loss of blood left me with little strength to resist his attack.

At that exact moment, the light in the bathroom went out as I heard the lock slide to the "unlocked" position. The knife missed me as Hyman quickly changed the angle of his attack in the darkness, assuming I would again turn my head to avoid contact. The knife cut into the drywall behind me. The door opened. Light from the cabin provided some illumination. A woman's arm swung into the bathroom. There was a coffee pot in her hand. Steaming hot coffee blew out of the pot into Hyman's face. He screamed in excruciating pain and covered his burning face with his hands. I pushed him out the now fully opened door and slumped on the toilet. I saw it was Kathleen.

Hyman's body was experiencing involuntary muscle spasms as he laid sprawled in the aisle. Kathleen put down the coffee pot and drove her knee into Hyman's solar plexus. He was now desperately gasping for air. Blisters had already formed and the poached flesh was peeling from his face.

One of the pilots came out of the cockpit and put plastic zip ties on Hyman's wrists, functioning as handcuffs.

Kathleen came into the bathroom with a warm towel.

"Mr. Bradford, stay with us. You're going to be all right. I'll stop the bleeding and help you up," she said in a soft, reassuring voice, as she put pressure to my wound with the towel.

"Everyone back to your seats... everything is fine and we are all safe," someone was announcing, as I sat back in my seat with Kathleen's help. Kim was in shock and I hated to see the look of dread on the faces of my kids, as they walked forward after hearing Hyman's scream.

"Thank you. Brian would have died if not for your attentiveness and quick action," Kim said to Kathleen.

"I saw that strange, little man follow your husband into the lavatory and knew something bad was about to happen," Kathleen explained. "I was in the galley, getting coffee and didn't want to waste time calling for assistance, so I just grabbed the coffee pot without thinking."

"How did you get into the lavatory?" Kim asked. "I assume Hyman locked the door once he pushed himself in. If the lock wasn't locked, the light wouldn't have gone on."

"On the outside front door of the lavatory, there is a four-inch nameplate that contains the word, 'LAVATORY.' It is attached to the door by both Velcro and a hidden wire inside the door. If you pull the name plate out from the door, the attached wire is extended and unlocks the door and the light goes out. A little trick of the trade," Kathleen explained.

"Well, thank God your experience and knowledge helped to save a life and avoid a hideous tragedy."

"I'm just happy it worked out. My training taught me to

act instinctively without wasting precious time trying to think about what I should do next. By the way, the Captain has decided to continue on without turning back. Mr. Bradford's bleeding has stopped and we will call ahead for medical help to stand by when we land in Providenciales."

Kathleen was right. I was feeling much better. We moved our seats a few rows back because the flight attendant strapped Hyman to the first row of seats. He was totally immobilized. My voice cracked as I told Kim that Hyman may have killed Detective Jack.

After a little rest, I decided to get up from my seat and say a few words to this pig of a human being. I walked up to the first row.

"Wake up, doctor, assuming you really are a physician. There are a few items of information I need to know before you get turned over to the police."

"Leave me alone. My face is bleeding and the pain is unbearable. Tell the flight attendant to give me something for the pain and a warm towel for the blood. I have nothing else to say to you," Hyman growled.

"I will get you some first aid, but you are going to answer me first. Remember the police in Provo are going to want a statement from me. I can make it very hard on you. The prison cells down there are one hundred degrees in the bright sun with no windows. It's not pleasant being a prisoner in a foreign country. But I can also make sure you get flown back quickly."

"Alright, alright. What do you want. Make it short," the doctor said.

"You made some comment in the lavatory about a former Detective. Were you referring to Jack Jarrett? What happened to him?" I asked, dreading to hear the probable answer.

"He was in the way. I had no choice. I wanted you and I couldn't do it with the Detective on the plane."

"You bastard. He was a dedicated, hard-working man whose only focus was to help me to the best of his ability. May you burn in hell forever."

"I don't want to talk anymore. I'm sorry about the Detective, but what's done is done," he stated with feigned contrition.

"Well, you are going to talk some more, like it or not. Either you tell me what I want to know or I'm going to take my pen and stick it up your nose until I pierce your brain. With my other hand, I will cram my handkerchief down your throat to muffle any desperate cries of pain."

Hyman's eyes widened. I had his attention as he sat there helplessly strapped to the seat. He was already a bloody mess so more blood from his nose would not be noticed. I took my pen and jabbed it into his nostril while pressing my handkerchief hard against his mouth. I only had a short amount of time before someone would notice. The flight attendants were in coach explaining the bathroom incident to the alarmed passengers. The other people in first class, including Kim, couldn't see over the seats unless they stood.

"I'm going to slowly push the pen deeper into the upper reaches of your nasal cavity. When you're ready to talk you can shake your head left to right, but you better decide quickly because I'm probably close to puncturing your cerebral cortex," I whispered into his ear, as he tried his best to scream in muffled agony.

I guess he got the point because he started to shake his head. The bleeding was substantial as I withdrew the pen.

"How did you kill Detective Jack?" I asked, as I uncovered his mouth.

"Injection and strangulation. First, I paralyzed him with a

drug and then choked him to death with a leather strap, once he was immobilized."

"So, he felt all the pain and fear of desperately gasping for air and being unable to breathe, while helpless to move in any way. You are truly a loathsome and despicable human being. I guess I'm lucky you didn't try the same method of death on me."

"It was too difficult to accomplish. It would be cumbersome to push the lavatory door open with a syringe in one hand and the leather strap in the other. I needed a free hand to push you against the back wall in the bathroom. The needle could easily have broken off, if there was a struggle. Plus, you were facing me. The detective had his back to me and didn't know what was coming. That made it easier to use the syringe."

"So, tell me, the fake story that both Martin Brown and you told me in my office the first time we met... was it orchestrated and planned by ZeiiMed from the beginning?"

"Of course. The plan was to get the Complaint served, then have ZeiiMed produce all its documents with the damaging emails hidden among the millions of electronic documents produced. The key was to make sure ZeiiMed could prove without question that it produced the inculpatory emails. Then, when the case settled after your untimely death, the records would be forever sealed and no one else could ever bring another civil action based on the same claims or documents. You can't be sued twice for the same matter by the same plaintiffs. You're a lawyer, you know that. Only if ZeiiMed had failed to produce all the emails could it remain a target. ZeiiMed didn't make that mistake."

"My untimely death? What are you talking about? Martin Brown never said the plan was to kill me whether or not I found the incriminating emails."

"Dr. Brown didn't know what he was talking about. ZeiiMed decided that you were to be killed in an accidental death within twenty-four hours after delivery of its emails and other documents. Then ZeiiMed planned to make a very generous settlement offer that Martin and I, as the clients, would insist on accepting, immediately halting all further litigation. ZeiiMed didn't want to take a chance that you might have miraculously discovered the inculpatory emails, despite the odds being a million to one. Plus, your death made it more understandable that Martin and I would be too distraught to continue to pursue the Complaint. We would tell everyone we wanted it to end and a settlement would achieve that result. And, by the way, don't think for one minute this is over. ZeiiMed will take another run at you. ZeiiMed will finish with Martin Brown shortly, then me. The final act will be you."

"But why? Now that the New York Attorney General is investigating, it will become obvious that ZeiiMed is the responsible party," I said.

"You don't get it. ZeiiMed is fighting for its life. It's like a wild animal backed into a corner. It is going to attack. Look what's happening in Washington. The proposed Health Reform Legislation will create either a federally-run public insurance company or insurance exchanges with government-run insurance plans. It will give health insurance to forty-seven million uninsured people at a cost of one trillion dollars over ten years, with the consequence that private health care insurers like ZeiiMed will be out of business. To help pay for universal insurance, the payments to the doctors will be significantly reduced, probably on the recommendations of a Medical Advisory Council that reports to the President. Lower payments to doctors will enable the insurance exchanges to offer reduced premium policies that everyone will jump at and drop the higher priced policies sold by ZeiiMed. ZeiiMed cannot compete with the resources and finances of the government. This is a war on several fronts for ZeiiMed and it doesn't plan to take any chances."

"I guess not. ZeiiMed seems pretty intent on killing everyone in its path," I said.

"That's true. ZeiiMed also is concerned that the New York AG will recruit you to assist in attacking ZeiiMed's continued existence. ZeiiMed doesn't want to deal with you, Health Care Reform and the NYAG all pushing the company out of business. It just comes down to dollars and cents, as usual."

"What about the doctors? I thought you were so concerned about the underpayments to your colleagues and their need to get paid a fair price for their services," I inquired.

"Nobody cares about the doctors. They will survive, they always have. All doctors know the system run by ZeiiMed and they know how to maximize their reimbursements by filling out mountains of forms. Even with Health Care Reform, they'll manage. Young doctors will accept the reduced payments dictated by the federal government, but eventually refuse to accept the insurance once they build up their reputations and their services are in demand. Pay cash or find another doctor. So, the world will have two types of doctors. The poor will get the inexperienced doctors and the rich can afford the skilled ones. But, of course, everyone will have health insurance."

I marveled at how Hyman could spew out such sarcasm while tied to his seat and suffering extraordinary pain from the open burns on his face.

I had no further use of Dr. Hyman. He had given me the information I wanted and now I hoped to never see him again. Then again, I guess I did have one parting comment for Dr. Hyman.

"Listen to me, Hyman," I said, noticing his eyes were now closed.

"Open your eyes or I'm going to get out my pen again and this time I won't be so gentle."

Hyman opened his eyes and stared at me.

"If either you or anyone from ZeiiMed ever goes anywhere near my wife or children again, I will focus my entire life on finding and killing you, assuming ZeiiMed hasn't gotten to you first. And it doesn't matter to me if you are in prison. I have friends with contacts inside the walls and anything can be done for the right price. So, beware. You tread on my family and you will be in hell a lot sooner than you ever thought possible."

I walked back to my seat. Kim was in her seat, but she didn't ask any questions about my conversation with Hyman.

I turned to her.

"It looks like everything is fine now. The bad guys have both been caught. Neither Brown nor Hyman will be back on the street any time soon. I'll give an interview to the police in Providenciales and we can catch a couple of well-deserved days in the sun. Then we need to return home for Detective Jack's funeral. I'm so sorry to tell you this, but Hyman confirmed that he murdered Jack."

Kim held my hand and quietly started to cry.

Chapter 24

I leaned back in my seat and closed my eyes. A number of thoughts were streaming through my head, bouncing back and forth like ping pong balls ricocheting off the walls of my brain.

First, I was disturbed by Hyman's warning that ZeiiMed wasn't done with me. If the plan truly was to dispose of me all along, I guess it's possible that ZeiiMed decided to complete the task, no matter what.

If this is the reality I'm facing, I had to devise a plan to encounter it and defuse it. I can't just continue to live life unworried and undistracted until finally faced with a life and death encounter when I least expect it. I don't know what I'm going to do to address this problem, but I committed myself to doing something affirmative to eradicate the threat.

I can't ask the police to help because I could never jeopardize the life of another officer after the horrible death of Detective Jack. Like it or not, my destiny was in my hands alone, with success or failure judged only by the course of action I decide upon.

Second, I can't help but beat myself up over the way I was so easily hand-picked for manipulation by Martin Brown, Stanley Hyman and ZeiiMed. I know I should stop flagellating myself over this, but I am ashamed at how easily I was targeted as a lazy, bored and exploitable litigator. Then, once selected, it became obvious that I was also highly receptive to false flattery and easily persuaded by honey and hype. I guess I could live with these shortcomings if they had merely led to personal embarrassment, rather than violent acts and needless death.

But maybe I've been reinvented and revitalized by the violence. Yes, I am reshaped and pledged to an aggressive course of action that will once and for all put an end to this disastrous sequence of events that started when I first met Martin Brown and Stanley Hyman. My weaknesses have created a platform for my strengths to appear. I am ready to end this madness and commence a plan of attack.

Third, I am in awe over the remarkable events that occurred over the course of the last few days. During that time, I have been saved from serious injury or death by three courageous women that put their own well-being at risk in order to save mine. Kim, Mary, and now Kathleen, came to my rescue in dangerous situations that required quick thinking and split-second reactions. How lucky am I to have crossed paths with such remarkable people? Women may have once been referred to as the "weaker sex" but, as far as I'm concerned, women are simply the better half of the male-female equation. May their elevated status on the ladder of human existence continue unabated.

On the lighter side, I guess it's just darn lucky that I have always enjoyed hanging out with women more than men... and now I've found it's also a lot safer.

At that moment, the thought struck me that Dr. Hyman may have brought a black medical bag on the plane with him. I got up and went to the aisle where Hyman had been sitting. Sure enough, his black bag was under his seat. I opened it and filled my pockets with packaged syringes and small vials of all sorts of drugs. I didn't know what the drugs were, but I would check them at later time to determine if they could be useful in my future plans. Before returning to my seat, I put all the vials and drug paraphernalia in my carry-on bag. Kim didn't seem to notice.

Chapter 25

When we landed in Providenciales, the local police boarded the plane as soon as the cabin door was opened. Hyman was placed in custody and escorted off the plane in custody. After Kim and I disembarked, the police politely asked me to answer a few questions to which I obliged.

I told them that Hyman admitted to killing Detective Jack at JFK. I couldn't be sure, but I think the cops had already figured that out. The airport police at JFK and the captain of our plane had both probably called ahead.

I also warned the police that Hyman believes there will be an attempt on his life as punishment by ZeiiMed because both he and Dr. Brown failed to extinguish my life, despite several attempts. I then gave a brief and concise summary of my dealings with ZeiiMed. I'm sure they thought my story was a little farfetched.

The authorities decided that Hyman would be incarcerated overnight, returned to New York with a local police escort on board, and turned over to the NYPD upon landing at JFK.

A doctor from the local Red Cross hospital had been called to the airport by the police. My puncture wound was bandaged rather than stitched because it had started to close on its own, with no subcutaneous tissue exposed. I promised to stop by the hospital the next day for a tetanus shot.

At that point, I was told I was free to continue my vacation as I pleased. I found Kim, went to Gilley's (the friendly

airport bar), bought two Coronas and grabbed a ride to the
Alexandra Resort.

182

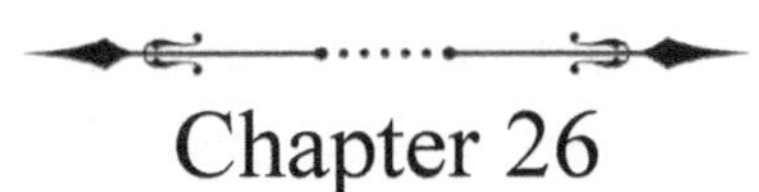

Chapter 26

For the next couple of days, we relaxed on the beach, visited local friends and enjoyed the food and cocktails.

I've found that sitting on the beach in a lounge chair with your wife, together under an umbrella, can lead to some fairly crisp conversations on current topics of interest. And I'm usually the one who does the most mouthing off. For example, on our second day on the beach, we had our first cocktail at 11:00 a.m. and were discussing our lunch plans when I started fanning the flames of controversy.

"Honey, remember when I was talking to Hyman on the plane after he was restrained and put in the first row?" I asked.

"Yes, I couldn't see you very well from my seat, but it didn't look like you were having much of a pleasant conversation."

"True, but it is curious that Hyman mentioned that ZeiiMed may be put out of business if Health Care Reform Legislation leads to the creation of the so-called insurance exchanges, each subsidized by unlimited taxpayer money. That's because an insurance exchange will charge lower insurance premiums than can be competitively offered by ZeiiMed, that needs profits to survive. The theory is that millions of people will jump to the federal insurance program once health insurance becomes mandatory."

"Well, to start at the beginning," Kim responded, "I think it's a wonderful idea to provide health insurance for everyone. It's long overdue and the American people shouldn't have been forced to wait for this benefit since Theodore Roosevelt first talked about it. I like the idea that no matter what your pre-existing health condition, you can get insurance and won't be cancelled because you go to the doctor too often."

"But what about the cost of such a plan? There are forty-seven million uninsured people and the cost to cover them ranges from nine hundred billion to a trillion dollars, and that's just for the first ten years," I said.

"You are right about that. Maybe we need to have a less ambitious program," Kim noted. "I think there should be universal hospital and emergency room benefits for students, the unemployed, the elderly, the self-employed, as well as all teachers and hospital employees. You set up an insurance exchange made up of competing, private, non-profit co-operatives that are subsidized by the government with tax revenues generated from a tax on the top Fortune 500 companies. The retired, over-sixty crowd can keep their Medicare coverage without any cutbacks or charges—the elderly are a strategic voting block the politicians want satisfied. Last, the poor should continue to get Medicaid, but expand the income eligibility for federal subsidies to families earning forty thousand dollars or less on an annual basis, as some politicians are advocating," Kim lectured, as if she was in a college classroom.

I guess she had been reading up on the issue. Next time, I'll pick a topic she doesn't know so much about.

"It sounds like you just solved the health care crisis. You should go to Washington," I teased her. "But I think your proposed program is going to need more funding. Maybe a federal tax on individuals with annual incomes over five hundred thousand dollars is a solution. Otherwise, the payments to doctors and the hospitals would have to be further reduced. And, as you well know, I am opposed to any reduction in pay to the medical profession." Kim didn't smile at my humor.

"Fine, tax the rich," Kim replied. "The money has to come from somewhere and I agree you can't keep cutting the fees paid to the doctors. It might as well come from the people that can afford it."

"I get it. The old 'Robin Hood' theory. I'm sure the White House would agree with you. The current administration loves the idea of taking from the rich and giving to the 'less rich' until everyone is equal. It's called a redistribution of wealth and the President seems intent on implementing it. And, since you just solved that national issue, I've now got a real 'life and death' problem for you to resolve," as I waded into the next hot topic of the day. Hopefully, Kim hasn't done any research outside of health care.

I began. "President Obama has sixty-eight thousand men and women fighting in Afghanistan. Now, after eight years of war with no prospects of killing and defeating all the Taliban insurgents, the White House is considering the shipment of fifteen thousand to forty-five thousand more troops. The number of new soldiers actually sent will probably be in the middle at thirty thousand. And what is the purpose of the additional soldiers? To protect the Afghan citizens from the Taliban in order to make them feel secure in their homes and villages? It's never going to happen and more Americans on the ground gallantly fighting for their country is not going to achieve an unattainable goal."

"But we just can't give up and leave right now. The Afghan government would eventually collapse in defeat to the Taliban," Kim responded.

"What you're missing is that it's going to happen sooner

or later. Why have more soldiers killed to relearn the same lesson that history has already taught us? The Taliban use guerilla tactics, coupled with sabotage operations and random IED bombings. They have no uniforms, they look like the local villagers, they speak the same language as the Afghan citizens and they know how to fight from decades of experience, all of which seems very similar to Vietnam."

I took a breath and continued, "The Taliban military strategy consists of roadside bombings, suicide bombers and isolated attacks on truck transports and police stations, coupled with the violent takeover of isolated villages one by one. The Taliban have no tanks, no jets, no navy and no formal military. Just like Vietnam, our troops are required to go from village to village trying to identify the enemy through the use of local informants and intelligence information. It is extremely dangerous warfare that is doomed to fail because of the Taliban's knowledge of the terrain, knowledge of the local people and decades of tactical knowledge from fighting foreign invaders."

"So, what's the solution?" Kim asked. "How do we fight an enemy that is committed to implementing another attack on America?"

"That is a very good question, and I'm not saying I have the answer and I'm not saying we should withdraw entirely from Afghanistan and Iraq. The Taliban would massacre the USA-friendly Afghan citizens. Some troop presence will be necessary, combined with jet attacks and unmanned drones. All I'm saying is the type of ground warfare currently being conducted will not conquer the enemy. It will not produce a stable government capable of providing for its people and it won't stop the Taliban from providing Al-Qaeda with a meeting place in a mountain cave to plan another attack on us. Russians fought against the Afghani militants for nine years trying to keep a Communist-backed government in power from late 1979 to early 1989. It was a failure. The Soviet war machine withdrew with a loss of over fourteen thousand Soviet soldiers. Why does anyone think we will produce a better result?"

"Can't we just back up President Karzai's police and soldiers instead of trying to attack the Taliban with American ground troops?" Kim asked.

"The problem there is the massive corruption within the Karzai administration. The Afghan people have no faith in the government's ability to provide a stable society and the recent election fraud proves that there is no hope that Karzai can be voted out of office. Fixed elections, ballot stuffing, corruption and inefficiencies... is this the government we want to fight for?

"Moreover," I continued, "the Afghan police and the Afghan soldiers can't be relied on. There was a recent newspaper article in the *New York Times* where an Afghan police officer poisoned eight of his fellow police officers that were protecting a police station. After disabling his fellow officers with the poison, the turncoat policeman called his Taliban buddies as part of a preconceived assault plan. All the poisoned officers were then killed and the police station destroyed by the Taliban. This type of insurgency cannot be stopped by U.S. ground troops, even if we continue our current pattern of warfare for another eight years."

I was rambling in a monotonous drone and realized I was in my self-righteous, over-bearing lecture mode that no one finds interesting in the slightest. Actually, I'm amazed my wife has endured my boring comments for as long as she has.

"Goodness, you paint a dismal picture. You're all criticism with no constructive solution. I don't see what that accomplishes at all. Let me know when you've thought this over more and actually have a plan for stopping the Taliban without the loss of American lives."

"I know," I said. "Nobody believes the solution to the problem will be easy. I'll change the subject, but what I can't change is my emotional revulsion each time I read about a young, healthy American soldier blown apart while on ground patrol in a foreign, desolate land on the other side of the world."

Now I had really worked myself into a downcast mood. I decided to take a walk.

"Kim, I'm going to walk to the front desk to pick up the paper. Do you want a rum punch on my way back?"

"Yes, thanks. I'm going to take a short nap. All this stupid drivel we have been exchanging is exhausting. Wake me when you come back."

I walked from the beach to a walkway lined by palm trees. The walkway goes past the outdoor restaurant/bar and around the inviting crystal-clear pool. On the other side of the pool is the reception area and I was fortunate to find an available newspaper from the States. I sat on a comfortable recliner by the side of the pool, next to a palm tree that curved very conveniently to provide just enough shade to read. At the bottom of the front page, my attention focused on a name, John Edison of ZeiiMed. Mr. Edison was the subject of a congressional hearing being conducted before a Senate Commerce Committee. The complete article on the hearing was on page ten of the paper.

I turned to the article and read that the Senate Commerce Committee had served a subpoena on John Edison to testify regarding an investigation into allegations that ZeiiMed has been underpaying both the medical profession and its own customers for health care services performed "out-of-network." The article also noted that Mr. Edison is now the Chief Executive Officer of ZeiiMed.

There was no mention in the article of any of the emails created in 2001 directing the programming of the database to reduce the payments to the doctors. Apparently, the congressional committee did not yet have all the documentation that the New York Attorney General now has. The paper also stated that CEO Edison was denying any knowledge of wrongdoing by ZeiiMed and denying any manipulation or scrubbing of data by ZeiiMed. In addition to the denials, the article noted that Mr. Edison had proudly announced that ZeiiMed was negotiating a massive settlement with doctors across the nation that will provide additional fees to the doctors and the implementation of a new database at ZeiiMed.

I closed the paper in disgust. Of course, ZeiiMed's tactic is to deny, deny, deny and then act as if it never happened. ZeiiMed will pay big money in settlement and continue its business without interruption, while looking for the next illegal scheme to create cash.

This means that ZeiiMed will never stop in its attempts to eradicate me and possibly my wife as well. I know the truth and ZeiiMed will make sure the truth dies with me. ZeiiMed won't take any chances with its future and I'm the one who could jeopardize it. ZeiiMed can't control me, so it must extinguish me. All of which reconfirms my conviction to take action to secure my family's safety before ZeiiMed makes another attempt on my life.

I must engage ZeiiMed at its highest level if I am to have any hope of cancelling ZeiiMed's plan to execute me. Only by pursuing the top person can I obtain any reassurance that ZeiiMed will call off its pursuit. The outline of a plan was now taking place.

My target is new CEO Edison. I will confront Edison to make sure he understands that I am capable of locating and harming him when he least expects it. I must face Edison to convince him to cancel the directive to kill me. It is the only way to end this. I either go after John Edison or spend the rest of my life wondering if today is the day that ZeiiMed succeeds in executing me.

As soon as I return home, I will put my plan into action. It will require finding out what Edison looks like and where he lives. With that information, I can then put together the necessary details to achieve our confrontation.

I looked down at the folded newspaper on my lap as I rose from the recliner to return to the beach. The paper just happened to be folded to the obituary page. There was a small article announcing the death of Dr. Stanley Hyman. It stated only that he had been admitted for hospitalization after experiencing chest pains and had a fatal adverse reaction to some medication. All lies. No mention of his facial burns or attempted homicide at thirty thousand feet. I guess the authorities hospitalized Hyman as soon as they landed back at JFK Airport. I warned them, but either they ignored me or failed to post sufficient security to counter the diabolical expertise of ZeiiMed. Without question, ZeiiMed poisoned him. Probably by someone posing as a doctor.

In the end, Hyman was right when he said ZeiiMed would kill him. That's exactly what happened. ZeiiMed is unrelenting and unforgiving. All I can hope is that my eventual 'meeting' with John Edison will be successful in cancelling ZeiiMed's death warrant on my life.

With my basic plan firmly in place, I walked back to the beach to tell Kim what I was going to do as soon as possible after our return to New York.

So much for a stress-free vacation.

Chapter 27

With two rum punches and double limes, I approached Kim as she slept on the beach.

"I brought you an eye-opener to ease you from pleasant dreams to current reality," I said, as cheerfully as possible.

"I'm not awake yet, but I'm glad to see you are carrying liquid refreshments that include alcohol. Yet I can tell from your somber tone that maybe I should chug the rum punch before you start," Kim responded.

"You're right, something important happened. The top guy at ZeiiMed testified before a congressional committee that ZeiiMed had done nothing wrong and if any mistakes were made in payments to either the doctors or patients, it was unintentional and minor. Then, despite the fact ZeiiMed claims it is completely innocent, ZeiiMed nonetheless announced a settlement with everybody for millions of dollars so the world is happy and business as usual continues."

"Well, I don't see why that should surprise you. You knew ZeiiMed was going to settle. The company's lawyer called you and told you so himself. Once ZeiiMed decided to settle, why would it admit to anything?" Kim commented, once again providing a quick and accurate evaluation.

"I agree, but here's the rub. The new CEO at ZeiiMed is John Edison. He is the same guy that started the stream of emails in 2001 that confirmed the intentional manipulation of the company's database to underpay doctors and its customers. Edison knows all the skeletons and dark secrets and he knows that I know them also. I guarantee Edison was told exactly which emails I identified during Finley's deposition. Thus, the problem. ZeiiMed is coming after me and maybe after you or the kids unless I can get to Edison and make sure he gives the command to back off. It's what I must do to guarantee our safety. We don't have any other choice in the matter."

"Now, Brian, I know you gave a lot of thought to this, but really... you're a lawyer, not an assassin. What makes you think that you have the know-how and the brawn to take on this guy, *mano a mano*, and force him to do what you say? Please don't take offense, but wimpy lawyer-types really don't make effective enforcers," she said, shredding my insightful dissertation on individual bravery blended with moral justification for permissible violence.

"I know you're thinking only of our best interests, but I can do this. I'm not sure how at the present time because I have to investigate where he lives, who he lives with and what he looks like. ZeiiMed started this and tried its best to kill both of us. ZeiiMed will not stop and will not forget unless and until I can convince Edison to cease and desist. I'm not looking forward to what I have to do, but there is no turning away from it. I need your support and encouragement because it will be too big a distraction if you disapprove," I stated in my best lawyerly presentation.

"I understand and will help anyway I can," she said quietly and without complete conviction.

After getting over the shock of her consent to my plan, I kissed her softly on the lips as our bodies hugged closely.

"If you're putting your life on the line for me and the family, I guess I should make sure we enjoy every moment we have together. Let's go for a walk on the beach," Kim said.

As we walked down the beach, the line of resort hotels ceased and fewer people were seen. Eventually, the beach became deserted. The strip of endless white sand narrowed to about ten-feet wide, with the dunes slowly encroaching as we walked. The dunes arose about three feet above the beach and were covered with a forest of palm trees, as far as you could see.

As we continued hand-in-hand, Kim suddenly stopped, planted a firm, lingering kiss and surprisingly commanded, "Take off your bathing suit, I want to go swimming."

"Excuse me, what if someone comes by," I think I responded.

"Look around you. It's deserted. No one is coming by. Let's get in the water."

I followed instructions and threw my bathing suit towards the dunes.

"You look handsome. The nautical setting works for you. It must be the sea and the sand," Kim said.

"It's not the sea and the sand, it's you."

"Well, I'm very glad for that. I'm ready to join you."

"You look beautiful. I hope no one has a cell phone camera around here. I don't want the rest of the world to see what I'm seeing," I said. Actually, the vision created an overpowering wave of intense desire that has never waned after many years of marriage.

We held hands and ran into the sea. When the water was up to her shoulders, we kissed and embraced. Surely, all this splashing around would attract the sharks. Luckily, no sharks disturbed us and our physical embrace somehow slowly translated into a deep state of contentment.

"I love you," I whispered, "but how do we get out of the water now that we are feeling a lot more modest than a few minutes ago?"

"We have nothing to be ashamed of. Remember, we're married and on a vacation in paradise. We will casually stroll across the beach to our suits and head to the nearest bar," my wife suggested and/or directed.

Who is this woman and where did she come from? I don't know, but I wasn't going to ask any questions that would spoil the moment.

We made our way back to the hotel, hand-in-hand, with our faces more radiant than the noonday sun overhead.

Chapter 28

We were back home in Port Jefferson for less than a week when I commenced the plan focused on Mr. Edison. I received additional motivation when I called the NYPD to inquire about the charges being filed against Martin Brown for attempted homicide. I was told he was dead. Details were very fuzzy, but Dr. Brown never made it out of the hospital alive, just as Hyman had predicted.

One thing is for sure, he didn't die from the bash on the head delivered by Mary and he didn't die as a result of my smashing his head into the wall. Again, ZeiiMed probably got one of its paid killers to put a toxic mix of drugs in his intravenous tubes, just as was probably done to Hyman. If ZeiiMed has you targeted, not even a police guard at the door of your hospital room will save you. It was time to get moving on the arrangements for my face-to-face meeting with Mr. Edison.

The first order of business was to find his home address. Since Edison had testified before a congressional committee, I knew his testimony would be easily found by typing his name into a search engine such as Google. But the transcript of the hearing didn't include a question and answer regarding the witnesses' home address, as a deposition transcript normally would.

However, prior to the hearing, witnesses are usually requested to make a written submission to Congress in preparation for the hearing. This material is often on the internet also, and can be easily obtained if you are patient enough to scroll through all the pages of the Google search results.

I got lucky. It was there. Edison directed his lawyers to prepare a sworn affidavit for submission to Congress that detailed in many paragraphs the reasons ZeiiMed never did any of the bad things it was being accused of. Sure enough, the first paragraph of the affidavit set forth his full name, current position, office address and home address, 60 East 84th Street, New York City, Apartment 5A.

Next, I needed to see what he looked like. Simple. My Goggle search conveniently found a video of his congressional appearance—a plump, round face with rosy cheeks that seemed inflated and swollen. In fact, his whole body seemed pumped full of air, giving the impression that a sharp pin would deflate him. He was middle-aged with bushy, thick hair combed back on the sides of his head, but totally bald on top. Perfect. He seemed to be just the type of person that would abhor the slightest pain, yet would bleed easily and profusely. His most distinctive feature were the eyes. Very small circular pupils were surrounded by a radiant ice-blue ring, creating a piercing stare with a haunting gaze.

For weapons, I searched the key word "Billy Club" and came up with numerous mail order vendors for all sorts of billy clubs and knives. I selected a silver, folding, razor knife and a nine-ounce, black leather billy club. Delivery guaranteed in twenty-four hours. I decided not to get the four-foot, curved medieval sword—just too hard to conceal in New York City. At the last moment, I remembered the metal handcuffs and added them to my "shopping cart."

I now needed to find out if he lived with a wife, and/or children. I didn't want to be unexpectedly confronted by family members when I paid my unannounced visit to his apartment. I logged on to Facebook from my computer by providing my name, email address and a password (my birth date). I found that John Edison had a homepage, but no useful information was available.

I needed to get into his Facebook profile by being invited as a "friend." I couldn't use my computer because it would leave a trail that could reveal my identity. The solution was to use the computer of one of the young female employees in my law firm.

So, one night I worked late and was lucky enough to find that a secretary named Patricia had forgotten to shut down her computer for the night. I used her computer to log on to Facebook, by inserting her name, her office email address and a request for a new password. Facebook immediately emailed Patricia a new code that I used to instantly receive a new password. I then logged in a second time using the new password.

Since I needed to persuade Edison to accept me (Patricia) as a "friend," I clicked the "Compose a Message" box on his Facebook page to see if I could trick Edison into extending an invitation to Patricia. I composed the following message and sent it to Edison with a friend request:

"Hi, John. I know you are a really important businessman with a very big company, one of the biggest in the world. I read a lot about you once I Googled your name after seeing a video of your testimony before Congress on YouTube. I'd really like to sign up as your friend so we can talk together and learn more about each other. I'm a secretary here and would love to know about what it's like to have such an

Then I went back to the Facebook page that automatically appeared for Patricia when I logged on under her name. On her Facebook page, I listed her age as twenty-one, female, blond and "searching" for a meaningful relationship with an experienced man. I then choose a "Privacy Setting" that permitted everyone to access Patricia's Facebook page.

All I had to do now was wait and hope that Edison was at his computer and would take the bait by inviting Patricia to be his "friend." Ten minutes later, it worked. Edison sent a response confirming Patricia as his "friend."

Facebook is a marvelous offspring of the internet explosion in the digital age. It's a daily ritual for millions of people of all ages and all walks of life. However, there are inherent dangers in exposing your private, personal information to "friends" that you hope will treat the information responsibly, especially when the very purpose of Facebook is to have everyone know everything about everybody. Security and confidentiality are not Facebook's best attributes.

I now had access to all the personal information Edison had included as part of his Facebook profile. He was single, with one child (apparently, without custody) and interested in "meeting women who would appreciate the wisdom obtained from my many life experiences." This confirmed that family members will probably not be in his apartment at night, although I will need to be on the lookout for possible girlfriends. It was clear that this dirtbag Edison was using his Facebook page to try to attract impressionable, naive teenagers.

I then deleted the automatic email sent by Facebook to

Patricia confirming her new account, new password and new "friend." Then I shut down her computer.

As far as I know, the New York Rules of Professional Responsibility haven't yet specifically addressed the ethical considerations of a lawyer gaining access to the private portions of a social networking page through a deceptive friend request. Luckily, the Professional Ethics Committee hasn't yet ruled such behavior improper. Then again, who am I kidding? I really don't care how many rules I break to accomplish my purpose. ZeiiMed and Edison aren't operating within the law and I can't beat them if I don't keep up with them. I'm going to do whatever I need to do and let society judge me after it is all said and done. I have no restraints. There are no out-of-bounds markers. I am restrained only by own moral code and right now that code has no limits. I will do whatever needs to be done to maintain the safety of my family. It's now time to continue my pursuit of Edison.

Last, but not least, is the problem of how to get in the front door of Edison's building, as well as the front door of his apartment. Since almost any problem or question can be answered utilizing the appropriate search engine, the answer was not hard to find. I found that over ninety percent of all locks in America can be opened quickly and quietly with a "bump key."

Bump keys are uniquely cut keys with a row of small, uniformly-sized teeth, except for a large first "tooth" on the front of the key. Bump keys were traditionally used by professional locksmiths to pick a lock efficiently and legally when requested by a homeowner. Now bump keys are more widely distributed and often used for illegal entry. The procedure is to insert the bump key into the lock and turn it slightly while tapping the key handle with a small hammer.

To make sure I would have a bump key that would work, I ordered a set of six bump keys from Amazon that supposedly would work with all six of the most popular locks manufactured in the U.S.A. Once again, delivery in less than forty-eight hours. I think Amazon home delivery will one day revolutionize how people shop.

I now had the tools and information necessary to carry out my plan. I had to remain focused on accomplishing my goal without letting any doubts cause me to hesitate.

The next step was to "case the joint" by doing a surveillance of Edison's building at 60 East 84th Street, including building access, the lobby, security personnel and pedestrian traffic in front of the building.

I resisted the urge to dress in the same stylish burglary ensemble worn by Cary Grant when on the prowl in the movie, *To Catch a Thief*. I didn't want to overdo it.

Chapter 29

It had been about ten days since Kim and I returned from our vacation. I went back to work, but the place seemed different. I found it hard to sit at my desk without reliving the terror of Dr. Brown's assault. The violence that followed saved my life, but nonetheless created a disturbing memory. I tried, instead, to concentrate on the heroism of Mary and the courage she demonstrated in delivering the blow that spared me from a lethal confrontation.

There was no question in my mind that Mary was also having great difficulty dealing with the violence she dispensed in her split-second reaction to my life and death situation. In fact, Mary hadn't come to work since she returned from St. Martin. I had her home number, so I decided to call.

She picked up the phone on the third ring. I was surprised she answered.

"Brian, so nice of you to call. I've been thinking about you," she said, sounding surprisingly upbeat and energetic. "Did you and your wife have a nice vacation in Turks? I've heard that Provo's beautiful water and the soft, white beaches can do wonders for a marriage."

"Yes, we had a short but pleasant time. But the reason I called is my concern for you. Your actions were very brave, but now that you've had plenty of time to think about what happened in my office, I'm sure you're very frightened. You have every reason to believe ZeiiMed may harm you, just as was attempted with me. In fact, I was wondering whether you were contacted by ZeiiMed's people?"

"Yes, some guy called me at my hotel and told me never to go back to work and never talk to anyone about the Complaint or the information obtained during the case. I was scared. The voice was very threatening. Then, a few days ago, I read about Martin Brown's mysterious death in the hospital. Now I'm really terrified," she said, her voice trembling.

"I understand. But I want you to come back to work and I'm going to personally make sure it will be safe for you. I can't give you the details now, but I will call you once I can assure you nothing will happen to you."

"Brian, what are you talking about? What are you going to do? What can you do? ZeiiMed won't stop and you're in more danger than anyone. Plus, I just learned today that Hyman is dead also. What do you know about that? Why is he dead?" Mary asked.

I hesitated to tell her the whole story, although it wouldn't be fair to hide the basic details.

"Hyman got on my plane to Turks and assaulted me in the bathroom. He was restrained for the rest of the flight and arrested when we landed." I left out that Hyman was actually trying to murder me. I didn't want Mary any more upset than necessary.

"Oh, my God! Both Brown and Hyman were actually ZeiiMed henchmen and both are now dead. What did we get ourselves into?" Mary asked, her anxiety rising.

"Look," I said, "it will be alright. I'll fix this by going directly to the top man at ZeiiMed and have a little chat with him. Like I said, I'll call you when it's done and hopefully I can guarantee your safety so you can return to work and your everyday life."

"Brian, they will kill you. You can't bully ZeiiMed into

doing what you say. Please don't try. I care for you and would be destroyed if, God forbid, something happened to you. Please tell me you'll change your mind," Mary implored.

"I can't. This has got to end and I think I know how to do it."

"Are you crazy?" Mary exclaimed, as she raised her voice. "These people are murderers. They would love it if you approached them. ZeiiMed's executives will say some crazy lawyer came on their property and threatened them with physical harm, so there was no choice but to kill him in self-defense. Plus, you're out of your mind if you think you can talk to the head guy at ZeiiMed and keep his attention while you politely explain why ZeiiMed should stop trying to harm you or anyone else. Great idea. I'm sure you'll be very convincing right up to your demise. And, after they dispose of you, Kim and I will be next on the list."

"I know you're saying this because you have feelings for me and want me to stay out of harm's way. But, like I said, I have to end this. I can't live my life wondering whether ZeiiMed's hit men are around the next corner. I'll talk to you soon."

"Be careful," Mary said. "I need to see you as soon as this is over. I'll be praying for you. I hope our lives can be restored to normalcy and we can get back to work without constant anguish and worry. Also, before you go, I need to know... We do care for each other, right?"

"Yes. I mean, no. Maybe. I'm not sure. Not like you mean, I think. Bye now." I certainly made a mess of that answer. I don't function well under pressure.

I hung up and tried to work for a couple of more hours. I couldn't concentrate on my job and didn't want to dwell on Mary. I was anxious to commence my plan for meeting John

Edison. I thought about all the variables that could go wrong and decided my odds of success weren't very encouraging. So, what? I was committed and I was ready.

Nighttime finally came. I gathered my tools (knife, billy club, bump keys, handcuffs, etc.) and several of the drug vials and syringes I had taken from Stanley Hyman's medical bag on the airplane. I then changed from business attire into black jeans, black polo golf shirt and dark sneakers.

I headed uptown at about 8:30 on a warm and clear summer night.

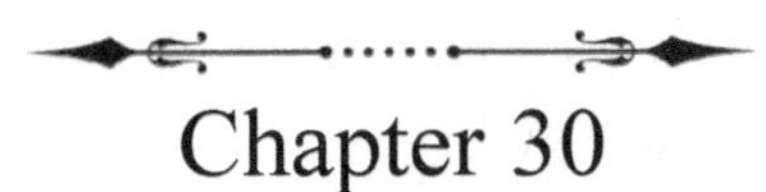

Chapter 30

I took the 7th Avenue subway from the Wall Street Station to 42nd Street. At 42nd, I switched to the shuttle to Grand Central Station. From Grand Central, I hopped on the Lexington Avenue subway to East 86th Street. From there, I surfaced to street level and walked two blocks south to East 84th Street. On 84th Street, I turned west, crossed Park Avenue and headed to Madison Avenue. Just before reaching Madison Avenue, I arrived at Edison's building at 60 E. 84th Street.

I walked to the entrance door of his building. It was a heavy glass door with no doorman. I put my face right up to the glass door and looked in. There was a lobby that extended straight back for about twenty feet, with a window on the wall to my left about twelve feet in. Once the first section of the lobby ended, it turned sharply to the left about two feet.

After the turn, the corridor then seemed to continue straight back another ten feet to the rear of the building. There was an elevator door just after the turn at the beginning of the ten-foot second section. The elevator was on the right side of the hallway. Because the lobby turned to the left before reaching the elevator, it was difficult to see from the building's front door anyone coming on or off the elevator.

The window on the left wall of the front lobby was puzzling. It couldn't open to the outside because the next building, a small French restaurant, shared the same interior structural wall. The front door to the French restaurant was about five feet down from the front door to Edison's building. I thought it bizarre that both front doors had the same address: 60 E. 84th Street.

The restaurant was named *"Très Bien,"* with a bright red awning in front. I walked in the front door. There was large open area with an unmarked, interior door on the wall to my right, with no window visible. There was an appealing wooden bar to my left with about twelve bar stools. The bar extended parallel to 84th Street with large picture windows providing an engaging, open-air atmosphere.

I took a seat at the first stool at the bar, closest to the unmarked door on the right-hand side of the restaurant. I wanted to eventually investigate the door because it seemed to be aligned with the window in Edison's lobby.

I had to figure out how to get in the lobby of Edison's building without entering through the front door. The traffic on 84th Street was very busy. I wouldn't have the time to insert the bump keys, searching for the one that would eventually open the door, while my fellow New Yorkers were mingling in front of the restaurant reading the menu on the front door. Someone would be on their cell phone to the authorities in a New York minute.

The bartender approached me.

"Hello. What do you care for, darling? The beer is ice cold, but a martini will get you there a lot faster," she said with a slight brogue and smiling, gorgeous green eyes.

"First of all, I was looking for some authentic French ambiance and apparently it's not available at the bar," I teased her. I couldn't help myself. She was very cute in a Celtic sort of way. An enchanting, round face with strawberry brown hair that curled outward at the ends. Add in a few freckles and, I'm sure, a tart tongue.

"You got that right, sunshine. You want to feel like you're in Paris, I can point you to the shuttle to JFK. You can be there before dawn. On the other hand, if you want a drink, I'm your gal."

Tart is right, I thought.

"I'll pick the latter. And since I now know that the IRA has invaded France, I'll take a draft of Guinness, poured slowly and patiently," I volleyed back.

"Well, Mr. Know-It-All, everybody's aware that's the only way authentic Guinness is poured, so you really should stop hanging out at French bistros giving instructions to the hired help," she countered.

I knew there was no way I was ever going to get the last word while talking to this sassy Irish lass with the "gift of gab." It didn't stop me from trying though.

"Well, I have plenty of time so pour it as slowly as you want. But I would appreciate if you get started now because all this conversation is making me thirsty."

"Coming right up," she said, as she walked the length of the bar to the beer tap at the other end. Nice legs. The beer finally arrived.

"Thank you. I really think this place is cozy and the food smells great. I was just surprised to find a bartender from Ireland," I explained again.

"Actually, everything in here is authentic French, except for me. The dining room is very nice. Just turn right at the end of the bar and the tables are in the back room, with a black and white tile floor and red gingham tablecloths. With the floor to ceiling mirror behind the bar, our view of the dining room is blocked. I'm sure you were expecting a bistro to feature a thin, European model type with flirtatious eyes as the bartender, but honey, you're not getting that here."

"You mean, what you see is what you get? Believe me, I'm happy not to deal with a distracted, haughty mademoiselle that thinks she is nouveau French. I'd much rather take on the sharp-tongued sarcasm of the girl from County Clare," I said.

"I'm not from County Clare."

"Where are you from and how did you get hired here anyway?" I asked.

"You know how many times I've been asked the same questions? It does get tedious. But, if you must know, my past is none of your business. I will tell you that the restaurant changed management a year ago and I just happened to walk in at the right time. I promised the boss I would develop a regular following that would keep the cash flowing. He fell for my blarney."

"And your nice gams."

"You keep your attention on your beer and off my legs. By the way, what are you doing here? I've never seen you before."

"Oh, I came by the neighborhood because I intend to break into an apartment upstairs and assault its occupant."

"That's a weird sense of humor. You're kidding— right?"

"No, I'm not."

"Yes, you are."

"Yes, you're right. I am kidding, of course," I said.

Having probably said much more than I should have, I realized I better get back to business and stop clowning around.

"The truth is," I said quite untruthfully, "I'm thinking of living in this area and was wondering if any of the apartments next store were available."

"I don't know, but I have been inside a couple of them. The layout is very nice, the view is great and the Park is only couple of blocks away. You walk into a small alcove as you enter the apartment and then it is straight through a very large living room until you reach the bedroom door. Open the door and you have the master bedroom with several large windows that look out right on 84th Street. The kitchen, bathroom and small second bedroom are on the other side of the apartment."

Good to know. Just walk straight until you get to the door of the master bedroom. Helpful information when the lights are out in an unfamiliar place and you don't want the occupant to wake too soon.

"Thanks," I said. "You'll probably see me around."

"Why don't you stay for dinner? The special is grilled beef fillet in a red wine sauce with morel mushrooms."

"No, not tonight. But I would appreciate it if you pointed me to the men's room."

"That's it right there," she said, motioning to the unmarked door I was interested in exploring, about four or five feet to the right of my barstool. "No one knows it's the bathroom because there is no sign on it. By the way, it's the only bathroom—for both men and women—so knock first."

"Will do. By the way, my name is Brian Bradford and I will definitely be back another time to eat."

"I'm Meadhbh O'Shea."

We shook hands and made lingering eye contact.

"No need to run off, you know. Finish your drink. I've got a couple of other customers to tend to," she said.

"Yes, I'll be here a little while longer. By the way, that's a very interesting first name. How do you spell it?"

"M-E-A-D-H-B-H, but it's pronounced MAYV. It's a very old Irish name that means 'intoxicating.' But I don't know if that means I'm intoxicating or I dispense intoxication."

"I'd say both," I commented with a smile.

"Aren't you a bit of a wild rover. I've got to go make some drinks and you need to chill down a little."

Meadhbh walked down to her other customers. I headed for the bathroom. I knocked. No answer.

I opened the door. Directly in front of me, just across the bathroom floor, was the same opaque window I observed from the front door of Edison's building. I closed and locked the door and headed over to inspect the window. It was a large double-hung window. The lower section of the window was designed to open by sliding it upward, but it was locked. If it could be opened, I was sure the opening would be large enough for me to crawl through, depositing me in Edison's lobby on the other side of the window.

I couldn't imagine why the window was located there, but it didn't matter because it served my purpose. The window had a sliding bevel sash lock. The locking device on the top of the lower window pivoted into a keeper base at the bottom of the upper window. The locking device had a flat metal handle that pivoted when pushed.

However, the lock was unable to pivot out of the base because a half-inch steel bolt had been inserted to block its movement. No problem. A strong screwdriver could be jammed under the locking device, raising it over the steel bolt and then sliding it out of the base mechanism by moving the lock handle towards me. I will need to return another night with a screwdriver added to my list of "must-have" items to accomplish my plan.

I went back to my bar stool to finish my beer. Meadhbh was down at the other end of the bar. There wasn't much else that could be accomplished that evening, so I was preparing to leave shortly. As I was waving to Meadhbh to signal my departure, the front door of *Très Bien* opened and in walked a familiar looking face. I immediately recognized the very distinctive contrast between the shiny bald spot on the top of his head and the unusually thick, wavy hair pushed back on the sides of his head, as if glued to his skull. Edison walked the length of the bar and then turned and headed into the restaurant in the rear.

I probably stared too intently.

Meadhbh noticed. She came down to my end of the bar.

"Do you know him?" she asked.

"No, never saw him before. But he looked familiar, like someone I knew in college," I lied.

"You had a fat, bald friend in college? What kind of food did your college dining hall serve, anyway?"

"Very funny. Can't I say anything that you don't turn upside down?"

"If you said something credible, I wouldn't be so glib."

"Whatever. By the way, do you know who that guy is?" I asked.

"I'm not friendly with him, but he's always in here for dinner. He lives in the building next door that you're looking to rent in. He's some big executive with money to burn. Always sits alone, orders right away and leaves by 10:30. Has creepy eyes that scare me. You want the owner to introduce you?"

"No, no thanks. He's not the person I thought he looked like. Just a coincidence. Actually, I think I'll be on my way, but I wouldn't miss a rerun of this show for anything. You'll see me again. What time do you usually close?"

"Closing is at 12:30 unless I have a lot of customers, then I stay open. I certainly hope to see you again. I enjoyed giving you a hard time and a second opportunity would be welcomed. Besides, I like your face."

"Thank you."

I again extended my arm across the bar to shake hands. As we touched hands, I leaned forward without thinking and kissed her on the cheek.

"Bye now," I said.

"Bye back to you, Mr. Affectionate. Take care of yourself."

I left the restaurant and grabbed a cab to Penn Station knowing it would only be a couple of days before I returned to 60 E. 84th Street.

Chapter 31

Thinking it over, it turns out my dry-run inspection of the building at 60 E. 84th Street provided significant information. Now I can gain access to the lobby of Edison's building and I know where the elevator is. I have the general layout of his apartment and fairly accurate confirmation that he lives alone. Maybe, most important, Meadhbh became a new friend.

But there are still many unknown factors with potentially life-threatening consequences. I don't know what I will encounter as far as security, once I'm in Edison's building. Also, I have no idea how the confrontation with Edison will play out, once I'm in his apartment.

I have decided to return to *Très Bien* in two nights. I will, of course, bring all my necessary tools and weapons, including a heavy-duty screwdriver for unlocking the window in the bathroom. Since it will be a Thursday night (a big bar night in New York City), I decided to arrive at *Très Bien* about midnight. If the bar is as crowded as I expect, I will be able to stand near the bar with a beer until the opportunity arises to slip into the bathroom without any of the customers or Meadhbh noticing. Hopefully, Meadhbh will assume I had left without saying goodbye while she was busy tending the bar.

There's no question that I was developing an increased anxiety level over my plan now it was about to commence. I need to be prepared for any consequence. I must work myself to a state of heightened consciousness where I will act and react in a split second to any eventuality, including an immediate dispensing of a force so violent that any resistance is eradicated simply and completely. I will not have had time to think about my next move. It must be instinctive and uninhibited.

I now realize that somewhere in my mind I have a door that can be opened to release a wave of destructive action, a door that I had previously been totally unaware of. The door will be opened on Thursday night and the animal within me will appear without any limiting emotions of compassion or remorse to restrict my physical force. Any and all obstacles will be confronted with an unthinking wave of pugnacious, aggressive punishment without concern for cruelty or shame.

The brutality that may result will not remake my identity or redefine my existence. It will not existentially reshape my sense of manhood or alter the outside world's view of my masculinity. Rather, it will merely be a conscious decision to open a particular door of my mind for a short period of time and release the chains that usually suppress and securely lock this violent compartment of my being. A compartment of every person's being.

I can and will rechannel my anxiety by adding its emotional energy to the dark and uninhibited forces pouring into my consciousness from the newly opened door.

I am ready.

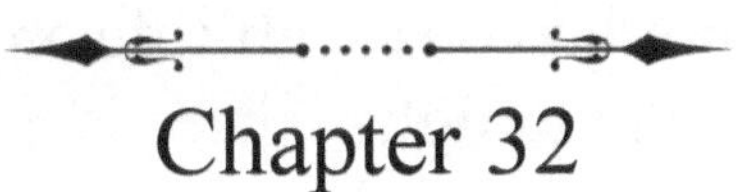

Chapter 32

It's about 6:30 p.m., Thursday night.

I plan to stay at work until about 11:30 p.m., before heading uptown. Kim doesn't know. I should have told her face to face, but I knew she would just try to talk me out of it. I have no choice now. I have to call.

"Hi, honey, it's me."

"You're still at work. Why aren't you on the train?" Kim asked.

"I'm going to be home very late tonight. I've decided to have my meeting with John Edison tonight. Of course, he doesn't know it yet," I responded.

"Look, I know I said okay to this, but maybe you should reconsider. God forbid you break some law and get caught. You're a lawyer—an officer of the court. The authorities will pull your license and then send you off to prison to make an example."

"The good news is that I won't need a license if I'm sent to prison. I'll be making them all day long, so I'll have plenty." Kim didn't enjoy the humor.

"Look, you've got to take this more seriously. Tonight's events may very well change your life forever."

"You bet it will. I won't have to worry every day that someone may be about to kill me, assuming I'm able to present my proposal to Mr. Edison and he accepts. Plus, you will be out of danger and that's really the most important aspect of what I hope to accomplish."

"I really don't understand how you planned this whole

thing yourself. It's not like you've had a lot of experience in this area."

"My plan is to rendezvous with Edison in his apartment, just the two of us, late tonight. There is a French restaurant that adjoins his building and the barmaid knows of him and has been very helpful. I have to admit I've been a bit of a flirt, but it's all in the line of duty," I said.

"You do whatever is necessary to accomplish your plan and come home safe. I don't care if you propose marriage to this woman so long as you get in and get out as quickly as possible, without getting caught."

"I love you. Always have, always will," I responded.

"Me, too. I'll be waiting up for you whenever you get home. Love you. Bye."

At 11:30 that night, I changed out of my suit and put on the same night-prowling outfit. I left my office and headed for *Très Bien*. I had the syringes, vials, bump keys, black gloves, handcuffs, heavy screwdriver, billy club and folding razor knife.

I really am out of my mind. I can't believe what I'm about to do. The next time I'm in a predicament like this, I think I'll hire someone to do my dirty work for me. That's usually what lawyers do.

Chapter 33

At just about midnight, I entered the front door of *Très Bien*. The bar was empty. I took a seat on the first stool, same as two nights ago.

Unfortunately, the first part of my plan had already gone awry. I anticipated that the bar would be packed and I could sneak into the men's room unnoticed without anyone wondering why I never came out. With the bar empty, I will have to chat with Meadhbh and she's going to think something is very strange when I don't return from the bathroom.

I immediately decided on a change of plan. I will tell Meadhbh what I am up to. I will skip a few of the details, of course, and then ask for her help in carrying out my plan. It's a gamble, but I feel it will work out. Something developed between us the other night that was palpable. I am confident I can convince her to assist me.

"Hello, handsome, what brings you in here so late?" Meadhbh greeted me from behind the bar.

"I was hoping to have corned beef and cabbage for dinner, but that didn't work out so I decided to visit my only Irish friend as a back-up plan," I responded.

"I'm glad you did. It's unusually slow tonight. I can use the company."

"By the way, I bet you call all your male customers 'handsome.'"

"Not all my male customers. But, if you must know, I don't say 'handsome' to a man unless he is fit, over six feet, has some hair and dresses in the same black shirt and pants with matching eyelashes as the last time I saw him."

"This must be my lucky day. I finally qualified for something and I didn't even know I was being tested."

"Enough of the snappy dialogue—how are you anyway?" she asked.

"I'm doing fine. It's good to see you again."

"How about a drink?"

"Yes, I'd love a beer."

I certainly needed to keep my senses tonight, but one beer wouldn't hurt.

Meadhbh poured the Guinness slowly and brought it right over.

"Are you still trying to rent an apartment next door? It would be great if you lived so close. We could run into each other all the time," she commented, revealing more than a superficial interest.

I tried to ignore the amorous signals she was sending and got back to business.

"Actually, my story about shopping for an apartment was a bit of an exaggeration. I'm not looking to rent an apartment upstairs. Actually, I'm intending to break into an apartment upstairs. I'm not a criminal though, I'm a lawyer," I said and waited for her reaction.

She didn't walk away and she didn't dial 911, so I guess she was willing to listen.

After a short pause, she commented, "I don't know the difference between a criminal and a lawyer, so you need to do a better job of explaining yourself."

"Point well taken. I'll start at the beginning. Remember that guy I recognized the last time I was in? His name is John Edison."

"Yes, of course I do, but I didn't know his name. In fact,

he was in tonight. He was again by himself, but he drank way too much and staggered out of here at about 10 p.m. He's in his apartment now. I watched him as he left to make sure he went right into his building without breaking his neck. But more important, what do you mean you plan to break into an apartment?"

"You see, Mr. Edison and I are having a bit of a disagreement. He runs a huge managed health care company that was involved in litigation I commenced by the filing of a complaint. Due to its life-changing consequences, I now refer to it as 'The Complaint.' After the litigation started, some very damaging documents were disclosed by Mr. Edison's company, called ZeiiMed. After the disclosure, ZeiiMed became unhappy that I had the documents because damaging information was disclosed.

I continued, attempting to keep it short, "ZeiiMed is now trying to kill me and my wife in the hope of eventually extinguishing anyone who has the legal leverage to use the documents against ZeiiMed. But ZeiiMed didn't stop there. In a cold-blooded act of shocking brutality, ZeiiMed ferociously killed a very fine NYPD detective who was investigating the attempt on my life. Also murdered were the doctors that had been my clients and were the named plaintiffs in the Complaint, although I later learned both doctors were really ZeiiMed stooges."

I ended my narrative with the realization that my story was probably too much for anyone to fully understand and comprehend upon hearing the first time.

"Wow, did you just make that up? Who would believe such a story? Next, you're going to tell me that the overweight, bald, lonely guy that lives upstairs did all this to you and the others?"

"I know it sounds beyond belief. But it's true and I'm here

tonight to end this nightmare. Edison is the top guy at ZeiiMed. If I can get to him and persuade him to stop, then hopefully my family can live in peace."

"I don't understand," Meadhbh said. "Why are you telling me this? I feel very badly about what you have been through, but I really think you should go back to the police."

"One detective is already dead because of me. I'm doing this tonight and I just need a little assistance from you. The best way for me to get into Edison's building is through the bathroom window. I know it sounds ridiculous, but there is too much activity in front of his building for me to chance trying to unlock the lobby door with the so many eyes around. All you have to do is let me break the lock on the bathroom window and climb through the window into Edison's lobby. I will leave the bathroom door unlocked once I am ready to go through the window. Then you can open the bathroom door and make sure the window is shut behind me. No one will notice that it's not locked."

"So, basically, all you want me to do is not rat you out once you go inside the bathroom and don't come out?"

"Yes, that is your biggest contribution to my plan. Plus, once I unlock the bathroom door, make sure I have two or three minutes before anyone enters the bathroom so I can get through the window unseen."

"By the way, you mentioned your wife. I didn't know you were married," she said, changing the subject. "You don't wear a wedding ring."

"The subject of my marital status didn't happen to come up. I know it seems hard to believe, but we've only met once before tonight."

"Since you've been ogling me top to bottom from the first time you laid eyes on me, I think you should have immediately said, 'Hi, I'm married so please disregard my lecherous glare and roaming eyes.' Then I would have, at least, known what I'm dealing with."

"I'm not really sure this is the time to be clowning around," I responded. "If you must know, I don't wear a traditional wedding ring because my college ring, which I wear on my left hand, was blessed at my wedding and serves as my wedding ring."

"Okay, back to business," Meadhbh said. "Please promise me that you are not going to kill or maim this guy Edison. Also, I noticed from time to time some very big security guys in the lobby next door, so how do I know you won't be killed or seriously injured?"

"I'm not going to kill anyone, but I will need to overpower and restrain the security guards. Believe me, Edison will not call the police. ZeiiMed doesn't want any publicity. I admit I may be required to put Edison into a little distress to get him in a compromising mood."

"So, you are the brave hero of the people about to save the world from the evil health insurance company? You ought to be in Congress passing health care reform with the public company option. Wouldn't that stop ZeiiMed by putting it out of business?"

"You know, I am trying to be serious here."

"Then I'll be serious also. I will help you and I will agree to let you climb through the bathroom window without telling anyone or sounding an alarm. I will just continue to serve drinks while humming a familiar Beatles' song dealing with the same subject. But I do need a kiss before you go. It will probably be a long time before you return to the scene of this crime, so to speak. And I don't mean a friendly peck or a cheek-to-cheek deal. I'm talking about a long, sensuous joining of lips that tenderly creates a passionate spark of erotic awareness. Or, to put it more succinctly, kiss me like you kissed your wife when you were both in your twenties."

"Are you serious? You must be kidding. That's a tall order. I'm not sure I can deliver. Besides, I don't remember my twenties. It was too long ago," I said with a sudden wave of shyness.

"Sure you can. It's all your fault. You batted those sexy eyelashes at me and now here we are. Well, get started and try to have some fun."

The bar was unusually narrow in width, so I leaned forward and she followed my lead. We touched lips as I tilted my head slightly. We lingered as I gently pressed harder against her mouth. She pulled back slightly, then renewed the contact eagerly. It was a soft, pleasurable moment of physical symmetry and affection. Bottom line, she was a damn good kisser. I hoped I was succeeding in satisfying her expectations.

I disengaged and opened my eyes. She continued to lean over the bar and her head remained at a slight angle, her eyes still closed. The laws of gravity graciously provided a memorable view of her well-formed bosom.

"Don't worry, you passed the test," she whispered.

"Okay, then. Let's get together and do this again soon," I joked, not knowing what else to say.

"Not bad, lover boy. You've had some practice over the years. I can teach you a few minor refinements in the technique, but overall quite good."

"It sounds like you're a judge at a swimming contest," I replied.

"I will put it another way. I think it will hold me over until we happen to meet again. It's certainly something to remember you by."

This relationship sure seemed to be getting complicated

very fast. My goodness. We haven't even had our first date yet and who knows if we ever will. Life is simply moving too fast.

"This has been a blast, but I have to change my focus and get started on my plan for the evening. I better begin with opening the bathroom window. I can't thank you enough for your understanding, your assistance and your lips. Our moment together was great and I won't be forgetting it for a long time. Take care. By the way, if you happen to hear me screaming in torment upstairs, feel free to call 911."

I couldn't help but depart with a bit of levity, but it seemed there was a grain of truth to my comment.

"Go, and be careful," Meadhbh said. "I'm worried about you already. May God's blessing be with you."

She then walked down to the other end of the bar without turning back.

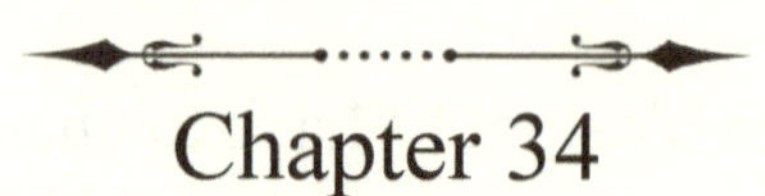

Chapter 34

Once in the bathroom at *Très Bien*, I locked the door and took out the screwdriver. Forcefully, I jammed the head of the screwdriver under the locking mechanism on the top of the lower window. I then pressed down on the screwdriver, allowing the locking mechanism to lift over the obstructing steel bolt and freely pivot out of the keeper base while moving the handle of the locking device towards me. The window was now unlocked.

I put my ear to the window. There wasn't any sound in the lobby. Very gently, I lifted the lower window up. There was a crackling sound as some crusty old paint cracked and broke free. The window probably hadn't been opened in years.

Once the window was opened, I leaned out to look into the lobby. There was no one in the lobby's twenty-foot section leading from the front door. To my left there was a wall and then a ninety-degree turn to the left before the second section of lobby continued towards the rear of the building. I could hear the elevator mechanism cranking. The door to the elevator was immediately on the right in the second section of the lobby.

All was clear.

The key now was to work quickly.

I unlocked the bathroom door then turned to face the window. Putting my hands on the window sill, I wiggled through the window head first. Halfway through, I put my hands in front of me and fell gently onto the lobby floor. I quickly stood, grabbed my billy club, and closed the window.

A security guard was probably stationed at or close to the elevator door. As soon as I made the short two-step left turn, I would be visible to anyone in the second section of the lobby. I had to be ready.

As I made the turn, my back hugged the wall. My right arm was cocked across my body ready to spring forward, with the billy club in hand.

It all took place in a split second. As soon as I made the turn, I saw the security guard just inside the elevator door reading a newspaper. With as much force as I could generate, I struck the guard with the club on the bridge of the nose. A bone cracked, blood squirted from his nostrils and his hands went to his face. Before he could scream, I delivered a second blow to the back of his head and gently lowered him to the ground unconscious. Inside his red suit coat was a wallet and revolver. His ID said he was employed by ZeiiMed. It was a relief to learn that he wasn't some off-duty cop who operated the elevator for a little extra cash.

The gun was a Ruger-GP-100, double-action revolver with a six-inch barrel and .357 caliber ammunition. Light, reliable and accurate, it had a very comfortable rosewood insert grip. This will come in very handy.

I pressed the elevator button for the fifth floor and pushed the security guard's frame to the rear of the elevator. He was also bleeding from the wound on the back of his head, but it wasn't fatal. At this point, in this situation, I'm committed to the singular objective of completing my flagitious task and no amount of blood was going to lessen my primitive fury.

I was sure there would be a second guard on the fifth floor. I was ready to strike without hesitation. The darkest, most remote door of my conscious being was now open wide, with an avalanche of rage flowing forth. It could be controlled, but not now, not at this point in time.

The elevator stopped and the doors parted open on the fifth floor. A guard was in the dimly lit hallway, his back facing me. He started to turn, not two feet from the opening doors. Luckily, he did not appear to have a weapon in his hands. Keeping low, I forcefully struck the side of his left knee with the billy club. The blow caused him to lose his balance. He started falling to the floor. He grabbed me around the neck with his arms as he descended, but I maintained my balance as he slipped down.

My arm circled above my head at full extension, allowing me to strike downwardly with speed and accuracy, billy club in hand. It struck him with intense force on the side of his face where the back of the jaw meets the front part of the ear. His whole jaw structure seemed to disengage and move sideways away from his face several inches. The pain must have been excruciating. The sound of the blow was chilling. His jaw hung loosely from his face. All the muscle and bone that previously held his jaw in place was now smashed and ripped.

I left him on the floor and pressed the "stop" button on the elevator.

Apartment 5A was straight ahead.

Chapter 35

I took out the set of six bump keys and inserted the first one into the lock on the front door of Edison's apartment. Using the handle of the folding razor knife, I tapped the handle of the key while turning. It didn't work. Same with the second key, then the third key. This was taking too long. A miracle. The fourth key worked, the door unlocked and I opened it quietly.

I took out the syringe I had obtained from Stanley Hyman's medical bag on the plane. There had also been several vials of drugs in the bag, including pancuronium bromide and tubocurarine chloride. Both drugs will cause muscle paralysis, but pancuronium bromide is too strong. It totally paralyzes the patient and prevents speech and eye movement. Consciousness and sensitivity to pain are not impaired by either drug.

Before I had left my office, I loaded a syringe with fifteen milligrams of the preferred drug, tubocurarine chloride. It causes skeletal muscle paralysis, with the subject still capable of eye movement and speech, although there may be some shortness of breath and sleepiness. It takes a few minutes to reach full effect after injection, with the condition then lasting about twenty-five to thirty-five minutes.

The syringe and the drug were apparently undamaged by my crawl through the window and the fights with the guards. I put the syringe back in my pocket and entered Edison's apartment.

There was a large living room with a door on the wall across the room. If Meadhbh's information was correct, it was the door to Edison's bedroom. The living room was lit only by night lights plugged into two electrical outlets near the floor. There were no apparent obstructions, so I walked straight across the living room to the bedroom door. I put the revolver in my right hand and opened the door with my left. I quickly and quietly stepped inside. The bedroom was brighter than the living room. The windows were unshaded and the city lights gave a soft glow to the room. Edison's head was on the pillow at the top of the bed directly in front of me. His eyes were closed. I placed the gun six inches from Edison's ear.

"Wake up, you rodent, and move very slowly. I have a gun pointed at your head and I would be quite happy to spend the rest of my life in prison for the pleasure of watching your skull burst open."

His eyes and his mouth opened wide in fear.

"Who are you? Why are you in my apartment?"

"You know damn well who I am and why I'm here. Now very gently sit up in the bed and put on these handcuffs. I suggest you do exactly what I tell you because I will pull the trigger if you deviate in the slightest."

I looked at his face, the first time I had seen him up close. His puffy, viscous complexion looked particularly unpleasant. The uncombed hair on the sides of his head was unruly and seemed to extend from his head parallel to the floor. His ice-blue eyes were saturated red from booze and his upper body swollen.

"What are you going to do to me?"

"Now that's a question that doesn't have an answer yet. You are going to just wait and see what develops. It all depends on how you respond to my questions," I replied. "I told you, put on the handcuffs."

Edison snapped the cuffs on his wrists with his arms extended in front of him.

"Please, I'll give you whatever money I have. My wallet is on the desk. That's all I have."

"Still pretending you don't know me? Keep it up and I swear you will regret it very shortly," I cautioned him again.

"I'm telling you the truth. I don't know you. I've never seen you before and I don't know your name or what you want," Edison pleaded, as he continued his charade of ignorance.

I had no time or patience for this guy. I quickly grabbed the syringe with my left hand and plunged it into his arm, while I screamed at him not to move. He started to roll to his side away from me, but I succeeded in getting all the drug into his blood.

"Christ, what did you do? Is that poison? Am I going to die?"

"No, I don't think so. But in a few minutes you will be paralyzed to the point that you will be unable to move your torso or limbs. I intend to then gently slice open the skin on your inner thigh and expose your femoral artery. I have a very sharp razor knife with a stainless-steel blade to assist me in making an incision. Then, if you continue to feign knowledge of why I am here, I will slowly and painfully cut into your femoral artery and watch it shoot a stream of your blood clear across the room. I'm sure your very rotund body has plenty to spare, but I guarantee that the volume of blood spewing forcibly into the air will soon drain you dry. Now, don't move an inch. I'll show you what I mean in a couple of minutes, but if you struggle I will simply cut as deep into the artery as I can."

I waited several minutes watching Edison sweat as the

drug took hold. I put the gun in my belt and immediately opened the blade of the knife. I threw off the bed covers. He was wearing only gym shorts. I felt nauseous at the sight of him. I touched the tip of the blade to the skin covering the femoral artery on the inside of his upper leg, right where the artery is unprotected by muscle or the femoral sheath.

"I am slicing into the skin. As you now understand, you feel the pain but can't move your leg due to muscle paralysis. I'm ready to cut into the artery. The funeral home won't have to waste time draining your fluids because you will already be on empty. Plus, the embalming fluid can be conveniently inserted right where I cut the artery. You better start talking fast. It's now or never."

"Okay. Okay, stop. I know you're Brian Bradford and I know of the Complaint you filed against ZeiiMed. But that lawsuit is about to be settled and over with," Edison said.

"You keep this up and this whole room will be red with your blood. You will have the agonizing torment of watching the life leave your body. This is your last chance," I warned.

"Yes, I know the hell that ZeiiMed has put you through. I know that an order was given to kill you and your wife, if necessary. I know you must be in constant fear for your life..."

"That's right," I interrupted, "and I'm here to get your promise to call off your killers. You now know I can get to you at any time. I swear there will be no conversation next time. You will be dead and I will enjoy every second of the killing process."

"I promise," Edison said, "no harm will come to you. And I can tell you why. ZeiiMed needs you. We have decided to double our settlement payment to the doctors and the New York Attorney General has agreed to discontinue the investigation of ZeiiMed. We hope to make a public announcement tomorrow. But we need you to help get the settlement approved by the Court. The Judge cannot approve the class action settlement without a Fairness Hearing and ZeiiMed needs you to convince the Court it is a fair, equitable and just settlement. You are the lawyer who was attorney of record for the plaintiffs during the litigation of the case and can provide a first-hand evaluation of the reasons this settlement represents an equitable payment for the losses suffered by the doctors. The Court won't approve the settlement without the essential testimony that only you can provide," Edison pleaded.

"So, you kill Hyman and Brown and you almost murder my wife and I. Now you somehow got the Attorney General to drop its investigation. I guess money solves all problems and heals all wounds."

"Yes," Edison said, "and you are entitled to a major fee payment because you're the attorney who handled the case right up to the settlement, although some of the fees will go to new counsel for the New York/New Jersey Medical Association. Christ, I can't move my arms or legs. I'm totally immobilized. Damn, please tell me this isn't permanent."

"I'll let you know after you persuade me that ZeiiMed will leave me and my family and my law firm alone forever," I said. "I don't want any of your money and I want nothing to do with ZeiiMed. I'll attend the Fairness Hearing and I'll tell the Judge that the doctors are entitled to the settlement money because its represents the money ZeiiMed withheld from them and should have paid years ago. I owe that to the other doctors I represented. They were cheated and the settlement comes close to evening the score. But I'm not doing it to help ZeiiMed. All ZeiiMed can do for me is get out of my life forever and leave my wife, my children and my colleagues alone forever."

"You have a deal, Bradford. I'm the boss and I'm telling you ZeiiMed will never harm you, your family, or work colleagues ever again," Edison repeated.

"And I'm telling you, if there is a next time no one will be able to keep me from getting to you and I will enjoy butchering you."

"Understood," Edison said. "Understood completely."

I accomplished as much as I could have hoped for. I never intended to kill Edison, merely to scare him and hope for the best. The fact that ZeiiMed needs my participation at the Fairness Hearing enhanced my bargaining power and secured the result I sought.

"I'm leaving. Our business is done," I told Edison. "The paralysis will wear off in another ten or fifteen minutes."

I left the handcuffs on his wrists and quickly walked out of the apartment with the key. I ran down the five flights of stairs and into the street.

The briefly opened door to my pernicious cognitive function closed. The primeval wave of heinous fury was once again contained and controlled in a deep compartment of my mind. For now, anyway.

Mission accomplished, I think.

I called Kim and told her I was fine.

Chapter 36

Two days later, I am back at work. The Court's docket revealed that the Fairness Hearing is scheduled for the first week of December 2009, several months from now. There is a lot of preparation that needs to be done and I can't accomplish it without Mary back at work assisting me. I will call her today.

New counsel for my former clients, the doctors of the New York/New Jersey Medical Association, have already filed substitution papers with the Court. Officially, I am no longer counsel of record for the plaintiff doctors.

One of my partners signed a stipulation agreeing to the substitution. The new counsel is Daniel Giulini. I've met him on a couple of occasions, but I know little of him. He is with a small commercial litigation firm of twelve lawyers on 28th Street near Fifth Avenue. Good luck to him. He probably has no idea what he has gotten himself into. If he's fortunate, he won't have to do much work other than getting the settlement approved by the Court and collecting his fee from the settlement funds paid by ZeiiMed.

As soon as I can convince Mary to return to work, we will go see Mr. Giulini to prepare for the Fairness Hearing.

No time like the present.

I need to get my legal staff back together.

I dialed her number.

"Mary, it's Brian," I began...

"It's about time you called," she interrupted. "I've been waiting to hear from you. I thought maybe something went wrong and you were injured by those ZeiiMed people. I can't live like this," she said.

When did our relationship go from employer-employee to some hybrid of co-equals mixed with a hint of tension usually found in long-term relationships? I certainly didn't have the answer.

"I didn't realize that you were so anxiously awaiting my call," I stupidly said.

"How can you say that? Let's review recent events. After escaping a life or death struggle in Baiting Hollow, you and your wife finally elude danger only to find yourself confronted by a lunatic doctor who intended to induce a heart attack while you sat at your desk in your office. I saved the day by cracking open the skull of that lunatic in the first and hopefully last act of violence in my life. On top of that, I'm threatened by ZeiiMed while on vacation. Then you tell me you are meeting with our tormentors and will shortly negotiate a long-term peace plan with the bad guys, with life rosy once again. Now tell me again how you didn't know I was eagerly awaiting your call."

"Yes, you're right. Of course, I should have called sooner."

"You're forgiven. Now please tell me what happened."

"I met with Edison, the CEO of ZeiiMed. He wasn't expecting me, of course, but I don't think there were any long-term ill effects from my 'pop-in.' Edison acknowledged, after some coercion on my part, that he knew of the attempts on my life and agreed that ZeiiMed would never again try to injure me, my wife or anyone at the firm, including you."

Obviously, I was sugar-coating the true version of my confrontation in Edison's apartment to make it palatable for Mary. There was no way she could handle more tales of violence in her distressed mental state.

"How can you be so sure Edison will keep the agreement? There's no way we can trust this guy," she responded.

"First of all, I clearly demonstrated to him his vulnerability to my extreme retaliation if he doesn't keep his word. Second, he needs us to appear at the Fairness Hearing to sanitize the proposed settlement and convince the Court to approve it. Only by settling with the doctors will the Attorney General call off his dogs and discontinue the investigation of ZeiiMed's dirty laundry. Edison knows that he needs our help to get it done."

"So ZeiiMed gets away with all this violence and mayhem by paying everyone to go away?"

"That's exactly what I said to Edison. But it's a great settlement for the doctors and it adequately addresses a wrong that will now end at last. Despite everything that's happened to us, something very significant was accomplished for the doctors by this settlement. Plus, there is no guarantee that a continuing investigation by the NYAG will succeed in overcoming ZeiiMed's whitewashing techniques. So, please come back to work. I desperately need your help in preparing for court and I truly believe it is now safe for you to get on with your everyday life."

"I will come back to work and I will focus on getting my life back to normal. But I'm not so sure I agree with your sudden acquiescence to ZeiiMed's felonious behavior. Sure, I want ZeiiMed to pay, but it shouldn't end until everyone involved is in jail."

"Look, I can't get into that discussion now. I did what I had to do. We can only hope that you and my family are safe from harm. The settlement with the doctors is just a very favorable side benefit. The result is not perfect, but it's better than living every day of our lives afraid of who might be waiting for us around the next corner."

"I understand, but I don't agree. We'll talk about it some other time. I appreciate all you did to protect me from ZeiiMed. I don't know how to repay you, but I'll think of something. I'll be in work on Monday," she finally said.

"That's great. See you then. After you review all the draft settlement papers, we'll go and visit with the doctors' new lawyer, Daniel Giulini. Bye."

I hung up the phone thinking about what could possibly be her idea of a repayment plan.

Chapter 37

Mary returned to the law firm on Monday, as promised.

In the next three weeks, we reviewed all the legal papers filed and to be filed in preparation for the Fairness Hearing, including detailed documentation providing notification of the settlement to all doctors across the nation.

Everything seemed back to normal and nothing had happened to even suggest that Edison might break our agreement. In fact, I was now able to enter my office in the morning and not have a flashback to the violent scene with Doctor Brown. All is good, so far.

The next matter on the agenda was our meeting with Daniel Giulini. Mary and I took a taxi to his office on 28th Street. Upon entering his fifth-floor law office, there was a small but very busy reception area. In fact, all seven seats were taken with people waiting to see one of Giulini's lawyers about some problem they had in life. It appears that the recession was creating very positive repercussions for Giulini's law practice.

Mary and I stood until someone approached and offered to escort us to a conference room. We were led down a narrow hallway with numerous small offices on each side. The lawyers inside the offices could barely be seen from behind the mountains of papers stacked high on each desk.

We entered a small, windowless conference room with shelves of legal books stacked from floor to ceiling against each wall. The chairs surrounding the cramped conference table collided with the bookshelves as we moved the chairs in our attempt to sit. I was barely able to slip into the seat. No coffee or water. Mary and I grinned slightly at our situation and waited silently for Mr. Giulini's appearance.

Several minutes later, the door to the conference room opened forcefully and banged into the interfering wall of books. He came in quickly, hand outstretched.

"Hi, I'm Danny. You must be Brian and, of course, by process of elimination, you must be Mary. My secretary already told me how pretty you are. Don't take offense, I'm way too old for you. Coffee? Water? Yes, no, maybe? Speak right up!"

We quickly shook hands and said we would like coffee.

"I'll get it for you. Gimme a second," Danny said. He stuck his head into the hallway and screamed, "Coffee! Milk, no sugar. Two."

"No answer. The usual," Giulini said to us.

"You hear me or what? Do I have to say it again?!" he bellowed again into the hallway, at an even higher pitch.

"Yes, I got it. Just wait a minute," came the loud reply from an unseen woman, presumably his secretary.

Danny closed the conference room door and sat on the edge of the seat at the end of the table without leaning back. He was only about five feet, four inches, with very short white hair. Probably close to sixty years old. He had a thin, long face with a slightly hooked nose and large ears. His olive complexion was remarkably wrinkle free, but the bags under his eyes ensured that no one would mistake his age. He was dressed in a black suit, with a black tie and black shoes. Only his white shirt broke the monochromatic wardrobe theme. I suspected that he always dressed the same and probably had done so long before it was made popular in the movies.

We quickly learned that Danny talked fast, walked fast and gestured with the swiftness of a young maestro.

"Coffee is coming. Let's get to work. I'll start. Six or seven weeks ago, I got a call from some guy at Tweed, Fox & Fortune," Danny said.

"Was the call from Charles Wadsworth?" I asked.

"I don't know, but I don't think so. Some other lawyer at the firm. The Tweed guy said they have a settlement in principle with your office, but the plaintiff doctors needed a new lawyer to finalize the settlement papers, notify the doctors, get the appropriate releases and oversee disbursement of the settlement funds. I was promised a flat fee of three million, maybe more, if I got it all put to bed faster than anticipated."

"Didn't you think it was a tad unusual for you to get an employment opportunity from an adversary?" I asked.

"Who cares? I'm not going to represent ZeiiMed. I'm the attorney for the doctors and I will make damn sure they get their money as soon as possible. Your office approved my involvement by signing the stipulation appointing me new counsel for the plaintiffs. Clean and simple."

"Well, Mr. Giulini, I did have an unfortunate incident or two involving a couple of doctor clients that caused me to take some time off. There is no question my law firm can no longer handle the matter." I did not want to go into too many details with him.

"That's great! No problem. I'll handle it from here so long as nobody tries to bribe me, assault me or kill me with kindness. All you have to do is show up at the Fairness Hearing. You understand?" Danny asked, probably thinking he was being funny.

"Yes, what do you want me to do at the Hearing?" I asked,

thinking that Danny has no idea how close to injury or death this case will bring him if he gets on the wrong side of ZeiiMed.

"Exactly what I tell you to do. No, I'm not kidding. Really. Seriously, I will address the Court, give an introduction, identify all the lawyers and then ask you to give a short talk. And I mean short, including a brief explanation about why you filed the Complaint and why the settlement is fair in view of the possible risk of loss if the litigation continues," he very rapidly stated, without taking a breath.

"But there is no risk of loss. We have proof that ZeiiMed is guilty as charged. It is undisputable and incontestable," Mary blurted out. "What about an admission of fault? How can a federal court approve such a massive settlement as fair and reasonable without some acknowledgment of guilt or wrongdoing by ZeiiMed?"

"I don't care. No one cares. We have a settlement, but we won't get the money, and it is a lot of money, unless you, Mr. Bradford, convince the Court there is a risk that the Complaint could be dismissed if the case isn't settled. Make it up if you have to. Okay? You good with this?" Mr. Giulini asked, as if every lawyer "makes it up" when they go to court. Maybe they do.

"I guess no one can guarantee what a jury will determine, no matter how good you think your case is," I mentioned. "Plus, the Judge did almost throw out the Complaint at the first Conference in Court. There is no guarantee the ZeiiMed emails I found will change his mind."

"That's right. Now you got it. Just keep talking like that at the Hearing and it will be over in no time and we'll all have our fees before Christmas."

"I don't want a fee. I don't want a dime," I said.

"I want everybody at ZeiiMed in jail, but no one is asking my opinion," Mary chimed in.

"Christ! Where is that coffee?" Danny turned quickly in his seat, grabbed the door knob, opened the door, and screamed for the coffee once again.

I saw this as an opportunity to start our departure.

"We're fine now. Forget the coffee. We have another appointment to get to. We greatly appreciate your help and we will see you at the Hearing. I'll get there a half-hour early so we can chat in the hallway outside the courtroom before the hearing begins," I said, as I stood up and nodded to Mary to do the same.

"Oh. Gotta go so soon? I thought we would grab a bite, but I guess not. Next time."

"One last thing," I mentioned, as we were leaving the conference room. "As I said, I personally will not take a fee for my work on the Complaint, but I still want my share of the fee to be given to charity. That's non-negotiable, so just do it."

"Yeah, sure, whatever you say. So long as the deal gets done and we all get our payday, nobody cares. Nice meeting you. I like classy guys and you seem like a classy guy. That goes for you also, Mary. Can't wait until we have another chance to talk. Always a pleasure," Danny stated in parting.

We left quickly.

Hopefully, we will meet Mr. Giulini only one more time at the Hearing and never again. On our way back to the firm, Mary went on at length about her varying degrees of dislike for the settlement, ZeiiMed, the Tweed law firm and Danny Giulini, although not necessarily in that order. Most of what she said was accurate and insightful.

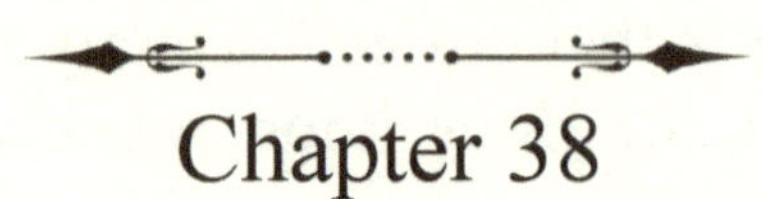

Chapter 38

Time flies and it seems all one can do is admire its unrelenting march forward at an ever-quickening pace.

Thanksgiving came and went. It is now the first week of December, 2009. Mary and I headed to court for the Fairness Hearing.

We found a cab on Pine Street, one block north of Wall Street, and headed for the Federal Courthouse on Pearl Street. Of course, even now, the morning of the scheduled Hearing, we were still evaluating the pros and cons of our support for the settlement.

"At this point, I think I should just say what Giulini told me to say and get this whole chapter in life over with. The doctors will have the settlement funds they deserve as full payment for the medical services they rendered, ZeiiMed will be off our backs and we won't have to ever speak with Danny again. I mean it. I've simply had enough. I want the whole mess to go away forever," I said to Mary, hoping she wouldn't try to convince me otherwise.

"I'm tired of talking about it myself. It's just difficult to struggle with the agonizing thought of ZeiiMed coldly killing the doctors, the Detective and almost you and your wife. Now, it's all going to be buried, with 'the truth' being the first item tossed in the grave. It's just hard," Mary lamented.

"I know, but life isn't fair and the settlement will finally end our involvement," I responded, hoping to end the issue.

No such luck.

"You have your opinion and I have mine. And there is no one who could ever convince me to just let it go and forget the brutal murder of Detective Jarrett. Enough said," Mary continued.

"Believe me, I will never again have a day on this earth that I don't mourn Jack Jarrett's death and say prayers in his honor. God bless him. Plus, it's repugnant that the authorities have not connected his death to ZeiiMed. I have looked and looked in the newspapers for any information on the investigation into his death. Nothing. ZeiiMed must have significant infiltration and influence in the police department."

I was getting too deflated before my court appearance, so a change of subject was in order.

"I have an idea, let's just end our discussion and watch the news on the television monitor," I suggested.

Several years ago, the cabs in New York were installed with touch screens that play various entertainment channels. It's mounted on the back of the front seat behind the driver, facing the passengers in the rear seat.

I touched the button that said, "News." On the screen appeared Senator Dean Delancy of New Jersey sitting at his desk in Washington, D.C., with an American flag in the background. His speech began, apparently live at that moment:

> "We all know that health care reform is a subject that provokes strong feelings on both sides of the fence. Many people are pleased that millions of uninsured Americans will now have health insurance, but there are also many others that are satisfied with the health benefits provided by their

private employer or union and don't want the anticipated additional expense of financing other people's insurance coverage. I understand the fears and concerns on both sides of the issue. And I'm here today to tell you about a health insurance company that also understands and appreciates the great divergence of thought that the President's proposed health care reform has created. The company is ZeiiMed and I'm sure you have heard of it before. But let me tell you a few things you don't know.

"Today, with the acquiescence and support of the Office of the Attorney General in New York, ZeiiMed will ask the federal court in lower Manhattan for permission to pay one billion dollars to doctors nationwide who have been providing you, the public, with the finest medical services in the world. It is these same doctors that will be providing you with their experienced medical opinions and medical techniques once health care reform is passed.

"Why will ZeiiMed do this? Because ZeiiMed wants to build a strong and lasting trust with the medical community in preparation for ZeiiMed's new role. What new role you ask? Well, I am pleased, no elated, to announce that ZeiiMed will be appointed as the national administrator to oversee, supervise and organize the state cooperatives, the insurance exchanges, the insurance marketplaces and the federal medical boards that are formed, created or designated to run the new national health insurance program to be passed by Congress and signed by the President.

"You may ask why the Senate Health Insurance Committee decided that ZeiiMed is the right choice. First, it is the biggest health insurance company and the most experienced in the field. Second, ZeiiMed already has the computer programs to calculate the rates to be paid to doctors and hospitals in fair return for their very capable medical services. ZeiiMed has spent years collecting data from the medical community to use in establishing its formula for paying the medical professionals for their services—fair payments to the doctors and fair to the American public that is now being insured on practically a universal basis.

"Now, please understand that ZeiiMed is not perfect. It has had some minor glitches in its past that regrettably caused some doctors not to get paid what they were worth, what they were promised and what they should have received. Because of that unfortunate incident, ZeiiMed is appearing in court today to proudly request the Court's approval of its one billion-dollar payment to its colleagues in the medical world. ZeiiMed has cleared up the minor problems with its computer data and that is now in the past.

"I congratulate ZeiiMed on its appointment as the top national administrator for the implementation and supervision of the new federal health care reform legislation. We are all very grateful that ZeiiMed eagerly accepted this massive responsibility to help all Americans live longer, more meaningful lives. Thank you."

I pressed the "off" button on the video screen.

"I think I'm going to vomit," were the first words spoken by Mary.

I felt the same.

"I can't imagine how ZeiiMed is able to pull these kinds of strings. It's beyond all belief. I am shocked. Previously, ZeiiMed was concerned that health care reform was going to drive it out of business. Now there is this revised health care law with ZeiiMed controlling and administering health care reform in whatever shape it finally takes when, and if, signed by the President," I said in disgust.

"Look, let's drop this subject, too. We may be in this traffic for awhile. There appears to be an accident with all the flashing red lights ahead. I'll start on a new subject and you can chime in whenever you like. By the way, I know this is out of the blue, but I do like your cologne," she stated quite unpredictably.

"What brought that on? You're not allowed to make such a comment. I'm not permitted to compliment your dress or perfume so why is it acceptable in a professional setting for you to say something about my cologne?" I said, pretending to be offended.

"First of all, I don't have any perfume on. But if I did, you would definitely make some off-color remark about it. Second, I don't care about or know about the office rules for taxi etiquette. I can and will say what I like, especially when it comes to you. Didn't we cover this subject once before? Just in case you don't remember, I personally saved your skin by inflicting a bloody wound to the skull of your assailant. That provides me carte blanche to say what I want when I want."

"Fine. I get it. When it comes to us, we're allowed to say to each other anything that pops into our heads."

"Pretty much," she said, "as long as it isn't a gross or

overly sexual comment."

"So, we're back to rules again?"

"No, call it a guideline and it applies only to you and not to me," she responded.

"I feel harassed by the sexual tension in this cab," I said.

"Wrong again," she responded. "It's not harassment because you're not offended, you enjoy it."

"How do you know?"

"Just a wild guess, but the libidinous expression on your face tells a woman all she needs to know. Never mind though. Forget this conversation—I think we hit another dead end. Let me give you my quick take on a current event I found very interesting."

"Proceed. I'm all ears," I lied, hoping the traffic would quickly clear. "By the way, what does 'libidinous expression' mean anyway?"

"You know, so don't ask," she answered. "Okay, here's my story. Let's start with the President of the United States. He's got a problem with the big banks. The federal government spent billions on the bailout and now the banks are on schedule to earn billions of dollars in profits and pay enormous bonuses to their executives. So the President summons the top executives of twelve of the biggest banks to Washington. The meeting was scheduled for Monday morning, presumably at 9 or 10 a.m.

"Guess what?" Mary continued. "Executives at three of the most prestigious banks in the world don't make the meeting. They call and tell the President, the President of the United States, that their scheduled flights out of the New York metropolitan area were severely delayed due to heavy fog at both Reagan National Airport and Dulles International Airport in D.C. So, three of the top bankers in the world simply don't show up for a scheduled meeting with the leader of the free world."

"That's silly. They probably missed out on a really nice lunch at the White House," I added, to lighten the mood.

"If you or I failed to show for an important meeting, mediation, court appearance or trial, we would probably lose our jobs," Mary pressed on. "The same goes for people in all walks of life: accountants, teachers, janitors, truck drivers— we all have to be somewhere that's important to our jobs and we make darn sure we're at the required place on time. But these bankers, scheduled to attend the most important meeting of their lives, don't bother to think that maybe the weather might delay their early morning flights on Monday and make alternate plans—such as going to D.C. the night before, on Sunday. Don't these guys listen to the weather reports for D.C. before Monday morning?"

"How do you know?" I interrupted. "Maybe the bankers had important family or health problems that made it impossible to travel on the day before the Monday morning meeting."

"Well, maybe that was the case, but you would think the bankers would have disclosed any excuse that was more palatable than fog at the D.C. airport. But the most interesting part of the story is what happens next."

Mary went on. "One month later, the President announces to great fanfare a 'financial crisis responsibility fee'—a tax to be imposed on the largest banks, the ones with more than fifty billion dollars in assets. The tax is estimated to raise more than ninety billion dollars over ten years to recover taxpayer losses from TARP. Based on early calculations, the three banks whose top bankers were held up by the fog are part of a group of five banks that will be levied the largest estimated annual fee. So, you tell me, do you think the President was roaring mad at the snub? I can see it now.

Right after Obama concluded his meeting with the bankers that made it through the fog, he calls his staff together and raises the roof. I can hear the President now:

> 'How dare those bankers embarrass the Office of the President? We'll show them. The White House will announce a new law requiring a payback of every cent that was spent bailing those ungrateful banks out of the financial crisis, with a tax on the largest banks. They will learn real fast who's the Boss. Oh, and just for good measure, let's also prohibit banks from making proprietary investments in high risk mortgage-backed securities using the hard-earned deposits of working-class Americans. As far as I'm concerned, from now on the White House is taking on the banks and we intend to win.'"

"Well, we don't really know what the President privately told his staff and I doubt Congress will approve the bank tax," I responded. "But I, for one, would have been at the White House an hour early in the hope I might have time to look around once I was let in the front door."

The traffic started to clear. Luckily, we had left early and had time to spare.

"I'm glad we had this time to ourselves," Mary commented.

"Yes, I always enjoy spending quality time with the employees," I said, instantly realizing my poor choice of words.

"Don't be so glib. You know darn well I'm much more than just another paid employee."

"Yes, you're right, I should have referred to you as an

associate."

"I like 'colleague' better. It correctly and accurately creates the sense that we are equals," she instructed me. "And don't deny that you enjoy spending time with me."

Unlike Bill Clinton, I'm not denying anything. In fact, I didn't say anything in response.

We were now at the courthouse. Finally.

I exited the cab first, stepping onto the sidewalk. Mary followed me out the same door, after paying. She immediately noticed someone standing next to me on the sidewalk.

I turned towards her, as she stood next to me after leaving the cab.

"Mary, I would like you to meet my wife, Kim."

I turned to my wife and said, "Kim, this is my colleague, Mary, about whom I've told you so much and who, quite simply, saved my life."

There was a moment of uncomfortable silence. Mary looked at me with a puzzled expression.

Finally, Kim spoke. "How nice to meet you, Mary. Brian always says you're the smartest associate at the firm. Also, I can't thank you enough for your heroic action in saving Brian from that lunatic doctor. You are very brave."

Kim gave Mary a brief hug and added, "Thank you again."

"It's a pleasure to meet you also," Mary responded. "Brian didn't mention you would be here today. I would have looked forward to meeting you. By the way, I want you to know that what I did to help Brian was pure adrenaline and instinct. I'm just glad Brian is okay and hopefully, I will never have to resort to violence ever again."

"True, but remember that I will always believe that your quick action in responding to a terrifying situation is the only reason Brian is here today," Kim continued.

The conversation was getting too sentimental for my taste.

"Kim," I interjected, "Did you tell me you were coming in the City today?"

"No, but I just couldn't resist this opportunity to see you eloquently mesmerize the entire courtroom with your persuasive legal reasoning and compelling argument. I think it will be very exciting."

"Well, thank you. Everybody in the office was saying the same thing this morning," I said, thinking it was funny, but no one seemed amused.

"Okay then," I continued, "why don't we head into the courthouse. I need to touch base with a couple of lawyers before I go into the courtroom."

Mary walked ahead as Kim and I followed.

"She is very pretty. You never mentioned that," Kim whispered to me.

"Is she really? I guess so. She has some appealing features," I answered, not really knowing how to appropriately respond to such a question from one's spouse.

"Honey, when we get to the corridor outside the courtroom, it will probably be pretty hectic. We may get separated. I'll just see you again after the Hearing is over."

"No problem, Brian. I understand you have to focus on what you have to do. Actually, I'm going to head to the Ladies Room and then take a seat in the back of the courtroom. Love you, I know you'll do great."

I gave Kim a quick kiss and hurried to catch up to Mary.

Chapter 39

I stood in the corridor outside the doors to the courtroom. It was crowded. It seemed a large number of doctors showed up to observe the proceedings and confirm their big payday, in addition to the usual army of lawyers for ZeiiMed. I hadn't yet run into Charles Wadsworth, but I needed to speak with him about that damn public statement by Senator Delancy. Charles should have called me to let me know it was going to happen less than an hour before the Hearing.

I found Daniel Giulini.

"Ready to go?" he asked.

"Yes, of course."

"Stick to the script we talked about, don't deviate, don't embellish," Daniel stated.

"Keep to the script? Obviously, ZeiiMed isn't sticking to the plan. Did you hear Senator Delancy's speech about the greatness of ZeiiMed and anointing the company as the next coming of Moses to lead all Americans out of the health care crisis. How did this happen? ZeiiMed is a ruthless, diabolical machine that destroys and eliminates everything in its path, including lawyers and other forms of life."

"Don't sweat it. Nothing has changed. Let's just get the deal sealed by the Court and we'll all go home. Don't mess up," Daniel said aggressively.

"Whose side are you on? I know you want your three million-dollar payday, but your doctor clients will be screwed for sure if the government gives ZeiiMed full reign over health care. Have you got a side deal with ZeiiMed?" I asked, as my blood pressure started to rise.

"I'm not discussing this. I will tell you one more time. Go into that courtroom and convince the Judge to approve the settlement. Who knows what will happen if you mess up."

"Is that a threat?" I asked.

Giulini stepped closer to me.

I felt a sense of apprehension.

"Call it what you want. I'm going into the courtroom. This is not the time to get cold feet. Just get the settlement done. You play hero and all hell will break loose," Daniel quickly snarled in my ear, as he walked away.

I turned and headed towards the doors to the courtroom as I continued to look for Charles.

I bumped into John Edison. We stopped and faced each other.

"I'm glad you're here. So far, you have kept your side of our agreement," he said.

"Well, yes, I have, but the Senator's speech today sure blindsided me. It's bad enough the Attorney General is dropping its investigation, but now you've gone a step further and got the federal government to put ZeiiMed in charge of health care reform. ZeiiMed's been given the keys to every doctor's office in America."

"Just leave it alone," Edison responded. "It doesn't concern you. ZeiiMed has fully lived up to its agreement. Your wife, your family and your work people have not been approached or contacted by ZeiiMed. You have only one more thing to do and then we're done with each other. Just go into the courtroom and charm the Judge into approving this settlement."

"Yes, I know. I'm hearing that a lot today. I need to speak to Charles. Where is he?" I asked.

"You mean Charles Wadsworth?"

"Of course, who else? He is lead counsel for ZeiiMed, right?"

"Come over here. I have something important to tell you."

Edison pointed to a quiet area by a window, away from the crowd mingling near the doors to the courtroom.

"It was kept very private, but I just assumed you knew. Charles passed away unexpectedly several weeks ago," Edison stated.

"I can't believe that. I didn't hear or read anything about it. How did it happen?"

"It was sudden and unexpected. In fact, he was at a meeting at ZeiiMed giving legal advice on the settlement we are about to ask the Court to approve. Charles suddenly felt very dizzy and went to our infirmary, but despite the best efforts of our skilled medical team he had a massive heart attack and died within minutes of its onset. His wife insisted on no autopsy and had him buried the next day. I hear she bought a lovely chateau in Tuscany and relocated there shortly after the burial."

"I see. It was all very smooth and efficient and very much the ZeiiMed way of conducting business," I commented.

"What are you talking about? ZeiiMed's medical staff did everything they could to save Charles' life."

"Don't you dare try to sell me your lies. I know you guys killed Charles, just like you killed the others. It's ZeiiMed's penalty for failure, you ruthless son-of-a-bitch. The most pathetic aspect is that Charles didn't know that Robert Finley would give such damaging deposition testimony because he didn't know the 'smoking gun' emails even existed until the deposition. ZeiiMed never told him and he had no idea of ZeiiMed's plan to plant Hyman and Martin as plaintiffs in my Complaint. You wasted a life for no reason and you couldn't care less," I said in utter disgust.

"I suggest again that you just keep out of ZeiiMed's business," Edison stated. "No one can prove your theory. Charles is dead and in the ground with no questions asked or explored. Think anything you want, but I wouldn't go mouthing off to others about things you know nothing about."

"Maybe you're wrong. Maybe it's not over. With his wife's permission, a body can be exhumed and examined for drug or chemical poisoning. My only problem is convincing his wife to do it, especially if her lovely chateau turns out to have been paid for by ZeiiMed."

"Don't even think about it. You will never find her or get near her. I can assure you that. She is very concerned about the welfare of her children and I have promised her continued care and comfort, financially and otherwise, as part of what I call a partnership between the Wadsworth family and ZeiiMed. Plus, you take this any further and I will treat it as a breach, a grievous breach, of our agreement," the ruthless animal responded.

"You're right. I have a lot of thinking to do and not a lot of time to make a decision. The Judge will take the bench in ten minutes. So just get the hell away from me now and forever. And remember, I got to you once and I can do it again. Think about that every time you go to bed at night," I said, as I turned to go into the courtroom.

My head was pounding. My palms were sweaty. I was confused and perplexed as to what to do next. Another murder that ZeiiMed was getting away with. No further investigations by the police or the Attorney General's Office. ZeiiMed had a new sponsorship with the federal government to supervise and govern all health care in America. How can I live with all this and just pretend it doesn't exist? All I need do is tell the Court that a great settlement was negotiated and shut my mouth about everything else. However, I don't know if I can and I'm running out of time to decide.

It was a decision that would alter my life forever.

Chapter 40

I stepped into the courtroom. The Honorable Whitman Peter White had decided to switch courtrooms since our last appearance. I guess he anticipated a large and active crowd for the Hearing. With the press release by the Senator earlier, I was sure we'd have more spectators and press people than anyone projected.

The courtroom had at least fifty wooden pews in front of the Bench with an equal number on each side of a long, middle aisle that was several feet wide. The Bench itself was elevated by a platform at least five feet above the floor level. Clearly, the Judge wanted to make sure he impressed everyone with his imperial majesty, as well as his omnipotent and omniscient presence.

The Bench was so high that the clerks sitting immediately in front of it would surely get a neck sprain tilting their heads to observe the Judge. It was like being in the first row of a movie theater.

The courtroom was packed. Not only was every seat in every pew filled, but spectators also lined up three-deep along the rear wall.

Every kind of electronic device was observable. Cell phones were not allowed in the Courtroom, but laptops, notebooks and BlackBerrys, with the phone capability disabled, were everywhere. Before such miracle devices, attorneys would interact with each other, exchange war stories and network face to face. In today's world, the attorneys never look up from their electronic devices, seemingly so immersed in the four corners of their internet world that it's impossible for them to comprehend and appreciate the presence of other human beings.

As the courtroom doors closed behind me, I heard my name called. I turned to my left. It was Kim. She was seated right on the aisle in the last pew.

"Brian, good luck! You have quite an audience here. Put on a good show for everyone," Kim said.

"Thanks, honey. I'll do my best. Your support means everything to me." I leaned down and gave her a kiss on the cheek.

As I pulled away, the woman sitting next to Kim spoke to me. "Hi, Brian, nice to see you again." It was Meadhbh.

"Oh, hi, Meadhbh. I'm very surprised to see you here." I glanced at Kim's eyes to gauge her reaction.

"This Hearing was all over the news today on CNN," Meadhbh explained. "I guess the media got a heads up on the Senator's press release and realized the Settlement Hearing was going to be a big story. I've never been in a courtroom and I couldn't pass up the opportunity to see my new favorite lawyer..."

I quickly interrupted her in mid-sentence. "Meadhbh, this is my wife, Kim. Kim, this is a friend of mine from... you know, I forget where from," I fumbled along. My mind went blank.

"Nice to meet you, Kim. I'm a bartender at a French Restaurant on the Upper East Side. Brian has been in a few times when he was in the area. Since I work at nights, I'm off in the mornings and thought I would stop by. Brian always talks about you. I feel I already know you."

"That's interesting," Kim said. "I hope he tells only positive stories about us."

"Absolutely, it's all good and all above board. Although I

think he did mention he never met anyone who could kiss like you," Meadhbh said to great embarrassment.

The embarrassment was mine and not Meadhbh's. I guess I should be thankful she didn't mention "The Kiss" over the bar—that would certainly have thrown off my concentration for today's Hearing.

"I can't imagine why my dear husband would say that to you. He really is such a clown," Kim said with a smile, but she scowled at me with a look that could stop a herd of elephants. "I'll make sure Brian takes me to your restaurant and we'll meet up then."

"Great idea, honey," I threw in with my usual dose of sarcasm. "Kim, can I talk to you for a second? Meadhbh, I'll see you after the Hearing. Thanks for coming."

Kim stood up and we faced each other. "Kim, let's talk about Meadhbh another time. Right now, I'm starting to have doubts about my scripted performance here today. I just learned, on top of everything else, they killed Charles and he was completely innocent. He didn't know anything about the emails that Finley testified about. Charles was just a mouthpiece, not a co-conspirator. I just don't know if I can stand in front of the Judge and tell the entire courtroom about the wonderful settlement with ZeiiMed and say nothing of the real reasons why it came about."

"Brian, I know its difficult and I want you to do what you believe is right. Just remember, though, you cross ZeiiMed and our deal with them is off. We become targets and, sooner or later, ZeiiMed will once again try to make us victims. It's just a matter of when. ZeiiMed will not stop. It's what those people do and it's all they know. But the good news is ZeiiMed already took its best shot at us and missed. Now we know what to expect, but not when to expect it. We have options. We can talk about them later.

But right now, you have to follow your conscience. By the way, Meadhbh is cute. Yes, we can talk about her another time."

"Thanks, Kim. I'm not sure how this will play out today, but I know I couldn't have taken another step without your steadfast support. I have to go sit at counsel's table now. The Judge will be out in a minute. By the way, don't you remember I mentioned needing Meadhbh's help in getting to Edison?"

"Yes, I remember. But I still want the details. You better go."

I walked down the center aisle. All eyes were on me as I approached the plaintiffs' table directly in front of the Bench, on the left-hand side of the aisle. Mary was already there with papers spread out everywhere on the table.

I sat next to her, facing the Bench.

"How do you feel? Ready to go?" she asked.

"My stomach is sour. My headache is excruciating. I'm sweating, yet have the chills. Aren't you glad you asked? And, I just told Kim that I'm having serious doubts about my puppet act today. Maybe the strings have been pulled too tight and are about to break. This may be my only and last chance to tell what really took place and reveal the truth about ZeiiMed."

"I'm with you, Brian. Yes, I'm pretty scared and was also looking forward to putting the entire ZeiiMed mess behind us all. But if you want to fight and you need me to fight with you, I'm in," Mary declared. "I told you they all belong in jail!"

This is some woman. First, she saves my life by cracking open the skull of a doctor gone insane and now she's ready to jump in the trenches for hand-to-hand combat in round two. I really need to buy Mary a drink and tell her how great a friend she is.

The cast was assembling in anticipation of the Judge's appearance. Daniel Giulini sat next to Mary at our table. I looked over at the defendant's table a few feet across from us. It was once again packed tightly with an armada of lawyers from Tweed, Fox & Fortune. It was obvious that ZeiiMed had been notified that the Judge moved the Hearing to a larger courtroom because even more ZeiiMed lawyers were sitting at the table. I wondered which one of these robots had been selected to be the mouthpiece now that Charles was six feet under.

As I watched, it appeared that one attorney at the table was getting most of the attention. He was an athletic-looking, well-built man who sat up perfectly straight in a stiff and unyielding posture. His hair was cut very short and his nose slightly flattened, furthering his militaristic look. If ZeiiMed ever decides to send out another bad guy to do me in, I hoped it wouldn't be him. All ZeiiMed would need to do is wind him up, program his mainframe, and then let this predator loose.

My thoughts were interrupted by the stenographer as she took her seat next to the Bench. The Judge's three law clerks likewise took their places directly in front of the Bench, facing the attorneys and spectators.

One of the clerks loudly banged his hand on the desk and announced in a loud, commanding voice:

"All rise. The Honorable Whitman Peter White, presiding. All who have business before this Court stand tall, face the Bench, speak slowly and give your full attention to the Court. Anyone observed using any electronic device will have it immediately confiscated by the court officer and destroyed. Anyone making noise while Court is in session will be escorted out of the courtroom by a Federal Marshal."

The Judge magically appeared from a door behind his Bench and took his throne, I mean seat. His upper body seemed more bent over than the last time I saw him, making him look more fragile. His white hair had grown longer on the sides of his head and seemed to be combed upward to partially cover his baldness on top. With his sunken cheeks, black robe and long thin face, he could easily be mistaken for a creepy butler in a dimly lit haunted mansion.

"Welcome back," were the Judge's first words.

Despite his appearance, his voice was strong and clear.

> THE COURT: I understand there is a settlement proposal on the table for my review. I will hear from counsel on the merits of the settlement and the reasonableness of the compensation to be paid the doctors before deciding if the Court needs a more formal hearing with expert testimony. I will hear from counsel for ZeiiMed first.

I had guessed right. The attorney with the crewcut and stiff posture stood quickly to attention.

> MR. CLARK: Good morning, Your Honor, Sir.
>
> THE COURT: You don't have to call me 'sir.' Your Honor is appropriate.
>
> MR. CLARK: Yes, Your Honor. My name is John Standish Clark and I am counsel for ZeiiMed.
>
> THE COURT: Where is Charles Wadsworth? He usually addresses the Court on behalf of ZeiiMed.
>
> MR. CLARK: Unfortunately, I must inform the Court of the very sad passing of Mr. Wadsworth unexpectedly at a young age. Sudden heart attack, I

believe.

THE COURT: I had no idea. The Court was totally unaware. Please accept my condolences to his family and Tweed, Fox & Fortune.

MR. CLARK: No notification was sent to the Court or to his professional colleagues and adversaries. His family wanted the entire matter to be kept very private. No newspapers were notified, so no obituaries appeared. There was no wake and the funeral mass was held at the Wadsworth home in Rye, New York. Certainly, I should have been more sensitive to this issue and quietly informed your clerk before the proceedings began today. But what's done is done. ZeiiMed is only interested in moving forward, not looking back and has instructed me to proceed as its counsel to bring this case to a conclusion today.

As I listened to Mr. Clark make his speech, I could feel my anger slowly rising.

ZeiiMed murdered Wadsworth and now considers his passing an annoyance that we should all get over as soon as possible. I wouldn't have been shocked to hear Clark ask the Court to have his own name put in the records of the earlier court hearings and Mr. Wadsworth's name erased as if he never existed. There seems to be no end to this madness. ZeiiMed continues to expand its web of brutality and deception, with everything to be gained and no one to stop it.

In fact, only Mary, myself and Edison have complete knowledge of the series of horrific events that resulted in this Hearing today. Worse yet, once the Judge approves the settlement and ends these proceedings with the bang of his gavel, there will no longer be anyone interested in learning of what occurred and no one interested in bringing ZeiiMed to justice.

Maybe if ZeiiMed got what it deserved, Detective Jarrett could spend the rest of eternity sleeping peacefully. I am tortured by my complicity in my adversary's plan for today. I abhor my lack of backbone and moral compass. I am repulsed at my role in enabling a result dictated by others. All because of concern for my own safety and comfort, regardless of the consequences of my silence. I cannot do this. I will not permit this.

THE COURT: Proceed, Mr. Clark, with your business before this Court.

MR. CLARK: My client, ZeiiMed, is very pleased to report that the parties have reached a settlement that compensates doctors nationwide for all underpayments that may have occurred over a period of fifteen years. The settlement amount is one billion dollars. The money will be placed in a Compensation Fund and will be dispersed directly to the doctors for each invoice that was submitted to ZeiiMed and paid less than the billed amount.

For example, let's say a patient insured by ZeiiMed visited a doctor and received an invoice for two hundred dollars from the doctor for the office visit. If ZeiiMed only paid sixty dollars, the doctor is now entitled to a full payment of one hundred forty dollars from the Compensation Fund. If the patient already paid the one hundred forty dollars balance with the patient's personal funds, then the patient will get one hundred forty dollars from the Compensation Fund.

Also, we request that the proposed class of plaintiff

doctors be certified to include all doctors nationwide. However, the doctors have the obligation to submit the paperwork demonstrating the underpayments.

THE COURT: Are you saying that ZeiiMed will pay the entire unpaid balance of each invoice regardless of whether the two hundred-dollar charge for the office visit exceeds the usual and customary charge for that particular medical service?

MR. CLARK: Yes, sir. Excuse me, I mean Your Honor. The point is, Your Honor, that none of these settling doctors will have to worry about that. If a doctor has an unpaid invoice, ZeiiMed will assume that the full charge on the bill was usual and customary and it will not be questioned, just paid.

Going forward, of course, ZeiiMed has a right to question excessive invoices and pay only eighty percent of the usual and customary fee, but not the invoices of the doctors for the last fifteen years.

THE COURT: If ZeiiMed is really being as generous as you say, why is it settling? ZeiiMed could save all this money and not have to pay anything until after the trial and all the appeals, years from now?

MR. CLARK: Because ZeiiMed feels a responsibility to the doctors and to the medical professionals. We want a healthy relationship, to coin a pun, with the professionals that provide important medical care to our insureds. This also why we want the class certified for settlement purposes to include all doctors nationwide so the allegations in the Complaint will be forever resolved, never brought up again and forever locked away in the bowels of the courthouse.

ZeiiMed wants this matter resolved forever and is willing to pay for the peace it seeks. Plus, as you may have heard today on television, we have reached agreement with the New York Attorney General to discontinue its investigation of ZeiiMed. Also, ZeiiMed accepted the federal government's request that ZeiiMed supervise and oversee the health care industry once it is overhauled by the proposed Health Care Reform law in whatever form it is finally passed and signed into law by the President.

THE COURT: Thank you, Mr. Clark. I now want to hear from counsel for the plaintiff doctors. You presented your position very clearly and skillfully. However, it does sound almost too good to be true.

MR. GIULINI: Good morning, Your Honor. I will make a short presentation as the current counsel of record for the plaintiff doctors. Then I will turn it over to Brian Bradford, the predecessor counsel who was personally involved in the filing of the Complaint and the subsequent litigation leading to commencement of settlement negotiations.

I was substituted as counsel for the Plaintiff doctors just as the settlement discussions were beginning.

I have reviewed the expert reports prepared at the request of Mr. Bradford's law office and I have evaluated the damage calculations contained therein. I have also evaluated the reports of the experts retained by ZeiiMed and exchanged as part of the usual discovery disclosure. While we certainly contend that the actual losses to the doctors exceed the settlement amount of one billion dollars, we also believe the settlement to be fair, reasonable and appropriate in view of the risks of litigation and the unpredictability of jurors.

If the case doesn't settle, the doctors will have a difficult evidentiary burden in establishing the exact amount of the underpayments to each group of doctors in different geographical areas. That is, the damages to be paid to each doctor based on the usual and customary charges in each of the major areas of the country can be very difficult to accurately calculate over a fifteen-year time period.

As this Court is aware, we nonetheless have indisputable proof established by sworn deposition testimony and streams of incriminating emails that the outdated Depressor Data was implemented by ZeiiMed for the express purpose of calculating grossly inadequate payments to the doctors and hospitals.

MR. CLARK: Excuse me, Your Honor, but I feel the need to interrupt here. We have a very large gallery of people here today, including the press and television media. So, for the sake of accuracy, I want to note for the record that ZeiiMed vigorously disputes Mr. Giulini's statements regarding what he refers to as the Depressor Data and further disputes the allegation that ZeiiMed engaged in any systematic, intentional manipulation of outdated Depressor Data pursuant to a pre-conceived plan to underpay anyone. We simply didn't do what Mr. Giulini alleges and find repugnant any comment to the contrary. It simply didn't happen, except in a few non-material, isolated instances that were quickly corrected.

Mr. Clark banged the top of the table with his open hand for emphasis. The Judge's eyeglasses dropped down the bridge of his nose, as his head tilted downward in a piercing glare at Mr. Clark.

THE COURT: That is not necessary, Mr. Clark. Keep calm and make your point in a civilized fashion. Such behavior will not be permitted in my courtroom.

MR. CLARK: I will, Your Honor. I apologize to the Court. But my client is sick and tired of these extreme accusations ungrounded without any proof whatsoever. There is not one ounce of proof to support the wild and unproven lies that are a product of the doctors' paranoia and illusion. The only reason we are settling is to get the doctors to shut their very big mouths and desist from their constant crying about not getting enough money to sustain their very expensive life styles. ZeiiMed is fed up with all their garbage and may this finally be the end of it.

THE COURT: Your comments are very adversarial and not in the mutual spirit of compromise that usually accompanies an application for this Court's approval of a settlement. I am perplexed by your words and disappointed in you. If ZeiiMed refuses to admit any fault or responsibility, it's almost impossible for me to determine the fairness of the settlement. You're agreeing to pay a billion dollars and then argue that there were only a few isolated and corrected instances of computer miscalculations. It doesn't make sense.

MR. BRADFORD: I feel the same way, Your Honor. But I have much more to say on the subject.

I was sitting down when I made my unsolicited comments

to the Judge. Interrupting the Court can get you in big trouble with this Judge. I can't let my emotions compromise the position I now had to take, but I needed to get the Court's attention while ZeiiMed was on the defensive.

I turned to Mary in the seat next to me and whispered, "I can't let this go on. I've changed my mind. I know this may jeopardize our future safety, but we'll be haunted to an even greater degree if we sit back and let ZeiiMed get away with it. We are lawyers. We took an oath to seek justice and uphold the law. We are governed by laws and the laws sustain our society. Justice cannot be administered here today without a full disclosure of the truth. I am obligated and compelled to do what is right, to do what is necessary.

> THE COURT: Mr. Bradford, please end your sidebar with co-counsel and address the Court. If you have something to say, please stand and present your remarks. Either do so now or you shall not have this opportunity again. Speak now or forever hold your peace.

I stood slowly and paused before looking straight at the Judge.

> MR. BRADFORD: Good morning. May it please the Court. I do have several remarks, most of which I had no intention of making when I prepared for this Court appearance.

I again paused, collected my thoughts and then pushed the papers in front of me aside.

> THE COURT: Proceed, Mr. Bradford. We are all

eagerly awaiting your words of wisdom.

MR. BRADFORD: So, as I was saying, I have no prepared remarks because I had not intended to make this statement. I had planned to inform Your Honor about how ZeiiMed had very fairly and magnanimously increased its settlement offer to a number considered very reasonable and acceptable when compared with my evidentiary burden of proving liability and damages on a class-wide basis sufficient to sustain a verdict on appeal. And I still believe the settlement is appropriate compensation for the decades of underpayments by ZeiiMed. The settlement should be approved and I join in the application seeking an Order that permits the settlement to proceed.

This is the point where I was supposed to sit down as instructed and shut up. That's what ZeiiMed wants and Mr. Clark wants and what even Mr. Giulini wants. Everybody gets their money and no more questions are asked. The matter is closed, the file sent to storage, the investigations cease and all suspicions of impropriety and criminality are forever buried.

However, I cannot accept that and I will not play my part in orchestrating such a result. There are few if any occasions in life when one is confronted with making a decision that will forever change the world we live in. When that time comes, there can be no forgiveness for making the wrong decision. There is emotional comfort only in knowing you made the right decision regardless of the consequences.

This is where I am as I stand here today before this Court. This is my last and best chance to change forever the destructive and ruthless business of

ZeiiMed. Violence, destruction, physical harm and death are all part of its daily routine conducted for the sole purpose of pursuing its goals and profits. Well, it's all about to change. The light of truth will change the unchangeable and shake the unshakable.

THE COURT: Let me cut you off right there, Mr. Bradford. Clearly, you are embarking on a very emotional and somewhat rambling presentation that may or may not be relevant to the simple issue of whether the settlement should be approved as fair and reasonable. That being said, I will let you continue, at least for a few more minutes. But I urge you to get to the point quickly, with less of an emphasis on eloquence and more of an emphasis on established facts. Proceed.

MR. BRADFORD: Thank you, Your Honor. I will get to the point. I will start with the most recent events and work backward in time from there. I came to court today having recently made an agreement with the Chief Executive Officer of ZeiiMed, Mr. John Edison. Mr. Edison is here today.

Mr. Edison quickly stood from his seat in the gallery.

MR. EDISON: You better be careful. If you make any disparaging remarks about ZeiiMed, we will sue you for defamation and report you to the Bar Association. As you know, any agreement you have with ZeiiMed regarding this litigation is highly confidential and will be voided immediately if revealed by you here today.

THE COURT: Sit down! Now! There will be order in this Court. You have no right to speak unless recognized by this Court. If you say another word without being invited to do so by me, you will be restrained and removed from the courtroom. Officer, please stand by and be ready to quickly remove that man from the Court on my command.

MR. BRADFORD: Your Honor, you have now had the pleasure of meeting the very refined and polite Mr. Edison. Actually, his outburst here today will bring more credibility to my tale.

As I was saying, I promised Mr. Edison that I would come to Court here today and express the virtues of the proposed settlement, as well as the pitfalls and risks of continued litigation. In return, Mr. Edison agreed that ZeiiMed would discontinue its efforts to kill me, my wife and my colleague here today, Ms. Mary Douglas. Your Honor, I am talking about a plan conceived and orchestrated by ZeiiMed for the cold-blooded murder of people whose only crime was learning the truth about ZeiiMed. Edison agree to terminate the plan in return for my testimony here today in support of the settlement.

There was an audible murmur of shock from the gallery behind me.

THE COURT: Order in the Court. I want silence, no gasps of alarm or other emotional reaction from the spectators in this courtroom today. I will not say it again.

MR. BRADFORD: By way of background, at the time I made the agreement with ZeiiMed, I was in Mr. Edison's apartment, quite uninvited. I had restrained Mr. Edison and I was threatening physical harm. I am sure you are wondering why I would confront ZeiiMed's top corporate officer in such a manner.

I will tell you why. Essentially, my discovery of the incriminating Depressor Data used by ZeiiMed triggered a series of events that included the use of explosives to destroy my condo building in Baiting Hollow in an effort to end my life. After ZeiiMed was unsuccessful the first time, I thereafter became locked in two additional near fatal confrontations that could have resulted in my death each time.

One such confrontation was in my office. The murder attempt was carried out by my former client and named plaintiff, Dr. Martin Brown, now deceased. The second confrontation was on a plane thirty thousand feet in the sky when another former client and named plaintiff, Dr. Stanley Hyman, tried to cut my throat after having strangled the police detective, who was protecting me, in the airport terminal. How do I know this was all ZeiiMed's handiwork? Because both doctors admitted it to me, just moments before their respective plans for my demise were foiled by the fortuitous intervention of two very brave women, one of whom is sitting right next to me, Mary Douglas.

Also, Dr. Hyman admitted to me that ZeiiMed killed Dr. Martin and fully expected that ZeiiMed would likewise kill him. Why? Because they failed to carry out ZeiiMed's instructions to end my life. According to ZeiiMed, I also wasn't supposed to have discovered the outdated Depressor Data and the emails confirming ZeiiMed's intentional use of the Depressor Data. Failure means punishment.

As a result, both my former clients, Martin Brown

and Stanley Hyman, are now dead. I should correct myself. I thought they were my clients—they were not. They were both taking their instructions from ZeiiMed as part of a scheme masterminded by ZeiiMed.

The scheme, as I now understand it, was to convince me to file the Complaint. In discovery, ZeiiMed would produce the inculpatory emails and outdated Depressor Data camouflaged in hundreds of pages of cyberspace junk that was essentially nonsensical gibberish. After the production, ZeiiMed would offer a very enticing settlement amount and Doctors Brown and Hyman were instructed to insist on settling. Once the case settled, the Depressor Data would never again see the light of day in a civil litigation. To preclude a future group of non-settling doctors from filing a new Complaint, ZeiiMed would demand that a settlement class be certified to include all doctors nationwide.

Next, the Depressor Data and the 'smoking gun' emails would be stored in a huge government warehouse in an unmarked crate until finally being destroyed. The Confidentiality Agreement and Order signed by this Court shortly after the filing of the Complaint required that all documents and ESI be destroyed at the conclusion of the case. As such, all records regarding the Depressor Data would vanish.

ZeiiMed wins and just keeps doing business as usual, although I'm sure procedures would be implemented to prevent the creation of any future emails discussing the Depressor Data on a going forward basis. Most of the scheme I have outlined was implemented by ZeiiMed, with a few dead bodies thrown in as collateral damage.

So, you may ask, what changed my mind? What was the deciding event that caused me to come forward and make this disclosure?

First, in a taxicab on the way to court, I learned that ZeiiMed was now in charge of the supervision and administration of the new federal health care program in whatever form it is eventually passed by Congress and signed into law. The fox is now truly in charge of the hen house and the hen house includes every citizen in America. I was shocked.

Second, the press release announcing the appointment again noted that the New York Attorney General was ceasing its investigation of ZeiiMed. All hope was now lost that ZeiiMed would ever be brought to its knees in the light of day.

Third, I received today the sickening news that Charles Wadsworth was dead. He also was murdered by ZeiiMed, but he knew nothing of ZeiiMed's scheme to manipulate the litigation so that all incriminating documentation against ZeiiMed would be buried forever. But it doesn't matter. Charles failed because the result demanded by ZeiiMed was not achieved. It wasn't part of the scheme for me to discover the 'hot' emails and send them to the authorities. In ZeiiMed's depraved view of the world, that was all that mattered. It was enough to condemn Charles Wadsworth to death, even though he was unaware of ZeiiMed's master plan.

And isn't it ironic that Wadsworth was killed in ZeiiMed's very own infirmary at ZeiiMed's headquarters? I cannot live with the knowledge of this blood bath without speaking out and requesting, in fact, begging this Court to take appropriate action to put an end to ZeiiMed's evil mayhem and bring justice and punishment to the executives that orchestrated this lawlessness.

THE COURT: That is truly a remarkable tale, unlike anything I have ever heard in civil litigation. According to your statement here today, as an officer of the Court, you had two violent episodes with your own doctor clients, as well as a threatening confrontation with the CEO of ZeiiMed, initiated by you in response to ZeiiMed's alleged attempts on your life. Also, a detective, the two doctors and opposing counsel are all now dead.

MR. CLARK: Your Honor, may I respond to this preposterous tale? ZeiiMed strenuously denies these unfounded allegations as complete untruths that no governmental authority has asserted despite extensive investigations. I would greatly appreciate any opportunity to elaborate.

THE COURT: I don't think so. I've heard enough. There is no way anyone could make up such an inconceivable narrative of events without a serious vein of truth. Besides, I don't believe you are going to contend that the four people that are dead have been miraculously restored to life. When was the last time two plaintiffs and counsel for the defendant all died in the space of a few months? I don't know what, if anything, the state authorities are doing, but it appears to me that federal law may have been violated. I have made up my mind. The Court's ruling is as follows:

The settlement is approved by the Court as fair, reasonable and adequate. The official transcript of this hearing, with Mr. Bradford's accusations, will be referred to the Department of Justice for entry of a possible indictment, if warranted, against ZeiiMed and any individuals at ZeiiMed that violated federal law in causing these events to unfold.

Since a criminal indictment of a health insurance company will void its authorization to conduct its insurance business in most states, I am directing ZeiiMed to immediately pay the one billion dollars in settlement funds to an escrow account to be administered by a Special Master to be appointed by this Court. The payment is to be made to the escrow account within ten business days. This will guarantee that the settlement funds will be available for distribution regardless of whether a criminal indictment of ZeiiMed causes it to file for bankruptcy and eventually liquidate.

I further order that a class of all doctors nationwide is hereby certified for settlement purposes and includes all doctors that have submitted bills to ZeiiMed in the last fifteen years. Notice to the class is to be expedited and must issue no later than fifteen days from now.

The Court is adjourned. Please clear the courtroom as quickly as possible. Order is to be maintained and I instructed the Federal Marshals here today to make sure it is maintained. Good day to you all.

Everyone rose as the Judge left the Bench. Once the Judge had exited the courtroom, everyone seemed to be talking aloud at once in agitated voices. The ZeiiMed lawyers and the ZeiiMed executives seemed shocked at the turn of events. Rather than being pleased at the Court's approval of the settlement, they were utterly dismayed at the thought of a possible federal prosecution and indictment. The newspaper and television media swarmed around the ZeiiMed executives and then headed up the center aisle to approach me.

"Mary, let's go. I said all I needed to say. I'm not talking to any reporters. I'm sure Kim is waiting for us out in the corridor."

I made my way through by pushing and elbowing the crowd. My only words were, "No comment."

The marshals were yelling at people to leave the courtroom, but no one was paying any attention. This was a circus and the elephants had been let loose. I finally got to the rear of the courtroom as I navigated by people as gently as I could. I opened the door leading into the corridor. As soon as I stepped into the corridor, I found myself face to face with John Edison. His scowl spoke a thousand words. I couldn't have been happier.

"You really fucked everything up. I told you, if you broke our agreement I was going to come after you. You're done now," Mr. Edison fumed.

"I don't think it would be too smart for ZeiiMed to attempt an assault on me in my new role as a confidential government witness in a federal Grand Jury investigation of ZeiiMed. It just might be a little too obvious. The Feds will figure it out. But then again, ZeiiMed never has been too smart when it comes to assaulting lawyers."

"You're actually right," Edison responded loudly. "You have a free pass until the federal proceedings are over, at which time the sand will have run out of the hourglass for you."

"You do love to make threats. Just remember, I could have drained your blood once before and I guarantee I can do it again. I can't think of anything more enjoyable than watching the panic in your eyes as the blood gushes from your body in a steady stream of red fluid. You've met your match, you son of a bitch. But I actually hope you die of old age in a federal penitentiary. That way, I won't go to jail for murdering you."

The people surrounding us in the corridor started to step back, leaving Edison and I in the middle of a large circle of people staring at us. Kim pushed through the crowd and stood next to me as Edison and I faced each other a couple of feet apart.

"Honey, what's going on?" Kim asked with evident alarm. "Everyone heard you two exchanging vows of endearing love and are quietly waiting to hear more. Let's get out of here."

"Not yet. But I'm glad you're here, Kim. You wouldn't want to miss this. Mr. Edison was just explaining how he intends to physically harm us assuming the Feds don't throw him in solitary confinement for the rest of his life."

"That's right," Edison interrupted, lowering his voice as he leaned closer to Kim, "and not just your husband is a target. We're going to hit you also and hurt you bad."

In a split second, Kim violently kicked Edison, striking him in the shin with the narrow point of her high heels. She struck with such force I'm sure she fractured a bone in his leg. In fact, the sound of the cracking bone echoed down the corridor. Edison fell to the floor, holding his leg.

"You do what you have to do, Mr. Edison. But just remember, we will be waiting for you and, when you miss, our revenge will be unmerciful," Kim said.

I grabbed Kim's arm and led her to the stairs.

"Time to go, honey. Let's not get arrested for assault and battery."

Edison was still on the floor, moaning in pain.

We left the courthouse and got into a cab.

"I'm very proud of you," I said softly to Kim, as the taxi entered the flow of traffic.

Kim seemed to be in shock so I put my arm around her as we proceeded in silence. I enjoyed the mental image of Edison collapsed in the hallway in the grip of agonizing pain.

Chapter 41

Five months passed quietly. It was early March 2010. I was fairly secure in the belief that ZeiiMed would keep its distance until the Grand Jury either returned an indictment or declined to do so. Since a Grand Jury functions in secrecy, I would not learn of its decision until a public announcement by the Department of Justice.

Nonetheless, I felt reasonably certain I would eventually be contacted by an attorney from the Department of Justice to talk about the DOJ's investigation of ZeiiMed. After all, I had become rather newsworthy as a result of my public statements at the Fairness Hearing. The media picked up on my accusations against ZeiiMed and the story seemed to be everywhere on the internet, radio and television. If I started a blog or made daily updates on Twitter, I suspect I would have quite a following. But I didn't embrace my notoriety despite my belief that the publicity helped to keep me alive.

Then, as I anticipated, the call came.

"Hello, Mr. Bradford, my name is Peter McAtee. I'm a Deputy Assistant Attorney General with the Criminal Division of the Department of Justice, specializing in Organized Crime and Racketeering."

"Nice to hear from you, Mr. McAtee. I figured I would get a call from the DOJ sooner or later. What can I do for you?"

"To quickly update you, let me tell you what happened after the Judge at the Fairness Hearing referred the transcript of the Hearing to the DOJ. The Deputy Attorney General signed a letter of authority directing me to convene a Grand Jury to determine if there was probable cause to believe a violation of federal law was committed by ZeiiMed and/or its officers and directors. The letter of authority was filed in Federal Court in the Southern District of New York and a Grand Jury of twenty-three jurors was empaneled. It wasn't easy because it seemed every potential juror had a conflict of interest because ZeiiMed was their health care provider. I'm now in charge of presenting evidence to the Grand Jury through documents and witnesses obtained by serving subpoenas."

"That's great. You don't need a subpoena to get my cooperation," I stated.

"I need to speak with you about the information I've accumulated to date and the best way to present that information to the Grand Jury. I'll be candid with you. I've run into some real roadblocks that I'll explain when we meet."

"I'll assist you any way I can. Where do you want to meet and when?"

"How about the St. Regis? Tomorrow night at 7:00?" asked Peter.

"That's fine. I'll see you then. How will I know who to look for?"

"Don't worry. I'll find you, Mr. Bradford. Your YouTube video has been played often enough. I know what you look like."

"Okay, see you then," I responded and hung up.

YouTube? I guess someone secretly recorded a video of the Fairness Hearing on a smart phone.

The St. Regis? I'm surprised by the choice. The government certainly won't reimburse his expense receipts for the high-priced drinks there. I guess Mr. McAtee assumes I'll pick up the tab. Actually, I liked the place a lot and have been there often. It's a New York City classic that's world famous and it's world famous because it's a New York City classic. The sophisticated lounge is called the King Cole Bar and it's located inside the landmark St. Regis Hotel, located at 2 East 55th Street.

The St. Regis, completed in 1904, has gold-plated revolving doors and a marble-paneled reception area. Just past the reception area is the elevator bank and then the elegant Astor Court adorned by crystal chandeliers. High tea is served in fine China on small tables with well-starched, white linen table cloths. A large harp is displayed below a high, gold-trimmed ceiling surrounded by colorful wall prints of majestic biblical scenes. On the far side of the Astor Court is the front door of the Bar.

Upon entering the King Cole Bar, your attention is immediately focused on a huge eight-foot-tall mural by Maxfield Parrish, copyright 1906, that extends the entire length of the thirty-foot wall just above the bar. The mural is about twenty feet from the entrance of the King Cole Bar. There are seven small cocktail tables to the left and right of a walkway in the middle of the room.

The mural features a smirking Old King Cole sitting on his outdoor marble throne with servants and jesters on each side of the throne providing music, comical entertainment and refreshments, while his feet rest gently on a regal cushion. Two guards, each with a six-foot gold spear, have a peculiar expression of dumbfounded skepticism regarding whether the King will appreciate his subjects' strenuous efforts to grace him with every worldly comfort.

The bar itself is small, with only seven or eight bar stools along its length. There are two additional stools at the end of the dark wood bar, after it turns ninety degrees and extends an additional four feet before connecting with the wall. Despite the very expensive drinks and the opulent ornamentation of this five-star hotel, the bartenders are down to earth and engaging.

I arrived early to select where we would sit. The two stools at the very end of the bar were empty and would afford us some degree of privacy, despite the fact that most of the patrons were there to gawk and critique the other patrons.

I had just taken my first sip of beer when Peter McAtee approached me.

"Mr. Bradford? I'm Peter. Nice to meet you."

"Hi. It's a pleasure to meet you. We're lucky to have two seats together. At this time of the evening the place is usually packed," I stated.

We shook hands. He sat and ordered the specialty of the house, a Bloody Mary. He was young, probably around thirty-two. His jet-black hair was short with an oily sheen to it. His eyes looked weary and his sunken cheeks darkened by the shadow of very thick facial hair that hadn't been shaved since early morning. I guess he had been working long hours on the case. His navy-blue suit was wrinkled and his red tie askew.

"Thanks again for meeting me here. I actually have my office at the DOJ in Washington, but got assigned this Grand Jury because I'm admitted to practice in the Southern District of New York. While I'm in town on the case, the St. Regis was on my list of tourist attractions to visit," Peter said.

"Good choice. There are few bars in the City with the unique combination of wealth, charm and friendliness. Everyone likes it here," I replied. "By the way, you don't appear Irish. The name threw me off."

"My father had one hundred percent pure green Irish blood. He married a lovely Italian woman with long dark hair right off the boat. It was love at first sight, I'm told."

"Interesting," I commented. "It's amazing how many times I've heard a similar story."

"I'm pretty tired, so if you don't mind, I'll get right down to business. As I said on the phone, I'm with the Organized Crime and Racketeering Section of the DOJ. I specialize in criminal prosecutions that allege an unlawful pattern of racketeering activity that affects interstate commerce through the fraudulent use of the mails or internet, all in violation of RICO, the Racketeer Influenced and Corrupt Organizations Act."

Peter continued, "RICO was intended by Congress to deter the unlawful activities of organized crime, but it has been broadened to include any criminal enterprise. My job is to convince at least twelve of the twenty-three Grand Jurors that ZeiiMed and its affiliated companies are a criminal enterprise with probable cause to believe that a crime was committed by a pattern of racketeering activity. To do that, I have to demonstrate a scheme to underpay the hospitals and doctors, with an intent to use the unlawful profits to continue the function of the criminal enterprise."

"It seems a bit vague and circular, but I'm sure you've done this successfully many times before," I commented.

"Well, yes. But my successful RICO prosecutions have been against organized crime, not a multi-billion-dollar corporation that provides health insurance to millions of Americans. In fact, it's kind of a joke around the office that the Irishman with his mother's Italian looks has a natural gift for putting members of the Cosa Nostra behind bars. Personally, I don't see the humor, but that's another story. The point is that I'm not dealing with the Mafia. I need to discuss with you the problems I'm having in getting evidence against ZeiiMed before the Grand Jury."

"Let me know what's been done so far and I'll see what help I can offer," I said.

"I'll start with ZeiiMed. Of course, I served a subpoena on the company to get every piece of paper and electronically stored information pertaining to the outdated Depressor Data. ZeiiMed responded that everything was destroyed because the case was settled. Turns out everything is gone, including every piece of paper that had anything to do with how the Depressor Data was accumulated and then utilized to underpay the doctors and hospitals nationwide."

"Quite candidly, it doesn't surprise me in the slightest. You are dealing with a formidable and ruthless opponent in ZeiiMed," I said. "But I'm sure my law firm still has most of the documents I obtained in discovery from ZeiiMed."

"No, there's nothing there either. When Mr. Giulini got the case from you and substituted as attorney of record for the plaintiffs, all the boxes of ZeiiMed documents in your office were delivered to him, including the Depressor Data and the inculpatory emails your office identified. Guess what?"

"Go ahead, I'm all ears."

"Giulini destroyed it all before we contacted him. Again, his excuse was that the case settled. Your law firm kept no copies and completely deleted from its computers the web site of documents produced by ZeiiMed, as well as every CD. Apparently, Giulini instructed your firm to do so in order to avoid any chance that some documents could be accidentally revealed to third parties in violation of the Confidentiality Agreement that was 'So Ordered' by the Court at the beginning of the case. Also, a revised

Confidentiality Agreement recently signed by Giulini and ZeiiMed specifically provided that all documents and ESI produced in the litigation would be destroyed once a settlement was approved by the Court. So that's exactly what they did once the case settled. That's the story I'm getting anyway."

"If you ask me, it seems likely that Mr. Giulini has some connection with ZeiiMed that makes me very uncomfortable. ZeiiMed may be telling him what to do and when to do it. When it comes to ZeiiMed, you just can't trust anyone and always work on the assumption that ZeiiMed has its claws in everyone," I stated.

"Since I don't have the Depressor Data or ESI to present to the Grand Jury, I need a new strategy for getting the indictment. Essentially, I'm left with the oral testimony of John Edison and Robert Finley. Assuming that I can get some damning admissions out of them, I can then follow up with your testimony to wrap up the whole story in a pretty package with a bow," Peter said.

"Don't count on Edison giving you anything. I guarantee he will fight you all the way and deny, deny, deny. Of course, Finley turned against ZeiiMed in his deposition and knows he can be hit with a perjury charge if he deviates from his prior testimony. And, you better have some police watch over Finley or he won't make it to Court alive. Do you have a copy of his deposition transcript?"

"Believe it or not, I don't. The DOJ had a hell of a time running down the stenographer and finally found her in Tuscany. Guess what? She has permanently relocated and has no record of the transcript. She had sent the transcript and a CD of the testimony to you and Wadsworth, but then deleted every trace of it in her computer. Wiped it clean with no Cloud backup. As I said, your firm has nothing left and

Tweed, Fox & Fortune also destroyed everything once the parties agreed to the settlement. The DOJ may go after Tweed, Fox & Fortune for spoliation of evidence, but I still have no incriminating documents to use against ZeiiMed.”

“Did the court reporter say why she moved to Italy? I’m curious because it seems to be ZeiiMed’s place of choice to send inconvenient ladies.”

“No. Just that she had an opportunity to change careers that she couldn’t pass up. Apparently, she suddenly owned acres of wine country and went into the grape growing business.”

“You’re learning a painful lesson about what it’s like to go up against ZeiiMed,” I replied. “Look on the bright side—at least ZeiiMed hasn’t tried to physically harm you.”

“Very funny.”

“It wasn’t meant as a joke,” I responded.

“I’m hoping we’ll find a copy of the transcript, but I’ll probably have to proceed without it. By the time I question Finley before the Grand Jury, maybe my investigator can find the video of his deposition.”

“Don’t get your hopes up,” I commented.

“I won’t. I’m a big boy and I understand that ZeiiMed is a formidable opponent.”

“How about the police? Has any evidence turned up that can trace the deaths of either Martin Brown, Stanley Hyman, John Jarrett, or Charles Wadsworth back to ZeiiMed?” I asked.

“No, nothing. The cops have gotten nowhere trying to figure out who committed the murders. The one that really bothers me is Jarrett. His death was a cold-blooded execution. The others died while in a bed, supposedly receiving medical care. Maybe they did die of natural causes,” Peter said.

"Not a chance. It was ZeiiMed, there is no doubt in my mind. You don't know it, but Detective Jack was a friend of mine and a day doesn't go by without a prayer for him. But no one will ever be able to prove that ZeiiMed was responsible. Speaking of proof, why can't you get from ZeiiMed all the documentation generated within the last six months in payments to the doctors or hospitals. Every day ZeiiMed issues checks to the medical industry. There has to be some recent records you can obtain by subpoena," I suggested.

"I did that. ZeiiMed produced all its documentation created in the last six months, including all emails, statistical data and paper files accumulated by ZeiiMed in creating its formula for calculating reimbursements in several different geographical areas nationwide. Guess what? My entire team of DOJ lawyers couldn't find a scintilla of evidence that ZeiiMed was underpaying. Obviously, ZeiiMed knows the heat is on and has temporarily changed its way of doing business."

"It won't last. That I can guarantee," I said. "ZeiiMed is an unrelenting, unforgiving machine that simply will not stop its way of doing business, although it may pause strategically for short periods of time, if necessary."

"By the way," Peter said, "I've read your comments to the Court during the Fairness Hearing a number of times. You seemed bitter at the Office of the New York Attorney General for ceasing its investigation of ZeiiMed."

"Yes, I believe ZeiiMed was let off the hook by the New York Attorney General's Office. I thought the NYAG was my last and best hope to get ZeiiMed and its executives exposed to the light of day."

"You shouldn't feel that way," Peter replied. "The Attorney General's Office did everything it could once you sent in your letter with the inculpatory emails. Their job was to make sure the harm done to the doctors and hospitals was rectified by a fair and equitable restitution, coupled with an injunction from the Court prohibiting future wrongful conduct. In fact, it was the New York Attorney General that got the settlement amount to the enormous sum of one billion dollars. Restitution and Repair—that's what the NYAG does and that's what they did here. It's now the DOJ's job to try and get a criminal conviction based on a breach of federal law."

"Sure, I understand. Between ZeiiMed's threats and the constant worry about what's around the next corner, I've gotten pretty paranoid that ZeiiMed has control and influence over everything and everybody, including the NYAG. Of course, I don't have any first-hand knowledge so I'm glad to learn that the NYAG did its job and did its best."

"One thing is for sure. ZeiiMed doesn't control the DOJ and I will do the best I can even though I don't have a lot to work with," Peter promised.

"Okay. So, you're set with the plan to compel Edison and Finley to give testimony before your Grand Jury?"

"Yes, that's the plan," Peter confirmed.

"I know the Grand Jury Rules prohibit me from being present during the questioning of witnesses, but I'll be waiting outside the Grand Jury room in case you need me for anything," I offered.

"Sounds good," Peter said.

"When and where is the Grand Jury next scheduled to meet?"

Peter double-checked his pocket calendar.

"March 23, 2010, at the Federal Courthouse on Pearl Street. Just ask the Federal Marshal when you enter through security. It's not in a courtroom because the public is not allowed access."

"See you then," I said.

"Now let's have another drink and talk about something interesting, such as how the Washington Nationals and the New York Mets stack up against each other this year," I continued. "And, by the way, it's my treat. It's the least I can do to thank the DOJ for joining my quixotic pursuit of ZeiiMed."

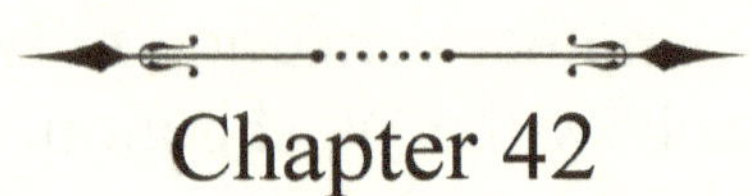

Chapter 42

Two days later, I dropped by *Très Bien* to see Meadhbh after I finished work. I took my usual place at the end of the bar. Meadhbh greeted me with a draft beer in a frosty cold glass.

"Nice to see you. It's about time you came to visit me," she said, in her usual piquant tone. She looked very nice. Her hair was soft and sensual. When she smiled, her green eyes sparkled as her dimples accentuated her glowing cheeks.

"Nice to see you, too. Is that for me?" I asked. "How did you know I was thirsty?"

"Just a lucky guess, but you are in a bar, you know," she responded. "By the way, before we continue with this theme of mutual friendship and fondness, I have a bone to pick with you. You acted like a total creep when you realized I was sitting next to your wife at the Fairness Hearing. The look of fear on your face couldn't have been more evident if you were face-to-face with a great white shark in Montauk. What did you think I was going to do? Tell your wife about the wild sex romps that we actually never had?"

"No, you just caught me a little off guard when I saw you there."

"Off guard? You were shell-shocked. You realized you had no choice but to reluctantly introduce us. You were then imagining that Kim and I would chat about you once you left to play super lawyer in front of the Bench. Wrong. It didn't happen that way. We didn't exchange war stories about you. For the record, I am not trying to break up your marriage and I don't want to be your mistress. We're friends and I like your wife a lot. Actually, I'm a simple girl. I'll be satisfied with an isolated 'roll in the hay' without any long-term emotional consequences."

Of course, I didn't know what to say. I may have said, "Okay," but I'm not really sure. I decided to go into the apology mode.

"I'm sorry I acted so awkwardly. I really was happy to see you and I have known Kim long enough to know she wasn't about to interrogate you about our relationship, although I'm not really sure what our relationship is," I said.

"You are hopeless," she said, without providing any illumination on the issue. "I mention a 'roll in the hay' and you don't say anything but apologize. Well, I am glad you stopped by anyway. I wanted to tell you how eloquently I thought you spoke in Court the other day. Also, I wanted to tell you what occurred after your little rendezvous with Edison in his apartment."

"Yes, I'm interested. There were no news articles about a break-in at Edison's apartment," I commented, "and thanks for the compliment."

"You didn't find any news article because the police never came. An ambulette showed up out front and carried a couple of people out. The vehicle had the words 'ZeiiMed Medical Services' on the side. It was over in a couple of minutes. The next morning, the window in the bathroom was filled with brick and mortar. Then, a couple of bulky looking guys approached me and provided a description of you. I said you had come in the night before and had a couple of beers, but I didn't know you and had never seen you before. It seemed to satisfy them. Now they have an army of security next door at Edison's apartment house. No way anyone is getting in there uninvited again."

"Which brings me to the reason I came here tonight. I need another favor," I said.

"Wouldn't you know? And I thought you dropped in because you simply couldn't live another day without seeing me. You really are a heartbreaker. Be right back, I'm needed down the other end of the bar. Can you believe someone actually wants a drink when I'm engaged in a conversation? The nerve of some people."

Five minutes later, she returned with a Guinness.

"Thank you," I said, putting a fifty-dollar bill on the bar.

"Don't mention it. So, tell me, what do you need? I've now gotten over your emotional shallowness."

"Does Edison come here anymore for dinner?" I asked.

"Yes, but he rarely eats alone and he's got this device that looks like a remote control for a car. It's actually some kind of silent alarm that can alert security next door if he needs help. I actually asked him about it one night because the device was sitting on his table and there weren't any keys attached to it."

"Here's what I'd like you to do," I said. "Call me the next time he comes in and is eating alone. I need to speak to him face-to-face, but not until March 23rd. Either the evening of the 23rd or any evening following the 23rd that he is in the restaurant. The best date of all would be the 23rd itself, so mark it on your calendar," I told her. "My number is on this piece of paper."

"Listen, honey, as much as I care for you and have enduring memories of our Kiss, I can't have you come in here and start beating up one of the customers. People around here have seen me talking to you and I could get blamed or worse, fired. It's one thing to make sure no one disturbs you while you go through the window in the bathroom, but it's another matter altogether for you to bloody Edison right here in the restaurant."

"No, I swear it's nothing like that. I only want to talk to him. No yelling, no screaming, no punches," I promised.

"What if he doesn't want to talk to you? What if he gets up and leaves or tells my manager to remove you. You said a lot of bad things about ZeiiMed at the Fairness Hearing and I was in the corridor outside the courtroom when he fell to the floor in pain. What happened to him anyway?"

"Kim kicked him. She probably cracked a bone."

"Good for her—but you see my point. Now that you mention it, Edison has been walking with quite a limp."

"Please believe me. I would never do anything that would cause you any trouble. You're my friend and I care for you. If he refuses to speak with me, I promise to leave quietly. I need this one opportunity and hopefully, I will never see him again. In fact, it's possible that something might happen on the 23rd that alleviates my need to speak to him, but I don't think I'll be that lucky."

"Alright, I'll do this for you. But what do I get out of it?' Meadhbh asked.

"What is it you want?" I responded, while thinking it was probably a mistake to ask such a question.

"I have to tell you? You're supposed to know. It doesn't count if I have to instruct you."

Now I was totally confused. But I've learned that admitting to confusion was a not a good idea. I decided to change the subject and hope for the best.

"I really do appreciate all the help you have given me. Assuming that I am eventually successful in getting ZeiiMed and Mr. Edison out of my life forever, we should go out and celebrate the conquest of good over evil," I said awkwardly.

"I get it. I have to wait for good to overcome evil before we can talk somewhere other than across the bar at my place of employment. I guess I'm in for a long wait."

"That's not what I meant."

"You do seem to have a hard time saying what you mean—no wonder you became a lawyer. But I will let you off the hook and merely say that I hope to see you soon."

"Yes, you will," I said. "On March 23rd or shortly after, depending on when Edison is here. Feel free to call me anytime at work."

"I do look forward to the next time. By the way, you can call me—it's in the dating manual."

I almost mentioned that we weren't dating, but luckily that didn't slip out.

"Bye now, love you. See you soon," I said.

"Love you back, I think. Say 'hi' to Kim for me," she responded.

I left the restaurant as bewildered as ever.

Chapter 43

The Grand Jury room at the Federal Courthouse on Pearl Street is located in an area separate and apart from the courtrooms. The purpose is to keep the Grand Jury proceedings out of public view. The proceedings are not open to the public and spectators are not permitted. The Grand Jury is intended to be shrouded in secrecy, with the Grand Jurors and the prosecutor prohibited from divulging anything that transpires during the proceedings.

The room where the Grand Jurors convene was institutional and unremarkable. There were twenty-three functional, plastic chairs placed around a long table in front of a raised, wooden platform with a box-like structure smaller than a judge's bench, but basically of the same design. The prosecutor from the DOJ sits in the box and faces the Grand Jury table and the Grand Jurors.

In the corner of the room was a chair for the witness. The witness chair is also surrounded by a box-like, wooden structure, but much less grand than that given the prosecutor. The witness chair faces the Grand Jurors and is only a few feet from their table. There is also an area for the Court reporter at the front of the room.

The waiting room for the witnesses is down the hall from the Grand Jury room. On March 23, 2010, I met Peter in the witness waiting room at 8:30 a.m.

"I'm going to proceed to question Robert Finley first today," Peter told me. "He should be here any moment now. Since the Grand Jury rules prohibit Mr. Finley from having his lawyer with him when he testifies, I'm hoping to get even more damaging testimony against ZeiiMed than you did during his deposition. Then I have Linda Santini coming to testify. I also subpoenaed your good friend, Mr. Edison."

"So, you probably won't need my testimony then?" I asked.

"That's right, I don't think I'll need your testimony. You could testify about the Depressor Data and the inculpatory emails you reviewed, but we don't have the documents themselves, except for a few, and that will impact your credibility. Also, you filed the Complaint hoping to get a big fee, so that makes you biased. I need a turncoat from inside ZeiiMed such as Finley to establish my RICO case and get an indictment," Peter responded.

"Did Finley's lawyer give you any clue as to how cooperative he will be?"

"No, he wouldn't tell me anything about how the testimony will go. But my staff did find the video of Finley's deposition, so I have some ammunition. By the way, it wasn't easy to find the video operator, but we finally ran him down. He's not in business anymore. He got a lot of harassing telephone calls trying to recover the original and all copies of the video. They paid a visit to his house. They said they were FBI, but it's clear they weren't. The video guy ended up selling them the original and all his copies, but one. He lied when he told them he didn't keep a copy. Then, he eventually gave the last copy to my investigator once he was convinced that it really was the Department of Justice that wanted the video," Peter explained.

"By the way, who is representing Finley?" I asked.

"Daniel Giulini," Peter said.

"He really gets around. One day he's representing the doctors and collecting a big fee, the next day he's representing a ZeiiMed employee. The guy has no ethics at all. He will do anything for money. What a sleaze.”

“I was pretty surprised myself. I’m sure ZeiiMed’s is paying him to defend Finley, even though Giulini can’t actually enter the Grand Jury room.”

“Well, I’m heading back to my office. Call me at the end of the day to let me know how it went,” I said.

“Will do. Let’s hope for the best and I’ll let you know how it turns out,” Peter said. “Thanks for your help.”

As I was leaving the courthouse, I ran into Giulini and Finley as they were entering. Giulini, the shorter of the two men, had his usual double-breasted, black suit and tie, but the bags under his eyes seemed more swollen and darker than usual. Finley looked much different from the last time I saw him. His stomach didn’t protrude as dramatically as it once did, but he had experienced significant hair loss, with a bent-over posture and grim look on his face.

“Hi, Danny. Fancy running into you here,” I started.

“Oh, hi, Brian. You remember Bob Finley. We’re in a rush. We’re late, we really have no time to talk.”

“I know you’re late and I know where you’re going,” I continued.

“The federal rules say it’s a secret who gets subpoenaed before the Grand Jury. You committed a crime if you discussed it with anyone,” Giulini said.

“I didn’t say anything about a Grand Jury, you did. I think I’ll report that disclosure. And if there is any questionable behavior, it’s yours. Have you ever heard of the Canons of Ethics or the Disciplinary Rules?”

“What are you talking about, Brian? I have to go.”

“I’ll tell you what I’m talking about. You are the lawyer for the Plaintiff doctors in the settlement of the Complaint against ZeiiMed. You pocketed a lot of money as counsel for the doctors. Now you're representing an employee of Defendant ZeiiMed with regard to the very same conduct that was the subject of the Complaint. You are once again getting paid by ZeiiMed, this time because you jumped ship and joined your adversary."

"So what? One case ended and I got a new client."

"No. You are a slave to money and you don't care what ethical rules you break to make a buck. You are an embarrassment to our profession. Plus, I think you've been on the ZeiiMed payroll all along. My guess is ZeiiMed paid you from Day One to paper the settlement quickly, get it approved and make sure I stopped mouthing off about ZeiiMed. Well, two out of three usually isn't bad, but when it comes to ZeiiMed no failure is acceptable, no matter how minor. You're lucky ZeiiMed was forgiving in your case. It won't happen again."

"Shut up and get out of my way," was all Giulini said.

"You better make sure Finley tells the truth. If you conspire with ZeiiMed to get Finley to change his testimony, you'll be disbarred and Finley will go to jail for perjury. On the other hand, if Finley decides not to conspire with ZeiiMed and tells the truth, then we all know his days are numbered. Quite a dilemma," I pointed out.

"Don't listen to Bradford," Giulini said to Finley, "He doesn't know what he's talking about. You'll be fine, just proceed as we discussed. If you have any questions or concerns you are allowed to stop the DOJ's questioning and consult with me in the separate room where I'll be sitting."

"Perjury? What does Mr. Bradford mean I may be charged with perjury? I don't want to go to jail. Why did he say my days are numbered," Finley inquired, with a tone of panic.

"You are not going to jail and no one is going to harm

you. Just proceed as we instructed you at the meeting in ZeiiMed's office," Giulini responded.

"Sounds like your witness is getting cold feet," I said to Giulini.

"We're leaving, get out of our way," Giulini answered.

"Sure, have a nice day. Keep in touch, Danny. We'll do lunch. I'm sure you can get ZeiiMed to pay," I said, unable to resist any opportunity to harass Giulini.

Danny and Finley proceeded on their way to the Grand Jury room.

I headed to my office with a sense of dread and a premonition that Peter and the DOJ were in for a very difficult day. ZeiiMed will do everything and anything to avoid indictment.

I have learned not to underestimate ZeiiMed.

It seems to always get what it wants.

Chapter 44

On March 23, 2010, Peter McAtee addressed twenty-three Grand Jurors from his seat at the front of the Grand Jury room. Mr. Finley was in the witness chair and the court reporter was present. It was 9:30 a.m.

BY MR. McATEE: Thank you, everyone, for being on time today. I am going to present live testimony from Mr. Finley, sitting to my right in the witness chair. Mr. Finley is currently employed by ZeiiMed. As you know from the documents I provided, each of you has a copy of a draft indictment against ZeiiMed. After the completion of the testimony today, I will ask you to vote to return the indictment against ZeiiMed based on your belief that there is probable cause to believe that a crime was committed, in this instance one or more criminal violations of RICO.

Also, for your review, you have been provided a copy of the federal RICO statute and some recent documents the DOJ obtained from ZeiiMed. As I mentioned before the live testimony today, the DOJ encountered great difficulty in obtaining the ZeiiMed documentation that reflects ZeiiMed's intentional use of outdated data to purposely underpay thousands of doctors that provide important medical care to you and your children. We have a few relevant documents, but most are unavailable due to ZeiiMed's illegal destruction of evidence.

Even worse, ZeiiMed then lied and misrepresented the criminal scheme to everyone. The few documents we do have are before you. I have played for you the videotaped deposition of Mr. Finley so you can compare it to his live testimony today. It is the position of the United States of America that the anticipated testimony you will hear today will be sufficient to support a return of the indictment.

However, I do want to mention that the DOJ has not met with Mr. Finley and does not know what Mr. Finley's actual testimony will be here today. Mr. Finley is represented by counsel, but the rules prohibit his attorney from being with him in the Grand Jury room during his testimony. Mr. Finley's counsel is sitting in the witness' waiting room and Mr. Finley is aware of his right to leave the Grand Jury room and consult privately with his counsel. I believe that covers all introductory matters, so let's begin.

EXAMINATION BY MR. McATEE:

Q. Good morning, Mr. Finley. How are you today?

A. Just fine. I'd rather be doing other things, but the DOJ has told me to be here, so here I am.

Q. And the government is glad you came. By way of introduction, my name is Peter McAtee and I am an attorney with the Department of Justice. I am here today to ask you some questions about ZeiiMed. I want you to relax and just answer each question as truthfully as possible. You are not the target of this Grand Jury investigation, so don't worry about that. Please remember you are under oath and sworn to tell the truth. Do you understand?

A. Yes, I do.

Q. What is your current position with ZeiiMed?

A. I have been with ZeiiMed for many years and I am now a Senior Vice President and the National Director of Computer Operations in North America.

Q. Do the computer operations that you are in charge of include responsibility for all payments made by ZeiiMed to all doctors, hospitals and other providers of medical services?

A. Yes.

Q. Please explain for the Grand Jurors your understanding of the terms old or outdated 'Depressor Data.'

A. I don't know. What do you mean?

Q. Yes, you do. You previously testified in a deposition what these terms refer to, after having given a misleading explanation when first asked the question.

A. I really don't remember, but I will say that some people at ZeiiMed use the slang 'Depressor Data.' But it's not an official term of art at ZeiiMed. ZeiiMed accumulates tons of data regarding the amounts charged by doctors nationwide and, in fact, all over North America. This raw data is referred to sometimes as the 'Depressor Data,' but it just refers to the data received from doctors regarding their billings. I never use the term and I don't personally know anyone at ZeiiMed that does. I don't think it's polite to collectively categorize highly trained doctors as 'Depressors,' which seems to describe the singular skill of using a tongue depressor to check for swollen glands. The term has a negative connotation that's not appropriate. Certainly, lawyers dislike it when people refer to them in negative stereotypes, such as ambulance chasers.

Q.   That is not what I am referring to. My question is this: For a period of time exceeding ten years, did ZeiiMed program its computers with obsolete data so that the reimbursements paid to the doctors were materially below the amounts that ZeiiMed agreed to pay in its health insurance contracts with the medical profession?

A.   That's a very complex question, with many parts. But my simple answer is 'No,' ZeiiMed didn't do what you said in your question.

Q.   Isn't it a fact that the data used by ZeiiMed to 'depress' or underpay the doctors was called the 'Depressor Data'?

A.   No, I'm not aware of that.

Q. Not   aware?   Didn't   you   receive   emails instructing you to use the oldest data available so the doctors would be underpaid and the profits increased. Isn't that correct?

A.   It's correct there are some emails that seem to say that. But it was all just a big misunderstanding. ZeiiMed never did that and never will. I suggest that if the DOJ has the so-called 'Depressor Data' you referred to, then show it to me and I'll tell you exactly what it means and what it is.

Q.   I'm in charge of this examination, not you. Your job here today is to answer my questions and not make suggestions. I have a videotape of your deposition. Are you saying that you lied under oath when you testified in your deposition regarding ZeiiMed's illicit scheme to intentionally underpay and cheat on payments to the doctors?

A. I was very ill during my deposition and the video reflects that. My attorney at the time actually cut short the deposition because I was so sick. So anything I said then should be disregarded. I was very disoriented and confused that day. Please don't hold me to anything I said because I didn't know what I was saying or why I said it.

Q. You are going to be charged with perjury if you don't withdraw what you just said and tell the truth. Are you going to do so?

A. I want to talk to my attorney.

Q. You have ten minutes, if you insist.

A. I insist.

Finley then left the Grand Jury Room to confer with Mr. Giulini and returned about fifteen minutes later. Mr. McAtee then continued with his questions.

BY MR. McATEE: Did you have the opportunity to consult with your attorney?

A. Yes.

Q. Did you provide false or inaccurate testimony to any question I asked you today?

A. (Pause.)

Q. Are you going to answer?

A. Yes, I will answer. The answer is a definite 'No.' I have not said anything that is incorrect, inaccurate, false or untrue in any manner whatsoever. I told you I was very ill at my deposition. I couldn't think coherently or speak accurately. Now that's the truth and the whole truth, as you lawyers say.

Q. In response to our subpoena, ZeiiMed

produced all your compensation records. I have determined from these records that ZeiiMed funded your 401(k) account with the sum of five hundred thousand dollars approximately thirty days ago. Is that correct?

A. Yes.

Q. Is it fair to say that this payment by ZeiiMed to your pension account was significantly in excess of the usual ten thousand-dollar pension fund payment made to you by ZeiiMed on a yearly basis?

A. Yes.

Q. Was this extraordinary payment made in return for your exculpatory testimony today in favor of ZeiiMed?

A. Absolutely not.

Q. What do you mean 'absolutely not'? You expect the Grand Jurors to believe that ZeiiMed did not make the payment to influence your testimony here today?

A. I'm not sure I understand the question, but I do a darn good job for ZeiiMed and earn every penny of the compensation I receive. ZeiiMed told me the pension bonus was in recognition of all my years of hard work and that's all there is to it.

Q. You are dismissed, subject to recall upon the return of an indictment against you for perjury. Do you understand?

A. I would like to thank all the Grand Jurors for your time and attention today. I know it may sound like I am changing my prior testimony, but I'm really not. The deposition was very adversarial, the attorneys were screaming at each other and I was so physically ill I couldn't think straight. I didn't know what I was saying that day. In fact, I couldn't think at all. Good day to you all.

Q. Mr. Finley, I said you are excused. Please leave and make no more self-serving and gratuitous statements to the Grand Jurors.

BY MR. McATEE: We will now take a fifteen-minute break. I will then begin my questioning of the next witness.

Peter left the Grand Jury room to see if his next witness, Linda Santini, was in the waiting room. She was present, sitting with her attorney. The attorney rose to greet Peter.

"Good morning, sir. My name is Lucas Bujoin and I am Ms. Santini's attorney. I think you'll find she doesn't have a lot of knowledge about the issues you are interested in and, hopefully, this will not take too long."

Lucas was a dashing figure with a firm handshake. He was very slim, of average height, wearing John Lennon glasses with thick lenses. His treated blond hair was long and shaggy, in contrast to the dark hair of his razor thin mustache and dense eyebrows. At first blush, he appeared to be a bookworm, but his tightly tailored suit gave him a European flair. He also stood inches from Peter's face so that the smell of the onions from his home fries that morning filled Peter's nostrils.

"Step back and take a deep breath. You are here because your client was served with a subpoena and I'll decide what she knows and doesn't know and how long it will take to determine each. Ms. Santini, we are ready for you now. I will accompany you to the Grand Jury Room. Mr. Bujoin, please make yourself comfortable. We will see you after we're done."

"Bye, Lucas. I'll be back in plenty of time for us to do lunch," Linda said in a street-smart Brooklyn accent.

The Grand Jurors were in their seats as Ms. Santini entered the room and walked to the witness chair. She was about forty-five years old, with very short hair that spiked straight up on the top of her head. She had ten studs in the lobe and outer rim of each ear, with bright and abundant blue eye shadow. Her dress was short, maybe a little too short for court, but she had a nice figure.

BY MR. McATEE: Good morning, Ms. Santini. Thank you for your attendance here today. For the record, is your appearance here today in compliance with the subpoena that my office served on you?

A. Yes, I was served with a subpoena and my lawyer, Mr. Lucas Bujoin, told me it was necessary to appear. He really is very cute and smart, too.

Q. Yes. I just met him. He seems very bright, although I don't think I'll comment on whether he classifies as 'cute' or not. Getting back to business, I will remind you that you are sworn to tell the truth and nothing but the truth. You will be subject to prosecution for perjury if you violate this oath. Do you understand?

A. Oh, yes, I understand completely. Lucas, I mean Mr. Bujoin, explained everything and I listened to every word he said.

Q. Did you meet today with Mr. Bujoin over breakfast to discuss your testimony here today?

A. Yes, we met at the diner and generally discussed the questions you might be asking me.

Q. How were the home fries at the diner?

A. Good. I mean they looked good. I didn't order

them, but Mr. Bujoin did.

Q.   Yes, I thought he did. How long did you spend with Mr. Bujoin discussing your testimony?

A.   Not long. Maybe half an hour. Hey, were you at the diner? How did you know what Mr. Bujoin ordered?

Q.   It's not important and, no, I was not at the diner and no one from the DOJ was observing you. Did Mr. Bujoin show you any documents to review?

A.   Yes, he showed me an email I wrote to Mr. Finley in April 2001.

Q.   Yes, I will ask you about that. It's one of the few ZeiiMed documents we have. But, I don't want you to tell me what you discussed with Mr. Bujoin regarding the email, because communications with your lawyer are privileged. By the way, are you paying for Mr. Bujoin's services as your lawyer?

A.   No. ZeiiMed is paying his law firm. I think it's called Tweed, Fox & Fortune. I joked to Lucas that he always looks like a 'fortune.'

Q.   And ZeiiMed is your employer, correct?

A.   Yes, I am a Senior Supervisor responsible for computer operations in the tri-state area.

Q.   In April of 2001, did you become aware that ZeiiMed had reprogrammed its computers to significantly reduce the payments to the doctors that treated patients with health insurance from ZeiiMed?

A.   At one time, I thought I had discovered some incorrect programming of the computer software that runs the doctors' reimbursement programs. It wasn't a big deal. People make mistakes all the time, but they were discovered and corrected with retroactive adjustments if there were underpayments or overpayments. I notified management, but before I could follow through on the issue, I was transferred to ZeiiMed's office in Vincennes, Indiana. I don't know what happened after I sent my April 2001 email to Mr. Finley, but I'm sure the computer problem was corrected quickly as is our custom and practice.

Q. Why were you transferred to Indiana?

A. I never really got a good answer to that question from my boss. I didn't want to go, but I was told I had no choice.

Q. Where are you currently living?

A. Both my home and the ZeiiMed office I now work at are in New Jersey. About six months ago, I was overjoyed to learn that I had received a major promotion to my current position and was transferred back to New Jersey. It was just wonderful.

Q. Did ZeiiMed provide you with financial assistance in connection with your move? I will give you fair warning that the Justice Department has obtained copies of all your banking statements and records.

A. Yes, ZeiiMed was very generous. Not only did the Company pay my moving expenses, but ZeiiMed also helped me find a beautiful home on a picturesque tree-lined street in Chatham and paid the down payment on the house. I am very, very grateful to my employer.

Q. So then, isn't it a fact that no matter what I ask you about ZeiiMed, you wouldn't say anything negative?

A. Well, that's probably correct. I'm not going to lie for ZeiiMed, but I certainly don't have anything but good things to say about my employer.

Q.   Even if you knew ZeiiMed was involved in an intentional criminal scheme that violates federal law, you wouldn't tell me, would you?

A.   That question really doesn't make sense. There is no such conspiracy or violation of federal law so how can I answer that? You are making up a total fabrication and then asking me to respond as if your fantasy world was true. How can I possibly do that? I can't. You told me I better tell the truth here today and that's exactly what I'm doing.

Q.   Thank you for your time here today. You are now dismissed. No more questions.

A.   Thank you. I don't mean to be difficult, but I can't testify about something that doesn't exist. You know what I mean? It's really simple. It was nice meeting you. So long.

BY MR. McATEE: Ladies and gentlemen of this Grand Jury, we are going to break for lunch. We will resume at 2:00 p.m. with the last and final witness before you commence your deliberations. Please return promptly from lunch.

After catching a quick sandwich, Peter went immediately to the waiting room to see if the next witness had appeared in response to the subpoena. As Peter entered the room, he was again met by the suave Lucas Bujoin.

"What are you still doing here? Your client finished before lunch and I dismissed her," Peter said.

"Yes, I know. I'm here with another of my clients, John Edison, and he is ready to proceed. He is a very busy executive, running a billion-dollar company. He has many time-consuming responsibilities so I would like to proceed as expeditiously as possible."

"Can I talk to Mr. Edison for a few minutes before we get started?" Peter asked.

"Come on, Peter. You know the rules. No sneak previews. Once he is on the stand, you can ask him anything you want, but you won't know his answers until he provides them in front of the Grand Jurors."

"Okay, okay. Let's get started. Tell Mr. Edison to come into the Grand Jury Room."

The Grand Jurors had reassembled after lunch. Peter took his seat. Mr. Edison walked in and sat in the witness chair in front of the Grand Jurors. Peter noticed that Edison's smug grin imparted a sense of superiority, with his ice-blue eyes projecting an intimidating presence. Peter suspected that his examination of Mr. Edison would be challenging and very adversarial. He would need to use all his skills and experience to keep this guy under control.

BY MR. McATEE: Good afternoon, Mr. Edison. Since the Grand Jurors may not be aware of your position, I will start by mentioning that you are currently the Chief Executive Officer of ZeiiMed.

A. Yes, and Chairman of the Board.

Q. Congratulations, I wasn't aware of your promotion. As the CEO of ZeiiMed, what are your current job responsibilities?

A. I try to efficiently run a very big company that employs a lot of people. I hire the best managers I can find because I certainly can't do everything by myself.

Q. As is my custom and practice for all witnesses, I will remind you that you are under oath and will be charged with perjury if you fail to tell the truth. Do you understand?

A. What's wrong with you? Of course, I understand. You don't need to intimidate me by throwing your perjury speech in my face. I showed up here today and agreed to testify without making a motion to quash the subpoena. I'm insulted that you feel the need to lecture me about the punishment you will inflict if I don't do exactly as I'm told.

Q. No more speeches please, Mr. Edison. Let's just move along. Isn't it a fact that your main purpose as the head of ZeiiMed is to generate profits?

A. Well, that is essentially correct, but within limits. ZeiiMed first and foremost strives to bring the best possible medical care to the people that purchase health insurance from us.

Q. But you can't provide medical care to anyone unless you make money. Making money is the objective—the primary goal, without which everything else falls apart. Correct?

A. I'm not going to argue the point. Yes, of course, we are out to make money.

Q. And what is the biggest expense at ZeiiMed? That is, what is the single biggest item on ZeiiMed's balance sheet that draws the most money out of ZeiiMed?

A. That's easy. ZeiiMed's biggest expense is the money it pays to the doctors and the hospitals for providing medical treatment to the patients that have health insurance with ZeiiMed.

Q. So the more money you pay to the doctors, the less your profits are?

A. That is an overly simplistic analysis, but essentially correct.

Q. So, the less you pay to the doctors, the more

money ZeiiMed gets to keep. Is that also accurate?

A. I think I just answered that.

Q. Isn't it a fact that you instruct your managers to institute procedures and practices to keep the payments to the doctors as low as possible?

A. I admit we do keep close watch on the money going out to the doctors. We make sure we are getting the best medical services for the lowest price possible.

Q. What I'm hearing is this. ZeiiMed wants greater profits and knows the best way to get it is to pay less to the doctors. Isn't that right?

A. Well, technically yes. But in reality...

Q. I didn't ask you to explain. Just answer 'Yes' or 'No.'

A. I don't think I can without an explanation. You are trying to intimidate me again.

Q. Yes, you can. It's simple. Just state your sworn answer on the record. Please do so now.

A. Within those strict limitations, the answer is 'yes.' But I'm not comfortable with the way you are manipulating my responses. Maybe I should talk to my lawyer.

Q. That's fine. But I have a few more questions before I finish this topic. Isn't it a fact that the easiest way to diminish the payments to the doctors is to instruct your managers to program your computers to automatically reduce across the board, the money paid to the doctors throughout the country?

A. Well, that would be one way to reduce ZeiiMed's costs and increase its profits, but I'm not admitting that I told my staff to illegally manipulate our computers in that manner.

Q. Isn't it a fact that in 2001, when you were an executive vice president in New York, you instructed Mr. Finley to use the oldest data available in calculating payments to the physicians?

A. Now that's a direct question and I will provide a direct answer. Of course, the answer is that I did not, except for a very limited test case we were conducting with respect to doctors in rural Alabama. I was concerned because I had been informed that these country doctors were charging rates below anything we had in our computer records going back ten years. I demanded an investigation and if it turned out to be true, I wanted to make sure we increased our Alabama reimbursements up to a reasonable minimum compensation, even if the actual amount paid was above the amount of their actual invoices. The point was that if ZeiiMed didn't make sure their compensation was at a basic level to sustain them, someday there would be no doctors left in rural Alabama. The doctor may charge ten dollars for the office visit, but I made sure our payment to the doctor was a lot more than that.

Q. So, you are telling me there was no intentional underpayment of doctors nationwide through the use of what has been referred to as the outdated 'Depressor Data' programmed into ZeiiMed's computers?

A. That is exactly what I am telling you. What don't you understand about my answer? How dare you drag me before this Grand Jury and ask me insulting and rude questions that clearly imply that I broke the law and my company broke the law. I am outraged. I need a break to compose myself. I want, no I demand, an opportunity to speak with my lawyer, Mr. Bujoin.

Q. We just began the questioning. I suggest we proceed for an hour or so and then take a break so you can confer with counsel. Agreed?

A. No. I know my rights and I want to speak with Mr. Bujoin right now. Please direct the stenographer to stop recording and permit me to leave the Grand Jury room. My understanding is you have no choice. You must grant my request.

BY MR. McATEE: Very well. We will now have a short adjournment so Mr. Edison can meet privately with his attorney. Let the record so reflect. You have fifteen minutes.

Mr. Edison exited the Grand Jury Room and headed to the waiting room to meet with Mr. Bujoin.

"I'm surprised to see you so soon. Did something happen out there?" Lucas asked.

"Don't be a fool. Of course, something happened. That stupid Justice Department lawyer just asked me if I intentionally manipulated the Depressor Data."

"In other words, he asked you if you committed a felony?"

"Yes, exactly right."

"Remember, we discussed that a question like that would be asked of you. We prepared for that," Lucas reminded Edison.

"I know, I know, but I got flustered nonetheless."

"So, go with the game plan we talked about. Stick to the script. The President himself has now made you one of the top federal officials in the country for federal health care programs. Don't mince words. Hit him with the news right between the eyes. The Justice Department can't touch you now. You are invincible," Mr. Bujoin coached him.

"Alright, exactly how do I handle this?" Edison asked.

"You go back to the Grand Jury Room and immediately say that you have a statement for the record. McAtee may try to stop you from speaking, but he can't stop you from making your statement. Just refuse to answer any further questions until you've made your statement on the record. Be tough. You're in the driver's seat."

"Okay. I understand. I'm ready to go out there and blow them away," Edison responded.

Mr. Edison returned to the Grand Jury Room to continue his testimony.

> BY MR. McATEE: Mr. Edison are you now ready to proceed after meeting with your attorney?
>
> A. I am. But before the questioning resumes, I have an important statement to make.
>
> Q. You are not running these proceedings, I am. You are here to answer my questions or be held in contempt. Do you understand?
>
> A. Yes, I do and I will answer all of your questions truthfully for as long as it takes. But first, I must insist on making certain remarks which will materially impact this Grand Jury. If you refuse, I request an opportunity to speak directly to the Judge in charge of this Grand Jury. My comments are that significant.
>
> Q. We cannot delay these proceedings in order to schedule an appearance before the Judge. But, in the spirit of full disclosure and compromise, I will permit you to make a short statement and we will then continue with my questions without any further

interruptions. Do you agree?

A.   Yes. I would like to be the first to tell everyone here that I am happy to announce that this morning President Obama signed into law the Patient Protection and Affordable Care Act. The Act will provide insurance coverage to over thirty-two million uninsured Americans and will forever prohibit insurance companies from denying coverage to children with pre-existing conditions. Coverage must now be made available and at affordable, subsidized rates depending on the family's income.

Q.   Isn't it a fact that ZeiiMed will now have millions of additional opportunities to implement its objective of underpaying the medical profession for the essential medical services needed by their patients?

A.   As I said, ZeiiMed vehemently denies any such intention and categorically denies your accusation. Also, I am proud to tell you that today I was nominated by the President to be the new Administrator of the Centers for Medicare and Medicaid Services, which will have over 16 million new enrollees by 2020, all of which are poor and/or elderly. The position will also include primary responsibility for the Children's Health Insurance Program.

This nomination is a personal honor that I humbly embrace, in addition to the previously announced appointment of ZeiiMed as National Administrator designated to oversee and supervise the new health care law. The new health care legislation now signed into law will bestow on me, as the newly nominated Administrator for Medicare and Medicaid Services, the legal obligation to reduce payments to doctors in these federal programs by over four hundred billion dollars without reducing benefits. So, you see, while the DOJ thinks ZeiiMed committed a federal crime by reducing payments to doctors, the President has personally directed me to do just that pursuant to the authority given me by the new law. I think your bosses should call the White House to make sure that your respective branches of the federal government are not taking positions inconsistent with the mandate of the President.

In fact, the DOJ will be the attorneys that prosecute any Medicare or Medicaid fraud while I am Administrator. So, Mr. McAtee, we will probably be working together in the future. I may take a two-year leave of absence from ZeiiMed in order to accept the position of Administrator, but I haven't yet made a final decision on that.

BY MR. McATEE: In view of these new developments, I believe I am required to suspend all further questioning. Since you have been asked to serve the Government as the Administrator, a conflict of interest may exist and further testimony is precluded. If you lied, a marshal will escort you back here to finish your testimony. You are dismissed.

Ladies and gentlemen of the Grand Jury, I am now going to ask you to begin your deliberations on whether to return the indictment against ZeiiMed. This requires a vote of twelve or more members. I have previously explained the law at issue and provided you with a folder of documents discussing the RICO statute.

Your only task is to determine whether there is

probable cause to believe that a crime was committed and that ZeiiMed committed it through the acts of its managers and/or employees acting at the direction of its executives. Please let me know when you have rendered your decision.

Peter slowly walked out of the Grand Jury Room, masking, as best he could, his severe disappointment in the job he had done.

Chapter 45

Peter McAtee was not surprised in the least when he learned at 4 p.m. on March 23, 2010 that the members of the Grand Jury had decided not to return an indictment.

Peter tried to convince himself that it wasn't his fault.

The witnesses were probably lying, but there was no evidence to disprove the lies. Of course, that was why the lies were told in the first place.

Without a "turncoat" witness and practically no documents to demonstrate the Depressor Data, it was a hopeless task. A handful of incriminating emails can sometimes result in a criminal indictment, but not always and not this time.

Of course, his bosses at the DOJ in Washington would not look at it that way. The outcome would be considered a mark against his career. He would just have to work harder and do better in the future.

Maybe it was a major miscalculation not to have Brian Bradford testify, but it was too late now.

Peter headed for Amtrak to take the train back to D.C. He had packed his bags the night before and was ready to go.

Before he got on the train, Peter called Brian to let him know what had happened. Brian expressed dismay, but told Peter it wasn't his fault. However, it was Brian's last comment that caused Peter some concern. Brian mentioned that his war with ZeiiMed was still far from over.

Chapter 46

It was 6:30 p.m. on the evening of March 23, 2010. Brian Bradford was still at his office in New York City. However, he didn't seem to be getting much legal work accomplished. The call earlier in the day from Peter McAtee of the DOJ was upsetting. There would be no indictment against ZeiiMed or any of its enablers.

Of course, Brian knew all along that somehow ZeiiMed would avoid indictment. ZeiiMed seems to always win and always knows exactly what's needed to accomplish its purpose. The threat of a perjury charge by the DOJ was just a mild annoyance to the witnesses when compared to the rewards given by ZeiiMed for obedience and the misery inflicted for disobedience.

Once again, Brian became abundantly aware that the only way to keep ZeiiMed at bay was to take matters into his own hands and do it himself. Now that the DOJ had packed its bags and gone home, he was once again a target. Edison would not forget and ZeiiMed would not relent.

The phone on his desk rang. Brian picked it up.

"Hello, cutie. I guess if I don't take the initiative and dial you up, our relationship would be over," Meadhbh said, in a lubricious tone.

"I didn't know we had a relationship," I responded.

"Not this conversation again—once was enough."

"Okay, I'll change the subject. It's nice to hear from you, as always. Are you at work?" I asked.

"Yes, I am, so this will be short. You asked me to call you

when Edison came in alone. Guess what? Tonight is the night. He's sitting at a table and no one is with him. I already brought him a drink and confirmed he was dining alone."

"Good. Thank you so much for the information. I'm on my way over. See you in a little while."

"I look forward to all our precious moments together," she said in her unique style of humor.

Before heading to *Très Bien*, there were a couple of items I needed to bring with me.

First, my four-inch, folding razor knife. I had promised Meadhbh no violence in the restaurant, but I may need the weapon to make my point of view more convincing during our discussion.

Second, I was taking with me one hundred milligrams of the drug ketamine, in a white powder form for oral consumption. On an empty stomach, it will kick in after about five minutes. Basically, the drug is used as anesthesia for animals. But, at the low dose I was going to use, Edison will experience a mellow, dream-like feeling of detachment and disassociation of mind and body, coupled with a sedating effect. It will also cause a slight loss of his sense of balance. Basically, the drug will keep Edison in his seat, forced to listen to me without a high level of anxiousness or a desire to walk away.

Ketamine is tasteless and quickly dissolve in a drink, with the effects lasting an hour or so. It can be easily bought on the internet from a supplier in China. While ketamine can be a very dangerous drug at higher doses, the amount I intended to give Edison will simply make sure I have a captive audience without any potential for physical harm— to him or me. After all, I did make a promise to Meadhbh of no bloodshed and I intended to keep it. I hoped so, anyway.

Chapter 47

I arrived at *Très Bien* and took my usual seat at the bar. Meadhbh finished serving a drink to a customer and came down to my end of the bar.

"Hi. Good to see you," I said and extended my hand.

"Handshake rather than a kiss? You must be kidding. I deserve a least a quick lip touch for the initiative of calling you," Meadhbh said, not waiting a moment before initiating a salacious comment.

I leaned over the bar and gave her a quick peck on the lips. "You've done better, but I'll take it," was her quick comment on my feeble performance.

"Remember? I'm married. But getting down to business, I am very glad you called me. I had hoped another meeting with Edison wouldn't be necessary, but the DOJ didn't get the indictment. Plus, Edison said that my 'free pass' would end once the federal proceedings were over. I can't just go through life waiting for ZeiiMed's next move against me or my family. I need to talk to him immediately."

"Well, he's here. He's had one drink and just ordered another. Scotch and water," she said.

"Good, because I would like to put a little something in his drink before you deliver it."

"A little something? What are you talking about. You want me to poison one of my customers?" she asked.

"It isn't poison. It's a drug called ketamine. It will not hurt him, but it will put him in a sedated state that will keep him listening and sitting for a short period of time."

"Isn't that the date drug everybody warns against?" she asked.

"It's the same chemical, but in a much lower dosage and its not combined with any other drug, such as coke or ecstasy. The commonly used date-drug dosage induces memory loss, a total detachment form reality, hallucinations and a possible loss of consciousness. None of those things are going to happen to Edison. I promise."

"What is it you want me to do?"

"Make him his drink. I'll give you the ketamine to put in it and I'll join him at his table after you deliver the drink."

"You promised me no violence, right?"

"Yes, and I will keep that promise."

"Also, I don't want him hitting his panic button releasing four goons that suddenly charge through the restaurant."

"Don't worry, I have a plan for that, too. And if everything works out as I anticipate, I'll never have to involve you in this mess again."

"Does that mean you'll never visit me again?"

"We don't have time to clown around. Of course, we'll see each other again. Let's get this done now. Here's the drug in a glassine envelope."

Meadhbh made the drink and poured in the ketamine.

I watched as Meadhbh walked out from behind the bar and then towards the tables in back. I couldn't see her actually deliver the drink to Edison's table from where I was seated at the bar, so I just waited until she returned.

Meadhbh was back five minutes later.

"He's all yours," Meadhbh said. "But I'll be a tough act to follow. I got him laughing and he's in very good spirits. Speaking of spirits, he gulped down half his drink in one sip. His pudgy cheeks have turned a brighter red than usual. I think he likes me. Try not to ruin the big tip I'm anticipating."

"You really ought to think about becoming a stand-up comic. If you can make me smile in a stressful moment like this, you're assured a successful career. By the way, Edison is celebrating because he wasn't indicted today and the White House announced his appointment as the absolute czar in charge of Medicare and Medicaid. Gotta go now. Time for my performance."

I walked to the end of the bar and made a right turn into the dining room. Most of the tables were taken. I saw Edison sitting at a small square table for two, pushed up against the back wall. The seat directly across from him at his table was empty.

Edison did not look up as I approached his table. Apparently, he didn't notice me coming. I sat in the empty seat without saying a word. Needless to say, he was surprised, but his alarm at my presence seemed to be dulled by the alcohol and the drug. The scotch and water was almost gone. He must have taken a second gulp.

"Congratulations. You've had a very successful day. First, you get appointed as the Administrator of the Centers for Medicare and Medicaid Services and then, later in the same day, the Grand Jury lets you off the hook. You've had a very big day," I said, trying to lessen, at least initially, the intense animosity between us by patronizing him. It didn't work.

"Bradford, you vile son-of-a-bitch. There are few people in the world I detest more than you and I will get my revenge for your off-the-script speech in Court that led to the Grand Jury proceedings. Damn you and damn your family forever," he bellowed at me.

This was not going well. I grabbed the remote-control panic button and put it in my pocket. I quickly unfolded the razor knife under the table and touched his knee with the blade point without cutting into the skin. I needed more time for the drug to kick in fully.

"Now listen to me. Don't raise your voice and don't make a scene. You won't need your panic button because if you had pressed it, I would have stuck this blade four inches into your leg and cut out your kneecap. And I would have kept cutting even after you passed out from the pain. Your knee would be on the floor when you woke up. The same will happen if you yell or scream. But we've been down this road before. You know the drill. We're going to have our little conversation no matter what, after which I walk out of here and never see you again."

Edison's eyes were becoming glassy and he seemed to have trouble focusing. The piercing menace of his ice-blue eyes had diminished. His hands were no longer clenched. The drug must be working.

"Yes, okay. I feel more relaxed now, despite the blade pressing on my leg. In fact, you are not upsetting me at all. I have mentally distanced myself from my body and seem to be floating pleasantly away. You know, you can't harm me now. I've been appointed the top man in the federal government in charge of Medicare and Medicaid. I'm personally in charge of the medical treatments and medical costs of millions of newly insured Americans. Plus, ZeiiMed will pick up most of the remaining 32 million uninsured Americans that must now sign up for a health plan or be penalized by the health care police," Edison said, slurring his words a bit.

"That's why I offered my congratulations."

"Your congratulations are misplaced," Edison responded. "ZeiiMed will never earn the billions of dollars of profits that it did in the past. The benefits that ZeiiMed has to pay out under the new health care legislation are a nightmare. ZeiiMed is forced to provide mandatory coverage for all children with pre-existing conditions—do you know what that means? All those kids with horrible childhood diseases now get full coverage for top specialists and special hospitals, all at the expense of ZeiiMed. And we can't even charge the parents an exorbitant premium. And that's only the beginning. All children are covered to age twenty-six on their parents' policy—that's fourteen million more people ZeiiMed has to care for without additional premium. Last, but not least, there is the insane requirement that eighty percent of each premium dollar we collect by law must be used to pay actual medical costs incurred for patient care. That leaves me a mere twenty percent to run my entire worldwide company and still make my money. Fat chance of that."

"I don't care about your lost profits and I'm very pleased that sick children have mandatory coverage. That's not why we're having this conversation," I responded.

"Actually," Edison continued, "I'm here because the White House put me personally in charge of Medicare and Medicaid. The federal government knows that universal coverage will not work without decreasing the payments to doctors and hospitals. More medical services to more people for less money. That's the plan. The White House is aware I'm the world's expert in cutting payments to doctors and that's why I was hired. The indictment was fixed to fail from day one. You wanted to put me in prison for cutting the doctors' pay and the White House recruited me to do the same thing in a full-time job as a federal bureaucrat with a fancy federal title. Pretty ironic. Actually, between you and me, I took the job so I can write new federal regulations that will limit and restrict this ridiculous blanket coverage for everyone, especially the children, under the new health care reform law," Edison said, in a verbal tirade fueled by booze and the drug.

"You are beyond question the most evil person on the planet. How could you possibly say that innocent, sick children in horrible pain shouldn't get the best medical treatment on earth? I ought to cut your knee off just for mentioning that. But I won't. The manager won't let me back in the restaurant if I get your blood all over the place—and I like it here, at least when you're not around," I responded.

"Don't be so self-righteous," Edison snarled. "The lawyers should be ashamed of the exorbitant fees they charged trying to write, explain and implement the new health care legislation. Then it is finally passed into law and new teams of lawyers commence litigation across the country alleging that Congress and the President didn't have the constitutional power to compel all Americans to purchase mandatory coverage or be subject to a penalty or tax. So the lawyers get rich creating the new law and the rest of the lawyers get richer trying to have the law ruled unconstitutional. You attorneys really are the 'worst lice' in America, as Michael Savage often said on his radio show."

"I'm surprised it took you so long to figure out the lawyering business. But that's another subject," I said. "I do want to know one thing. Is it true that ZeiiMed robbed all those doctors of all that money over so many years?"

"You're an ass. What did you think?" Edison growled. "And, hopefully, ZeiiMed and I will continue our way of doing business for many more years, now with the backing of the federal government. So all your efforts at revenge for the attempts on your life amount to nothing. ZeiiMed wins everything, every time. So get out of here and wait for your time to come. You know, ZeiiMed never misses a target. Sooner or later we succeed."

"That is exactly what I came here to talk about," I said, as his naturally irritating presence started to get to me. "I'm telling you once and for all... leave me, my family and co-workers alone or else. If anything happens to anyone, I will hunt you down and never stop until I finish with you. You know, you can't hide from me and you can't keep me from getting close enough to shoot, stab or drug you. And now you've got your fat federal job, you'll be more exposed than ever. Even now, in a public restaurant, I could slit your throat in a split second. Bottom line, I want an agreement that ZeiiMed will get permanently out of my life. If you don't agree, both of us will have to live out our days wondering when, how and if I will kill you before you succeed in killing me."

"So, you want to make a pact with the devil? Didn't we already do this and you broke the agreement? How do I know you won't break the agreement this time also? You know how lawyers have a tendency to renege on deals," Edison responded.

I personally didn't think it was a good time for Edison to make lawyer jokes. Then again, he was high on booze and drugs.

"I'm offering to make a deal. The past is the past. I am out of options because of my concerns over the safety of my family and colleagues. ZeiiMed will never hear from me again and I will never again speak of the Complaint or the lawsuit against ZeiiMed. Yes, we did have a pact, but recent events, including Wadsworth's death, caused me to suddenly change course as I was addressing the Court. I felt my last recourse against ZeiiMed was a DOJ investigation. The deaths and mayhem caused by ZeiiMed warranted it.

But now you have won the last round and I'm out of bullets. So, we have an understanding—ZeiiMed stops trying to kill me and my family and I won't drug and slice you up in slow and agonizing torture," I stated, in terms as basic as possible.

"Okay," Edison responded. "We have a deal—another deal. Now take that knife away from my knee. But I'm warning you, ZeiiMed will be watching and now I have access to the vast surveillance network of the federal government. I will hear everything you say in the office, in the house, and in the streets. We will be observing you with cameras wherever you are. You won't know how we do it, but don't ever think for a second that we aren't doing it. Pardon me if I don't shake your hand, but I don't like you and I'm sure you despise me. Have a good life—you just got an extension. And one last matter, how long before this drug wears off?"

"You'll be fine in about thirty minutes. Don't try to get up until then. Goodbye, I'll be following your new career in the federal government with great interest. Please make sure my firm's health care plan doesn't get cancelled," I said, as I left the table and returned to the bar. I didn't look back at Edison as I walked away.

My favorite bar stool was empty, thank goodness. The confrontation had been physically and emotionally exhausting.

"How did it go?" Meadhbh asked.

"Good, I accomplished all that I had hope to. Here is his panic button, please return it to him."

"No problem."

"I have to go now. If I stay here and happen to run into Edison again, I'll probably stab him in the gut just to finally end all this. It's what he deserves. Of course, you would be a witness to a homicide and have to testify against me at my criminal trial," I said.

"Would the prosecutor make me testify to the jury about our love affair?" Meadhbh asked.

"What love affair? We don't have a love affair."

"Well, don't tell the jury that or I'll get busted for perjury," she replied.

Now I had a headache in addition to being tired. I gave her a quick kiss on the lips and stood to leave.

"You're finally learning the technique. Thanks for the tasty kiss, but just press harder next time. When do we see each other again?" Meadhbh asked.

"I'll be around. I always enjoy your company and you've been a great help to me with regard to Edison. I can't thank you enough. My wife told you she wants to visit you here, so I'm sure we will. Bye now."

"Take care of yourself, and when you do return, please don't bring your wife. I like her, but three is a crowd," Meadhbh said.

She winked at me as I walked out the front door.

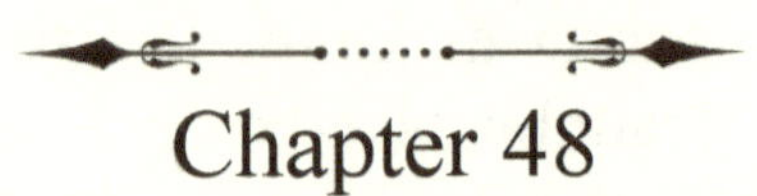

Chapter 48

I arrived home in Port Jefferson very late that same night. Kim was still up, reading in the kitchen.

"You said you were going to be late, but it's unusual for you to come home past 11:00 p.m.," she commented.

"I had another meeting with Edison," I said.

"Oh, no, now I'm worried. No more bloodshed I hope—you don't look injured, thankfully," Kim said.

"Everything is fine. I interrupted his solo dining experience at *Très Bien*. The Grand Jury didn't indict ZeiiMed so I needed a face-to-face with him. I had to make sure ZeiiMed keeps away from you, me and everyone else we care about. In summary, Edison and I agreed to leave each other alone since we both know the other is capable of inflicting severe harm. That's what I wanted to accomplish. I emphasized that no matter where he goes or what he does, I can always get to him. He said the same thing to me about ZeiiMed," I explained.

"Now that I know you're not injured, I'm mad as hell that you didn't tell me you were meeting with Edison. He is a very dangerous man and could have killed you on the spot."

"That's why I met him in a public place with lots of people around. I had no choice other than to try and get a truce from him," I responded.

"You're wrong. You did have a choice. You could have decided not to make a deal that guarantees ZeiiMed gets away with murder. I was so proud of you at the Fairness Hearing when you spoke so eloquently and forcefully about the horrible acts committed by ZeiiMed. You filled the courtroom with your persuasive plea for justice. Every person in that courtroom, except for Edison, was touched by your humanity and zealous earnestness. You endured personal anguish and soul searching in reaching your life changing decision to speak out in Court that day."

Kim took a deep breath and continued, "Then, you force a meeting with Edison and agree to never speak a word about ZeiiMed again. Well, I think you shortchanged your moral conscience and just abolished the basic difference between right and wrong. Lawlessness is never permissible, acceptable or condoned in a just society. You just set jurisprudence back two hundred years."

"I did what I thought was right and fair for the family," I feebly responded.

"But you didn't make the right decision. Two inconsequential people like us don't mean a darn when compared to the big picture of life. And I'll tell you exactly what I'm talking about. I received a call today from Detective Jack Jarrett's widow, Lisa. Remember, we spoke to her at Jack's funeral mass? Lovely lady. She called to ask a favor. Her nineteen-year-old daughter, Lori, whom we also met at the funeral, plans to marry next month at a small civil ceremony at City Hall."

"That seems a bit rushed, doesn't it?" I asked.

"Yes. I got the feeling there was some urgency to the timetable," Kim continued. "but that doesn't matter. Lisa said Jack has no living sisters or brothers. She asked if you would give her daughter away at the ceremony. She said Jack often talked often about your perseverance and fortitude in dealing with ZeiiMed's life threatening ordeal and often mentioned how much he enjoyed your company. She said Jack worked so hard, they didn't really have any friends and all of her family lives in Europe. She said she will never forget Jack's comments about you and decided to take a chance on calling us. She hoped her request wasn't too much of an imposition."

"My goodness, I feel like crying. I'm so touched," I said. "I need to sit down."

"There's more. She asked us over to dinner at her house next week. Lori and her fiancé will be there. I accepted for us."

"Yes, of course. This is rather overwhelming."

"But, here's the point," Kim stated. "Jack Jarrett risked his life protecting yours. He risked everything in the hope you would be safe. He lost it all, his life, his future, his family and the joyous anticipation of being at his daughter's wedding. And what do you do in return? You make a deal, a truce with the people that arranged his death. Brian, this can't be happening."

"You're absolutely right. I've got to re-examine everything. But I'm totally overwhelmed emotionally. I can't think straight right now. I'm going to bed. We have a lot to talk about tomorrow," I said.

"Yes, let's turn in. It's been a very hard day for both of us," Kim responded. "We can figure this out tomorrow. Just one more thing. Did Meadhbh help you again in arranging your meeting with Edison? I remember the last time you had a 'chat' with him, Meadhbh was essential to making your plan work."

"Yes, she helped me again. As I mentioned, I met with Edison at *Très Bien*. She had called to tell me when he was in the restaurant alone. I forgot... she asked about you and said to say hello," I explained, trying to sound sincere.

"You seem uncomfortable, just like when you noticed Meadhbh sitting next to me at the Fairness Hearing."

"Oh, that was nothing and tonight was nothing. I'll explain as we walk upstairs. As I told you, I was just surprised to see her at the Fairness Hearing. Plus, I had talked to you about the fact that I needed her assistance in getting to Edison."

"Yes, I remember. But men are still such pigs as a rule."

"I'm just happy you are willing to sleep with this pig."

"I am, at least for tonight. Check with me tomorrow about how I feel going forward."

I think she was kidding, but I can't say for sure. Anyway, being self-centered and short-sighted, I decided to just live for the moment. Kim slipped into bed in a beautiful, transparent silk and lace nightgown.

She didn't appear sleepy.

Kim is just as assertive, determined and confident in bed as she is out of bed. I have no problem going along for the ride. She enjoys waves of passion and it's my job (pleasure) to assist in reaching each crest. I've learned to take care of the Lady and the Lady will take care of you. My devotion to the task was once again rewarded with Kim having rhythmically attained an exhilarating, multiple peak experience.

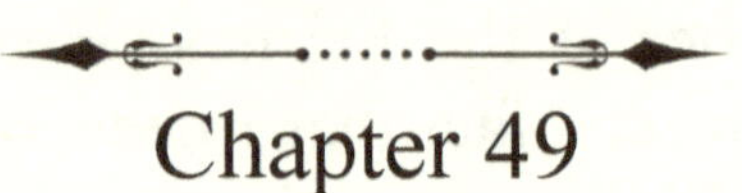

Chapter 49

Actually, it was a couple of days before I returned to work. There were a lot of issues for Kim and I to discuss—including the question of how we envisioned the rest of our lives would play out. You can't predict the future and certainly can't predict the obstacles and hurdles to be encountered, but you can work out a general attitude to be embraced in reacting to the future. We attempted to do this.

How successful we would be in translating our conceptual discussion into reality was totally unknown. Heck, I could have a heart attack tomorrow and all that talk will turn out to be nothing more than a lot of hot air. Regardless, I guess it's constructive to have a lengthy heart-to-heart dialogue with your spouse every twenty years or so. I'm already looking forward to the next time two decades from now. I should put a note in my diary, although I don't think I can buy one for a time period so far away. I guess I'll just have to remember.

In all candor, I returned to work after our impromptu marital retreat with a renewed sense of affection and devotion to Kim. It truly was a comfort.

My workday hadn't progressed far before Mary came by to say hello.

"Nice to see you, Brian. Last time I saw you was at the Fairness Hearing. Things got a little out of control at the end, but your presentation to the Court was outstanding. Without question, you did the right thing and the only thing.

You took the morally just and correct path. Congratulations."

"Thank you. I appreciate your comments. I was struggling to get the words out coherently and at the same time battling with my internal rationale and justification for speaking the words. It took its toll emotionally. But, according to Kim, I've once again fallen off the morally correct path, but that's another story."

"By the way, what exactly happened in the corridor outside the courtroom after we adjourned for the day?" Mary asked. "All I saw was a bunch of medics taking Edison out on a stretcher. What did I miss?"

"Something did happen to Edison and that something was Kim. He was making threatening remarks to us and Kim reacted by forcefully kicking him in the shin. The bone probably fractured. Believe me, I was surprised as hell, while at the same time relishing the moment."

"My goodness. That little incident will now be permanently engraved in the firm's folklore. Congratulations also to your wife. That reminds me of another question I had. Who was that woman sitting next to your wife at the Fairness Hearing? I saw you enter the courtroom and turn to talk to your wife sitting in the last pew—than all of a sudden you looked dumbfounded and off balance. What happened?"

"Nothing much. Kim was sitting next to a friend of mine who works at a bar on the Upper East Side. I was surprised to see them sitting together because they had never met in person."

"I get it," Mary stated. "Two separate and distinct parts of your world collided and you were shaking from the big bang. You really should be more careful about having the women in your life overlap. Plus, I was there watching and could have also run into your East Side friend. By the way, what is her name and how did you meet her?"

"Her name is Meadhbh and she works at *Très Bien* on East 84th Street, right next to where Edison lives. She was a big help assisting me in making direct contact with him."

"It sounds plausible, but you are blushing a bit. I may have to go and visit her some time."

"What?"

"Only kidding. I'll drop this sensitive topic as long as you pay attention to my next story."

"Go ahead, I'm ready for a change of scenery."

"Did you happen to see the picture on the front page of the *New York Times* today?" Mary asked.

"Yes, I believe I did, but I'm sure my answer will only be the beginning, not the end, of whatever discussion we are about to have. By the way, you sure give a lot of thought to the front-page pictures each day," I commented.

"You're right and I will continue to," she said. "The picture shows several marines in an open field in Afghanistan assisting a wounded soldier into a hovering helicopter for transfer to a hospital. It reminds me once again that our soldiers are getting killed at an alarming rate in Southern Afghanistan. U.S. troops go on patrol through rugged terrain and small villages and then get attacked by Taliban sniper fire as soon as an open field is reached. This is in addition to the many fatalities caused by roadside bombs. It's simply not getting better—you can't kill every member of the Taliban. It's been nine long years of this now and we are nowhere close to success. Soon it will be a ten-year war. How far are we from the mind-boggling Hundred Years' War that started in 1337? We should just maintain a presence in the major cities and stop trying to eradicate the Taliban from every corner of Afghanistan."

"I know it's heart-wrenching to think of the unrelenting pain experienced by the family members of each lost soldier," I mentioned. "But I don't think we will be able to start substantial withdrawals until at least 2020, if then. I guess the government is doing the best it can to try to keep America as safe as possible. As I said, we can't just pull out on a moment's notice and abandon the Afghan citizens. That would result in a slaughter—everyone knows that."

"But President Obama promised us 'change we could believe in' as a catalyst of hope for a better America and a better world. What did we get? Millions of people have lost their jobs, oil is gushing out of the ocean floor at a rate of fifty thousand barrels a day in the Gulf of Mexico, Iran's nuclear arsenal is growing and the federal deficit is beyond anyone's wildest projection," Mary countered.

"Well, this Administration certainly has had its successes. Health care reform, financial reform through the Financial Stability Act and an arms reduction pact with Russia," I pointed out.

"Don't get me started on financial reform that was long overdue. The SEC finally filed a civil lawsuit against one investment banking firm alleging wrongful acts in connection with the structuring and marketing of a series of synthetic CDO(s) whose performance was tied to 'securities backed by residential mortgages.' The residential mortgage portfolio selected by the bank's hedge fund was of such a negative character that significant losses were experienced. The bank supposedly was aware that the collateral selection process would generate losses yet, nonetheless, misrepresented to its potential investors that the portfolio had been selected by an independent third party."

"Those are serious allegations. I'm amazed an investment bank would conduct business in that fashion," I commented.

"It gets worse," Mary continued. "After the hedge fund played a significant role in the selection of a subprime residential mortgage portfolio likely to experience losses, it took a short position that created profits once the investors in the CDO(s) inevitably lost their money. I guess I shouldn't be shocked by such behavior, but I am. Another shocking corporate scandal that will go away because settlement money is paid and the file closed. But the business culture doesn't change, so there will always be a repeat of the behavior."

"I know, I know. It does seem the whole world is going to hell in a handbasket. But I need to talk to you about another matter—one that impacts our lives to a much greater degree—ZeiiMed," I said, changing the topic to the only subject I was truly concerned with.

"ZeiiMed was not indicted," I said. "As a result, I felt it necessary to speak again with Edison and warn him to keep ZeiiMed away from us."

"What did he say?"

"I believe we reached some sort of an understanding," I responded. "It was an agreement to mutually keep away from each other. I tried to convince him I had the ability to get close enough to harm him no matter how well guarded he may be. I think he bought it, although I can't be a hundred percent sure because he was high on booze and drugs."

"How do you know he took drugs?" she asked.

"Actually, not drugs, a drug. A drug that I concealed in his cocktail and he guzzled down enthusiastically."

"You drugged him?"

"Yes," I said. "It was all part of the plan to create a sense of vulnerability and insecurity in him. It appeared to work."

"If I was Edison, as soon as I woke up the next day, I'd give instructions to an army of ZeiiMed robots to destroy you at any cost."

"Maybe, and that takes me to the next part of my story. Once I got home after meeting with Edison, I told Kim everything that had occurred that day. She didn't agree with my strategy in dealing with ZeiiMed."

"You mean she was mad as hell that you met with Edison without talking to her first?" Mary interrupted.

"Exactly," I replied. "She liked that I had her safety and welfare in mind when I decided to once again confront Edison. But she didn't like not being given a choice. She wanted the opportunity to decide that maybe a truce with ZeiiMed isn't the right option to take, especially when we really have no way to hold ZeiiMed to any such truce."

"So what does Kim want you to do now?" she asked.

"She wants no let-up on ZeiiMed. Kim feels I owe that to the family of Jack Jarrett, the Detective who was killed protecting me, and to all the other people that have been cheated, harmed or killed by ZeiiMed. She explained that I can't give up and surrender, while permitting ZeiiMed to reload and start all over again. ZeiiMed will never stop doing what it does and it looks like I may be the only person to cripple, if not kill, this monster."

"I agree with Kim," Mary said, without hesitation.

"You do?"

"Yes, I do," she said again. "As you know, I wanted these criminals in jail, although I eventually became fearful of ZeiiMed and just wanted all the mayhem to stop. But the reality is that people are dead and ZeiiMed can't be allowed a free pass. History will only repeat itself without our efforts to change it."

"Okay. I understand. You and Kim think alike."

"Let's review what's occurred," Mary went on. "I bloodied one ZeiiMed guy who was trying to kill you in your office. You bloodied another ZeiiMed guy on the airplane and inflicted a little torture for good measure. Your wife kicked Edison at the courthouse. I can only imagine what else you did after putting a drug in his drink at *Très Bien* a few days ago. I think we've done a pretty good job so far. Let's keep up the good work. I'm ready."

"Alright then, what's the next step?" I asked.

"There are many things to be done next. But the plan itself is short and simple: Educate, reveal and expose. Like a vampire, ZeiiMed cannot survive the light of day. By constantly drawing attention to ZeiiMed and explaining to one and all what it does and what it did, we have a fighting chance of containing ZeiiMed and maybe even disabling it," she said.

"Okay, but what do we do first?" I asked.

"What we do is use your fame as leverage to provide a high exposure platform. You're now a fairly famous lawyer from your cases against ZeiiMed and I'm sure Larry King, Charlie Rose and other television hosts would be pleased to have you on their programs. Interviews with newspaper reporters can be arranged. I can start a legal blog to tell our story. And I bet you would be quite a star speaker at the next AMA convention. We might even get some new doctor clients with new lawsuits to file. You can become a legal expert on litigation against the health insurance industry. Last, but not least, you can always write a book in a muckraking style about ZeiiMed."

"Of course," I noted, "ZeiiMed is not going to let all this happen without a reaction. It will fight back and hard. We will be in constant danger. But I have a plan to help address that. I need to talk to Kim before I tell you, but I'm sure she will go along with it."

"Okay," Mary said, "We'll talk later. In the meantime, I'll

make some calls to arrange the media exposure."

I called Kim.

"Honey, I have an idea I'd like to speak with you about. Mary had many of the same suggestions you made regarding our campaign against ZeiiMed. In addition, why don't we move into the City right next to Edison? Edison lives in an apartment building adjoining *Très Bien*, but there is another apartment house on the opposite side of *Très Bien* that has a vacancy. I can be right in Edison's face. If Edison wants to watch me and intimidate me, I'll be right at his doorstep watching him and confronting him. When he walks out of his apartment house in the morning, I'll be standing there in his face, drinking my coffee. I'll look into his building every night on the way home from work. We'll dine in full view of each other at *Très Bien*. And he can't do anything to harm us because he would be the first and only suspect in any investigation. What do you say?"

"I think it's a marvelous idea. Call the broker now. I love Port Jefferson but we are just too isolated here to battle ZeiiMed this far from the City. I'm ready to move right next to Edison if that increases our chances for success," Kim replied.

"Great, I'll get working on it and call you as soon as the broker gets me the details," I said.

The phone rang almost the instant I put it down. It was Meadhbh.

"Hi. We haven't talked in a few days. I thought it wouldn't hurt if I gave you a buzz to update you on Edison," she said.

"That's very nice of you. I hope Edison didn't cause any problems at the restaurant after I left," I replied.

"No. After you left he just sat there for thirty minutes staring at the wall. Then he left without saying a word, although he was a little wobbly on his feet."

"That's good. I didn't want him to think for a second that you were involved," I commented.

"No, I'm pretty sure he has no idea about our relationship... I mean, our friendship. Actually, that's what I wanted to let you know. Since Edison probably has no knowledge of my complicity with you, I'd be glad to assist if you need another uninvited get-together with him."

"Thanks for the offer, but I don't think it's necessary at the present time. Plus, I have good news. I'm moving into the apartment building that adjoins *Très Bien*—not the one Edison lives in, but the one attached to the other side of the restaurant. We're going to be neighbors very soon."

"I can't wait. It will be nice to see those long eyelashes on a regular basis. By the way, is your wife moving in also?" Meadhbh asked.

"Of course. The three of us are going to have a wonderful time together."

"Like I said, I can't wait," Meadhbh repeated. "I always love a challenge. Are you coming by the bar tonight?"

"No, can't make it tonight. But soon I'll be waving to you every day as I pass on the sidewalk outside the restaurant."

"If you wave from the street rather than coming into the restaurant and greeting me, you will be permanently banned from the bar. I expect the personal touch. And, by the way, bring in your wife anytime you like. I was only kidding before. I enjoy her company and my private conversations with you will not be repeated to her or anyone else."

"Now that the rules of engagement have been established, do you want me to draft a written agreement so that we can both sign it?"

"Very funny. I'm only trying to convince you there is no guilt in our seeing each other more frequently once you are in the neighborhood."

"That's because so far we haven't done anything to be guilty about."

"Yet," she added. "Talk to you later."

Chapter 50

Three days later, I was home after work when the call came in. I was in the bedroom thinking about the move to New York City and what items to put in which box.

After picking up the phone on the third ring, an unfamiliar voice began speaking.

"Hello, is Brian Bradford there?" a young female voice asked in a serious, business-like tone.

"Yes, I'm Brian. Who is this, please?"

"You don't know me. My name is Judy. I work as a waitress at *Très Bien* on 84th Street. Meadhbh asked that I call you. I have some bad news. Meadhbh was seriously hurt two days ago..."

"Jesus, I'm shocked to hear this. It can't be. What happened? How serious is it? Sorry for all the questions, but this is very upsetting."

"She is getting top-notch care at the Neurological Institute of New York Presbyterian Hospital up at Columbia University Medical Center. I was there today and she seems to be doing much better."

"Neurological? What do you mean? Please explain."

"I know it's a lot to take in on one phone call, but I'll do the best I can. Meadhbh was attacked by two men outside the brownstone where she has an apartment in Brooklyn. It was late at night. She was returning home from work at the bar. They grabbed her and beat her viciously on the head with bats and broke her arm as she tried to resist. She was left unconscious lying in a small garden next to the sidewalk. It was dark. No one saw anything and no one came to her rescue. The street lights had been smashed the night before, so they may have been following her and planning the attack. It was horrible. The garbage men found her a few hours later as dawn broke. It's hard to go on, I can't stop crying."

"Take your time. Of course, you're at an emotional meltdown. I can't believe it myself. I just saw her a few days ago."

"Yes, I know. When I was at the hospital today she mentioned your name and gave me your number. She reminded me to call you a number of times."

"Thank you for the call. The news is unbearable, but I'm so glad you got in contact with me. I'm going to go see her tomorrow. What's her current prognosis?"

"The doctors aren't positive yet—but they are some of the best in the world. All I know is that there was a bruising of her brain tissue from the impact of the blows, with mild bleeding in and around the brain. She experiences an occasional loss of consciousness, headaches, nausea, and a slurring of words. She had an MRI and a bunch of CT scans so the doctors can figure out exactly what's happening inside her head. That's about all I know."

"Judy, thanks again for calling. I'll say lots of prayers and visit her tomorrow."

"I'm glad I was able to get hold of you. It will make Meadhbh happy," she responded. "Maybe I'll run into you at the hospital. Bye."

I was barely able to return the 'Good-Bye' before my head collapsed into my hands in shock, sadness and concern. Plus, my mind was racing ahead with thoughts about the identity of the perpetrators and their possible motivation.

In the deepest recesses of my cerebral cortex, the heavily barricaded door to my most repressed emotions of rage, violence and unrestrained vehemence slowly opened.
Again.

Chapter 51

Shortly after my telephone conversation with Judy, I went downstairs to find Kim. She was watching television in the family room.

"Honey, do you have a few minutes? I just got an unsettling telephone call I'd like to tell you about."

"Yes, of course. What happened?"

"A waitress at *Très Bien* just gave me a call about the bartender Meadhbh."

"Yes, I met her at the Fairness Hearing. She sat right next to me. Remember? You acted very ill at ease and aloof. When I asked how you met Meadhbh you couldn't remember. You expected me to believe that? I could see darn well how pretty she was. The only reason you were so uncomfortable was concern over what she might tell me. So spill the beans. What was it you were so afraid she was going to say to me about you?" Kim asked.

"Nothing, nothing at all. She is just a very good friend. We talked about this the other night. I really don't understand why we need to discuss this again. As you recall, I made the effort to connect with her because I needed her help in getting to Edison. I mentioned to you that I had recruited her assistance. But it is possible Meadhbh misinterpreted my overtures. However, none of that is important right now. The purpose of the telephone call was to let me know that Meadhbh suffered a very serious injury. She was assaulted a couple of nights ago outside her apartment and suffered neurological damage as a result of blows to her head.”

“I’m so sorry. She was such a pleasant person. I liked her right away. Was it a robbery or some drugged lunatics?”

“I don’t know. I’m going to go see her at the hospital tomorrow. She is at the Neurological Institute of New York Presbyterian Hospital.”

“Get some flowers and sign both our names on the card. I will ask the priest for some special blessings tomorrow at mass.”

“Kim, you know my involvement with Meadhbh may have put her in harm’s way. If so, I’m going to have to rectify it.”

“I understand. You can’t ignore it and you need to know who is responsible. It has to be addressed.”

“Yes, exactly,” I said.

“You better be darn sure you know what you’re doing,” Kim warned. “As we both know very well, we are up against extremely dangerous people. Don’t underestimate them and don’t think for one second you can outsmart them or somehow get the upper hand. And one final thought—don’t get arrested. I can’t guarantee I’ll stick around if you get a harsh sentence for a serious crime. I will bail you out and show up for your trial each day. But if you are put away for a year or more, I won’t be here when you get out. I know it sounds harsh, but you should know the truth.”

“You won’t be getting rid of me that easy. Besides, I don’t even know for sure that ZeiiMed has any connection to Meadhbh’s injury. I’ll let you know once I talk to her at the hospital, assuming she is well enough to talk with me.”

“I’ll keep something out for dinner tomorrow night. I’m sure it will be late by the time you go to the hospital after work and then head home.”

“Thanks. I love you so much. But, to be completely

honest, I could have done without the mental picture of you being with another man while I'm in prison."

"Try not to think about that. Just remember how much I love you and will continue to love you in your present unincarcerated state," Kim said with a slight grin.

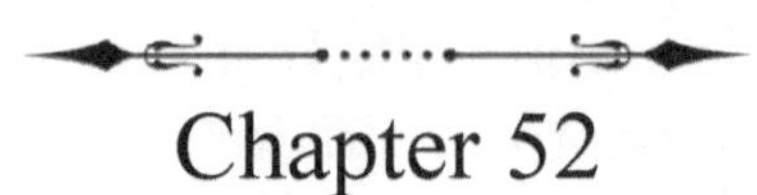

Chapter 52

The next day, I took the subway to 168th Street and walked to the Neurological Institute of Columbia University at 170 West 168th Street.

The front desk clerk told me that Meadhbh's room was on the top floor and to speak with the attendant there. I asked a couple of times for her room number, but it was not provided and no explanation was offered.

I was given a plastic identification card that had a large capital letter "P" on it in bold print. I was told to press the "P" button when I got into the elevator while inserting the card into the slot next to the button. I proceeded to the elevator bank.

Upon entering the elevator, there were twenty-five buttons, each consecutively numbered, except for the "P" button at the top next to a slot. I put the card in the slot and pressed the "P" button.

The elevator stopped at the "P" floor, the top penthouse floor. As the doors opened, I was greeted immediately.

"Hello, Mr. Bradford, nice to make your acquaintance," said a professionally dressed young woman with dark-rimmed glasses and brunette hair pulled tightly back. She had a clipboard with several sheets of paper in her left hand and extended her right hand. I gently shook her hand.

"My name is Ms. Taylor and I will escort you to Meadhbh's suite. Please follow me," she said, in a business-like tone without a smile.

We walked from the elevator bank into a huge room with

a vaulted glass cathedral ceiling that drenched the area with brilliant natural light. It was elegant. There were velvet couches and leather chairs clustered in several spots on the richly textured maroon and gold carpet. It was a perfect place for patients to meet with friends and relatives in a relaxed, comfortable setting.

"This is lovely. What a great facility. The top hotels in the world don't have lobbies as spacious and inviting as this," I said to Ms. Taylor, as we walked across the room.

"Yes, it really turned out well. We are very indebted to our benefactors to have this penthouse facility, along with the best medical care in the world," Ms. Taylor responded.

After we crossed the room, we continued walking until we reach a corridor. It didn't look like the usual hospital corridor. It had no medical equipment cluttering the hallway, no monitors outside each room. Only bright oil paintings of New York landmarks and landscapes were noticeable.

"I am very glad to say that Ms. Meadhbh is doing much better," Ms. Taylor said, as we walked down the corridor. "She suffered terrible blows to the head, but the doctors have her stabilized and she is able to speak, although slowly and with some difficulty. You will have about fifteen minutes with her. I will let you know when your time is up."

"Thank you," I said.

Ms. Taylor stopped and pointed. "This is her suite, please go right in."

The first room of her suite was a pleasant living room with two arm chairs, a couch, table and a large LCD flat screen television. I put the "get well" card on the table. Meadhbh wasn't in the living room, so I proceeded to the next room.

The bedroom had a large window with an impressive view of the Hudson River and the George Washington

Bridge.

Meadhbh was asleep in the bed, her face swollen and the top of her head wrapped in white bandages. Fiber optic monitors were behind her bed, with a fiber optic probe and electrodes from an electroencephalogram attached to her scalp.

I pulled a chair next to her bed and gently touched her hand.

Her eyes slowly opened.

"Hello, Meadhbh. How are you feeling?"

Her mouth opened to talk but no sound was made. Slowly, pausing between words, she spoke.

"Brian... Brian... I'm so glad you came by. I feel better already, but I know I don't look very nice."

"Oh, yes, you do. Your gorgeous green eyes are sparkling and beautiful as ever."

"You never said that before. How nice."

"It looks like you're getting great care here and I'm told you're doing much better."

"Yes... Yes... I am doing better each day. The doctors are exceptional. They relieved the pressure on my brain and are monitoring the blood flow around my brain. They say the brain will eventually rewire itself and make new connections around the destroyed neurons."

"That's great. I'm saying all the prayers I can for a speedy recovery. Then again, this penthouse floor is so luxurious you may never want to leave. What kind of a Cadillac health insurance plan do you have?" I asked.

"It is really nice here... The funny thing is that I don't have health insurance. My family doesn't believe in health insurance. My father says we only pay cash and cash buys the best doctors in the world. So, dad made all the arrangements and wires the money directly to the hospital.

I learned long ago not to try to change my father's mind when he has a head of steam up."

"Well, he sounds like a wonderful person who wants you to have only the best. That is very special."

"Yes, he really is. But the one thing my father can't understand is why I want to be a bartender rather than a captain of industry as he is. My father always says that the winner in life is the person who earns the most money. Of course, I don't agree."

"Meadhbh, if you can't talk about it let me know. But do you know who attacked you or why?"

"It is all such a blur... but I do know one of them said something before I lost consciousness."

"What was said, Meadhbh?"

"Now, don't start blaming yourself, Brian, but the man said, 'Send Brian Bradford our regards' or something like that."

"I'm so sorry. I never should have involved you."

"Stop it. I'm a big girl and I regret nothing... I especially don't regret meeting you."

"You're very special. I have to go now. I'm only allowed to stay a few minutes. I'll be back soon. Love you."

I leaned over and kissed her on the cheek. She squeezed my hand in return.

I left the suite.

Ms. Taylor was standing as motionless as a statue in the corridor, ready to escort me back to the elevator bank.

Chapter 53

The door to the cranial chamber containing my most base primal emotions was now unlocked and open wide. A wave of retaliatory rage flowed into my frontal lobe and translated into conscious thought and premeditated action. The disgust and anger were uncontrollable. The desire to inflict pain, injury and torment, with an unrelenting obsession for revenge, was uncontainable.

I was haunted by the disturbing vision of Meadhbh's neurological injuries and her courageous efforts to overcome her affliction. The misery she endured suffocates any reasonable expression of grief and transforms my being into a monstrous instrument of gruesome reciprocation.

The object of my obsession was Edison. I needed to find a way to surprise him at a location where there was little chance of being observed. The security at his building is much more extensive after my break-in of his apartment. There is no chance of getting anywhere near his front door. I could once again abruptly interrupt his dinner at *Très Bien*, but there would be many customers calling 911 at the first sight of Edison's blood.

No, I had to make sure he was at an isolated location, without a security detail, before I revealed my presence to him. Preferably, but not necessarily, at night. Of course, I was abundantly aware that this basic outline of a plan was not going to be easy to execute.

I started by observing Edison's apartment building in the

mornings, both during the week and on weekends. I walked up and down 84th Street near his building, crossing the street several times and circling the block. This approach had no chance of success. On only one occasion did I see Edison leave his apartment building and walk, with a noticeable limp (thank you, Kim), to a waiting sedan.

Security guards followed his every movement. Were they actually waiting for me to approach Edison? Who else would be on the prowl for him? I didn't know, but I hoped Edison and his entourage were losing sleep worrying about my next move.

Having decided that Edison apparently does not take morning walks with his sore leg, I shifted my stakeout to the evenings after 6:00 p.m. Diagonally across 84th Street from Edison's building is a street-level coffee shop with twenty-five floors of apartments above it. It sells fresh breads, salads and soups in addition to a large variety of coffees. Its primary attraction, however, are the large windows that run from floor to ceiling along the entire length of the store's front. Inside there is a wooden counter attached to the windows, with stools in front of the counter. This configuration allowed me to sit on a stool, put my coffee on the counter in front of me and observe from a perfect vantage point the everyday activity on 84th Street.

I became a regular at the coffee shop. No one seemed to mind that I would sit on the stool for at least two hours on weekday evenings. However, Kim was starting to get annoyed at my consistently late arrivals at home, but so far she had accepted my story that I needed to work late preparing for a major trial.

Yet, I should just tell her exactly what I'm doing because she probably suspected anyway. She knew I felt responsible for Meadhbh's injuries and she certainly remembers that I intended to do something to even the score. Nonetheless, I didn't want to tell Kim of my plan so she wouldn't be responsible at any level in the event something went unpredictably awry, such as police involvement.

Each night I watched the front door of Edison's building to figure out a pattern to his movements. At about the same time each night, he came home in the back of a black town car with a security detail. It seemed his new job with the federal government did not yet require his appearance in D.C. on a regular basis. I assumed the driver took him each day to ZeiiMed's world headquarters in the Grace Building on 42nd Street between 5th and 6th Avenue. I'm sure the town car and the thugs are all part of ZeiiMed's mandatory security detail for ensuring Edison's safety.

When the town car pulls to the curb in front of his building each day, two guards exit the sedan first and look around. I can't imagine what they expect to find. They then hold the front door of the apartment building open, while Edison follows with another guard. Once he is home, he stays home, except for dinner next door at *Très Bien* three nights a week. On those occasions, he walks out of his building on 84th Street, takes a few steps to the entrance of *Très Bien* and enters with his corporate groupies. On the return trip back home, Edison often appears a bit wobbly and one of the guards keeps a hand under his elbow.

The frustrating part is that the guy never seems to deviate from his routine. Doesn't he know there are hundreds of restaurants on the east side of New York? Nonetheless, I keep on watching from my observation post in the coffee shop, with my trusted billy club wrapped in newspaper inside a plastic Century 21 department store shopping bag. The razor knife is in my pocket. I decided not to carry a gun because there is too high a probability of getting caught by the authorities. The New York City police maintain a significant presence around town post-9/11 and have the legal right to conduct random searches.

After about three weeks of nightly vigils, I finally made progress. The evening was wet with a mist of rain blowing mildly in the air. Edison had one of his customary dinners at *Très Bien* and returned to his building. I was about to call it a night when quite unexpectedly Edison came back outside with his raincoat, khaki rain hat and an unopened, full-size umbrella that he was using as a cane. Although it was dark, the sidewalk was illuminated by both the street lights and the front light of *Très Bien*. I could see him clearly. He was by himself. No one seemed to be following him.

He walked west on East 84th towards Central Park. Once he crossed Fifth Avenue, he took a left turn and headed south on Fifth Avenue. Central Park was to his right as he reached the Metropolitan Museum of Art at 82nd Street. He passed the Museum and continued south on Fifth Avenue until the intersection of Fifth Avenue and East 72nd Street.

He paused when he reached Fifth Avenue at 72nd Street. He looked around and then turned right into the eighty-three acres of parkland called Central Park. After walking a short distance into the Park, Edison headed north on East Drive towards the Loeb Boathouse and Boathouse Restaurant. Only pedestrians were around since vehicles are not permitted on East Drive north of 72nd Street after 7 p.m. on weekdays. After walking another four or five minutes, Edison reached the Boathouse Restaurant, situated beautifully on the northeastern portion of "the Lake" consisting of twenty acres of water created from a swamp which, despite its grandeur or because of it, was never given a name.

So far, I had been very lucky not to be noticed. Although Edison seemed alert to the possibility of being followed, I was fortunate to be able to retreat out of his line of vision when he turned his head. A light post, tree, building doorway or tourist usually provided the momentary camouflage necessary to avoid detection.

Edison entered the front door of the Boathouse Restaurant. I waited a few minutes and looked inside from an adjoining snack bar area that is separated from the Restaurant by another door. Edison was sitting at the elevated bar overlooking both the dinner tables on the lower level and the picturesque Lake directly in front of the tables. The water directly in front of the restaurant was beautifully surrounded by overlapping trees and ancient rock formations. I waited outside a fair distance from the exit door in order to spot Edison upon his departure from the Boathouse.

I waited about twenty minutes. Edison left the Boathouse, but didn't head back to the entrance of the Park on 72nd Street. Rather, he proceeded along a three-foot-wide asphalt pathway on the northwest side of the Boathouse.

He was heading to the Ramble, a densely wooded area of approximately thirty-eight acres with tall, overhanging tree limbs and wandering, leafy bushes that protrude shoulder high onto the pathways. A sign states that the Ramble is a "New York City Ecosystem" known for bird watching, but warns all walkers to "stay on paths."

Once he was in the Ramble, Edison walked west past an elevated rock formation called "Willow Rock" and continued into one of the many heavily wooded areas containing a thick grove of trees. There were no other people on the pathway and no other pathways could be seen through the woods. I was only thirty feet behind him, but luckily he hadn't turned around.

Edison then unexpectedly left the paved pathway and diverted onto an uneven, trampled dirt trail created over the years by the feet of many hikers. The trail was totally secluded and obscured from view, with the darkness making it particularly treacherous.

The rage simmering within me since visiting Meadhbh at the hospital suddenly consumed every inch of my being. I knew the time was now or never. I started running to quickly close the gap between us. Edison seemed unaware as he continued to walk at an unchanged pace. I was within five feet of him, billy club in hand, when I stumbled on a tree root that had protruded a couple of inches above the dirt trail. I fell. As I hit the ground, I lost my grip on the billy club, but it landed close by.

I looked up from the ground. Edison had now turned around and was moving rapidly towards me. He removed a concealed metal pipe from inside his umbrella like a sword being removed from its sheath. He lifted the pipe over his head as a maniacal grin distorted his face. I rolled to my side and covered my head with my arms in a protective reaction to imminent impact as I lay helplessly on the ground.

The pipe struck my left elbow, crushing the bones in the joint. My arm became lifeless as the piercing pain almost caused me to black out. I fought to clear my head and focus on survival. I heard Edison barking angry words at me as my mental fog started to clear.

"Did you really think I didn't know about your silly little stakeout? My guards were actually watching you as you spied on me. I knew you would follow me if I walked off alone without any security. ZeiiMed wanted to quickly and efficiently stamp you out once and for all. But I wanted you alone, with no witnesses, so I could inflict such misery and torment that you will beg me to stop. You followed me like a meek lamb heading to the slaughter. I was trapping you by letting you think you were trapping me."

Before I had a moment to react, Edison had cocked his arm a second time and struck me with the pipe just below my knee. I was seriously hurt and totally vulnerable to a third and probably fatal blow. I didn't know if my leg was broken, but I certainly couldn't move it. I managed to grab the razor knife from my pocket with my right hand as I shrieked in pain to hopefully gain a little time.

I flipped the knife open and lunged my arm forward, thrusting the pointed blade clean through Edison's shoe and foot until the knife embedded in the dirt, nailing him to the ground.

I felt a surge of hope, as Edison made a guttural groan of distress. The warmth of his blood bathed my hand as I continued to wedge the knife blade deeper by moving it back and forth, cutting more flesh in his foot with each movement. Edison dropped the pipe. He bent down and grabbed his bleeding, anchored foot with both hands as he tried unsuccessfully to free it while howling in agony.

As he bent over, Edison's face was only two feet from mine. I released my hand from the immovable knife and quickly picked up the billy club, smashing it full force into the side of his nose. Blood poured out of his nostrils and into the pool of blood that had already formed around his punctured foot. He couldn't balance himself and fell backwards with his foot still anchored by the knife.

I was able to lift myself onto one knee, the injured leg dragging uselessly. As Edison's head lay on the ground, I viciously pounded his face a second time with the billy club, this time using a more powerful downward motion. His cheek bones collapsed and seemed to push his face inside his skull.

I stopped. Another blow would surely kill him. He was unrecognizable.

"That was for Meadhbh. You will probably bleed to death. But, if not, don't you ever go near her again. If there is ever a next time, I won't treat you so gently. That is a guarantee," I said.

I could barely see Edison's lips move under the swollen mass of red flesh on his face, but I did hear him weakly utter, "ZeiiMed will get you for this. No one wins against ZeiiMed."

I almost changed my mind and killed the bastard right then and there. But I decided not to. With his injuries, Edison's life will be a painful hell for years to come and I wanted to fully enjoy his suffering. Plus, on the practical side, there would be a police investigation if he died. The last thing I needed was a manslaughter charge.

I now realized the seriousness of my own injuries. I was forced to crawl back to the Boathouse Restaurant. On the way, two good Samaritans found me and provided very able assistance. I made up a story about how I had fallen on one of the many rock ledges in the Ramble. The ambulance was allowed to enter Central Park to pick me up. Someone made a call to Kim from the hospital.

As I was being prepared for surgery, I thought about my pending move to the apartment on 84th Street and wondered if it would now be delayed. I hoped not. I was looking forward to living next to Edison and planning my next villainous assault on the iniquitous ZeiiMed and its Chief Executive Officer, assuming someone finds him in Central Park with enough blood to survive.

Then again, I'm only kidding myself. My only true desire is to return to the gentle monotony and enjoyable simplicity of my everyday life before I agreed to file the Complaint. The structure and pace of my professional and personal endeavors and relationships was a great blessing which I clearly failed to appreciate at the time. Perhaps the key to life is not making the same mistake twice. I'll work on that. I'll do whatever is necessary to turn the clock back to when the cadence of life was uncomplicated and agreeably predictable. I will restore my existence to how it was before ZeiiMed, and this time treasure every minute.

The anesthesiologist said something to me that I didn't understand because his voice was muffled by the surgical mask. I felt a pinch on my arm and everything went black.

Chapter 54

I regained consciousness. I was lying in a hospital bed with a drawn curtain blocking my view of the room. I don't know where I am. I don't know how long I've been here.

I am in pain from my head to my feet. My arm is in a fiberglass tube that extends from my shoulder to my wrist, with the elbow bent at a ninety-degree angle.

There is a table next to the bed. A small clear vase is on the table with a single daisy. Leaning against the vase is a note in large handwriting. It's from Mary. It says, "Get well and looking forward to working with you on our next big case against ZeiiMed." I guess that's her sense of humor.

Next to the flower vase was a Hallmark card and a folded newspaper. I reached for the card with my one mobile arm. It's a "Get Well" card from Kim. She wrote a long message in the card that continued on the back cover:

> Brian, I love you and always have. I will visit again soon. Meadhbh called the house today to ask how you were. She read the article in the *New York Press*. I left the paper for you. Meadhbh said she will call again after you are discharged. She mentioned that her brain injury was slowly healing.
>
> I hope that your new celebrity status doesn't impact our life together, but I do need to talk to you about some changes that have occurred. My view of our marriage has recently altered. All the violence and

mayhem caused by ZeiiMed have made me re-evaluate my life and re-think the person that can provide me comfort from the emotional strain. We'll talk. The article is on page 5 of the *New York Press*.

I picked up the newspaper. It was already turned to page 5.

RUMBLE IN THE RAMBLE

What could possibly be the reason that a downtown lawyer and the Chief Executive Officer of the largest health insurance corporation in the world decided to settle their differences by hand-to-hand combat with knives and clubs in an isolated, wooded section of Central Park late at night?

According to the police, the answer is not known. But enough is known to conclude that these two idiots aren't bright enough to let the Courts decide whatever dispute they may have.

The police reported that John Edison, the boss at ZeiiMed, everyone's favorite insurance company, was found in the Ramble with a foot wound that bled excessively from a knife that ripped through his foot. Also, his face was a bloody mass of flesh that made him practically unidentifiable.

Although close to death, Mr. Edison was resuscitated and rushed to the hospital. After receiving treatment, he told the hospital staff that Attorney Brian Bradford had assaulted him with a knife and a billy club in a surprise attack while on an evening walk in the Park. Mr. Bradford has not provided his version of the occurrence, but it has been confirmed that Mr. Bradford was also hospitalized with injuries.

It has also been confirmed that Mr. Bradford recently commenced a massive lawsuit against ZeiiMed and then settled the case for one billion dollars several months ago. We can only guess that Mr. Bradford was very disappointed in the fee he received from the settlement, although no one knows for sure.

Mr. Edison's face will be surgically repaired and reconstructed, with his foot requiring several operations. Hopefully, this incident is not reflective of a new trend by lawyers to beat up their adversaries not only in the courtroom, but also in the streets and parks of the City.

It is not known when Mr. Bradford will be questioned by the police."

This is not good.

The police are going to question me about a crime I committed against Edison? I can't believe the police think I'm a criminal. At least Edison is alive... there won't be a murder investigation.

Kim apparently needs to discuss a new outlet (presumably male) for her emotional stress. I can't believe she tells me in a card left next to my hospital bed.

Meadhbh is recovering from severe brain damage, but may never fully recover.

I am in unbearable physical agony and can't possibly face any of these problems now or in the foreseeable future. So much for my plan to eagerly return to the repetitive, boring routine of my everyday life prior to the Complaint.

I should just close my eyes and pretend I'm asleep for the next year or so. Maybe it will all just go away.

Then again, with my luck, the problems will continue to escalate and the challenges will continue to mount. Actually, I better get well real fast. I have a ton of obstacles to overcome and I can't get started lying in this bed.

Where is my nurse anyway?

There must be a nurse call button here somewhere. I need pain killers and discharge papers now. I've got to get out of here.

I'm sure ZeiiMed knows where I am.

THE END

Afterword

At the time The Complaint was first published in October of 2013, the primary criticism was that the story ended too abruptly, leaving the read up in the air with many unresolved story lines.

As they say in the law business, I plead guilty. There's no question that the reader should have been left with a more satisfactory plot resolution, rather than so many dangling issues.

My father, who was ninety-six years old in 2013, was the first to inform me of the uncomfortable ending to the novel. After reading the many pages, he wanted a conclusion that created closure for at least one or two of the book's characters. I promised my father the sequel would continue the story and not end in the same disappointing fashion.

In May of 2016, The Device Trial was published, with Brian continuing his treatment at Lenox Hill Hospital for his wounds. With regard to the ending, I made every effort to not make the same mistake twice.

My father peacefully passed away a month before The Device Trial was published, but I'm sure he obtained a copy at whatever library or bookstore is available in the heavens. Hopefully, he'll be satisfied with the concluding chapters and epilogue.

Thanks for Reading,

Tom Breen
January 2024

www.ingramcontent.com/pod-product-compliance
Lightning Source LLC
Chambersburg PA
CBHW060515160726

47991CB00001B/49